Berkley Prime Crime titles by Cleo Coyle

Coffeehouse Mysteries

ON WHAT GROUNDS
THROUGH THE GRINDER
LATTE TROUBLE
MURDER MOST FROTHY
DECAFFEINATED CORPSE
FRENCH PRESSED
ESPRESSO SHOT
HOLIDAY GRIND
ROAST MORTEM
MURDER BY MOCHA
A BREW TO A KILL
HOLIDAY BUZZ
BILLIONAIRE BLEND
ONCE UPON A GRIND

Haunted Bookshop Mysteries
writing as Alice Kimberly

THE GHOST AND MRS. MCCLURE
THE GHOST AND THE DEAD DEB
THE GHOST AND THE DEAD MAN'S LIBRARY
THE GHOST AND THE FEMME FATALE
THE GHOST AND THE HAUNTED MANSION

Praise for Cleo Coyle's *New York Times* Bestselling Coffeehouse Mysteries

"Coyle's Coffeehouse Mysteries are always good."

—*Kirkus Reviews* (starred review)

"Coyle's Coffeehouse books are superb . . . Highly recommended for all mystery collections."

—*Library Journal* (starred review)

"This series continues to mix clever and intricate plots with a regular cast of characters who become more enjoyable with every episode."

—*Booklist*

"Charming . . . vivid and memorable."

—*RT Book Reviews*

"[A] terrifically written, can't-put-it-down series."

—AnnArbor.com

"Fun and gripping."

—The Huffington Post

"A delicious mystery!"

—*Woman's World*

"Cleo Coyle's Coffeehouse mystery series is among the best of the foodie/cozy mystery genre."

—Fresh Fiction

"What a pleasure to read a book by this author."

—Portland Book Review

"A tasty tale of multigenerational crime and punishment lightened by the Blend's frothy cast of lovable eccentrics."

—*Publishers Weekly*

"Clare and company are some of the most vibrant characters I've ever read."

—*Mystery Scene*

"[A] suspenseful mystery, witty dialogue, and fabulous characters."

—Cozy Mystery Book Reviews

continued . . .

"Coyle displays a deep understanding, not only of coffee . . . but also of coffee shop culture . . . If you have not yet discovered the Coffeehouse Mystery series by Cleo Coyle, you should . . . I heartily recommend them." —Eric S. Chen, BARISTO

"A wonderful series with plenty of local color, great characters, and a setting so real that readers will be scouring the streets of Greenwich Village looking for the real Village Blend."

—The Mystery Reader

"Anyone who loves coffee and a good mystery will love this story. Rating: Outstanding." —Mysterious Corner

Once Upon a Grind

Cleo Coyle

BERKLEY PRIME CRIME, NEW YORK

An imprint of Penguin Random House LLC
375 Hudson Street, New York, New York 10014

ONCE UPON A GRIND

A Berkley Prime Crime Book / published by arrangement with the author

For more information, visit penguin.com.

ISBN: 978-0-425-27086-8

PUBLISHING HISTORY
Berkley Prime Crime hardcover edition / December 2014
Berkley Prime Crime mass-market edition / September 2015

PRINTED IN THE UNITED STATES OF AMERICA

10 9 8 7 6 5 4 3 2 1

Cover illustration by Cathy Gendron.
Cover design and logo by Rita Frangie.
Interior text design by Kristin del Rosario.

There are two means of refuge from the miseries of life: music and cats.

—Albert Schweitzer

This book is dedicated to the memory of Turtle, a little New York stray who brought joy to our lives for nineteen years. She sat on my lap through the writing of every tale in that time, including this one.

ACKNOWLEDGMENTS

Once Upon a Grind marks the fourteenth entry in our Coffeehouse Mysteries, and Marc and I thought it fitting that a fairy-tale mystery set in New York City should begin in Central Park, a storybook world unto itself. From the towers of Belvedere Castle to the Ramble's shadowy woodland, the Park's eight-hundred-plus acres operate under the care of the Central Park Conservancy, and we thank them for answering our questions, and more importantly for the work they do in preserving our nation's first major landscaped public park. To learn more, visit them at centralparknyc.org.

Our interaction with New York's Finest has been nothing but the finest, and we thank them for providing answers to our questions, especially about the NYPD's Mounted Unit. As to the Ps and Qs of police procedure, this is a light work of amateur sleuth fiction. In the Coffeehouse Mysteries, the rules occasionally get bent.

The rest of the research behind *Once Upon a Grind* emerged from our decades of living and working in New York City. Although the Queen Catherine Café is fictional, you can visit two places that inspired it: Seher (aka Old Bridge/Stari Most) in Astoria, Queens; and Bosna Express in Ridgewood, Queens. You can also visit the Papaya King's original hot dog shop on Manhattan's Upper East Side (papayaking.com); go to a poetry slam at the Nuyorican Poets Café on the Lower East Side (nuyorican.org); and even try Gardner's favorite chicken and waffles plate at Amy Ruth's in Harlem (amyruthsharlem.com).

The staff at Penguin's Berkley Prime Crime is among the best in the business, and we sincerely thank them for shepherding this tale into publication.

We send special thanks to Wendy McCurdy, our longtime editor, whose ongoing encouragement and trust in us has kept us writing. Thanks also to her assistant editor, Katherine Pelz, for all her help.

A beautiful shout-out goes to Cathy Gendron for her magical cover art; and the brilliant Berkley Prime Crime team who helped craft this book: art director Rita Frangie; interior designer Kristin del Rosario; production editor Stacy Edwards; and copyeditor Joan Matthews.

We salute our agent, John Talbot, for his thoughtfulness, professionalism, and unflagging support.

Last but far from least, we tip our hats to Nancy Prior Phillips, whose courage and optimism has been an inspiration to us.

To everyone else whom we could not mention here by name, including friends, family, and so many of you who read our books and send us notes via e-mail, our website's message board, and the social networking sites, your kind encouragement keeps us going as writers, and we cannot thank you enough for that.

Our virtual coffeehouse is always open. You are welcome to join us at coffeehousemystery.com.

—Cleo Coyle,
New York City

If you ever find yourself in the wrong story, leave.

—Mo Willems, *Goldilocks and the Three Dinosaurs*

Prologue

Turn back, turn back, young maiden fair.
Linger not in the murderers' lair . . .
—THE BROTHERS GRIMM, *THE ROBBER BRIDEGROOM*

In the fading light of the dying day, the Princess glided along the tree-lined path, gossamer gown sparkling as if sprinkled with fairy dust. When she reached the Oak Bridge, she stopped.

"This way . . ." the Predator called.

The Princess studied the shadows. Little white teeth gnawed at pink fingernails. Finally, she stepped off the path, onto uncertain ground.

She had agreed to this meeting in the Ramble, the oldest section of Central Park. There were towering trees here and menacing boulders; cloudy streams and historic bridges. Most of all, there were thirty-eight acres of landscape magic—rustic paths that made an entire city disappear.

"Did you . . . did you make decision?" the Princess asked, her sweet voice betraying her Russian accent.

Forcing a smile, the Predator began a practiced speech, telling the girl everything she hoped to hear.

"Thank you," the Princess replied, eyes filling with grateful tears. With a hard yank, she broke the valuable chain around her neck. A golden key dangled at the end of it. She held it out to the Predator.

"Now that deal is off, please take back."

The Predator frowned. "I can't take your key, Anya."

"But you said I was free."

"From me," the Predator lied. "The rest is not my business."

Anya hesitated. Then she nodded and turned to go, content in the belief that at least the deal between them was dead.

Not exactly, *the Predator thought. "Anya, stop! Don't move."*

The Princess froze. "What is problem?"

"Your gown is caught on a branch. Another step will ruin it."

"Gown is special," the Princess wailed. "I was told to take care!"

"Don't worry. I'll free it."

Squatting in the dirt, the Predator pretended to fuss with the expensive fabric. "Princess Pink" is what they called it—more like bubble-headed bubble gum, *the Predator thought, for it wasn't the dress that was caught, but the girl who wore it.*

"You are so kind to help," the Princess said.

"Almost done," the Predator promised, getting the needle ready. Leaning closer, the Predator whiffed the girl's scent. She even smelled like all the others, the cloying perfume of eager sheep . . .

"Ouch!"

"Did I prick you? I'm sorry . . ."

"Is okay," Anya said. "I am free now, yes?"

The Predator didn't answer, simply watched the sparkling shroud drift away, through the trees and whispering leaves. In mere minutes, shadows would lengthen; the late afternoon breeze would take on a corpselike chill. That's when the drug would do its work, and this beauty—like the troublesome little pet she was—would be put to sleep.

The Predator smiled at a job well done, barely hearing the tinny speakers of the Delacorte Theater, quieting brats with an ancient phrase.

"Once upon a time . . ."

One

Control your own destiny or someone else will.

—JACK WELCH

Once upon that morning . . .

"What's the matter with you, Clare? Don't you want a little magic in your life?"

My ex-husband thrummed his fingers on our coffee truck's countertop.

I refilled the napkin holders, ignoring him.

"Come on," he pressed, "nearly every member of our staff has visited our resident gypsy, everyone but you."

"I've told you, Matt. I've sworn off fortune telling."

"But today is special—"

"What will it take to get through to you? Maybe I should text you? Adopt our daughter's favorite way of indicating emphasis by using periods after every word: *I. Am. Not. Reading. Coffee. Grinds. Today.*"

"And I'm not asking you to. I simply want Madame Tesla to read *yours*."

I took a breath for patience. This morning had started out so perfectly. The brisk October dawn had painted the sky with a golden light, making Central Park's dewy grass glisten like a fairy glen. Even the chill in the air was ideal for enjoying my freshly roasted coffee.

New York's favorite waking potion was something I usually brewed downtown, among the picturesque lanes of the historic West Village. But today I'd joined a few of my baristas on our coffee truck. By 8 AM, we were stocked up and parked in our assigned spot with the other food vendors near Central Park's Turtle Pond, a stone's throw from the Delacorte Theater, home of Shakespeare in the Park.

The only real challenge facing me at this early hour was Matteo Allegro—my former partner in marriage and current partner in business.

"Look, Matt, I realize you're trying to get some buzz going for these so-called 'magic beans' you've sourced from Ethiopia, but you're the one handling the Seer's tent. Why do I have to be involved?"

"Our gypsy knows you learned tasseography from your grandmother. If you don't let her show off for you, she'll be insulted, and—"

"Tell me the truth."

"I did. That's the reason!" One look at my expression and he threw up his hands. "Look, even if it isn't, what harm is there in humoring a nice old lady?" Matt's big, brown bedroom eyes were now blinking at me. This was his "hurt little boy" look, the one designed to make me feel guilty.

Unfortunately, it did. But like a lot of things that preyed upon me lately, I ignored it.

"I'm too busy," I said.

"You are not—" Matt tapped his watch. "The Kingdom doesn't open for another hour . . ."

"The Kingdom" was New York's inaugural Storybook Kingdom, a weekend festival celebrating the Brothers Grimm, Mother Goose, and classic literary characters beloved by children of all ages. In sixty minutes, families would be streaming into this Central Park compound for arts and crafts, costume contests, even a Fairy Tale Village with jugglers, puppeteers, and knights in shining armor. The whole production was dreamed up by the mayor's office. And since Matt's mother—our esteemed octogenarian employer—happened to sit on the Fairy Tale Fall events committee, we were roped into service.

"You're done setting up, aren't you?" Matt pressed.

"Yes, but the festival staff has kept us hopping since we parked. Here comes another wave . . ."

Matt stepped back as Esther and I filled coffee drink orders for two knights, a court jester, and a half-dressed dragon. When I looked up again, I saw that Matt's focus on fortune telling had finally shifted—to a slinky princess in scarlet.

The young woman's gown had a full, filmy skirt that sparkled in the morning sun. Its stunning red color was repeated in the bright streaks streaming through her soot black, chin-length hair.

"Has Pink Princess come by for coffee?" she asked Matt, her low voice hinting at a Russian accent.

"I don't know. What does the Pink Princess look like?"

The Red Princess laughed. "If you saw her, you would not be asking! My friend is gorgeous. Long blond hair, nearly to waist, and she is very much taller than I."

"Sorry, I haven't seen her," Matt replied.

"If you do, tell her to call Red."

Matt smiled. "You have a phone in that getup?"

"Is strapped to my thigh," the girl informed him with a playful wink. "*And* is set on vibrate. Want to see?"

I shook my head, hardly surprised by the flirtation. Well into his forties, my ex was old enough to be the young woman's father, yet his muscular good looks and world-traveler ease made him the most attractive man in sight.

When we were married, Matt's standard uniform was paint-stained jeans and a flannel shirt. Now that he'd hitched himself to a fashion-forward spouse, Matt was slicker than a *GQ* cover model.

Today's ensemble featured a jacket of stag brown suede tailored to his broad shoulders. His dark hair looked rakish against his bronzed complexion, burnished from a recent sourcing trip to East Africa. His toothy smile dazzled and his dark eyes smoldered. The true trick to Matt's appeal, however, was his appetite. When Matt liked a woman, he let her know it. And he pretty much liked them all.

Of course, none of these things enchanted me. When

you've lived behind a magician's curtain long enough, tricks lose their thrill.

What did surprise me was my ex-husband's rejection of Red's less than subtle invitation to watch her phone vibrate.

"Ah, no, that's okay . . ." He told her, rubbing the back of his neck. He actually looked a little embarrassed. "But I'll keep an eye out for your friend."

Red didn't appear bothered in the least by Matt's response.

"You are a prince!" she declared, and in a gesture that would prove astoundingly prophetic, she raised her fairy wand and tapped Matt's forehead before gliding away.

Two

"WHO was that young woman?"

"The Red Princess," Matt replied with a shrug. "She's looking for her friend, the *Pink* Princess. How many princesses are in this Kingdom anyway?"

"I don't know, but do me a favor and keep your pants on. This is a fall fantasy, not a male fantasy."

"Give me a little credit, will you? That girl is our daughter's age. Now where's Dante?"

Dante Silva was my *artista* barista—fine arts painter by day, java jockey by night.

"Why do you need Dante?"

"I want him to relieve you so you can visit the fortune-telling tent."

I resisted the urge to scream. "He's busy inflating the balloon Giant out back."

"Balloon Giant?"

"It's part of our *Jack and the Beanstalk* theme." I used my finger to draw a giant air circle. "Are you blind?"

"Oh, is that what these dangling vinyl vines on the truck are for? And the fake cow by the picnic tables?"

"Perceptive, aren't we?"

"Not entirely." Matt smirked. "For instance, I have no idea why you're dressed like a Tyrolean peasant. Unless your boyfriend has a secret Alpine fetish."

"Leave Mike Quinn out of this."

"I don't know . . ." Matt made a show of looking over my ruffled white blouse, laced bodice, and Oktoberfest-worthy dirndl skirt. "It's kind of sexy."

"Are you kidding?"

"Not entirely. Who wouldn't go for the shapely wench at the rustic tavern? Your flatfoot certainly would—if you grabbed a beer stein, showed a little more cleavage, and lost the babushka."

"I think it's time *you* got lost."

"Touchy this morning, aren't you?" Matt regarded my outfit again. "Who are you supposed to be playing anyway, Eva Braun?"

"I'm Jack's *mother*."

"Fine, Mrs. Beanstalk, then answer me this: Why does Esther have a musical instrument in her beehive?" He pointed to the large and lovely barista pulling shots at our espresso machine.

"Hey, I heard that!" Esther Best pushed up her black, rectangular glasses and pointed right back at Matt. "No *harping* on my headgear, *Signor* Boss-o!"

"That's not an answer."

"Esther is playing the part of the Magic Harp," I explained. "Given her fondness for reciting urban epics, we all thought it was apropos—and so did her rapper boyfriend."

"Thanks to Boris, my harp actually plays!" With a tilt of her high-haired head, she plucked out a tinny version of "On Top of Old Smokey."

Matt gawked. "I don't recall a harp in *Jack and the Beanstalk*."

"You would if you'd read it to our daughter repeatedly for the better part of her fifth year," I reminded him. "The year you practically lived in Hawaii."

"That was business!" The hurt look was back on the man's face, but this time it was genuine. "Those were boom times for Kona, Clare, and I was setting up trade with Japan."

"Now who's touchy?"

Okay, I confess chastising the man about his failures as a

father was low. Matt had worked hard in recent years to make things up to me and Joy—and, honestly, with my daughter's ongoing culinary career in Paris, he now saw her more than I did. I was about to apologize when a high-pitched scream rang out.

We all froze—until we saw Nancy Kelly, our youngest barista, barreling out of Madame Tesla's colorful little tent. She ran right for me, wheat braids flying, arms flapping.

"Boss, boss! You *have* to visit Madame Tesla. She's so amazingly authentic!"

Matt arched an eyebrow. "I told you."

"She gave me a *great* reading!" Nancy said. "And she told me to tell you she's waiting for you!"

Matt raised his arm and (not unlike the Grim Reaper) pointed at the tent.

"I can't! I'm too busy!" As I frantically resumed swabbing the counter, Nancy climbed back into the truck.

"Ms. Boss, you look white as a ghost. What's your problem?"

"Only one," Matt said. "She's crazy."

"Tell me." Nancy touched my shoulder. "Why are you so afraid of reading coffee grinds?"

I met the girl's gaze. "Because I can see bad things."

"What kind of bad things?"

"Death. I can see it coming."

THREE

MATT shook his head. “Stop being melodramatic.”

“It’s true,” I said. “Have you forgotten? I saw *your* death.”

“But I didn’t die!”

“You almost did!”

“But I didn’t.”

For several seconds, we glared in silence at each other. Then he tilted his head at Esther and Nancy, who’d gone wide-eyed over our nonmarital spat.

“Let’s not do this in front of the children.”

He was right. I could see our employees wanted details. Esther began to ask, and Matt changed the subject—to Nancy’s head.

“Speaking of death,” he said. “Why is Nancy wearing a dead bird?”

Nancy touched her elaborate headpiece. “That’s not a dead bird! It’s the Goose That Laid the Golden Egg.”

“And your face is painted gold because—”

“I’m the Golden Egg, silly!”

“You’re dressed as an egg with a goose as a hat, and I’m silly?”

“She wanted to play the Golden Goose,” Esther noted, “but her costume couldn’t fit behind the counter.”

“So I compromised,” Nancy explained.

“Because Nancy is a good egg,” I said simply.

Matt folded his arms. "Well, I hope you don't expect me to play Jack because I have *no* intention of putting on some ridiculous—"

"Dante is playing Jack," I said, "even though you have more in common with the role."

"Excuse me?"

"She's right," Esther said. "You were sent into the world at a tender age by your widowed mother—"

"And you forged your own destiny by obtaining 'magic beans' from faraway places," Nancy added.

There was a third parallel I could have made, but I kept it to myself.

Like Fairy Tale Jack, Matteo Allegro had developed a dangerous addiction. For Jack, it was the giant's wife. For Matt, the addiction was *cocaine*, which led to that near-fatal overdose, the one *I'd predicted* in a reading of his coffee grinds.

It was a miracle Matt had survived, and after months of rehab, he was finally able to chop down his need to get high. He'd remained clean for over a decade—and I continually prayed, along with his mother and daughter, that his feet would stay firmly on the ground.

"I don't care how much I have in common with Bean Boy," Matt groused. "I am not putting on a costume today—"

"Well, you can rest easy," I said. "Dante is happy to play Jack."

"And I'm happy to report our cow hasn't run dry," Esther declared, sliding a steaming cup across the counter. "Enjoy our 'Milky White' Latte."

"You named a drink after Jack's cow?"

"That's nothing!" Nancy bragged. "We've also got a Snow White Chocolate Mocha, Cinderella Pumpkin Cake Squares, and—"

"We Storybook-ified the menu," I finished for her.

Matt glanced around. "What menu?"

"Isn't it out there?" I sighed. "Give me a minute . . ."

As I located the stand-up chalkboard in the back of the truck, I felt my cell phone vibrate. (No, not against my thigh à la Red Princess—but in my peasant skirt pocket.) Hands full, I ignored the call, and instead wrestled the large sign out our truck's narrow door.

That's when I saw the vision . . . *in pink.*

Twenty feet away, the flap to Madame Tesla's colorful gypsy tent opened and a young woman stepped out.

Tall and lithe, she moved with regal steps that made her sparkling layered skirts seem to float through the air. Her gossamer gown was nearly identical to the dress worn by the Red Princess, except for the more innocent shade, which was fitting because this Pink Princess was likewise more refined, her beauty surreal, as if God had created another species.

Her blond hair fell in a curtain of gold down to her waist and her ocean turquoise eyes appeared exotic with their slightly almond shape—Tartar-esque, I realized, like many of the women I'd met who'd emigrated here from Eastern Europe.

Remembering Red's message for her friend, I was about to call out when I realized she had a cell phone pressed to her ear. She was talking fast and seemed to be upset. Was she crying?

Great, I thought. *Another reason I wanted nothing to do with telling fortunes. It was far too emotional . . .*

I'd seen similar reactions years ago with my nonna, who'd played fortune-teller therapist in the back of our family's Italian grocery. Every few days some neighborhood woman would rush in teary-eyed, until Nonna steadied them with that special cup of coffee before drawing them out, helping them see . . .

And that's when I saw—

A hulking knight, one of the two who'd stopped by our truck earlier, was sipping his brew slowly and staring directly at the Pink Princess.

While a man checking out a woman was as old as time, this was different. He held my take-out cup steady, as if deliberately hiding his lower face from view. With the helmet covering much of his head, only his eyes were visible. And the way the man's dark gaze tracked the Pink Princess looked downright predatory.

It sent a chill through me.

When my phone vibrated again, I actually started. Pulling the cell out of my skirt pocket, I checked the caller ID and tensed.

Why is Mike Quinn trying to reach me at this hour?

I hit the answer button and put the phone to my ear. When I looked up again, the predator knight was gone.

And so was the Pink Princess.

Four

"MIKE? Is anything wrong?"

"Everything's fine, Clare, except . . . I'm sorry about today. I was looking forward to being with you and my kids."

"I'm the one who's sorry—I'm sorry for your loss. In fact . . ." Moving the phone to my other hand, I glanced at my watch. "Shouldn't you be heading to Virginia by now?"

"I'm on my way to the car . . ."

I pictured Mike Quinn striding across the parking garage of his Washington high-rise. The man would have shaved close this morning, and his light brown hair would be in military trim. Given the somber event ahead of him, he would be wearing his charcoal suit, the worn leather shoulder holster creasing a crisp, white shirt beneath. His blue eyes would stay flinty cold all day, unreadable as a slab of city concrete. But during the funeral service, I knew they'd go glassy with held-back tears—and none of his coworkers would ever know it.

His *current* coworkers, that is.

As a decorated narcotics cop, Quinn was still the head of his own NYPD task force. In fact, he'd been based in New York for his entire career, until a U.S. Attorney drafted him for the temporary assignment in Washington, DC.

Sadly, that same attorney stepped down a short time later, when he was diagnosed with an aggressive cancer. He lost the battle a few days ago, which changed our weekend plans.

"You didn't work with the man long," I said, "but I know you respected him, unlike your new boss—"

"Let's not go there. Not now, anyway . . ."

(That was fine with me. Katrina the blond battle-ax had ruined more dinners and weekends than I could count. Why let her ruin this phone call?)

Mike paused. "I need a favor."

"Shoot—not literally."

I could hear Mike's little laugh. Then he took a long breath and let it out. "Leila rang me a few minutes ago—"

"Your ex-wife?" I bristled (couldn't help it). Leila was far from my favorite person, and I knew she felt the same.

"Leila is at your Storybook Kingdom right now. She's waiting at the entrance ropes. Is it possible to wave her in early?"

"Why in the world would she need to get into this festival before it opens to the public?"

"If you'd rather not do this, I completely understand—"

"No, it's okay. I'll take care of it."

"Thanks," Mike said. "I mean it. I'll owe you—"

"Oh, I like the sound of that."

"I thought you might." I could almost hear him smiling over the cellular signal, and that made me smile, until he added: "Can you do me one more favor?"

"I'm listening."

"Leila should be bringing her mother's helper along. If not, can you keep an eye on how things go with the kids today?"

"Mike, I love your kids, and I'll do what I can, but won't Leila want to look after her own kids?"

"She's been flaking out lately," he confessed. "She's late for things, forgets to pick up the kids when they're visiting friends, going to the movies. I'm a little worried she's . . ."

"She's what?"

"I'll tell you more when I see you. You're still coming down tomorrow, aren't you?"

"Are you kidding? I can't wait to get on that train."

"Then help me out today, okay?"

"I'll go right now to speak with Leila."

"Clare."

"Yes?"

He lowered his voice. "I know you, sweetheart. And what you do in the absence of answers. Do not investigate Leila. Whatever she's up to, *let it go.*"

"Let *what* go?"

A familiar beep-beep sounded. Mike had auto-released the lock on his SUV door. "For the moment, you'll have to let *me* go." He paused again. "Remember, no matter how obnoxious Leila is . . . I love you."

"I love you, too."

"Hold that thought."

Five

I found Leila Carver Quinn Reynolds waiting on the lawn at the rear of the majestic Metropolitan Museum of Art, where velvet ropes marked the entrance to our little park Kingdom.

A crowd had gathered already, but Mike's ex-wife was easy to spot. A svelte redhead with the complexion of latte milk and exquisite makeup skills, Leila looked uber chic with her chunky platinum jewelry, designer skinny jeans, and forest green cashmere sweater coat to ward off the morning chill.

Molly and Jeremy were at her side, along with their adorable collie, Penny, straining at her leash.

A few weeks back, Molly had mentioned a girl named *Annie* had become her mother's new part-time helper, but I had never met Annie and I didn't see a young woman.

Leila spied me in my peasant dress and snapped her fingers, beckoning me over like a duchess commanding her scullery maid.

I gritted my teeth, indulging in a moment's fantasy of strangling the woman with her own chunky necklace.

Patience, Clare. Be an adult.

I'd already talked to Samantha Peel, the busy festival director, who approved three guest passes. Now I was trying to keep my focus on Mike's kids—although it was Penny who ran to greet me first, breaking Jeremy's hold on her leash.

With a bark and tail wag, the little collie clearly remembered me from our past Sunday together. Mike and I had taken his kids on an apple-picking outing north of the city, and I'm sure Penny *also* remembered those warm, fresh apple cider doughnuts I'd shared with her.

"Sorry, no doughnuts today, girl." Petting her copper-patched white fur, I gathered her leash and returned her to the kids.

Eleven-year-old Molly threw her arms around me in a tight hug. She had her mother's pretty features and flawless complexion, but (thankfully) not the haughty poise of the fashion model her mother used to be.

That unguarded innocence of childhood was still evident through her joyful smile (despite the newly acquired braces). Her shoulder-length hair was like mine, on the chestnut side of auburn. And like me, she'd brushed it back into a neat ponytail, sunny yellow ribbons matching her sweater.

At Molly's age, my own daughter had leaned toward being a tomboy. Molly preferred girly things—ballet, figure skating, fashion. Even her outfit was feminine with a lemon-and-cream-plaid skirt and matching tights.

Her older brother, Jeremy, in blue jeans and windbreaker, had his father's strong chin, light brown hair, and striking blue gaze. Since he'd turned thirteen, he'd even started taking on Mike's reserve.

"Cool outfit, Aunt Clare," he said, hands in pockets.

"Wait till you see our coffee truck!"

Both kids lit up at my description of the balloon Da[illegible] had designed of a giant coming down a beanstalk. I hande[illegible] the kids a program for the day and pointed out the knights, jousting in all-day tournaments, including NFL stars.

"Awesome!" Jeremy said. "I'm totally up for that!"

"And I want to see the Princesses!" Molly insisted. "Annie told me she's going to be the Pink Princess!"

"Well, there is a Pink Princess," I said. "But I'm pretty sure her name is *Anya*, not Annie."

Leila sighed with profound impatience. "Molly calls Anya 'Annie' as a nickname."

"You're telling me that Anya, the Pink Princess, works part-time as your mother's helper?"

"Wow, Clare, you're *right* on top of things, aren't you?" Leila rolled her eyes. (And yes, I controlled my urge to take a poke at one.)

"Annie said there would be twelve princesses," Molly continued, "just like her favorite Russian fairy tale, where the beautiful girls secretly dance all night around trees with leaves of silver, gold, and diamonds. Have you heard the story of the Secret Ball?"

"No, honey," I replied and focused back on Leila. "So let me get this straight. You have *no* mother's helper with you today?"

"*Obviously*," Leila said to her French manicure. "I knew *you'd* be here."

Before I could respond, Molly tugged on my peasant sleeve.

"Aunt Clare! Aunt Clare! What is this twisty part on the map?"

"That's the Ramble," Jeremy answered. "I'll take you to see the ducks at Oak Bridge—"

"No," Leila snapped. "You two *stay away* from the Ramble. Those woods are confusing, and they're not part of the festival."

"Molly can see the ducks at Turtle Pond," I suggested. "We're parked right next to it."

"See?" said Leila. "Now go with Aunt Clare to see the ducks and funny beanstalk coffee truck. I have something to do."

Molly grasped my hand, swinging it happily, as Jeremy studied the festival program, Penny wagging her tail at his side.

"Leila," I called as the woman's stiletto boot heels clicked swiftly away from us, "you *do* know I have a business to run?"

"Have fun," Leila sang as she hurried down the tree-lined path and toward the Delacorte Theater.

Now why in the world is she going there? I wondered. The first *Mother Goose Storytime* show wasn't due to start for another ninety minutes . . .

Mike's warning came back to me: *"Do not investigate Leila. Whatever she's up to, let it go . . ."*

"Okay," I whispered to the absent Mike. "I won't spy on Leila."

Instead, I led Molly and Jeremy back to my truck, and set them down at a picnic table with mugs of hot cocoa.

Then I sent a *casual* little text to my assistant manager, Tucker Burton, who was on vacation this week. Tuck also moonlighted as a professional actor and director, and he *just happened* to be at the Delacorte right now with the rest of his *Storytime* cast, preparing for a long day of kiddie shows . . .

Mike's X heading 2 Delacorte.
Keep I on her.
X-tra paid vacation day in it 4U . . .

There you go, Leila. How's that for being on top of things?

With a satisfied smile, I slipped my smartphone back into my peasant pocket, ready to handle the day. That's when I saw the next crisis coming at me.

"Clare! Clare Cosi! I need your help!"

Six

Rocketing toward our coffee truck was festival director Samantha Peel.

An intense, middle-aged brunette, Sam was the commanding general brand of socialite. Instead of a riding crop, she carried a clipboard and her "war room" was a Bluetooth dangling from one ear, connecting her with a small army of festival workers.

With her designer safari jacket belted tightly around her waist, her long dark hair scraped back into a battle-ready ponytail, and her knee-high riding boots swishing swiftly through the park grass, she was dressed for the day's challenges. She also wore a strained expression, one I knew well. This poor woman was in desperate need of caffeine!

"What can I get you?" I asked.

"Prince Charming—and fast."

Over the years, I'd heard nearly every slang term there was in this coffee business from the "Ben Franklin" (black iced coffee) to the "Little Lydia" (small latte). I even knew about the "Osama Bin Latte" (quad cappuccino with raw cane sugar). But a Prince Charming?

"I'm sorry, Sam, but what exactly goes into a Prince Charming?"

"What goes into a—" She burst out laughing. "Oh, no, Clare! I'm not talking about some crazy coffee drink! One of my actors called in sick. I sent out an emergency text, and your employer answered. She said her son—" Sam glanced at the clipboard propped on her leopard print hip. "Matteo? Is that right? She said he would be willing to step in and play the part."

"Let me get this straight. You want *Matt Allegro* to be your Prince Charming?"

"Exactly!"

I shook my head. "Take it from a woman who knows, you're better off with a crazy coffee drink."

Matt protested, of course, but his mother *insisted* that he pitch in to help, and with one wave of her bejeweled hand, his fate was sealed.

Off came the tailored jacket and on went the belted silk tunic with the royal crest.

Gold crown (check). Fake sword (check)—he actually *liked* both of those (no surprise). But he categorically refused to wear the green tights, so the folks from the House of Fen provided black leather pants and knee-high male fashion boots with oddly pointed toes.

After one of his sourcing trips to the godforsaken wilderness, Matt looked less like a son of royalty than a member of Captain Hook's crew. But I had to admit today he looked the part of a fairy-tale prince, all broad-shouldered and darkly handsome.

Samantha declared him *perfect* for the role of escort to one of the festival's twelve Princesses, hired to enchant every little girl in today's audience. Then she leaned toward me and lowered her voice—

"And I do believe Matt will do the same for the *mommies*."

A few minutes later I noticed Matt futzing with his pointy boots. "What's wrong?" I asked. "You look like you're in pain."

"Not any pain, Clare. *Royal* pain."

Many hours later, the sun was sinking below Central Park's trees and my ex-husband was back, thrumming fingers on my truck's countertop again.

"Got any of those Black Forest Brownies?"

"Not today."

"How about those Kahlúa thingies?" He adjusted his crown. "They're like vanilla brownies, and you swirl chocolate and coffee liqueur into them."

"My Cappuccino Blondies?"

He waved his plastic sword. "That's right!"

"I don't have those, either."

"Haven't you got *anything* with alcohol in it?"

"Matt, this place is packed with children. Why would I be serving anything spiked with alcohol?"

"Because after a *very* long day of touchy dragons, cranky trolls, and screaming kids, we *adults* could use it."

"Sorry, Charming, you are cursed with sobriety—at least for another hour."

"Oh, boss! The natives are getting restless." Esther pointed at the flash mob forming in front of our truck. "If those are kids, we're fine. But if they're cannibal pygmies, we're dinner!"

I faced Matt. "Are you ready to hand out my gingerbread cookie sticks? They already announced the giveaway over the loudspeakers."

"I have to wait for my *Pink Princess*." He tapped his watch. "She's late."

"Since when do medieval princes have Breitlings? Shouldn't you consult a sundial or hourglass, maybe a magic mirror?"

"You got a magic mirror with white powder, I'm game."

"Don't even joke about that."

"Cough up an Espressotini and I'll go away."

"No deal. I *really* need you to hand out these goodies."

"We Princes have protocols. I'm not allowed to hand out anything until a Princess does her spiel. It's some kind of marketing gimmick for their designer gowns. That's why the House of Fen is one of the sponsors bankrolling this shindig." Matt rechecked his watch and scanned the crowds. "This isn't like Anya."

"Anya?"

"The Pink Princess."

"I know who the Pink Princess is." I narrowed my eyes

at the man. "I wasn't aware you and she were on a first-name basis."

"I was paired with Anya for most of the day, Clare. She's sweet, and she loves all this fairy-tale stuff."

"I hope you *behaved*," I said, "because she's also a part-time mommy's helper for—"

"Look, Sam's coming." Matt pointed. "Do you think she reassigned Anya?"

Samantha Peel looked frazzled after ten hours of conjuring up solutions to problems, but when Matt explained the situation, she went right to her magical Bluetooth.

"Bitsy, where the heck is Pink? . . . Well, if she's not answering her phone, try her friend, Red. Maybe they're together."

"Aunt Clare!"

Turning, I found an excited Molly Quinn looking up at me.

"Is Annie here yet?"

"We're looking for her, honey."

"I've been waiting all day for her to tell the story of the Secret Ball and the dancing princesses. It's my favorite, and she said she was going to tell it especially for me."

I brushed Molly's bangs. "She must like you very much."

"She likes Jeremy, too. She wants to be a teacher someday. But Annie needs lots and lots of money to pay for her education."

Lots and lots of money, I thought. *That doesn't sound right.* Between CUNY and SUNY plenty of young people with little money were able to earn college degrees. But I let that topic go in favor of another—Jeremy.

"Where is your brother? I don't see him."

Molly jerked her thumb toward the crowded ball field. I caught sight of Mike's son near the edge, giving their little collie, Penny, a chance to tag trees.

"And where's your mother?"

Molly's shrug surprised me.

"You don't know where your mom is?"

"We're supposed to meet her up at the castle, after we watch the knights joust."

"The Emerald Princess is on her way!" Samantha announced, looking relieved.

"Good," Esther said, eyeing the gathering crowd. "A mob is an ugly thing."

But Molly tugged my sleeve, and as I leaned down, she whispered in my ear.

"I don't like the Emerald Princess. She tells the same story about the frog prince—and she doesn't even tell it right."

"Well, I still need you to stick around," I insisted. "I don't want you running around this festival alone—"

"But Annie is *so much* better! She told *four* stories today. One about Baba Yaga, a witch with iron teeth who eats children. She lives in the forest, in a hut with chicken legs—that's probably why she told that one at the chicken nugget stand." Molly laughed. "And Father Frost—she told that one at the frozen yogurt truck. Do you know that story, Aunt Clare?"

"I don't, sweetie—"

"A girl is nice to Father Frost and he gives her treasure and a fur coat. But when another girl is rude to him, he freezes her!" Molly concluded with great relish.

I noticed the Emerald Princess jogging toward us, green skirt hiked up in a seriously un-Princesslike fashion.

"Molly, honey, after the goodies are handed out, I'll take you and Jeremy to see the knights, and then we'll find your mother."

And I'll find out what's more important to her than looking after you kids!

Molly shrugged in such a noncommittal way that I *should* have been suspicious—but too much was going on. Esther called for help and we swung into action, bringing out trays of cellophane-wrapped treats.

As Molly predicted, a rather lackadaisical story followed from Emerald Girl about a frog prince, then came the handing out of our frosted gingerbread "beanstalk" cookie sticks and bags of "magic beans" (chocolate-covered raisins) by Prince Matt, who was indeed quite the draw for the mommies.

Things went pretty well, after all. Then the excitement was over, the crowd dispersed—

And I couldn't find Molly or Jeremy.

Seven

"HAVE you seen Mike Quinn's kids?" I asked Matt. "I told them I'd take them to see the knights."

"The jousting started fifteen minutes ago. They probably took off because they didn't want to miss anything."

Before Matt even finished his sentence, I was pulling out my cell phone and tapping Jeremy's number. He didn't pick up, so I left a message to call me *immediately*.

"Clare? What's wrong?"

"Mike asked me to keep tabs on his kids today. Can you help me find them?"

"Of course. Come on . . ."

THE Fairy Tale Village was a collage of noise, color, and manic activity. While pastel Princesses strolled among their subjects with their Prince Charmings, jugglers entertained the crowd, and families swarmed in and out of rainbow tents with crafts, puppets, and carnival games.

A loud crash startled me, and I turned to find an armored knight on the Great Lawn being swept off his black mare. Atop a white steed, the victor raised his lance to loud applause.

"I didn't know they'd be jousting with *live* horses!"

"They're pros, Clare, from that '*Meat*-dieval' Tournament and Feast in New Jersey." He gave me a brochure that grinning jesters were handing out. "Shows six nights a week and a matinee brunch on Saturdays."

Hundreds of kids crammed the perimeter of the jousting field, cheering for their favorite knight. A half-dozen celebrity pro-football players were here, too, dressed in shining armor and posing for photographs.

We searched through the throng but saw no sign of Molly or Jeremy.

"They probably found their mother and went home," Matt said.

"I hope so."

To make sure, I called Leila. She didn't pick up so I left a voice mail message—nothing alarming, simply a request to call me back.

By the time we returned to our coffee truck, the festival was winding down. The crowd was thinning, and the park lights were flickering on.

I checked and rechecked my cell phone.

Nothing. No messages from Leila or Jeremy.

Hoping to get my worries under control, I climbed inside our truck to find my staff reduced to one—Nancy.

"Where is everybody?"

"Dante took off for his overtime shift at the shop."

"What about Esther?" I spied her musical harp on the counter.

"She was here a minute ago, until she saw Tucker Burton rushing toward Madame Tesla's tent. She said she wanted to know the reason Tuck was hurrying to have his fortune told—career or romance."

As I darted for the truck's back door, Nancy frowned. "Now where are *you* going?!"

"To find out!"

But it wasn't Tuck's "career or romance" business I was interested in. It was Leila's.

Eight

TUCK had a chance to observe Leila this morning at the theater, where she'd rushed to go (sans kids). Now was my chance to find out why.

But when I got to the gypsy tent, I found Esther half crouched at the door flap, one ear cocked.

"What are you doing?"

"Eavesdropping, of course."

"You should not be listening to another person's fortune-telling session. That's private business."

"Just think of me as the NSA."

"Esther—"

"Chill-ax, will you? I'm only trying to find out if Tucker got as lousy a fortune as I did."

"You had a dark prediction?" Concerned, I stepped closer. "What was it?"

Esther smirked. "Didn't you just say fortune telling is private business?"

"Yes, but I do happen to care about you."

"It's my romantic life." She grimaced. "There's a bumpy road ahead."

"Oh, is that all."

"Hey, I may not be the kind of female who dots her *i*'s with little hearts, but I do have one. Boris is my world."

"Of course he is. What I meant was: When it comes to

romance, there's *always* a bumpy road ahead. So don't take your reading too seriously, okay? Now go back to the truck and help Nancy close up. I have business with Tucker."

(And yes, I conveniently left out the part about my business being even more like the NSA's than Esther's, although my surveillance scheme was a tad more serious. I was truly worried about Mike's kids.)

I drew back the flap, and stepped into the heady aromas of brewed coffee and potent incense.

"Hello!"

Laughing voices abruptly stopped. Then came whispering and silence.

A batik-draped partition divided the tent into a main room and smaller anteroom, which was where I now stood. A greeter was supposed to be here to welcome customers. But at this late hour, she was gone. The only thing here was a doily-covered table and a framed sign that read:

MAGIC COFFEE BEAN READING
$20.00 TICKET DONATION
ALL PROFITS TO THE
CENTRAL PARK CONSERVANCY FUND

"Hello?" I called again.

This time, an ominous voice boomed a reply—

"Enter, you who seek the council of Madame Tesla!"

Well, I thought, *she certainly sounds authentic* . . .

Quelling my queasiness about the whole fortune-telling thing, I moved around the fabric-covered wall and into the dimly lit tent.

Nine

A single candle glowed on a table covered with white lace. Behind it, the old woman's violet eyes gleamed with arcane wisdom.

Swathed in multicolor robes and a pirate plunder's worth of bangles and necklaces, the gypsy's silver pageboy shined in the flickering light and her long earrings of moons and stars jangled above her narrow shoulders.

"Come, seeker of truth . . ." Madame Tesla beckoned me forward with a bejeweled hand. "The spirits have been accommodating today. Who knows what they may predict for your future?"

"Absolutely nothing," I assured her. "Because I'm not here for a reading."

"Oh, too bad, dear, because I've been getting raves!"

Slipping out of character, Matt's mother grinned. Today she was Madame Tesla, but every other day she was Madame Dreyfus Allegro Dubois, octogenarian owner of the Village Blend, and my employer.

There aren't many women who can say that the best thing about their marriage was their mother-in-law, but for me that was true.

Madame had taken me under her fiercely protective wing when I was a young, naïve, *very* pregnant small-town girl. By nineteen, I'd read through my school's entire library. I'd earned a scholarship and traveled to Italy to study art history, yet in far too many ways, I wasn't very smart.

With wisdom and patience, Madame showed this art school dropout how to survive and thrive in big, bad New York City. Along the way she taught me everything she knew about the coffee trade, shepherding me into a vocation that enriched me in countless ways.

Her own life was an inspiring story of triumph over adversity—from the loss of her family during wartime to the loss of true love in midlife, when Matt's father died. But with every setback, she rose again.

Knowing adversity had made her the perfect Mother Hen of Greenwich Village—historically a neighborhood of cast-offs and outlaws; misfits and miscreants; free spirits and free thinkers.

In the years I'd known her, she'd amazed me with hundreds of tales from her eventful life, and still she managed to surprise me. For instance—

"Can you guess who I chose as the inspiration for my character?"

"No idea."

"Alma, the wife of a former Turkish ambassador to the UN. She's the one who taught me the art of tasseography."

"Really?"

"Alma was wise, in her own way—and she knew how to play the crowd."

"Whatever your inspiration, I have to agree, your act was a sensation."

"It was the talk of the festival!" a voice boomed from the shadows.

Tucker Burton burst into the light so suddenly, I nearly jumped out of my Tyrolean peasant shoes.

"And *look* at Madame Tesla's giant pickle jar!" He shook the large container. "It's packed with tickets!"

My assistant manager was still dressed in his last stage costume of the day: the Pied Piper of Hamelin—that or a very tall, floppy-haired Santa's elf.

"What in the world were you doing lurking in the corner—with a pickle jar?"

"I asked him to step back there," Madame noted. "You see, when he stopped by to collect my tickets for the festival raffle, we got to talking, and—"

"And when she heard you coming in, she wanted you to see her fortune-telling performance without any distractions," Tucker added.

I was dying to ask him about Leila, but—given my lecture to Esther—I felt a little self-conscious.

"Um, Tuck . . ." I began carefully, "did you happen to get my text message?"

"I got it, CC, but late in the day. Your message came during our dress rehearsal, and my phone was turned off."

"So were you able to do *that thing* I asked?"

"Oh, yes . . . I saw *that person* you asked about. She met with *someone else* at the theater."

"Someone else?" I prompted.

A long pause followed, but it was more than careful hesitation. Tucker actually looked *frightened.* "Can we please talk about it *later*?"

"Talk about *what* later?" Madame broke in. With a miffed tone, she turned to face me. "What is going on?"

That's what I wanted to know. Tucker Burton loved gossip. He also trusted me and Madame. *So what could Mike's ex-wife possibly be doing that would put fear into him?*

"Hel-lo-oo! Mr. Pied Piper! Are you in there?"

Before any of us could answer, Tuck's boyfriend burst in, feathers flying (literally). As one of the best drag performers in the city, Punch had been receiving raves for playing the title character of Tucker's latest cabaret show, *Goosed!*

His standing-room-only act made him a natural choice for the role of "Mother Goose" in the Fairy Tale Fall week of *Storytime* kiddie shows, which kicked off today at the Delacorte. The performance involved so many pratfalls, stunts, and belt-em-out ballads that a wiry Hispanic actor in a gray wig, giant petticoat, and feather-covered French mantua was actually better suited for the role than a woman of a certain age.

"They want Madame Tesla's tickets ASAP for the raffle," Punch informed his beau. "And a VIP is asking for you."

"A VIP?"

"I'll explain on the way. Now come on—or do I have to blow that Pied Piper piccolo of yours to get you to follow me?"

Tuck blushed. "Sorry, CC, I've got to go . . ."

Madame pointed a beringed finger to the empty chair across from her.

"Sit down, dear. You look a bit frazzled."

"I should be going, too—"

"But you haven't even tasted Matt's new coffee . . ." Madame poured me a cup. The earthy aroma was irresistible—and it *had* been a long day. I took the cup, but I didn't sit.

"Matt did a nice job on the roast," I admitted as I sipped. "And he was right about these beans. The profile is nothing like the typical bright Ethiopian."

"What notes do you taste?"

"Bittersweet chocolate, plum wine, cloves . . . and something else." I sipped again. "Some kind of spice . . ."

As a master roaster, I prided myself on my sharp palate. It was rare for me to taste something I couldn't decipher—frankly, it bugged me, and I took more hits, trying again and again to nail down the elusive flavor.

"Matteo told me he sampled one cup of these pan-roasted beans under the African moon and bought half the harvest."

"I know," I said, still not certain of that strange spice. But when I reached for a second cup, Madame stopped me.

"Are you *sure* you don't want a reading?"

"Yes, I'm sure!" I grabbed the pot so fast to refill my cup, dark liquid sloshed onto the snow white lace. "Oh, no, I'm sorry . . ."

"Not at all, dear. I can see you're upset. Calm yourself. Enjoy your coffee break. I'm going to change," she said, rising. "My clothes are in the coffee wagon. Please sit down, put your feet up . . ." She pushed two chairs together. "Close your eyes, take a little nap. You'll feel much better."

I had no intention of taking a nap, but I did take a load off. As I finished my coffee, I even put up my peasant-soled feet. That's when I heard the young girl's voice.

"Aunt Clare? Are you in there?"

Molly?

ten

"Aunt Clare, we can't find our mom!"

Mike's daughter looked frantic. Jeremy looked scared. He'd stepped in after his sister, holding Penny's leash.

I got to my feet and embraced the children. "Where have you two looked for her?"

"We went to Belvedere Castle, like she told us to," Jeremy said.

"But she wasn't there!" Molly cried.

"Okay, calm down. We'll find her . . ."

I led the children out of the tent. Then they took the lead. Night had fallen fast, but the park seemed especially dark. Mike's children headed for the castle again.

"Slow down, kids! Wait for me!"

They didn't. They kept moving. At the crest of the hill, I reached the castle grounds, only to find the pair racing for a set of stone steps on the other side. At the bottom of the steps, they took a dirt path, one of the many entrances leading into—

Oh, no . . .

"Molly! Jeremy! Come back! Don't go in there!"

The Ramble was confusing in daylight. At night, the thick woods and maze of winding paths were downright stupefying. I did my best to catch up, but Mike's kids were moving at a preternatural pace.

Freestanding park lamps glowed along the path. They

were few and far between. The children would appear in a pool of light and quickly disappear again, as if swallowed up by a black beast. And then—

No!!!

They were gone. I had completely lost them!

I saw a fork in the trail. Both paths branched off into thick woods—one sloped upward, the other down.

Which way do I go?

Both routes seemed right. With tears of frustration, I searched for any sign of which path to take. And then I saw the light—literally.

A flickering glow emanated from far down the descending trail. Was it a flashlight? Someone signaling for help? I hurried along the dirt path only to find an incomprehensible sight.

A traffic sign hung on a huge oak tree, blocking my way, its blinking bulbs spelling out the words *Bridge Detour.*

"Clare . . ."

Now someone was calling my name. Off the path, I heard leaves crunching, saw branches moving. Then came a flash of sparkling pink.

Between two gnarled trees, a slender woman appeared with her back to me. Against the black trunks and brown leaves, the glistening fabric of her gown seemed to glow with its own illumination.

Then the woman turned.

"Leila!"

At the sound of her name, Mike's ex-wife took off.

"Stop," I shouted, following her off the path and into the woods, "your kids are looking for you!"

The brush grew thicker, but I kept going. Then the ground began to give, like quicksand. With tremendous effort, I tried to push forward but couldn't. That's when I felt it—

The cold.

Not the icy bite of harsh weather, but the black, empty chill that freezes you from the inside out.

A presence loomed nearby. I didn't need to see it because I *felt* it. And whatever it was, I knew it meant harm.

Shaking with fear, I watched a specter begin to materialize.

The black shape started out as human then it began to transform, its essence bending and twisting until it became a monstrous animal.

I was about to scream when somebody beat me to it.

"Help! Help me!"

I fell off my chair and onto the floor.

What the—

From my padded derriere, I rubbed my eyes. No longer in the Ramble, I was back in Madame Tesla's fortune-telling tent. My chair was turned over, my empty coffee cup on the ground beside me.

"Help me! Help me! Please!"

The woods had been an illusion, but these cries weren't part of a dream. They were real.

I scrambled to my feet and bolted for the lawn.

Eleven

THE cry for help had drawn a costumed crowd. A dozen Storybook Kingdom residents converged in front of my coffee truck. I elbowed my way through Jack, Jill, and Little Miss Muffet (sans her Tuffet).

Pushing into the center of the fairy-tale ring, I found Mike Quinn's ex—in a clinch with mine.

"What happened?!" I cried.

Matt stepped back and Leila faced me, topaz eyes pooling.

"I can't find Molly or Jeremy. They were supposed to meet me at the castle. When they didn't show, I searched everywhere, but I couldn't find them!"

She buried her face into my ex-husband's princely tunic.

That's when it hit me like a sucker punch: *Lost kids. In an urban park. At nightfall.* And they weren't just any kids. They were *Mike's kids.*

"Did you try calling them?"

"What are you talking about, Clare? Molly doesn't have a phone."

"But Jeremy does!" I reminded her.

"Not since I took it away."

"You what?!"

"My son sneaked his phone into school two days ago," Leila said. "And that's prohibited!"

"Mike never told me that!"

"That's because I haven't had time to tell him."

I clenched my fists so tightly my nails dug into my palms. "Leila, if Jeremy *had his phone now*, we could *contact him*."

"Stop yelling at me. They're *my* children. Not yours."

"And what about their father? Maybe you should have consulted him before you took the phone away."

Leila shook her scarlet mane, and her tone turned shrill. "What does that matter now? I can't find my babies. That's *your* fault, not mine. I left Molly and Jeremy with *you*. You agreed to watch them!"

A wall of muscle stepped between us. "That's enough. Bickering and blame aren't going to help us find two lost kids."

Leila's eyes flashed at Matt. "They *also* had their collie with them."

"Okay, and their little dog, too."

Leila demanded the police be called, and a perpetually grinning Cheshire Cat stepped up, informing us he'd already spoken to 911.

(The cat was actually James Elliot, whose popular portobello mushroom burger prompted his embrace of the *Alice in Wonderland* theme, complete with inflatable hookah-smoking caterpillar atop his bright orange sandwich truck.)

Within a minute an electric buggy with two park policemen rolled up, while in the background an NYPD sector car approached along the narrow road circling the ball field.

Samantha Peel arrived with her handy Bluetooth—and a bearded man in a navy blue blazer (the festival's legal advisor).

The police were serious and professional, but they were not overly alarmed; in other words, no Amber Alert, not yet. They calmed Leila and launched some basic protocols.

A smartphone alert was sent to Sam's staff, and an announcement was made over the loudspeakers for "Jeremy and Molly to please come to the coffee truck . . ." Meanwhile, Leila was instructed to ring her building's doorman *(no sign of them)* and the kids' friends. *(No luck.)*

Finally, the police shared their plans for a systematic

search of the entire festival area, as well as the museum's grounds near the festival's entrance. If the kids didn't turn up, the hunt would be widened.

The Mad Hatter joined the Cheshire Cat in offering to help search, as did Jack and Jill, Snow White's Huntsman, and Little Bo Peep (who clearly took her role to heart). But while the police outlined their plan, I felt a cold itch at the back of my skull.

That little dream I'd had in Madame Tesla's tent had involved Mike's kids, and they hadn't led me to any of the places the police were about to search.

It bothered me. But what was I supposed to do about it? Tell the police to base their response on a coffeehouse manager's naptime musings?

Rationally speaking, I had no idea where Molly and Jeremy were. And I certainly didn't want to divert official resources on *this* mother's "goose chase."

Yet my dream had seemed *so real.* I couldn't let it go . . .

That left me with one solution. But first I had to call Mike Quinn and tell him the truth. There was no getting around it—

I'd let down the man I loved.

TWELVE

Quinn picked up on the first ring. As soon as I explained the situation, he went into full cop mode, peppering me with questions on the official response, the name of the officer in charge, the search procedure, and a dozen other things.

"I'm sorry this happened, Mike. You warned me about Leila's flaky behavior, you asked me to keep an eye on your kids. I should have been more careful—"

"Stop. It's not your fault—"

"I don't care what you say. I feel responsible—"

"Let me finish, Clare. It's not your fault for a very simple reason. It's mine."

"How could it possibly be yours? You're four hundred miles away."

"Exactly."

I closed my eyes and took a breath. "Mike, I'll find them. I promise—"

"I'm coming to help."

"In the morning?"

"Now. I'm already in the car. If I can't book a seat out of Dulles, I'll go on standby. Call me anytime, okay? If you can't get through, I'm on the plane. I'll call you back as soon as I can . . ."

We said our good-byes and I turned my gaze skyward.

The night felt especially dark with the glow from Manhattan's lights painting the horizon an eerie purple.

I hurried to my coffee truck and climbed in the back door.

Esther looked up. "Nancy and I already emptied the thermal Air-Pots—"

"Fill them again," I commanded. Then I told them about Jeremy and Molly. They were both upset and asked to help. "Take care of the truck. And after the coffee is ready, notify the officer in charge that free java is available to all police and park personnel helping with the search."

Rummaging through the utility drawer, I found a heavy Maglite. I tested its beam—and accidentally blinded Esther.

"Yow!" she howled, rubbing her eyes. "Why do you need the flashlight?"

"It's dark outside!" I called, dashing for the door.

On the grass, my legs began eating up ground until something caught my arm. "Whoa, Nellie!" Prince Matt stared down at me with suspicion. "Where are you galloping so fast?"

"Where do you think? To find my boyfriend's kids!"

"Yes, but *where*?"

I told him my destination and Matt frowned.

"Clare, I'm not about to let you wander around Central Park's woods alone."

"Then I guess you're coming."

Thirteen

Using my dream as a guide, I started at Belvedere Castle—where Molly and Jeremy *should* have met their mother.

The Victorian folly was perched on top of Vista Rock, the second highest point in the entire park, and Matt complained about stiff boots and sore feet during the whole climb.

"Molly! Jeremy!"

A howl of wind was the only reply.

It set me to shivering (and kicking myself for not covering my peasant costume with a nice, warm hoodie). Ignoring the chill, I adjusted my babushka, untying the strings from beneath my ponytail and retying them under my chin. Now I looked like Baba Yaga, but at least my ears were warm as I led Matt across the brightly lit observation deck to stone steps cut into the steep hillside.

After the castle's bright lights, our descent felt like a plunge into a black abyss. Cold, damp air hung like a fog around us, and the strong scent of earth and autumn leaves wafted up from the forest below.

At the bottom of the rustic staircase, we followed the downward sloping dirt trail and entered the wooded maze known as the Ramble.

I activated the Maglite. Its powerful beam seemed

impressive back at the truck, but in these thick shadows, the light was easily dispersed.

"Molly! Jeremy!" I called as we moved deeper into the darkness. A wind gust rustled the dry leaves, sending another chill through me. After more minutes of silent walking, I glanced at Matt.

"You're awfully quiet."

"These woods are creepy."

I sent the flashlight beam across his face. "You look tense. Are you scared?"

"No. Just . . . uneasy."

I couldn't believe it. "The fearless world traveler is rattled by a few trees?"

"*These* trees, growing out of *this* earth."

"Is that supposed to mean something?"

"When I was a kid, I told my mother that I was spending the night at a friend's apartment, but I really spent it in these woods. Three of my buddies and I did it on a dare."

"And?"

"An old homeless guy saw us horsing around. He gathered us together and told us New York ghost stories for hours, including the true history of an early Dutch director general who ordered the massacre of two villages of Native American families. Men, women, children, grandparents—they were all killed right here on Manhattan Island, most while they slept."

"That's horrible."

"The Dutch official was ordered back to Amsterdam, but he never got there. His ship sank in a storm with everyone on board. The old man said he was cursed. The ghosts of the murdered families pulled him into the dark, icy depths." Matt shivered. "I had nightmares for weeks."

"That massacre probably occurred in lower Manhattan, not way up here."

"It happened on this island, this land. You never wondered why the Manhattan population is happiest on concrete? Why the entire island is paved over? It's a layer of stone between the residents and the cursed earth, which we do not have the advantage of at the moment."

"You actually believe there's a curse on Manhattan earth? You never mentioned this to me before."

"We've never been alone, at night, in the Central Park woods before—"

An animal chuffed from the bushes and we both nearly jumped out of our shoes (in Matt's case, pointy boots). I aimed the flashlight at the sound and saw a pair of shiny eyes on a masked face. The creature blinked calmly and scurried away.

"A raccoon," Matt whispered.

"At least it wasn't a rat."

"Rats don't bother me. I'm more concerned about wild dogs."

"What's next?" I cried. "Gators from the sewers? A killer-eyed cockatrice? You can't scare me with these silly fear tactics. I'm not leaving this park until I find Molly and Jeremy."

Matt stopped me. "They're not here, Clare. There's no sign of them. And the police are back on the festival grounds with a search plan that makes sense. This doesn't."

"Can't you trust me?"

"Yes—if you tell me why you think they're out here."

My dream, I thought, but what I said was—

"Mother's intuition."

"What does that mean?" Matt folded his arms. "Are you flashing back to some incident in Joy's childhood you never mentioned?"

Actually, there were plenty. When Joy was thirteen, she failed to come home from school. For hours, I knocked on doors in our Jersey neighborhood. I finally found my daughter in a tree house. She wasn't alone, and while Joy and her classmate Stewart weren't exactly playing doctor, they were definitely in the waiting room.

"I often wonder how many of Joy's secrets you've kept from me," Matt mused.

Only one, I thought. *And his name isn't Stewart. It's Emmanuel Franco.* But what I said was, "Not everything can be explained." And I continued down the path, calling—

"Molly! Jeremy!"

Nothing.

"Clare!" Matt shouted, standing his ground. "Let's turn around—"

"Wait, Matt! Look!"

When he caught up to me, I passed the flashlight over two items lying on the dirt path: a cellophane wrapper and a piece of broken cookie. I picked them up and sniffed.

"It's one of our frosted gingerbread sticks. Mike's kids were here. I'm sure of it!"

"You gave hundreds of those away, Clare. Anyone could have dropped it here. You don't expect me to believe—"

"I expect you to back me up. That's what good partners do. Now come on!"

Fourteen

After some fast walking, we came to a fork in the road. Just like my dream, the trail split into two paths. Each curved out of sight.

"So? Which way does your 'mother's intuition' tell you to go now?"

I closed my eyes and tried to conjure those dream images. I saw the giant oak tree, and the huge lighted sign hanging on its trunk.

"The blinking traffic sign was on a downward grade," I said, opening my eyes. "So let's follow the descending path."

"Did you say something about a *blinking traffic* sign? In the *woods*?"

Leading with the flashlight, I hurried down the trail.

"Clare?"

I faced him. "I had a dream, okay?"

"Last night?"

"No, I nodded off in your mother's tent. I didn't tell you because I *know* it's not rational. But I can't get it out of my mind, and—"

"Before you had this dream, did you drink my coffee?"

"Excuse me, but this is no time to discuss the quality of your—"

"Answer me, Clare! Did you *drink the coffee* in the gypsy's tent?"

"Yes! I had two cups and the dream came after that. I must have dozed off because—"

"You didn't doze off. And you didn't have a dream. What you experienced was a vision."

I studied Matt's face. "You're serious, aren't you?"

He nodded, and I realized he looked more than serious. He looked *excited.* "Are you telling me those so-called 'magic' beans you brought back from Africa really are—"

"The beans don't work on everyone. In Ethiopia, the village shaman told me the drinker must have a 'special spirit'—essentially a natural gift of insight. Let's just say she convinced me."

"How?"

"Trust me, Clare. After what I witnessed, I became a believer."

"A believer in *what* exactly?"

"In the coffee beans' ability to . . ." He looked away. "I know it sounds crazy, but I sent a sample to a friend. He's a chemist—and a coffee aficionado. I want to know what properties in these beans help certain people read . . ."

"Read the *future*? Is that what you're trying to say?"

"*Now* do you understand why I was trying to get you into that fortune-telling tent?"

"No. I do not understand. Mike's kids didn't go missing until the end of the day. What kind of future were you hoping I'd see?"

"Yours." Matt shifted from one pointy boot to the other. "My mother and I were both hoping the fortune-telling session would help you make an important decision . . ."

My stomach clenched. *They couldn't know about Mike's question. I was keeping it from them.* "I have no idea what you're talking about."

It was a weak lie, and Matt knew it. "Come on, Clare."

Oh, for heaven's sake. "How did you find out?" I demanded. "Did Tucker tell you?"

"That's not important. What *is* important is your peace of mind."

"Listen, *now* is not the time to discuss my future!" I walked away.

He gently grabbed my arm. "You asked me to be a good partner. I failed at that in marriage, but I won't in business—or as a friend. After we know the kids are safe, you and I—and mother, if you like—will sit down and help you figure out what to do, okay?"

I took a deep breath. "I just hope those kids *are* safe."

"What makes you think they aren't? Talk to me. After you drank the coffee, what did you see?"

I told him my vision, but not from the beginning. It was the *end* of the vision that disturbed me most.

"I remembered being very cold. Not so much temperature as temperament. It was a black, empty cold, the kind that chills you from the inside out. And there was a presence . . ."

"What does that mean?"

"It was a feeling at first and then I saw this black specter . . ." I described how it first appeared human and then transformed, twisting into a beastly thing.

"You saw Death in the woods?"

"Not Death. Someone who has no problem using it. *Now* do you see why I'm so desperate to find Mike's kids?"

Matt grimaced and his tone changed. "Tell me more about your vision. You said something about a traffic sign?"

"A giant oak tree was blocking my path. A sign hung on it with blinking bulbs. The lights spelled out *Bridge Detour*."

Matt pulled out his smartphone. "Let's try something . . ."

"What are you doing?"

He tapped the phone's screen a few times and showed it to me. "These are photos and descriptions of all the bridges in Central Park. Scroll through them and tell me if anything looks familiar."

"Balcony Bridge at West Side Drive—*No*." I continued down the list. "Bow Bridge across the Lake; Bridge Number Twenty-four across the Bridle Path; Gapstow Bridge across the Pond at Fifty-ninth Street; Oak Bridge across Bank Rock Bay—"

"Stop," said Matt.

"What?"

"Didn't you tell me the *Bridge Detour* sign in your vision was attached to—"

"An oak tree! Matt, I remember now: This morning Jeremy said something about showing Molly the ducks at Oak Bridge! Where is it? How far?"

He grabbed back the smartphone, tapped up a map. "We're very close. Look—"

"It's just ahead!" I bolted down the trail.

"Slow down!" Matt yelled. "Don't make me look for you, too!"

I picked up my pace instead (which may have been a tad reckless). Hitting a patch of wet leaves, I slipped, skinning an elbow as I fell.

Footsteps sounded behind me. Then a hand appeared in front of my face.

"Really, Clare, hasn't your boyfriend taught you the value of *backup*?"

With a sigh, I took Matt's hand and hauled myself up. "I'm just so worried about them."

"I know. Let's go . . ."

Together we continued along the trail until the Ramble's famous Arch appeared. Flanked by massive boulders, this narrow stone bower reminded me of a giant keyhole, and I felt like a shrunken, shivering Alice as we passed through—until I saw another breadcrumb (so to speak).

"A hair ribbon!"

I moved the flashlight's beam over the object. The ribbon looked like Molly's, except the sunny yellow color was half-buried in blackness.

The sight of that innocent little thing soiled and ground into the dirt sent a deathlike chill through me, and I took off again.

"Clare!"

"Come on!" I shouted, unable to stop myself.

By now, I could see a glimmer in the distance—lamplight reflecting on undulating waves. I jogged toward the light until I reached a small section of Central Park's Lake.

The landmark Oak Bridge spanned the inlet. Flanked by

beaux-arts lampposts, the beautifully restored bridge had been carrying people safely across the brackish water for well over a century.

In the middle of its wooden deck, I spied a boy and a girl in a pool of golden light, leaning against its cast-iron railings.

"Molly! Jeremy!"

With a shriek of joy and relief, I ran to them.

Fifteen

Molly threw herself into my arms.

She's crying, I realized, *and not tears of joy . . .*

"We tried to find Annie!" she said between heartrending sobs. "Someone told us they saw the Pink Princess in the Ramble, but when we got here—"

"Penny ran away, Aunt Clare," Jeremy said in an emotionless tone (not unlike his father's).

"She took off after a squirrel," Molly added through tears. "The leash slipped out of my hand!"

Molly wiped her nose with a tissue she pulled from her pocket.

I noticed something shiny coming out with it—a chain of silver and gold links with a broken clasp. I tucked the broken necklace back into her pocket and continued to comfort the inconsolable girl.

"It's my fault, Aunt Clare," Molly wailed. "Now Penny is lost!"

Jeremy squeezed her shoulder. "Don't cry, Mol. I told you I'd find Penny, and I will."

By now, Matt had caught up with us and was on the phone with Samantha Peel. In record time, an electric buggy appeared on the far side of the Oak Bridge.

Samantha rode in back with a fuming Leila Quinn. Up

front, a police officer sat behind the wheel next to the festival's legal advisor.

I sighed. *Has our society turned so litigious we need lawyers to oversee the reunion of lost kids with their mothers?*

The buggy rolled to a halt and Leila jumped out. No greeting, no thanks. The woman simply pushed me aside and grabbed Jeremy's arm.

"What were you thinking?!" she yelled, shaking the boy. "I was worried sick—"

"Leila, stop!" I dived in, pulling the woman off her son. "Penny got lost. They've been searching for the dog ever since."

Leila's eyes flashed. For a second, I thought she was going to shake me, too—she even balled her fist.

Oh, go ahead, I thought, balling my own. *Give me a reason.*

It was eleven-year-old Molly who acted like the grown-up. "Stop fighting!" she shouted. "We have to find Penny!"

The little girl's eyes filled with tears, and Leila's maternal instincts finally kicked in. "This policeman will find your dog," she cooed.

The officer's expression was doubtful, and Molly—a detective's daughter—immediately picked up his negative vibe.

"We have to find Penny *ourselves*!" she told her mother in a firm voice.

"We can't. It's late and you're both going home."

While Molly and her mother argued, the festival's attorney climbed out of the electric buggy, resplendent in casual-Saturday lawyer wear—navy blue sports coat, open-necked shirt, nicely pressed jeans, and highly polished loafers. To my surprise, he didn't approach Leila. Instead, he pulled Matt and me aside.

In his late forties, Harrison Van Loon (pronounced "Van Loan," or so he said at last week's vendors' planning meeting) lived on the leaner side of trim with a thick head of salt-and-pepper hair, a fashionably close-cropped beard, and horn-rimmed glasses through which his intense hazel green eyes were (unfortunately) studying Matt and me with open suspicion.

"From your costumes I'm guessing you're festival staff?" The toothy smile looked friendly, but the tone of voice was disturbingly serious.

I gave him our names, and he pointed at Matt.

"Allegro? You're the one Samantha signed up this morning, aren't you? I told Sam you should have been vetted first. Everyone who works around children has to be vetted. We don't want the festival to be exposed to legal action . . ."

This I knew from the aforementioned vendors' meeting, where Van Loon had handed out a long list of *do's* and *don'ts* in dealing with the public (emphasis on the *don'ts*) . . .

Do be courteous; *don't* be argumentative;
Do smile at the children; *don't* touch the children;
Do offer children food; *don't* hand the children food;
Do hand it first to a parent or caregiver *in loco parentis . . . et cetera, et cetera, ad nauseam.*

"Look, I signed a bunch of papers," Matt told the lawyer. "I followed your rules. I didn't know you wanted DNA samples on top of it all—"

"There wasn't time for formalities," I hastily added. "Samantha was in a bind and Matt volunteered to help out. You should be thanking him."

"You say you *found* these kids?"

"We didn't *say* we found them. We *found* them." Matt pointed to the children. "Ask them."

He glanced at Molly and Jeremy, who were continuing to argue with their mother. When he turned back, his suspicious lawyer gaze was no longer on Matt. Now he was focused on me.

"Exactly how do *you* know these children, Ms. Cosi?"

"Through their father, an NYPD police detective on assignment with the Justice Department in Washington."

Van Loon continued to frown down at me until Matt pointedly added—

"Clare is in a *relationship* with the man."

"Oh, I see . . ." Van Loon's stiff posture instantly relaxed.

"I was trying to cognize why I witnessed the hostility toward Ms. Cosi from the children's mother. But now that you've explained the *personal* situation . . ." He shook his head and actually broke into a smile before suppressing it.

Oh, brother. Before I could give him something else to *cognize*, he lowered his voice.

"Let me ask you something. Did the children tell either of you how they got here? I mean, did anyone—especially members of our festival staff—*lure* them into the woods?"

"No, nothing like that . . ."

As I explained how the search began first for the Pink Princess, and then the lost dog, Van Loon began patting his many pockets. Finally, he came up with an engraved silver case, out of which he produced two cards with little loons on them (the feathered kind).

"For the record, I may have to contact you two again, after I speak with the kids and get *their side* of tonight's events."

Gritting my teeth, I reminded myself that lawyers—like cops—had to get everyone's side of the story. It was the naked condescension I could have done without.

Van Loon handed over his cards. "It's merely a formality. We want to avoid exposure, and protect the festival from legal action. I have your contact info, now you have mine, and—"

Jeremy's strong voice interrupted the lawyer. "No way, Mom. We're not leaving the park without Penny."

With a frosty look, Leila tried to silence her son. It didn't work.

"I told Molly I would find Penny and I'm going to do it," he declared, his expression displaying a determination beyond his years. *Like Mike*, I thought again, and almost smiled—*almost* because the kids' distress over their lost dog was heart-rending, and their mother's attitude wasn't helping.

I pushed past the lawyer and stepped up to Molly.

"We'll find Penny," I promised her. "Matt and I will bring her home tonight."

My ex shot me a dubious look. But Molly's face brightened, and that was all I cared about.

"Can you really find her, Aunt Clare?"

I squeezed Molly's hand. "I'll do my best."

"If you can't find Penny, *I'm* coming back, first thing tomorrow," Jeremy declared.

Leila opened her mouth to speak—and for once thought better of it.

Samantha Peel never said a word during the encounter. She sat in uncomfortable silence, hands in her leopard print lap, obsessively playing with one of her chunky rings while Leila and the kids climbed aboard the cramped buggy.

Is Sam embarrassed by all this? I wondered. The woman was a socialite who traveled in elite circles. Charity balls, celebrity fund-raisers, black-tie galas—these were the tent poles of her year. I'd served coffee and croissants in Manhattan long enough to know how her species acted (and reacted). For someone like Sam, appearances were everything.

Did she think the story of two lost kids would hit the papers? I couldn't imagine why. They weren't lost for very long. It all seemed like very small potatoes.

Oh, well, one glass of imported vino, and Samantha Peel would forget all about this little hiccup in an otherwise smoothly run event. And Harry Van Loon, attorney-at-law, would be relieved that Mike's ex-wife had no grounds to sue the festival.

"Excuse me, folks . . ." The policeman sidled up to us. "The mother gave us a description of the dog. I'll notify Animal Control to look out for the collie in and around the park, but . . ."

Matt sighed. "Don't get our hopes up?"

The cop shrugged his shoulders. "Give it your best shot, your royal highness, but don't stay in Central Park too long. In that getup, you never know what kind of trouble will come your way."

Sixteen

As the electric buggy rumbled away, I waved good-bye to the kids. When the vehicle was out of sight, Matt turned to me.

"Mission accomplished," he declared. "Let's go home."

"Some Prince you are. You go. I'm staying to look for Penny."

Even in this gloom I could see the frustration on Matt's face.

"Don't tell me," I said. "I already know. It's like finding a needle in a haystack—"

"A needle with four legs and a will of its own."

"We have to try. I told Molly I'd do my best."

But it wasn't only that; I was spurred by the thought of what could happen to a little lost dog in a city where human beings sometimes vanished without a trace.

Matt noted my resolve and rolled his eyes to the starry sky. "Gee, I can't think of a better way to spend a Saturday evening in Manhattan. Can you?"

"You're a prince."

Matt snorted.

"Just let me call Mike and we'll go."

"Where?"

"Back through the Arch and into the Ramble. That's where Penny ran off."

Matt nodded and crossed to the middle of the bridge to give me privacy. He didn't have to. Quinn didn't pick up. I left a voice mail message, letting him know his kids were okay.

He was likely in the air by now, which meant our weekend plans in DC were ruined. But his kids were safe, and I thanked their guardian angels for our lucky outcome.

"Let's go, Clare, it's getting late . . ."

Leading with the Maglite, Matt guided us back through that giant stone keyhole and into the woods.

"HERE, Penny, Penny. Penny!" I called. "Come on, girl . . . Come to Mama . . . Here, Penny, Penny, Penny!"

This went on for some time until the yelling and the hiking became too much, and I paused to take a breath.

"Thank you," Matt said. "I was getting a migraine."

"Don't you ever get tired of whining?"

"I can't whine on the job," he replied. "Obsessing about a bad hotel room or a busted Rover in some underdeveloped country is flat-out indulgent. I mean, I'm living like royalty compared to the hunger, disease, poverty, and lawlessness I see on my coffee-sourcing trips. For me, whining has become a first-world luxury I only enjoy at home in New York, surrounded by the people I love—"

"Shhh!" I cut in, not that I minded Matt's complaint about complaining, but I thought I'd heard—

Bark!

"Did you hear that? Here, Penny, Penny!" I shouted. "Come to Mama!"

Bark, bark, bark!

Before Matt could react, I snatched the flashlight and leaped into a bush.

"Clare? Are you nuts? Stick to the path!"

"You stick to the path! Try to circle around and meet me on the other side."

I lost Matt's reply in my headlong juggernaut through the brush.

I hopped fallen trees and rocks, and crashed through low-hanging branches, their fingers shredding my babushka. I pulled it off completely and nearly screamed when the creepy silk of cobwebs tickled my face. Frantically shaking them off, I kept moving, toward the sound of Penny's bark.

"Come here this instant!" I commanded, using my "stern manager" voice.

In reply, I heard a whimper and saw that Penny and I were separated by a tangle of shrubbery too dense to break through and too high to clamber over. As I sought a way around the foliage, I was stopped by an ominous growl.

"Penny, is that you?" I whispered.

Suddenly Matt's crack about wild dogs seemed believable.

This is silly, I told myself. *It's only Penny.*

That's when a snarling ball of fur burst through the shrubs and knocked me backward!

My head hit something hard and the purple sky was suddenly bursting with meteors and flashing with comets. I raised my arms to fend off tearing claws, dreading the sharp fangs that were about to close around my throat.

Instead I felt a wet, warm tongue on my cheek, accompanied by lots of heavy breathing.

"Bad dog," I moaned, wincing when I touched my head.

The little collie sprawled on the ground beside me, wagging her tail and whining in canine gratitude. Penny was still trailing her leash, and I wrapped the strap around my wrist.

"Let's see you slip away now!"

The knock on the head made me weak, and when I sat up, a wave of nausea hit me. Next came a blast of chill air that cut right through my peasant costume.

I'd been cold for the past hour, but I'd hid it from Matt, fearing he'd drag me back to the coffee truck. Now I could no longer control my shivers, and my teeth started chattering.

"Let's g-g-go home, girl."

I rolled onto my hands and knees—and spied an eerie glow through the branches. I blinked to make sure they weren't concussion fireworks and realized the Maglite had been knocked from my hand into the brush.

As I reached for it, I saw the brilliant beam illuminating a figure. A young woman's body was sprawled on the ground.

Oh, no . . .

I crawled backward, the shock of the adrenaline rush rattling my already aching head.

Penny strained against her leash to get to the motionless form.

"Penny, sit," I commanded, pulling her back. Reluctantly the dog complied.

Now I was the one hurrying to get to the girl. Gently, I touched her skin. The alabaster flesh felt cold as winter stone, and I flashed on a life-sized porcelain doll, cast into the wilderness. But this wasn't a doll.

Holding my breath, I held two fingers on the underside of the girl's slender wrist. There it was! The flutter of a pulse—

She's alive!

The wind had piled leaves around her face and body. I brushed them aside to reveal long golden hair and a pink Sparklewear gown. The hope in my heart from the proof of life instantly plummeted to a dark, tangled place.

It can't be . . .

With frantic fingers I freed the Maglite from the brush and lit the young woman's face. This was no stranger. This was Leila's mother's helper, Molly's much-beloved "Annie," and Matt's missing partner, the Pink Princess.

Now I knew what had kept Penny in the woods. The little dog had found her friend and was trying to guard her from harm.

Like Penny, I had found Anya.

But was I too late to save her?

Seventeen

WITH all speed, I dialed 911 and explained the situation.

Other than a faint pulse, there were no signs of life. Anya's eyes were closed, her hair matted with leaves, and her complexion whiter than egg shells. I shook her motionless form, called her name over and over, but she never reacted.

"What's your location?" asked the emergency dispatcher.

In frustration, I struggled to answer: "Up the hill from the Oak Bridge, near the curvy trail by the big rock, but not on the path, in the bushes near a tall tree . . ."

How are they going to find us? I silently wailed. That's when I heard the heavy pounding of horse's hooves and whirled in the direction of the sound.

Either my head injury was far worse than I suspected, or a mounted knight in shining armor, plumed helmet, and flowing cape was heading right for me.

With a steamy snort, the galloping horse skidded to a stiff-legged halt. Penny barked once as the knight slid effortlessly off the saddle and dropped to the soft loam. Before the man in armor approached, he lifted his visor and raised a gauntleted hand.

"Ms. Cosi? Don't be afraid. I'm Officer Troy Dalecki—" The horseman flashed a badge on a cord. "I ran into Prince Charming on the trail back there. He sent me to—Oh, jeez . . ."

Dalecki noticed the Pink Princess. Slipping off his heavy armored gloves, he moved past me and dropped to one knee.

"What happened?"

I shook my head. "I just found her. She's alive, but . . ."

Dalecki used his own flashlight to check the girl for injury. He found nothing, even when he gently turned her on her side. Finally he opened an eyelid and checked her pupils.

"I think she's drugged."

He made sure Anya's air passage was clear and there was no danger of suffocation, then he covered her with a blanket he drew from a saddlebag.

While Penny happily bumped noses with the twitching mare, Dalecki spoke into a radio strapped to his breastplate. He rattled off codes and a GPS position, and then demanded paramedics, ASAP.

When he was done, Officer Dalecki shined the light on my face.

"Oh, jeez, your lips are blue. I think you're going into shock."

"Naw, I'm f-f-f-fine," I said, teeth still chattering.

Dalecki whipped the flame red cape off his shoulders and wrapped it around me. He tucked a generous amount of material close to my throat and made sure my arms were covered.

"Warmer now?" he asked.

Suppressing another shiver, I nodded, but Dalecki was no longer focused on me. He was staring again at the Pink Princess, his expression wracked.

"She's so beautiful," he murmured. "What could have happened to her?"

Meanwhile, from somewhere along the trail I heard Matt's call.

"Here, Clare, Clare, Clare . . . Come to Papa!"

Eighteen

Fifteen minutes later, four paramedics were hauling Anya's stretcher through the woods to an ambulance waiting on one of Central Park's well-lit traffic lanes.

The medics hadn't been able to revive her, though they kept trying. In silence, I watched them work, saying prayers for the girl as they loaded her into the ambulance, slammed the doors, and sped away.

I feared for Anya, and my heart went out to Molly. She loved her "Annie," and this news would be devastating.

PO Dalecki and his horse, O'Brian, had followed Matt, Penny, and me to the road. By now, the young officer had slipped out of his tunic, armor, and chain mail jerkin to reveal a rumpled gray NYPD sweatshirt and black jeans.

Sans steel helmet, Troy Dalecki displayed a prominent jaw, French brown eyes, and hair cropped so close I couldn't tell you the shade.

Rubbing his cheek where the plumed helmet had left a mark, he sat me down on a park bench beside his tethered horse, opened a notepad, and began writing down my statement.

For every question Dalecki asked me, I had one for him.

He told me was a member of the Mounted Unit. I remembered Mike describing them as an elite, high-profile group, one the NYPD thought of as their "ten-foot-tall cops." Dalecki was a rookie member, following in his father's footsteps—or hoof-steps, depending on how you looked at it. The "noble knight" costume was part of his moonlighting gig, he said, and the Storybook Kingdom was only part of it.

"I do three shows a week at the Meat-dieval Tournament and Feast . . ."

During our talk, Penny cemented her friendship with Dalecki's mare. The little collie didn't mind that O'Brian outweighed her by a thousand pounds, or that the mare towered over her like a giant fresh off his beanstalk. Penny made such a fuss to get O'Brian's attention the horse shook her mane and whinnied in playful response.

Matt, on the other hand, was chomping at the bit to make new *enemies,* and for once I couldn't fault him.

Every police officer who passed us (about half the Midtown force, it seemed) had a derisive crack or snicker for my ex and his "Prince Charming" getup.

The situation deteriorated when Dalecki was summoned by radio back to the horse trailer. He passed his notes to another cop and rode off, leaving Matt and me to wait for the chief investigating officer without our friendly knight.

Meanwhile, a group of uniforms gathered under a nearby tree to sip Village Blend coffee. Soon Matt, the long-suffering Prince, became the butt of their jokes as well.

"I wish you'd poisoned that coffee," Matt groused. "I'm having fantasies of mass cop-i-cide."

"I have two words for you, Matt. *Anger management.* The police are armed. All you've got are tight pants and a plastic sword."

Matt scowled.

"Forget about them," I said. "Focus on Anya. When did you see her last?"

"She took off after the giveaway at the Cotton Candy Patch. We were supposed to mingle at the joust for a couple of hours, but Anya said she had something else to do, and she'd meet me at the coffee truck at five sharp."

Matt punched a tree and shook his fist. "Of course she didn't show. How could she? She was lying half-dead in the woods."

The intensity of his reaction surprised me, until I considered his position.

At his "coronation" this morning, Samantha Peel had explained that all the Prince Charmings were expected to protect their Princess partners from unwanted attention (and their couture Fen gowns from grubby hands).

Matt had failed to protect his partner—*from what exactly?* That was the question.

"You shouldn't blame yourself," I told him. "We don't know what happened. But I'll find the truth . . ." (I'd also have to *tell* the truth to poor little Molly, and I wasn't looking forward to it.)

Matt shook his head. "Some prince I turned out to be."

I hated to admit it, but it was easier dealing with a smug Matt than a disheartened one. For one thing, in this situation, *Smug Matt* would be far better use.

"Cheer up," I commanded. "Plenty of women think you're a prince." I tugged his sleeve. "Look over there."

I directed Matt's attention to the white CSU truck that had parked twenty feet away. A small group had already gone back into the woods to gather evidence. For the past ten minutes, however, these two female techs—a short blonde and a tall brunette—had been sorting the same equipment over and over while they continued to check out Prince Charming and whisper to each other like high school BFFs with a secret crush.

Matt cleared his throat. "I see what you mean."

"Why don't you pump them for information?"

"Like their phone numbers?"

Mental forehead slap. "Like what they think happened to Anya. Or if the medics managed to revive her in the ambulance, on the way to the hospital. Or if they've found evidence of foul play."

Matt caught the brunette's eye and she smiled.

"Good thinking. I'll get right on it."

Nineteen

Matt wasn't gone a minute before a sleek gray BMW pulled up. An unmarked passenger van parked behind it, and a tight knot of uniformed police poured out and approached the luxury vehicle.

The cops were so fresh-faced that I (correctly) surmised they were cadets from the 20th Street Police Academy, uptown on a teaching tour; and the blue serge wall was so tall that I could barely see the man now at its center.

"As I was saying . . . a good police officer needs a sharp mind, along with an eye for detail that rivals an electron microscope!"

Oh, lord help me. That insufferable voice could only belong to one man—Detective Sergeant Fletcher Stanton Endicott, bestselling crime-writer and creator of the fictional "Forensic Detective," a moonlighting gig that made him known derisively around cop locker rooms as Mr. DNA.

"You couple that with a steel-trap memory, and a superior detective can instantly recall the name or occupation of anyone he encounters in the line of duty—"

"Excuse me, Detective Endicott," I called into the group. "I'd like a word with you."

By the way the man's face fell, I detected his "steel-trap memory" was recalling our previous encounter.

"Gentlemen, this is Chloe Coswell. Miss Coswell is a

private investigator." Endicott eyed my peasant costume and Dalecki's scarlet cape still draped over my shoulders. "Working undercover, presumably."

"It's Clare . . . Clare Cosi," I corrected. "And I'm a barista, not an investigator."

As the blue wall surrounding me reacted with barely suppressed guffaws, the embarrassed detective tugged me aside.

Always nattily dressed, Endicott had chosen an autumn theme for his evening seminar, with a brown plaid sport coat over a pine green cable crew, and khaki chinos. During our short stroll away from the rookies, he checked his Rolex.

"Cute undercover costume, Ms. Cosi—if you plan to get close to the Seven Dwarves."

"I'm not undercover. I was working at the Storybook Kingdom. Now would you please tell me what you think happened to Anya?"

Endicott adjusted his wire-framed glasses. "Nothing more sensational than an overdose. Self-induced, accidental, or criminally administered remains to be determined."

"Overdose? On what drug?"

Endicott paused then responded to my questions with a question. "How do you know the victim, Ms. Cosi?"

I didn't see the need to drag Leila and Molly into this, so I replied with less than full disclosure. "Anya was working as a costumed model at today's festival, and I was working at the same festival."

As I spoke, Endicott wagged a finger to summon his partner, a heavyset detective in a gray raincoat. The man slipped him Officer Dalecki's notes, and Endicott paused to read through the pages.

"Yes, we have already verified that fact," he said. "But unless you are a member of the victim's family, I don't see how the investigation is any of your concern."

"I found the young woman, Detective. If it hadn't been for me, she would still be lying out there, maybe dying. Maybe dead. I think you owe me some consider—"

A bellow interrupted us, one from an all-too-familiar source.

"Get your paws off me, flatfoot!" Matt roared. "I didn't do a damn thing, and I won't be manhandled by a pair of fresh-faced fascists!"

Twenty

Two stalwart cadets hauled Matt over to Detective Endicott. Though my ex was spitting mad, he wasn't resisting—*yet.*

"We've got a problem, Fletcher."

The speaker was Endicott's heavyset partner. While the man spoke, he flipped through Matt's snakeskin wallet.

"I caught the Prince here trying to *charm* information out of two CSU ladies. He's a local with an upscale address named Matteo Allegro. I'm running a background on him now."

Endicott's blond eyebrows rose high enough to contact his receding hairline. "A most interesting development, considering we have an eyewitness stating the victim was last seen at four o'clock, speaking to a man in quote 'medieval garb'—"

"Sorry," I said. "But clearly you have Matt mixed up with *another* man in *quote medieval garb.*"

Endicott narrowed his eyes. "Mr. Allegro was with you when you found the body, correct? Why were you searching for this woman, Ms. Cosi?"

"We weren't looking for Anya. We were looking for a lost dog—" I untangled Penny's leash from around my leg. "*This* dog. In fact, Penny knew Anya. She discovered the young woman and led me to her."

"So you and Lassie found Sleeping Beauty while working in tandem with Prince Charming?"

"I wasn't 'working in tandem' with anyone. Prince Char . . .

I mean Mr. Allegro was simply helping me look for this lost dog."

With a dismissive wave, Endicott resumed his professorial tone as he addressed the cadets. "What we see here is a ham-handed attempt by the perpetrator to establish an alibi."

"What?!" Matt and I cried together.

"Crime scene investigations often involve a spouse or lover who happens to 'stumble across' the victim's body"—Endicott made finger quotes—"it is this person who then alerts the authorities to divert suspicion, because this person is *actually* the guilty party."

"Hey, Ellery Queen," Matt snapped. "I am not a 'spouse or lover.' I hardly knew Anya."

"You hide the truth," Endicott proclaimed, poking Matt's tunic. "You were seen with the girl before she disappeared. 'A tall man in medieval garb,' our witness said. You certainly fit that description."

"I worked with Anya most of the day," Matt stated through clenched teeth. "But we split up at three o'clock."

"So you say. How long did you know the victim, Mr. Allegro?"

"I only met her this morning—"

"That's true," I confirmed. "Ask Samantha Peel. She's in charge of—"

"Ms. Cosi, your blatant attempt to establish an alibi for your paramour becomes more transparent each moment. On top of that, according to your statement"—Endicott tapped Dalecki's notes—"you betray knowledge of the crime possible only if you were *involved*."

I blinked. "And what would that be?"

"You know precisely when the girl went missing—"

"Of course I know when the girl went missing! The Pink Princess was supposed to show up at my coffee truck. It was Matt who reported Anya missing."

"Proving my point," Endicott loudly declared. "Mr. Allegro alerted the authorities to divert us from the fact that he is the guilty party."

Endicott narrowed his eyes. "What illegal substance did

you feed that poor girl, Prince Charming? A deadly form of heroin? Bad cocaine? Some sort of date rape drug—"

"I didn't give her the time of day."

Endicott frowned. "I should detain you on suspicion. Charge you, even."

"Charge him for what?" I demanded.

Endicott pointed to the sword. "Your boyfriend is armed."

"It's plastic!" I cried. "And he's not my boyfriend!"

"It's all right, Clare. I wouldn't need a sword to take this idiot down. I'd just shove this kinky boot right up his—"

The uniforms on either side of my ex tightened their grips, while I spoke loud enough (I hoped) to drown out Matt's threats.

"Sure! You *could* arrest him, Detective, but you and I both know you have no real cause to detain Matt, and I suspect you know that, too, don't you?"

Before Mr. DNA could reply, his partner in the gray raincoat waved a notebook computer. "Fletcher, I think we got something."

Endicott tipped his head. "Proceed . . ."

The detective began with Matt's multiple arrests in high school—underage drinking, fighting, misdemeanor vandalism (i.e. graffiti). He jumped a decade to Matt's overdose on cocaine and near death, even though no charges were ever filed in that incident.

The detective failed to mention Matt's three-month rehab stint, and the fact that he hadn't touched drugs in over a decade. (With the exception of caffeine and alcohol—the latter to the dismay of his twelve-step sponsor, though Matt seldom drank to excess.)

With relish, the detective then announced Matt's profession in the import-export business. But he saved the biggest revelation—and a broad grin—for last:

"Both Mr. Allegro and Ms. Cosi were scooped up in a DEA sting a short time ago. They were kicked loose without charges, but I smell something."

"So do I," Endicott said, rubbing his bony hands together.

"That charge was a mistake," I protested. "Don't make

another one, Detective Endicott. If you'll *just* speak with Samantha Peel—"

"I already did," Endicott's partner cut in. "She informed me that the victim, Ms. Anya R. Kravchenko, was scheduled to appear at the Fairy Tale Village with Mr. Matteo Allegro from three to five o'clock this afternoon, but neither of them showed—"

"But—"

"Don't you understand, Ms. Cosi?" Endicott smirked. "Ms. Peel is our eyewitness. *She* is the one who last saw the victim speaking to the man in 'medieval garb' at four, which bolsters *our* theory, not yours." Endicott faced the cadets. "Cuff Mr. Allegro, and read him his rights."

To my surprise, Matt behaved like a prince. He accepted his fate. As they slapped handcuffs on him, his gaze met mine.

"Don't bother Mother with this, Clare. Let my wife's lawyers handle it. I've got nothing to hide, and I'll be free in a few hours, guaranteed."

Endicott stepped between us. "Count yourself lucky, Ms. Cosi, that you're not joining your boyfriend—though you may end up in my interrogation room yet."

As the police loaded Matt into a squad car, I watched in helpless frustration.

"One last word of caution," Endicott added, leaning next to my ear. "If I see you or your little dog anywhere near a crime scene again, I'll have you charged with interference of a police investigation, and Lassie here sent to Animal Control."

Twenty-one

Oh, how I wanted to throttle that sanctimonious martinet, but I knew nothing would be gained by landing myself in jail and Penny in the pound, so I bit my tongue.

But I did leave a message for the smug detective.

As Endicott led his cadets into the park to "observe the crime scene," I moseyed over to the man's shiny new BMW and encouraged Penny to lift her leg and tag the driver's door.

"There it is, Endicott, a nice, warm puddle for you to remember us by . . ."

Alas, I could not coax the little collie to contribute anything more substantial to the cause.

Still stewing, I exited the park at West 72nd Street, near Strawberry Fields. Across the street from The Dakota, I paused under a cast-iron lamppost to check my messages. A text came in from Mike.

IN NYC. ON MY WAY TO HUG KIDS. CU SOON.

Oh, thank goodness. I could not wait to see him. And I was relieved he'd be at Leila's apartment. At this hour, Molly was likely in bed, and *somebody* had to stop me from strangling her mother.

It took me a few minutes to hail a cab—possibly because I

had a dog; on the other hand, I *was* wearing a blood-red, floor-length cape wrapped around a bizarre peasant costume.

While the cabbie made the forty-block detour around Central Park from West to East, I placed an unpleasant but necessary call to the current Mrs. Allegro, Breanne Summour.

I was hoping to leave a brief message with Bree's assistant or housemaid, but both were apparently out for the evening. The disdainer-in-chief of *Trend* magazine answered on the first ring—and though her staff was off duty, her caller ID was working just fine.

"Well, Clare, I'm home from a frantic Saturday meeting and Matt's not snoring in front of the HDTV or whipping up a high-caloric meal I can't touch. Presumably you're calling to tell me what you've done with my husband. Or should I wait to read all about it in the *New York Post*?"

"Hello to you, too, Breanne. And as for Matt's situation." I paused. "Well, it's rather complicated."

"It's always complicated when you and that misfit asylum of a coffee shop are involved."

"There is a bright side," I promised her. "If you act fast, we might be able to avoid an ugly mention on *Page Six*."

I explained the state of affairs, starting with Matt's "coronation" and ending with his arrest "on suspicion." Breanne was surprisingly unsurprised. She took down the name of the arresting officer and his precinct, and agreed to deploy her "legal team" ASAP.

"Okay, we're done," she said at last. "Buh-bye!" I could almost feel the cocktail party air kiss.

Though I was relieved that particular call was over, Breanne did give me an idea.

When she mentioned her "legal team," it occurred to me that if I played my cards right, I could have a legal team, too—or at least a legal water boy. *More like water bird*, I thought, remembering the loon on Harrison Van Loon's business card.

I fished around in my peasant blouse until I found the attorney's number. Though physically exhausted and emotionally frazzled, I summoned my best customer service voice for this performance.

"Mr. Van Loon? It's Clare Cosi. We met earlier this evening, in Central Park."

"Yes, I remember. You're the peasant girl."

"Coffeehouse manager, actually, and master roaster, but I'm calling now in my capacity as one of your official vendors."

"Go on."

"A situation has emerged that might expose the festival to legal risk."

That grabbed Mr. Van Loon's attention. "What sort of situation?"

Now to pour it on. "Actually, it's two situations, Mr. Van Loon, and they are both quite serious."

I told him about finding Anya's unconscious body in the park, and the subsequent police investigation. Van Loon seemed more relieved than surprised, and I found out why.

"A tragedy," he said, "although your news does solve one problem."

"Really?"

"When that young woman disappeared on us, Samantha and I feared she'd pilfered the gown, or peddled it to fashion pirates, which could have put the festival at great risk. Securing the property should forestall any legal action on the House of Fen's part."

"Oh, is that so?" I shook my head in disgust. "Well . . . thank *goodness* for that," I said, though Mr. Van Loon failed to catch my sarcasm. "There is another problem, however."

Van Loon expressed appropriate concern about Prince Allegro's arrest—*after* I pointed out that Matt was technically an employee of the festival, and his arrest would reflect badly on it.

I also mentioned that if Matt was falsely incarcerated (which he was), then he was within his rights to sue for damage to his good name.

"Such a suit could be forestalled," I pointed out, using Van Loon's own jargon, "if someone from the city's Fairy

Tale Fall committee took action before news of the incident reached the media."

Harrison Van Loon hastily agreed with my summation.

"Rest assured that police harassment of any festival employee seriously concerns me, Ms. Cosi, and I shall deal with this matter personally, starting with a phone call to the mayor's office."

Yes! I silently cheered. *Take that, Mr. DNA!*

I ended the call with a feeling of accomplishment, and relaxed back into the cab seat for the first time. Penny was curled beside me, and I was ready to enjoy the city scenery going by and the prospect of happy reunions ahead.

Molly and Jeremy would be overjoyed to see Penny. And my own heart felt lighter knowing I'd be reunited with Mike. Then I remembered Anya, and the thought of that beautiful young woman, lying close to death, sank my spirits, which failed to lift at the thought of seeing Mike's ex-wife.

The woman wanted to murder me with her bare hands.

The feeling was mutual.

In public, Leila and I could pretend all we wanted, but there was no getting around the ugly truth. Under our barely polite talk, we both knew the score: a cold war was raging between us.

And speaking of Cold Wars . . .

The spy job I gave Tucker came to mind, and I sent him a fast text message, asking for the skinny on Mike's wife. Maybe he could shed light on her shady behavior. With hope, I stared at the screen.

No reply.

Right about then, the cab rolled to the curb and I realized I was on Park Avenue, in front of Leila's apartment building.

"No traffic," the cabbie said, beaming.

My grin was more of a grimace. "Lucky me."

Twenty-two

"GOOD evening, Ms. Cosi . . ."

Felix Ortiz, the doorman at Leila's luxury apartment building, was one diplomatic guy. Holding the door for me and Penny, he didn't even make a crack about my absurd costume.

In the mirrored elevator, I discovered how tactful the doorman really was. With my babushka gone, my hair was a mess, my cheek was smudged, and a leaf was growing behind my ear. I shook out the vegetation, finger-combed my tangles, and spit-cleaned the smudge.

As I pulled off Dalecki's cape, I realized I'd also lost the top button on my peasant blouse. Matt's "tavern wench" comment about my costume reared its embarrassing head, but the cape was itchy and hot, so I folded it over my arm.

While composing myself, I couldn't help comparing my disheveled state to Leila's oh-so-perfect life: perfect clothes, perfect makeup, perfect husband, and the "right" address. No princess in a fairy tale had it better. Yet Quinn implied his ex was restless and unhappy, which begged the question—

When did the ball end?

Was Quinn wrong? Or was Princess Leila's enchanted marriage turning to cinders?

Stepping out of the elevator, I saw the carpeted hallway

was empty, but I knew Quinn was here. My first clue—his battered NYPD gym bag lodged in his ex-wife's front door.

By now Penny was so thrilled to be home she could no longer contain herself. The little collie dug her claws into the thick pile and dragged me by her leash through the door. (Anyway that's my story and I'm sticking to it.)

I was now standing in the bone-spare, skull white entryway of Leila's meticulously minimalist apartment. Devoid of décor, the area's recessed lighting made me feel as if I'd entered that tunnel of light people describe after a near-death experience. But instead of comforting words from my dearly departed, I heard Leila's strident voice at the other end of the hall.

"I cannot believe she called you!"

I was about to move toward her screeching complaint when I noticed the woman's designer handbag yawning open on the console. Next to the bag's mouth was a small box. Lacquered shiny, the pretty square was painted in shades of purple from light to dark, like the evening sky at twilight.

A note card sat beside it—

As discussed, your key is enclosed.

Invitations to come. ~ BB

If memory served, Leila was married to Humphrey (with an *H*) Reynolds (with an *R*), Esquire (with an *E*)—manager of a roundly successful hedge fund. Not one *B*, let alone two, in that name.

"So who is BB?" I asked the little collie.

Penny didn't appear to know or care. Happy to be home, she simply swept her tail back and forth across the supernaturally spotless marble floor.

The letters *BB* were also engraved on top of the mysterious purple box. I ran my finger lightly over the raised letters and whispered to Penny—

"Let's keep this between us, shall we?"

Lifting the lid, I spied a golden key nestled in a little coffin of purple velvet. A diamond winked at me from the key's top, where a clasp connected it to a chain made of silver and gold links in little diamond shapes.

Molly has a chain like that . . .

It had fallen from her pocket in the park. But Molly's chain had no key attached, only a broken clasp.

"Will you listen?! You're not seeing *my* side of it!"

Leila's piercing voice startled me back into action. I replaced the lid on the box, tightened my grip on Penny's leash, and continued down the hall—stopping at the narrow archway leading to the living area.

Another keyhole, I thought, *like that stone gateway in Central Park. Only this keyhole isn't leading me to two lost children, just a bickering ex-married couple . . .*

Their voices brought me back to those years when I was at war with my ex. (And yes, come to think of it, we did sound a little like lost children . . .)

When Penny nudged my leg, I glanced down. *Easy, girl*, I thought, patting her head. *I'm not eavesdropping. I'm just waiting for the right moment to interrupt . . .*

"That woman is not their mother. I am!" Leila cried.

"And I'm their father," Quinn calmly countered, "which is why Clare believed I had a right to know they were missing—"

From this angle, I couldn't see Quinn, though I could hear him. His tone might have seemed controlled, but I could tell he was tired and impatient.

"They weren't *missing*," Leila insisted. "The only reason she called you in Washington was to make me look ridiculous and her like a big hero. I was in complete control of the situation, and she had no right to—"

"She had every right," Quinn shot back. "She cares about them and she was concerned enough about their welfare to tramp through the woods and find them. I hope you thanked her."

"Thanked her?" Leila's fingers curled into fists. "That padded pastry pusher is the one who lost them!"

Padded pastry pusher?! Okay, now I'm eavesdropping . . .

I moved forward and peeked around the arch. Quinn stood tall at the far end of the room, arms crossed, frowning down at his ex.

Like her chic entryway, Leila's silk lounging pajamas were white, her red hair the only splash of color in the pale beige living room. The sight of her twig-thin form made me realize how hungry I was. With that big, red head on top of her stick-like body, all I could think of was a cherry Tootsie Pop.

Every so often, she'd check herself in a Victorian vanity mirror, a prized antique with an ornate frame of gold and silver. It even had its own pedestal.

I could barely hear Quinn's low reply to Leila's insult of me. Whatever it was, Leila didn't like it.

"What's that supposed to mean?" she demanded.

"It means I suspect you're up to your old tricks . . ."

Old tricks? What old tricks? I took another step closer.

"What I do—or don't do—is none of your business," Leila said. "Not anymore."

"It's my business when our kids are involved," Quinn stated. "So listen up because this is your reality check: *You* took Jeremy's phone away without telling me. *You* let the kids run around unsupervised with no way to reach them—"

"I refuse to listen to this!"

"You're the one who lost the kids, Leila, and you lost their dog, too."

"My God, Mike. Who cares about that damn dog anyway?"

My fingers tightened around Penny's leash. But before I could shout out, *I do, Twiggy Pop!* Quinn replied—

"Jeremy cares. I had to promise him we'd canvas Central Park together at the crack of dawn. He'll be out there on his own if I don't go with him."

"Only because Jeremy wants to be a big hero, like his old man."

Words like that would make any father proud, but coming from Leila, they sounded like an accusation.

"Molly cares, too," Quinn said, letting the dig slide. "When I left her, she was still crying."

Leila flipped her scarlet locks. "I'll buy Molly a smartphone and she'll forget all about that mutt."

"Molly isn't like you, Leila. She's . . ."

Not a self-obsessed sociopath? I thought.

Leila's refined features froze. She blinked a moment. Then twisted her mouth like a crushed tween girl. "You're . . . you're picking on me . . ."

Mike shook his head. "Don't even try it."

"You're *heartless*, picking on me after the ordeal I've had . . ." Wailing like an Oscar nominee, Leila threw her arms around her ex-husband's neck. "Hold me," she commanded through artfully paced sobs.

Gritting his teeth, Mike rolled his eyes to the heavens for strength then patted his ex-wife's bony shoulder. "Stop crying, okay? The kids are safe now. We just need to find Penny."

Hearing her name, Penny barked and bounded into the room. Leila hastily disengaged from Mike and gawked at the little collie.

"Excuse me," I said, trying my best for a clueless tone. "Did I interrupt something?"

Twenty-three

"Clare!?"

Quinn nearly bowled over his ex to get to me. He was still dressed in the charcoal suit he'd worn to his former boss's funeral, and his hard blue eyes widened so noticeably at my attire I feared I'd lost another button or three.

But those Irish eyes were smiling before he crushed me to his chest, and I finally dropped the leash I'd been clutching so tightly.

"Everything okay?" he whispered.

I pressed my cheek against his warm lapel. *No. Everything is not okay. Molly's beloved Pink Princess is lying in a hospital and Matt's been arrested.*

I was tempted to pour out the entire tale right then. But if I spilled it all now, Leila would hear about it, too; and I didn't trust that woman not to blab it to Molly. That little girl didn't need to lie awake with trepidation, wondering what had happened to her beloved "Annie." With any luck, by morning, Anya would awaken and *tell* us what had happened. So my reply was simply—

"I'm fine . . ."

Meanwhile Penny was yelping and running a swift circle around the room, steering clear of Leila's precious antique mirror but nearly knocking over an ultrachic chrome pole that passed for a floor lamp.

Leila ignored the dog. Tearful-mother act forgotten, she aimed her loaded gaze at me. "Well, aren't you the perfect little snoop. How did you get in here anyway? Do you pick locks, too?"

Oh, please. "The door was open."

Leila's chunky-ringed hand went to her silk-draped hip. She stepped closer, ready to make another accusation. I clenched my fists, prepared to take her on, when her daughter burst in—

"Penny! Oh, look! It's Penny!"

Jeremy was right behind his sister, wearing his Rangers pj's, hair mussed by sleep.

The collie ran into Molly's arms, tail wagging so furiously it cooled the room and (for the moment) the flaring tempers.

Penny licked the girl's cheeks and pawed her posy-print pajamas.

Jeremy hugged his dog. "See, Mol, I told you Aunt Clare would find Penny."

With Leila glowering silently, Quinn suggested the kids take Penny to the kitchen for something to eat.

"I'll go with them," I said, "and let you two finish your . . . *discussion.*"

In the kitchen, the kids filled Penny's dish with a can of beefy chow. Then Molly gave me a tight hug.

"Oh, thank you, Aunt Clare, for finding Penny. Thank you, thank you!"

"You're welcome, honey."

Jeremy nodded. Too adult at thirteen to join his sister in a girly hug, he extended his hand. "Good job, Aunt Clare."

"Uncle Matt helped," I said, giving the boy a firm shake. "We both wanted to see Penny back home safe."

"I would have helped, too," Jeremy said, shifting on his feet, "if my mom had *let* me."

"I know you would have. But she was right to get you out of the park. It's no place for kids at night . . ."

While the dog ate heartily, I petted Molly's hair. "Honey, can I ask you a question?"

"Sure, Aunt Clare, ask me anything."

"Do you remember when I first found you both? Something fell out of your pocket—a silver-and-gold chain with diamond-shaped links. It had a broken clasp. Was that your chain, Molly?"

The little girl shook her head. "I found it near the Oak Bridge."

"We both did," Jeremy said. "We thought it might belong to Anya."

"Why is that?"

"She wore a chain like it around her neck," Molly said. "It must be hers."

Jeremy nodded. "Since she went into the Ramble, we figured she must have lost it in there."

"I'm going to give it back," Molly said, "when she picks me up on Monday after school. I wasn't going to keep it or anything."

"I know that, honey, that's not why I asked. I was wondering because it's such a unique chain. I might want to get one like it. Tell me, do either of you remember what she wore on that chain? Was it a charm or . . . something else?"

Like a golden key maybe? I silently added.

Jeremy shook his head. "Whatever was on Anya's chain, she always had it tucked inside her shirt."

"Not always," Molly volunteered. "I saw it a few times."

"Saw what?" I asked.

"The key. She wore a pretty gold key on that chain."

"But you didn't find the key, only the chain?"

Both of them nodded and I frowned. *Was Anya's key lost or did someone take it? And why was Leila given one exactly like it? Coincidence? Were they both involved with the same man? Did this "BB" give both of them keys?*

"One last question, is that okay?"

"Sure," they said.

"Do you remember who exactly told you they saw the

Pink Princess go into the Ramble?" I held my breath, hoping for a break, like maybe a credible witness with more info. But Molly shrugged and said—

"Just some kids."

Jeremy nodded. "We didn't know them—a couple of girls and a little boy. We were asking around and they remembered seeing her pink gown going into the woods, that's all."

Penny barked and Molly hugged her. "All done already?" she sang. "You're really hungry, aren't you? How about a special treat for dessert!"

As Molly went for the dog biscuits, Jeremy studied me. "Why do you want to know who saw Anya go into the Ramble, Aunt Clare? Is everything all right?"

"Everything's fine."

He stepped closer and lowered his voice. "When you were looking for Penny, did you see Anya?"

"I saw her, yes," I said carefully. "Don't worry about it, okay?"

But the detective's son did worry about it. He glanced toward his sister and back to me, as if to say: *You don't want me and Molly to know that something is wrong, do you?*

"I better get going," I said quickly. "It's getting late. Have a good night's sleep, *both* of you. I'll see you soon . . ."

THOUGH I managed to avoid more questions from Jeremy, hurrying back to the living room failed to put me in the clear. Like an underfed predator, Mike's ex-wife couldn't wait to pounce—

"And here she is again, our dog savior! You and Mike were made for each other, you know that, Clare? The big cop hero and the wannabe heroine. Well, now that you're both reunited, you can go save the day *somewhere else*."

God, the woman was awful, and I wanted nothing more in that moment than to be somewhere else, but this was my chance to ask about Anya. So I swallowed my pride and stepped forward—

"Look, Leila, I think we got off on the wrong foot today."

"Oh, you think so?"

"Yes, I do. I'm sure if your 'mother's helper' had been with you, none of this would have happened."

"Trying to skirt blame, Clare?"

"The young woman's name is Anya, right?" I pressed.

"Brilliant memory."

"Did you know she was a part-time model when you hired her?"

Leila crossed her arms. "What does Anya's résumé have to do with anything?"

"I was just wondering if the girl came with good references, and from what agency—"

"Just wondering? You're not *just wondering*. You're poking around where you don't belong!"

"Don't get defensive, all I want to know is—"

"Enough butting in! You delivered the dog, now it's time for you to go!"

Leila rushed me, manicured claws thrust out. Luckily, Quinn stepped between us, saving me from acrylic impalement.

"Clare and I are leaving," he said. "Get a grip and get some rest. I'll be back tomorrow morning to take the kids to brunch."

Leila threw up her hands. "Oh, so now you suddenly have time to—"

"Tomorrow." Like Father Frost, Quinn's icy look apparently froze the woman's larynx because she finally shut up.

Twenty-Four

Quinn stopped in the kitchen to hug his kids and say good night, but after we left the apartment, he didn't say a word. Jaws clenched, he stewed in quiet fury.

As we rode the elevator in deafening silence, I pulled out my phone. *No messages.*

I knew the lawyers were working their legal magic to free Prince Matt from evil Endicott's clutches, and there wasn't much I could do, but waiting for word wasn't easy. I wanted to discuss the situation with Quinn, get his advice, even his help. But he didn't appear to be in the talking mood.

When we crossed the building's grand lobby, I wished the doorman a good evening. A scowling Quinn barely noticed.

On the sidewalk outside, I stopped him. "Are you all right?"

He looked ready to punch the *No Parking* sign. "Leila should have *thanked* you," he bit out. "Instead, she nearly *attacked* you. You did not deserve to be treated like—"

"Calm down. Leila and I don't get along. That's the way it is. What matters is those kids. How were they when you spoke to them?"

Quinn shook his head, loosened his tie.

"Jeremy was afraid I'd be angry, but he did the right thing. He remembered the Oak Bridge was a well-lighted area, so he followed the downhill paths until he saw the lights. Then he kept Molly calm and safe, watching the ducks, while he waited for a police officer or park worker—someone he could trust."

"Jeremy's a smart kid."

"He's a good kid. I'm proud of him."

"They're both good kids, Mike, and they have good hearts."

"So do you." He tugged me close. "But right now I'm more concerned about your mind."

"My mind?"

"Yes, your recurrently *curious* mind. You were asking Leila some pointed questions about Anya . . ."

For a split second, I was surprised he'd picked up on that, but I shouldn't have been. Quinn might be wearing a G-Man suit these days, but he'd spent years reading into things—from witness statements to suspect denials.

"Are you going to tell me why?" he pressed. "Or do I have to . . . coerce it out of you?"

"Tempting as coercion sounds, I need to tell you what's going on. But it's a long story, and I'm not telling it out here on the sidewalk."

Quinn nodded, "You've had a tough day. Let's get you home." Turning toward the curb, he raised his arm to hail a cab. I pulled it down. The cool night air felt refreshingly good against my flushed face, and I took a deep breath of it.

"How about we stretch our legs instead? I think we could both use a moment's peace after that pressure cooker upstairs . . . and maybe a snack?"

"Great idea, but you'll have to choose the restaurant. My stomping ground was the West Side, not Upper East. The only restaurant I've heard of around here is Babka's."

My mouth watered at the mere mention of that legendary eatery—a cozy, comfort-food paradise with lines around the block at its adjacent bakery.

"While Babka's food would be amazing"—I tapped my watch—"we'll never get a table at this hour. That's true of most of the places around here."

"Then let's take a walk and see what comes."

"Promise me one thing," I said as Quinn looped his arm around my waist. "Wherever we end up, let's sit in a back booth."

"You want privacy, eh?"

The man's thrilled little smile made me realize he'd gotten the wrong impression about my request. It wasn't for intimacy. My festival costume might have been a turn-on for Quinn, but to the general public, I would still look like Eva Braun at a *biergarten.*

TWENTY-FIVE

WE headed downtown and toward the river, away from Park Avenue's sedate royal forest of grand stone towers, and toward the "lesser" avenues of neon lights and bustling life.

"So how much did you overhear tonight?" Mike asked.

"Excuse me?" I snuggled closer for warmth—and camouflage.

The chic locals we passed smiled at me as if I were making a quaint Yorkville fashion statement. Cold as I was, however, I knew covering my peasant dress with Dalecki's floor-length red cape would have pushed their passing glances into disapproving "What a kook!" stares, so I kept the cape under my arm and myself under Mike's.

"You walked in on us while we were arguing," Mike pressed. "I think you overheard more than you're letting on."

"Maybe a little . . ."

"Or maybe a lot?"

"Well, I *did* happen to hear her refer to me as a pastry pusher. What do you think that means?"

"My fashion plate ex-wife doesn't eat carbs. In her world, Cosi, you're worse than a drug dealer."

"I see. What if I started giving out valium and diet pills with my espressos? Would I be in like Flynn with her pack?"

"Absolutely. The fashion-forward crowd adores pharmaceuticals. It's brownies and scones that scare them silly."

"That's it then. The next time I see that redheaded vampire, I won't bring a silver cross, I'll wave a chocolate chip cookie."

I was glad to get a smile out of Quinn, but the underlying sentiment was no laughing matter: the reigning royalty of Fashionista Land loved making women believe in order to feel superior they (ironically) needed to be reduced. In their world, any female over size 6 should be banished to "the racks."

At my age, it was easy to dismiss their sneering attitudes with a mental eye roll. What I couldn't forgive was their influence on young women. Anorexia, bulimia, diet pills, plastic surgery—I'd seen enough of it in this town to want to torch any billboard showing a model who looked like she'd stepped out of Auschwitz.

"You know," Quinn confessed, "when I was a young, dumb rookie, Leila's 'poor me' sobbing act worked like a charm. Tonight I just wanted to throttle her."

"For Leila, old habits die hard."

"Well, they're wearing thin on me."

"Speaking of Leila's habits, do you remember that phone conversation we had this morning when you told me about your ex-wife's flaky behavior, and you advised me not to spy on her?"

"Yeah, I remember. And I knew you would. Go on."

"Wait." I stopped him again. "You *knew* I would? Michael Ryan Quinn, did you *want* me to spy on your ex-wife?"

I studied the man's face. Even in the dim street lighting I could see the amusement was back in his eyes.

Quinn shrugged. "Let's just say I know you." He put his arm back around my waist, urging me forward. "So what did you find out?"

"Actually, not much. I'm waiting for Tucker to get back to me. He has some kind of scoop on her, something that seemed to *upset* him, as mysterious as that sounds. What do you think is going on?"

"Nothing mysterious at all. I can't tell you what upset Tucker. To me it's a simple deduction. Leila is acting the same way she did when she cheated on me."

"So you think she's having a torrid affair?"

"I do."

"Well, I don't. She dumped you for a rich new husband, didn't she? Isn't this the lifestyle she wanted? Why risk jeopardizing it?"

"Why do you think?"

"I don't know, unless . . . Where was that husband of hers?"

"Business trip. He's gone all the time."

"Sounds like you believe Humphrey Reynolds is cheating on her."

"Yes, and factor this in, Detective Cosi: Before Prince Humphrey of the Hedge Funds married my ex-wife, he insisted on a prenuptial agreement."

"Okay, revised theory: You think Leila has found some replacement Prince Charming, someone to keep in reserve in case the old one reduces her to mere middle-class alimony?"

When Mike nodded, I told him about the key necklace in the purple gift box. "Do the initials *BB* mean anything to you?"

"No, but that's probably her new paramour."

"I don't know, Mike. Something about the box and note seemed very peculiar to me."

"Who else but a love interest would send a woman a diamond-encrusted key necklace?"

"The note wasn't personal," I pointed out. "It was very businesslike. 'Invitations to come.' Don't you find that odd?"

"Not if some hapless assistant wrote it. These high-finance guys have a cast of thousands working for them, you know that. The assistant was the one who probably bought the necklace and wrote the . . . hot dogs!"

"Wrote the what?"

Quinn stopped me. We were standing on a desolate block between Lexington and Third. The shops were mostly dark. The few apartment buildings we passed looked quiet, their canopied doorways giving off little light.

He pointed past a bus stop poster for *Red Riding Hood: The Musical*, toward the corner of Third, where a papaya drink oasis glowed like a neon beacon in a midnight squall. It was a no-frills joint with a short-order grill and a few padded stools.

"When I was a precinct cop, these papaya joints were my second home."

The place served good hot food and fresh-squeezed fruit drinks, and given my very odd attire—not to mention my growling stomach—my reaction was immediate.

"Sold, American!"

Twenty-Six

New York was the only city in the world where a big yellow sign that read *Papaya* automatically implied hot dog.

Over the years, dozens of these stands had peppered the city: Papaya Dog, Gray's Papaya, Mario's Papaya—all spin-offs of the original "Papaya King" on the Upper East Side, hailed by Julia Child, no less, as serving "the best hot dog in the world."

We were about twenty blocks south of that eighty-year-old landmark to culinary doggery, waiting on line in a Papaya Palace, one of the knockoff shops.

"This is actually a very romantic choice," Quinn claimed as I studied the giant menu board above the busy grill.

"Oh, I can see that," I said. "The artful lighting"—bright as an operating room—"the clientele"—cabbies, ambulance drivers, tattooed teenagers—"the menu"—dogs, burgers, fried pickles, and paper cups of curly fries.

On the other hand, I had to admit, I was certainly dressed for peasant food.

"So don't you want to know why I think this place is romantic?" he asked after we placed our orders.

"Um . . . because cops hook up with long-lost parole violators here?"

"There's that, too." He shot me a half smile that crinkled

the crow's feet around his eyes. "But *this* romantic story is about an immigrant named Gus and his wife, Birdie."

"You're talking about the original Papaya King?"

"You already know the story?"

"Vaguely. I remember something about hula girls?"

"Good memory."

"Hula girls and hot dogs? This story isn't obscene, is it?"

Quinn laughed, placed his strong hands on my hips, and gently pulled me back against him. As we watched our food being prepared, he put his lips to my ear—

"Once upon a time, a young Greek immigrant came to America . . ."

Like many New York success stories, especially in the culinary world, the Papaya King's tale was one of grit and gumption. In Gus Poulos's case, he'd come to New York in the 1920s with no money, no family, no friends.

"He worked hard enough to buy the deli he worked in," Quinn went on, the rumble of his voice sending vibrations all the way down to my Tyrolean peasant toes. "Then came his first vacation to Miami, where he fell in love with the papaya, came back to New York, and opened the city's first tropical juice stand. Trouble was, nobody was buying. So Gus put young women in grass skirts in front of his store with free samples."

"Let me guess. He had lines around the block."

"He did indeed."

"So when did the hot dog come in?"

"That's the romantic part. A German-American woman named Birdie encouraged Gus to sample her favorite foods in their Yorkville neighborhood. Gus wedded Birdie, along with the idea of serving German frankfurters with his tropical juice drinks. And there you have it: The love of a good woman created one of the most iconic foodie combinations in the city."

"The love of a good woman *and* a Miami papaya," I pointed out. "It's a classic New York fairy tale of rags-to-riches success. Funny, though, I don't recall seeing any hula girls in Florida."

"Maybe not, but they worked like a charm for Gus."

"Lesson learned. If business gets slow, I'll put grass skirts on Esther and Nancy."

"What about Tucker?"

"Well, it is the West Village, but I don't think he has the legs to pull it off."

Our orders came up, and I sighed at the loss of Quinn's warm hands on my hips. But he gallantly picked up my plastic tray before I could, carrying them both while I grabbed us stools at the counter running along the immense picture window.

As we sat facing east, I noticed a stretch limo coming from the direction of Second Avenue. It turned the corner onto Third, its sleek chassis moving uptown with the showy pomp of a sovereign's white stallion. A few minutes later, I noticed another limo, this one black, taking the same route.

Limousines were common in this city and I didn't think much (at the time) of seeing two in a row. Besides which, I was quickly distracted by Quinn, who was devouring his hot dog with relish—and yes, that condiment was slathered on his four frankfurters, along with every other extra on the menu: chili, cheese, sauerkraut.

My own stomach growled at the smell of sustenance and I took a hearty bite. My bun was fresh and my dog had a good snap to it; but compared to Mike, I was a purist on the extras with only a thin line of mustard and a simple splash of "New York onions," which I found far superior to ketchup when it came to dressing hot dogs and hamburgers.

This one-of-a-kind New York sauce—a mix of onions cooked with spices, vinegar, and tomato—was much like the streets where it was born: sweet, sour, and ultimately complex enough to be satisfying. As I feasted, it occurred to me that was exactly how I felt about my life in this city.

To a Park Avenue princess like Leila, who wouldn't eat in a working-class place like this if her life depended on it, my career managing the Village Blend would seem small and pointless. But to me it was hugely gratifying and, most of the time, pure joy. I loved mothering my baristas and creating new coffee blends for my customers, and I was especially proud of following in Madame's footsteps, providing cups of cozy comfort for all the Village people (conventional and un-).

Meeting Mike Quinn during an accident investigation had been an accidental miracle of sorts. At my age, I honestly hadn't expected to find a meaningful connection with a mature man. But Quinn's sensibilities—especially after his failed marriage to that spoiled underwear model—weren't that of a perpetual playboy. By his very nature, he was the polar opposite of my ex-cocaine-using ex.

Where Matt was reckless, Quinn was thoughtful. Where Matteo was emotional, Quinn was controlled. Where Matt was easily distracted and (at times) superficial, Quinn was steadfast and patient enough to look below surfaces.

Granted, Matteo Allegro was an exciting guy, full of fire and passion—not an easy man to turn down. When I'd first moved back to Manhattan after a decade raising our daughter in New Jersey, he'd even tried to win me back. But I wasn't biting. When the choice came down to these two men, I chose Mike Quinn.

Now Mike was asking me to make another choice. Only this one wasn't so easy. Two weeks ago, on one of my Washington weekends, he proposed that I leave my life and work in New York and move to DC to be closer to him.

I'd asked for time to think. So far, he hadn't pressed me, yet I knew the subject of my future (our future) would come up again. Frankly, I was dreading it.

But there were more pressing dreads in tonight's mental queue—for one, telling Quinn about Molly's beloved Pink Princess.

As Quinn polished off the last bite of his fourth dog, he leveled his gaze on me and I could almost feel his mood shifting.

"So, Cosi. We're sitting down. We ate our food. Are you ready to tell me that story now?"

I nodded. "Unfortunately, mine doesn't involve frankfurters or hula girls."

"I had a feeling it wouldn't."

I paused, taking a fortifying breath. "I'm sorry to tell you this, but when I went looking for Penny, I found the little dog guarding Anya."

"Our Anya? Leila's mother's helper?"

"Yes. She'd collapsed in the Ramble . . ."

Twenty-seven

Quinn's light mood left him. I could practically see the emotionless cop curtain coming down.

"Where is she?"

"In the hospital. The police say she was drugged."

"Drugged?!" The iron curtain cracked, a rare thing for Quinn.

I leaned closer. "Mike, what can you tell me about Anya? Was she a drug user? An addict?"

"I spent most of my career as a narcotics officer, Clare. Do you think I would let a junkie near my kids?"

"She's clean?"

"Yes. She came to Leila with good references, and believe me, I checked them out . . ."

Quinn proceeded to give me the background on Anya R. Kravchenko: She'd emigrated from Moscow about two years ago, had no criminal record, no history of problems, and came with good employment references. They were plain facts, delivered in the detached tone of a detective.

"That's all paper stuff. What about her lifestyle? If she didn't take drugs herself, is it possible she had a boyfriend or another friend who used drugs? Someone you don't know about?"

"It's speculation but, *yes*, of course it's possible."

"I hope so, Mike, because if not, then something very

bad happened to Anya in those woods, which is awful enough. But there's more to the story."

"It gets worse?"

I filled Quinn in on Matt's arrest.

"And who did the honors?"

"Detective Fletcher Stanton Endicott. He even topped it off with a threat to throw Penny in the pound and me into Central Booking."

Quinn's frown deepened into dangerous territory. "Endicott *threatened* you?"

"Take it easy. I can't imagine he was serious. In fact, Penny and I left a little warm puddle of affection next to his car door—just to show him there were no hard feelings."

He shook his head. "You sure like to push it, don't you, Cosi?"

"That man is an ass, and you know it. How did he get so far on the force anyway?"

"He's a cousin of Mayor Stanton's," Quinn reminded me. "And he's been paired with smart partners."

"Now that you mention it. Endicott's partner was the one who dug up Matt's drug-related past."

"I know you don't want to hear this, sweetheart, but your ex-husband's past is going to sink him."

"Excuse me, but nobody's past should sink him, not when he's taken pains to reform and make amends. Do you really think it's right to arrest a man based on nothing but his past?"

Quinn shifted. "The way you tell it, Matt was paired with Anya most of the day."

"Yes, I grant you. The circumstances aren't in his favor. But he didn't do anything to that girl, and Mr. DNA will have zero physical evidence."

Quinn looked away, as if seriously studying the traffic flow on Third. I knew better. When he aimed his focus back on me, I braced myself.

"I have a question for you . . ." *(Here it comes.)* "Try to be objective, all right?"

"Go on."

"Anya is a beautiful young woman. Given Matt's history

as a skirt chaser and drug user, given that he was paired with her all day, isn't it *possible* that *maybe* he did do a little partying with her in the Ramble? She might have looked fine when he left her, and he didn't think she'd—"

"No, no, no!" A few heads turned, but I didn't care. "Matteo Allegro may be a lot of things, but he would never put a woman in harm's way. Matt loves women—maybe a little *too* much—but he's *ferocious* about *protecting* them. His very identity is wrapped up in it—"

"Calm down, Clare. I asked you to be objective."

"I am!"

Quinn arched an eyebrow.

"Look," I said, "*you* know your ex-wife, don't you? Her little games? Her fake crying? Her evasive behavior?"

"Yeah, unfortunately, I do."

"Well, I know my ex just as well. I would never have gone into business with him if I didn't think he could be a good partner and a good friend; if I didn't think that underneath his faults he was a good person. Matt has been on the wagon for over a decade. He hasn't touched cocaine."

"You're sure?"

"I'm sure because I knew him when he *did* touch it. Now it's your turn to be objective. What kind of person would leave a young woman in Central Park like that? If I hadn't found Anya, she might have died of exposure. You know Matt pretty well now, don't you? Can you honestly say he would do that?"

Quinn took a breath. "I think Allegro is careless, and he's not too smart. But you're right. I can't see him doing something that cold-blooded."

"That's the word for it. Whoever did this is *cold-blooded.* A guy might have partied with her and left her like that. Or it could have been much worse. What if he gave her a date rape drug and planned to assault her but got interrupted or scared away by passersby?"

Quinn's neutral expression cracked again. *Good*, I thought, *he should have a reaction!*

"Mike, as we speak, Endicott and his partner are trying to press their case. But it wasn't the father of my child who did this, and the longer the detectives focus on Matt, the less chance they have of getting the true guilty party. We could have a real predator on our hands here, and we've got to find this monster before another girl is harmed."

"I don't disagree."

"Is there anything you can do?"

Once more he studied Third Avenue's traffic flow.

"Let me make a few calls," he said at last. "I'll find out where Allegro is in the system. I can't get him sprung, his lawyer has to do that. But I can get Emmanuel Franco over to Endicott's precinct. Sergeant Franco can try to start the process of having the case reassigned."

"Thank goodness."

"With Anya an employee of my ex-wife, I'll have to recuse myself from supervision of the case. But Sully is acting chief of my OD Squad while I'm in DC, and Franco officially reports to him, so it shouldn't be an issue."

As he pulled out his cell, a raucous group of teenagers burst into the shop. "I better step outside where it's quiet," he said, rising.

"I'll be here for you."

He stopped and leaned close. "You always are," he said softly. "That's why I want to return the favor."

Twenty-eight

Feeling the strength of Quinn's support (and the residual pleasure of his warm breath at my ear), I sipped the sweet dregs of my tropical smoothie and gawked with some relief out the hot dog shop's window.

That's when I saw another limousine turning the corner. Then came a taxi, a car service sedan, and another limo. The final luxury vehicle pulled right up to our Papaya Palace. The back door flew open and a middle-aged couple emerged, both wearing evening clothes.

Laughing, arm in arm (and looking more than a little drunk), the pair slurred orders for hot dogs and "coconut champagne" to go, gathered up their late-night munchies, and stumbled out the door. During all this, I noticed the woman's necklace—a chain of silver and gold links in diamond shapes, holding a golden key with a diamond embedded at the top.

Exactly like the one in Leila's purple gift box.

I felt a tap on my shoulder. "Excuse me, lady, is someone sitting in that empty stool?"

A tattooed twenty-something girl loomed over me with a loaded tray. Her multipierced boyfriend stood behind her, drumsticks in one hand, a guitar case in the other.

"Take the seat," I told the girl. "And you can have mine,

too," I told the boy. Then I asked them both, "Do either of you happen to know if there's a nightclub down that block?"

"Yeah, some kind of club," the girl said with a shrug.

"It's private," the boy added, lightly drumming the stool top with his sticks. "That's all I know."

I bussed our trays and stepped outside. The night had gotten cooler, and I put on Dalecki's flowing wrap. (If this neighborhood could take an inked-up Sonny and Cher, they could put up with a middle-aged tavern wench in a floor-length scarlet cape.)

Quinn was standing a few yards away from the door, focused on his call. I caught his attention, put up my index finger, and mouthed: *One minute, I'll be right back!*

I sprinted across Third and moved down the side street, toward Second Avenue, where the limo parade had come from. The block was deserted, an odd place for an exclusive club; yet the teens seemed to be correct.

Farther down the street, the bright lamps of car headlights pulled up to the curb. Within seconds, a well-dressed couple exited a doorway. They were laughing as they entered the vehicle. When it glided past, I saw it was yet another limo.

I walked swiftly along until I reached the doorway. There was no sign, no velvet rope line, not even any lights. Only a steel door.

How odd.

Stepping closer, I saw the door itself was deeply recessed into the dingy brick building. Thick and black, the door had a diamond-shaped window. But the glass inside was reflective—more of a mirror—and I saw no door handle.

"So how do I get in?" I murmured. *Okay, I give up.* "Open sesame!"

"SHOW ME YOUR KEY."

Surprised, I glanced around. The shadowy street was empty. Composing myself, I cleared my throat and called out—

"Say that again please!"

"YOUR KEY. I NEED TO SEE IT."

The deep voice was male. Now that I was ready for it, I

realized the sound had come directly out of the diamond-shaped mirror on the dark door. I scanned the recessed area for a speaker or camera eye but saw neither.

"I'm sorry," I said to Mr. Mirror, "I forgot my key. May I come in anyway?"

A long silent minute passed and then the mirror spoke again—

"MOVE ALONG, LADY, OR WE'LL MOVE YOU ALONG."

Good grief, how rude.

I stepped back (way back) and hugged the side of the building, waiting for someone to go in or out again. But the mystery door remained shut.

Around me, office buildings were dark, apartment windows blocked by closed curtains and drawn blinds. The street's eyes were shut, its inhabitants departed or in dreamland.

An evening breeze rustled branches on a sidewalk tree, and its leaves cast strange shadows. The air around me felt radically colder, and I shivered as if I were back in the murky realm of my dream-vision in Central Park.

Then the leaf shadows began to move in eerie ways, joining together at my feet, staining the pavement with inky blackness. I blinked several times, but the vision would not go away. The shadowy leaves coalesced, pooling to form a yawning void.

Teetering on the edge, I felt dizzy, close to falling in. I squeezed my eyes shut, hoping to regain my balance. When I opened them again, Anya was standing on the sidewalk a few yards away.

Her eyes were wide, swirling pits. Her hair blew wild, and her Pink Princess gown rippled in a howling wind that I heard but could not feel.

She opened her mouth to speak, but couldn't. Then she took a step toward me, but something stopped her progress.

I looked down and saw the terrible wound on her left calf, a hole that leaked blood. The flow of red streamed toward me across the pavement and into the black pool at my feet.

Anya's lips moved again, and I strained to hear, but her

voice was scratchy and distant, barely audible above the roar of the wind around her. I wanted to approach her but the black void threatened to swallow me up.

"What are you saying?" I called across the dark chasm. "Please tell me!"

When her lips moved again, I barely heard the words—

"Free me . . ."

Like a ghost, she became transparent before fading completely. Then the black pool turned bright red.

Woozy, I shut my eyes to keep from falling in. That's when I heard the heavy footsteps approach. Someone big was coming.

Heart pounding, I opened my eyes to find Mike Quinn barreling toward me. "Clare, what is going on?"

Unable to speak, I shook my head, trying to clear it.

"You're shivering!"

Only when Quinn put his arms around me did the bone-deep cold begin to fade. My head started clearing, and I shook it again to help things along.

"What are you doing here?" he asked.

"I saw Anya," I said, my voice cracking. "She was right in front of me."

"You mean you flashed back to the crime scene where you found her?"

I shook my head. "She was standing right here, on the sidewalk . . ."

Still gripping my shoulders, Mike broke our embrace. "Answer me a question, okay?"

"Okay."

"Do you know what day it is?"

"Mike, I'm fine. I don't need you to—"

"What day is it, Cosi?"

"Saturday! We just ate hot dogs and played footsie at the Papaya Palace. I told you, I'm fine!"

"I don't think you are. Let's hail a taxi and get you home—"

My pocket vibrated. I pulled out my cell.

"It's Matt. He sent me a text . . ."

"What does it say?"

SPRUNG: Going home 4 long, hot shower and tall, cold, ALCOHOLIC drink. See U mañana. We need 2 talk.

"He's out," I said, relieved.

"Good. I was told they were cutting him loose."

"Then it's over?"

"No. I'm sorry. Matt's freedom may only be temporary."

"Why? What else did you hear?"

"Endicott and his partner are dug in. I talked to a friend in their precinct. Allegro's lawyers got him released, but Endicott's determined to find wrongdoing and pin it on him."

"How?"

"He's waiting for the toxicology report. If it comes back with cocaine-related results, your ex could be behind the eight ball again."

"Behind the eight ball or behind bars?"

"Both."

"What about your man Franco?"

"He's on his way to Endicott's precinct now, and I'm heading over to the West Side, where they took Anya."

"To check on her?"

"More than that. Sergeant Franco will need ammunition to get Anya's case reassigned to my OD Squad. I'm saving him time by getting details on her condition. And if we're lucky, Anya might have responded to treatment."

"You mean she might be awake enough to tell us what happened?"

"Yes."

"Then I'm going with you."

"No. I'm taking you home. I think you're having some kind of post-traumatic stress reaction—"

"I'm going to the hospital. I want to find out about Anya."

"But—"

"Look, if I actually do need a doctor, I'll find a few there, won't I?"

Mike rubbed his jawline. "You got me on that one."

"Then let's go."

twenty-nine

St. Luke's–Roosevelt Medical Center occupied several blocks near Columbia University on the Upper West Side. Quinn flashed his NYPD gold shield, and we made our way to the Intensive Care Unit.

He flagged a doctor going off duty, she collared an overnight physician, and we all moved to an empty waiting room.

The doctors explained that Anya's condition had not changed, but she was stable, and they'd moved her to a private room off the ICU. A nurse brought Anya's charts and they pored over them.

Anxious to see the girl for myself, I set Officer Delecki's cape on a chair and quietly stepped away. A shift change had reduced the nightshift staff, and the halls were eerily quiet, the beeps and pings of medical monitors the only discernable sounds.

A sturdy nurse with tight cornrows and a cherubic face approached me with a question in her eyes.

My presence after visiting hours—not to mention my peasant costume—needed an explanation, and I quickly conveyed how I'd been working at the festival where Anya had disappeared.

"I was the one that found her," I explained, "and I'm here with an NYPD officer."

"You're talking about that poor child they brought in from the park?" she said, her melodious island accent thick as burnt sugar syrup. "Down the hall, dear, first room on the right."

WHEN I approached Anya's door, I was surprised to find it closed. Hearing something going on inside, I put my ear to the wood. A sharp hand clap sounded, followed a moment later by a second.

I assumed a member of the hospital staff was administering a stimulus test, clapping hands to see if Anya responded to a sudden loud noise.

I pushed the door gently, but it hardly budged. It wasn't locked, more like blocked. *That's odd.* I applied a little more pressure and the door soundlessly cracked open.

"Come on, Anya, wake up," a voice whispered. "Wake up, and listen to what I've got to say or I'll slap you again."

Slap? I've heard of a clap test, but a slap test?

The murmured command was followed by another sharp blow. "Sign it, Anya! Wake up, and sign it!"

Sign it? What in the world?

With all my strength, I shoved the door. The chair blocking it tumbled over, and I charged into the room.

"What's going on here?"

Towering over the hospital bed, a shocked brunette in a nurse's uniform froze in place, right hand poised to strike. Now this woman was a lofty mug of java—six feet tall, with a forehead as wide as Cineplex screen, heavy foundation makeup, and a reach long enough to swat me from across the bed. All I could think of was that awful nurse from *One Flew Over the Cuckoo's Nest.*

Between us, the beautiful Anya lay unconscious, swathed in white, a string of IVs dripping a clear liquid into her bone-pale arm. The only color was in her cheeks, which glowed redly from the slaps.

Then I noticed the ballpoint pen forced between Anya's limp fingers, and the legal-sized document spread open on her stomach. My eyes went from the document to the giant nurse and back to the document.

My opponent realized I was going for the papers, and when she swung her hand again, it was at *my* face, not Anya's.

I ducked.

On the way down, I snatched at the papers lying on the sheets. I managed to snag a page or two before the giantess grabbed the other end. A brief tug of war ended when the pages split like a flimsy wishbone.

And I came up with the short end.

With a howl, the slap-happy nurse bolted for the door. But she had to get past me. Channeling my pop's favorite Civic Arena wrestler, I aimed the butt of my head for her midriff and tackled her with as much force as I could muster. She grunted as the air shot out of her, and we both tumbled to the floor. On the way down my foot slammed the nightstand, and a pitcher of icy cold water doused me—

"Aaahhh!"

Shaking off the freezing shock, I lunged for the document again.

It was a full-blown cat fight now, and as we rolled around on the floor, the absurdity of the situation was not lost on me. With my sodden, flimsy peasant dress, and my attacker disguised in a nurse's uniform, the whole thing was less like a WWF match than a tableau out of Robert Maplethorpe's kinky imagination.

Thankfully, the scene didn't last long. As the nurse tore away the last of my buttons, my grip slipped on the papers. She pulled them out of my hands, and I grabbed a clump of her thick hair. I did it to restrain the woman—but I ended up with nothing more than a fistful of wig!

I tried to ID her actual hair color—black? brown? auburn?—but she was wearing a tight skullcap. That's when I noticed a reddish brown scar on the back of her neck, in the shape of a crescent moon.

Free from my grip, the giantess scrambled to her feet while I snatched at her ID necklace. Its dangling string broke the second before the nurse stomped my thigh with her sneaker and fled the room.

Leg aching, I picked myself off the polished floor and went after her.

"Mike! Somebody! Help! There's an intruder in the hospital!"

In the very next moment, two things happened.

At the far end of the hallway, double doors opened and Mike appeared in response to my cries. On the opposite side of the corridor, I saw the fake nurse pounding the elevator button, trying to summon the next car.

When she spotted me, she abandoned the whole elevator escape and opted for the stairs. Rather than wait for Mike and maybe lose her, I followed the nurse into the stairwell.

Ignoring the pain in my leg, I clutched together the tattered ruins of my costume and hurried down the stairs, past one, two, three exits. Below me, I heard the fake nurse making a phone call. She was cursing, saying something about coming out. Her voice sounded closer, so I knew the call had slowed her down, and I was catching up!

At the ground floor she pushed through another steel door, and I was right behind her. We both ran through a hall lined with elevators, toward a glass door that exited to the street.

I was about ten steps from tackling the woman when an elevator opened in front of me. Mike stepped out and shouted—

"Clare, get down!"

No, I thought, *I'm too close to give up!*

But Mike's strong arm hooked my waist. Momentum spun us and we tumbled to the sea green linoleum—just in time apparently.

I was so furiously focused on catching the nurse that I'd missed her accomplice. Now I spied the fat man at the exit, a wool ski mask over his face and a very large gun in his hand.

The shot was deafening inside the narrow hall.

I curled into a ball, Mike protectively on top, when the clock on the wall above our heads exploded, raining plastic and glass. Ears ringing, I saw Mike's lips move as he ran his hand over me. I could tell he was asking if I was hurt, and I shook my head.

"I'm all right. Are you—"

He was already up and running. Two hands on his gun, he plowed his shoulder into the door and burst onto the chilly sidewalk.

I arrived in time to see a black SUV speeding away.

Legs braced, Mike was aiming at the wheels when an MTA bus lumbered through the intersection on Amsterdam, blocking sight of the fugitive vehicle. With a curse, he lowered his weapon.

By the time the bus passed by, the SUV had vanished into the night.

Thirty

When the police arrived, two uniforms separated us. Mike already called in a description of the suspects and their car. Now the cops wanted our full statements.

Meanwhile, Anya was moved to a new room, a security guard posted on her door. A doctor checked her over and deemed her fine—with the exception of her comatose state.

Then the Crime Scene detectives went to work. They searched Anya's old room for evidence, retrieved the bullet from the hallway, and the sopping wet clothes from my body.

By the end of it, my festival costume was living in an evidence bag, and (thanks to the hospital staff), I was handed a clean pair of OR scrubs. I got into the dry clothes and went looking for Mike.

I found him in the hallway with his suit jacket off. Arms folded, sleeves rolled up, he leaned against a wall, watching the Crime Scene people work.

When he saw me, he tugged my hand, pulling me back into the waiting room where we'd started out.

After a day working in a Fairy Tale Village, and a night chasing through (what felt like) cursed woods, I thought I'd be ready for anything, even a wicked witch disguised as a *Cuckoo* nurse.

What I hadn't expected was a goon with a gun, waiting

in a getaway car. And when the dust settled, I realized the heavyset man in the ski mask wasn't necessarily near-sighted.

"He deliberately aimed above our heads, didn't he? To keep us from following."

Mike nodded an affirmative, but I was no less grateful. Who knew where that man would have aimed if I had continued running for the door? Mike had saved my "pastry pushing" rear, and I told him so. He touched my cheek.

"One time or another, sweetheart, even the toughest of us needs backup. Unless, of course, you're a superhero."

"Well, you may see that yet."

I pointed to Delecki's cape, still folded on the waiting room chair. "The police took my peasant dress, these OR scrubs are flimsy, and the only other thing I have to wear looks like I pinched it from Superman."

Mike smiled and handed me his suit jacket. "In case you get cold."

"Thanks."

"So . . ." he said, leading us to two chairs. "Do you have an opinion about what happened?"

I rubbed my sore jaw. "Either it was the most aggressive health insurance broker in history, or some woman and her partner were trying to coerce Anya into signing a legal document."

"I'm guessing the latter."

"Me too. Did they find any of the pages I tore?"

Mike nodded. "One ripped page was mostly blank, but the other had a sentence about the undersigned waiving, quote, 'all further litigation,' and a space for Anya to sign."

"If she's involved in a lawsuit, it can't be that hard to find out the details, right?"

"That depends. Both parties could have been negotiating in private. But someone close to Anya might know the facts."

"It's too bad about the ID photo, the one I yanked off her neck."

"You said the photo was fake?"

"It wasn't the woman I saw. Not even close."

"Sounds like a semiprofessional job," Mike concluded.

"*Semi*professional?"

"Yes, it would have been easy to take a picture of the woman with the wig on, and stick it on the ID. But this pair grabbed some anonymous photo off a social site. They knew enough to manufacture a convincing ID without exposing themselves—that's professional-level thinking. On the other hand, trying to slap her awake was a downright stupid ploy."

"Stupid and desperate," I said. "Who would do something so risky?"

"A cut-rate private detective agency maybe."

"What? Like someone good enough to close a divorce case, but out of their depth for this job?"

Mike nodded. "Or it could be private muscle in the employ of some shady law firm, even a respectable one. Or someone's relative doing his or her cousin a favor. The possibilities are endless."

"What about the SUV?"

"They're looking for it, but I'll bet a steak dinner at Peter Luger's the vehicle was stolen for this job."

We both fell silent, and then I said what we both were thinking.

"This doesn't change anything for Matt, does it? I mean, these two wanted some kind of legal release. It's unlikely they were the ones who drugged Anya, only to pull this stunt to get to her again."

"I agree. I doubt they had anything to do with her overdose."

"Then I'm right. This doesn't let Matt off the hook."

"No, but the toxicology report might. We'll have to be patient. The lab results should be back within the week."

I cocked my head. "And the doctors are absolutely certain it's drug intoxication?"

"According to Anya's medical records, she has no history of illnesses, although they're running more tests. But there was no sign of violence. Anya wasn't molested in any way. No needle tracks were found on her body and no bruises, only some minor scratches on her leg, which they attribute to the brush in the woods."

"Her leg . . ."

I flashed back to the disturbing vision I'd had on the sidewalk outside that club. Anya had been bleeding from a hole in her leg—her *lower left* leg.

"Clare? What's wrong?"

"Was it Anya's left leg where they found the scratches?"

"Yeah." Quinn nodded. "Her lower left leg. They bandaged it up."

"And no needle tracks?"

"None—not that visible tracks prove anything. Intravenous narcotics can be shot under the tongue, where the tracks are harder to detect."

I shuddered. "I can't imagine."

"I don't have to imagine. I've seen it."

"Can't the doctors find a way to wake Anya up?"

Mike rubbed his eyes. "She didn't respond to flumazenil, which is unusual."

"That's what they used on Matt all those years ago when he nearly died of an overdose."

"Which means it may not be cocaine or heroin, and that's good for Matt. The specialists are ready with more specific treatment once they know what kind of drug they're dealing with."

Just then, a beefy young cop called into the room. "You two ready to go?"

"Go where?" I asked.

He shrugged. "That's up to you, Doctor. My sergeant said to take you wherever you like."

Mike arched an amused eyebrow. "Where to, Doc?"

"Home," I said. "But before we go, will you do me a favor? Ask a *real* doctor to reexamine those scratches on her leg. I have a strong feeling they'll find something there."

"What?"

"I don't know. Call it a hunch."

Mike studied me—seriously this time. "All right. I'll ask."

"It may mean nothing, but it bothers me, and—"

"It's okay, Cosi. One thing I've learned on this job. Never argue with hunches."

Ten minutes later, I was sitting in the back of a chilly police cruiser, tugging Mike's suit jacket closer around my flimsy OR scrubs.

Delecki's folded cape sat on my lap. I could have put it on, but I wasn't in the mood to fend off one-liners from our chauffeurs in blue. Besides, I was getting too much respect dressed as a doctor, even if I was freezing my padded ass off.

Mike had been leaning forward, chatting with our driver and his partner, when he noticed my shivery shifting. Without a word, he sat back and put his arm around me.

"Thanks," I whispered. "You're getting pretty good at this."

"Practice makes perfect," he murmured in my ear.

The evening had grown colder with a low fog rolling in from the Hudson, yet up ahead the Village Blend's windows glowed steadily golden through the shifting gloom, its flickering hearth making the red brick shop look like a welcoming cottage in a dark forest.

"Almost home," Mike whispered.

Snuggling closer to his big, warm body, I sighed. *Home* was exactly how I thought of my coffeehouse, and I was glad to hear him use the word.

In all our conversations tonight, he had yet to bring up the question of my moving to Washington. Frankly, I was relieved. I was still holding out hope that he'd find a way around his difficult boss in DC and come back to New York for good.

As fairy tales went, that would be *my* wish come true.

Mike thanked our escorts as they pulled over the cruiser, then he took my hand, and we crossed the sidewalk, toward the four-story landmark building that housed the Village Blend.

Thirty-one

Matt's wife, Breanne, had called the Village Blend an asylum, and I thought of it that way, too, just not the kind of asylum she'd meant.

Like Greenwich Village itself, this century-old coffeehouse was a refuge, a place where people of all kinds were welcome without judgment. I even had my own private asylum upstairs. The beautiful duplex apartment came rent-free, as long as I managed the business below.

That business had been close to ruin when I'd come back to it. These days it was purring along like an Italian sports car. Even now, twenty minutes before closing, nearly every table was occupied, and I wasn't surprised. Gardner Evans was on duty.

A young, African-American jazz musician, Gardner was my star night manager. He always came to work with sultry playlists that enticed customers to stick around for an extra cup or two.

Athletically built with a trimmed goatee, cocoa complexion, and liquid brown eyes, Gardner was a favorite of NYU co-eds and jazz aficionados alike (and there were plenty of both in the Village).

Gardner sometimes spoke about missing his family back home, but he enjoyed his barista work, especially the late shifts, which gave him a chance to "caffeinate up" (as he put it) before going out to midnight jam sessions. He'd play all night with his group, treat himself to fried chicken and waffles at Amy Ruth's in Harlem, sleep through the morning, and wake up, ready to pull shots by early evening.

Now I knocked on our French windows and waved good night. But when Gardner looked up from behind the counter, something bizarre happened.

As a crack of thunder shook the sky, a sharp shock rocketed through my body. The jolt came with a feeling of elation followed by loss, and then great sadness.

When it passed, Gardner was gone. He simply *vanished* before my eyes!

I blinked hard, trying to bring him back. But he didn't come back, and I felt frozen in place. "Clare?! What's wrong?"

I shook my head, unsure of where I was. Mike's hands were on my shoulders, and I was gazing up into his furrowed brow.

"Are you okay? You zoned out. Didn't you hear me calling you?"

"I'm fine. But Gardner, he *vanished* right in front of me. He's gone!"

"No, he's not."

I looked through the window again. Gardner was standing behind the counter, chatting with a customer.

I tried not to panic. "Mike, you have your key to my apartment, don't you?"

"Sure."

"Go around to the back stairs without me. I want to check on the shop."

"No, Clare, I think you should take it easy. Come up with me now. You obviously need to rest." He took my hand and held my eyes. "I was hoping we could talk—remember that question I asked you two weeks ago? About moving to DC?"

Oh, no, not now.

"Have you given it any thought?"

"I have. But—" I swallowed hard, "can we please talk about it in the morning, after we've both had a good night's sleep?"

He paused, face unreadable. Mike Quinn was a patient man, but even his patience was running out.

"Tomorrow morning," he said tightly. "Now come upstairs. We're about to get a downpour."

I pulled lightly against his grip. "First I need to check on the shop. I have a feeling something's wrong. This place is my responsibility. You understand, right?"

If anyone was familiar with the weight of responsibility, it was Mike Quinn. He didn't like my answer, but he didn't argue. Letting go of my hand, he turned away.

"I won't be long," I called after him.

Thunder rumbled again and the air filled with dampness. Wet drizzle brushed my cheeks and I squeezed my eyes shut. For weeks now, I felt as though my future was in the hands of a fickle fortune teller. I would decide one thing, sleep on it, and change my mind in the morning.

Okay, Clare, deal with the shop, then get it together and talk to him.

Opening my eyes, I headed for the Blend's front entrance. As I reached it, the door swung wide, and an attractive young woman burst out.

"Excuse me," she said, hurrying by.

Her face looked familiar, but I couldn't quite place it. Then lightning flashed, and I saw the streaks of red color in her soot black, chin-length hair.

The Red Princess!

She'd swapped her sparkly gown for black jeans and a scarlet sweatshirt, but I remembered her from this morning when she'd flirted with Matt and told him she was a friend of *Anya's*!

"Wait!" I called.

Ignoring me, she flipped up her red hood, rounded the corner, and disappeared.

Dodging sluggish raindrops, I followed. "Miss, please wait!" But as I made the turn, the girl was already ducking inside a big Lincoln Town Car, the vehicle of choice for practically every car service in the city.

She slammed the door, and the driver smiled, greeting her

in a friendly, familiar way. He was a thirtyish Caucasian male with shaggy brown hair topped by an *English bowler*—not something you saw every day, even in Greenwich Village.

As the two sped away, I saw the license was a standard Taxi and Limousine issue. But it was the odd bumper sticker that drew my attention.

Many of these livery drivers hailed from other countries, and the bumper sticker looked like a national flag that was slapped on the car out of pride. This one displayed a right triangle on a field of blue with a line of five twinkling stars along the hypotenuse.

I mined my memory, running through all the UN flags on a scarf my daughter had bought for me during a grade school field trip. She and I had memorized them all, quizzing each other for fun, but the bowler-wearing driver's flag eluded me, along with the obvious question—

What was the Red Princess doing at my coffeehouse?

As the downpour struck, I pulled Mike's jacket over my head and dashed inside for answers.

Thirty-two

As I shook off the cold rain, smooth jazz washed over me.

The lights were low, the fireplace crackling, and all around me date-night Saturday was evident with couples nursing lattes and cappuccinos at our marble-topped café tables, their heads bowed in intimate conversations.

Moving behind the counter, I approached Gardner.

"Hey, boss, you okay?" he asked. "Esther said you had a rough night. What's with the hospital clothes?"

"I'm fine—forget the clothes. Did you happen to notice the young woman who just left?"

Gazing down at me, Gardener gave me a little smile. "I always notice young women."

"Not *that* kind of notice." I described her. "Red hoodie, red streaks in her hair."

Garner rubbed his trimmed goatee. "Sounds like the girl who was talking to Esther."

"Wait, back up. *Esther* was here? Tonight?" I glanced around. "Did she leave?"

"No. She's been here for the past few hours."

"But Esther's off duty tonight. Why isn't she home with Boris, getting some rest?"

"Couldn't tell you."

"What about you?" I asked anxiously. "Everything okay with you?"

"With *me*? Never better." He flashed a toothy grin. "In fact, I got some fantastic news today . . ."

Thank goodness, I thought. *That strange vision of Gardner disappearing was obviously a stress reaction, nothing woo-woo about it.*

"Remember my auntie? The one who makes the best Caribbean Black Cake on the planet?"

"How could I forget?" Gardner had created a Black Cake Latte one Christmas season (with homemade Burnt Sugar Syrup), which now had a permanent spot on our holiday menu.

"Ten years back, my auntie and her husband went their separate ways, but they never divorced, and when he passed away, she got everything, an estate in the Islands and a big pile of stocks and cash."

"I'm sorry for her loss," I said sincerely, "but I'm happy as long as she is. And you are."

"And my cousin."

"Your cousin?" I studied Gardner's excited expression. "I'm not following you."

"I'm leaving, boss. My dream is coming true."

"What dream?"

"When my cuz and I were kids, we hatched this dream to open a club together. I want it to be a jazz club, and he's down with that. Now that his mama's got some money, we're gonna try it."

"Here in New York?"

"No, closer to home."

"Home as in?"

"Baltimore—or somewhere close by. He's got a handle on a few places up for sale that might be right. We're still talking it through."

"But you're really going? Your mind's made up?" I felt like a mother hearing about her child's acceptance to college in some faraway land, where she'd never see him again.

"When a dream's this close, you've got to give it a shot, don't you?"

I forced a smile. Gardner was right, and I wanted him to

thrive, but my heart was sinking. His departure would be a hard loss for the Village Blend family. And then it hit me—

What I saw outside was true. Well, part of it anyway. I felt loss after Gardner's elation, and he was literally going to disappear from my coffeehouse. But he wasn't profoundly sad about it. *So why did I have that feeling, too?*

"Hey, you two, something's up!"

Dante Silva hurried toward us with a five-pound bag of freshly roasted beans in his hands and a look of distress on his face.

"I saw Esther in the roasting room and—"

"In the roasting room?" I said. "What's she doing down there?"

"Crying like a baby!"

Gardner and I glanced at each other then looked to Dante.

"I've never seen her like that before," he said.

No kidding, I thought. My resident slam poetess had mood swings that rivaled Sylvia Plath's, but none of us had ever seen her that upset.

Gardner appeared skeptical. "Esther's not the crying type."

"Well, she is now," Dante replied. "And it's kind of scary."

"Did you talk to her?" I asked.

"I tried, but she told me to hit the road, so I grabbed the beans and backed away."

"I'm going down there . . ."

After swerving to grab a stack of Village Blend napkins, I headed for the back of the shop. Behind me, the two young bachelors sighed loudly with relief. It didn't surprise me.

The heart was a mysterious organ, and the men I knew didn't have the first clue how to investigate it. Most would rather face a fire-breathing dragon than try to comfort a Goth girl in tears.

Thirty-three

On the steps to our ancient basement, I recalled my own purgatory spent down here, sobbing over one or another of Matteo Allegro's indiscretions.

Close to the bottom, I spied Esther, slumped on the raised concrete base that supported our big roasting machine, a few lost beans littered like cinders at her feet. She was crying so hard she hadn't heard my approach.

I cleared my throat (loudly), and she froze.

"Esther?" I called, trying to sound casual. "Are you down here?"

"Yeah, boss," she replied after an awkward pause.

My zaftig Cinderella had changed from her festival outfit into black jeans and a *Poetry in Motion* tee the deep purple shade of a day-old bruise. Her raven hair was still in its beehive, but it stood about as straight as the Tower of Pisa.

When she heard my approach, she turned away. I stepped forward and sat beside her, gently nudging her ample hips to make room.

"I'm fixing my makeup," she said with a sniffle.

I held out that stack of Village Blend napkins. "Then I guess a few of these will come in handy."

Esther took them all. The thick mascara had run down her cheeks. Lower lip quivering, she swiped at the black tears.

"Won't you tell me what's wrong?"

She stared at me, as if I'd spoken Greek, then threw her arms around my neck and broke down.

The smell of freshly roasted beans and the racking sobs of a young female brought it all back, those early married years when Matt had sent my heart through the grinder.

The young embarrass easily, and like Esther, I'd thought I wanted privacy. It was those times when Matt's mother sought me out. Madame offered her counsel, a shoulder to cry on, and (yes) a stack of Village Blend napkins.

My mother-in-law was the one who kept me going, because it was her open arms that told me I was still valued, still loved . . .

"I'm worried about you," I now told Esther, holding on tight. "Talk to me."

Sitting back, she dabbed her raccoon eyes with a crumpled napkin.

"You know my roommate is moving out at the end of the month," she began. "Not to bring up that *raise* again, but I still need help with the rent."

"Stated before, and duly noted. Go on."

"Well, last week, I got up the nerve to ask Boris if he wanted to move in with me. He's working at Janelle's Bakery so many hours now it made sense. He crashes at my place four nights a week already because it's easier than trekking all the way back to Brighton Beach."

"What did he say?"

"He claimed he was tired and we'd talk about it the next morning. But instead of a heart-to-heart, Boris snuck out while I was still snoring."

"Didn't you bring it up again?"

"Only every day! He kept putting me off, saying he needed to think things through—which made me feel like crap, by the way . . ."

I tried not to show it, but her words shook me up.

I couldn't help flashing on Mike and the fallen expression on his face when I'd put him off yet again. It was a hard realization, but the rapping Russian baker and I were in the same position, with the same unintended result. We were hurting the people we loved by our inability to make a decision.

"Tonight, I texted him," Esther went on. "I said I was tired of waiting and wanted an answer. I asked Boris to meet me here to talk it out. He texted back. Look—"

Sorry. Have given much thought.
Mind made up. Will explain tomorrow night at Poetry Slam.
See U then. –Boris

I kept my tone upbeat. "Sounds like he's finally going to answer you. That's good, right?"

"That's bad, boss. Very bad . . ." Esther's Tower of Pisa hair fell even more as she violently shook her head. "Don't you see? I pushed him too far. Now he's rethinking our whole relationship. He's not only going to say *no* to living with me. He's going to dump me!"

Thirty-Four

FRESH tears sprang up, and I pulled Esther into my arms.

"Oh, Esther, do you really think so?"

"Boris has too much integrity to break it off in a crummy text. But face-to-face, in a public place, while I'm distracted with my MC duties at the Slam and can't make a scene, that's when he's going to finish us."

"Maybe you simply need to be patient and hear what he has to say."

"Why are you taking his side? That doesn't help me!" Esther broke our clinch and grimaced. "Even Madame Tesla predicted it in my coffee reading. My love life is on the rocks!"

"First of all, you told me your grinds showed a 'bumpy road ahead'—which this clearly is, but the ride's not over yet. You need to hold on; have a little faith in Boris; and not let some silly fortune-telling session make you believe something is happening when it may not."

"No. I'm doing what I have to, avoiding total humiliation at the Poetry Slam tomorrow by facing my feelings now . . ." She reached for the Village Blend cup beside her and groaned. "Look at this. With all my stupid bawling, I let my perfect latte go cold."

I saw the sad remains of the latte art Esther had created—a heart with a ragged crack down the middle. She noticed my stare and shrugged.

"What can I say? Turning misery into art is what I do." She blew her nose into a fresh napkin.

"You're a poet, Esther, which means you have a great imagination. But I think you're using it too much in this case."

"Better to prepare yourself for the worst, I say. And I *will* be. I'm sorry I asked Boris to live with me—and I'm beginning to *hate* him, which is good. I'll be totally ready for him when he dumps me. I'll have plenty to say to that jerk!"

There it was. If hurt was anger turned inward, then it was only a matter of time before it turned outward again.

"And if you're not careful, Clare, it's going to happen to you and your blue knight . . ."

It was Madame's voice that issued the haunting warning in my head.

I ignored it, refusing to believe a thing like that could happen between me and Mike. I still couldn't believe it was happening to Esther and Boris.

When those two first met at a Brooklyn Poetry Slam, it was love at first phrase. In the years after, I saw the adoring passion in Boris's eyes whenever he gazed at his Esther, rapping on the stage, doing her work with inner-city kids, or pouring her perfect latte art.

"I know that young man loves you," I told Esther. "You two were made for each other. I'm sure Boris is on your side. You'll see . . ."

With a hard shake of her head, Esther rose.

"Let's give it a rest, okay? It's late. I better fix myself up and go home."

"Then I'll see you tomorrow." I gave her another hug. "Look, no matter what happens, I'm here for you, and I'll even try to finagle that raise, too."

Before I headed for the steps, I glanced at the roasting schedule near the Probat. It was the bright red color of the machine that reminded me—

"Esther, I'm sorry, but I need to ask you something. Were you speaking with someone earlier? A dark-haired young woman wearing a hoodie—"

"You mean Red?" she garbled, bobby pins in her teeth as she righted her leaning tower of hair.

"Her *name* is Red?"

"Her name is Roz something. I'm not sure. Red is what she wants to be known by—it's her performance handle. She updated it recently to Red in the 'Hood now that *Red Riding Hood: The Musical* is bringing in major bucks on Broadway."

"Is she in the show?"

"No, she's *using* the show. It's so popular that she's making the most of it on the Slam circuit. Wears the red hoodie, raps what she calls 'urban fairy tales' in English and Russian. They like her in Manhattan; they *love* her in Brighton Beach."

"So she's Russian?"

"She came over when she was a little girl. I actually know her through Boris. She's one of his sketchy friends."

"Sketchy how?"

Esther shrugged. "Her income fluctuates more than a bipolar torch singer. She's in a thrift shop coat one week and a designer outfit the next. She's taking the subway one time and the next she's got a hired driver chauffeuring her around. Same with her living sitch. From month to month she seems to move from posh digs to dives and back again."

"And you have no idea why?"

"Hey, when it comes to Boris's Russian friends, I learned not to ask questions. Red's a first-class rapper. That's all I know, and all I *want* to know."

"So were you two talking about Boris and your situation?"

Esther shook her head. "She came in asking about Mr. Boss."

"Matt?"

Esther nodded. "She saw him at our coffee truck this morning and asked me all about him. Then she asked if he was going to be at the Poetry Slam tomorrow night. I said I didn't know."

"Is she *interested* in Matt?"

"You mean like *hot* for him? No, I don't think so. She wasn't dreamy. She was upset."

"Upset how?"

"Nervous, gnawing at her fingernails. And angry. She kept muttering in Russian."

"What sort of mutters?"

"Run-of-the-mill Russian curses. The kind of things Boris spits out when he cuts himself shaving. Except for an odd phrase—*Ya budu ryadom. Ya budu ryadom.* She kept repeating it."

"What does it mean?"

"No clue. A new curse maybe?"

"Do you at least know where she lives now?"

"She bounces around too much. But I can text her."

"Good. Tell her that Matt is absolutely going to be at the Poetry Slam tomorrow. Do it right now."

"It's that important?"

"Trust me, it is."

THIRTY-FIVE

WHILE Esther communed with her smartphone, my mind raced.

If this "sketchy" girl rapper had drug connections, then she could very well be the reason Anya was lying in a hospital bed tonight. She could be the key to Matt's release.

"Okay, boss, I sent the text."

"Good," I said and headed for the stairs.

"Hey," she called.

I turned. "Something else?"

"I was wondering about Mr. Boss. Is he okay? I heard the cops were questioning him tonight."

"They let him go. For now anyway . . ."

Esther shifted. "You know, he's the reason I'm still working here."

"What do you mean? You're not harboring a secret crush on him, like Nancy, are you?"

"Nothing like that. It happened before you came back to manage the place. This awful guy was in charge."

"You mean Flaste?" I shuddered at the memory.

"That jerk actually fired me."

"I never knew that. Why?"

"No real reason. He wanted to hire a crony, and I was some 'chubby young nobody'—I overheard him leaving the snotty phone message for Mr. Boss. I was easy to dispose of and Flaste threw me out like a pile of trash."

"But when I took over, you were still working here."

"That's because your ex-husband blew a gasket. He flew all the way back from God knows where, didn't even change his clothes. He called me up from the airport, told me to meet him at the shop, and he chewed Flaste out right in front of me. He told the jerk we weren't some corporate franchise. We were a family. And anyone the Village Blend hired *stayed* in the family unless there was a *very* good reason to kick us to the curb."

Esther shook her head with pleasure at the memory. "Flaste was stuttering by the end, totally red in the face. But he was scared of Mr. Boss, who made him apologize and give me my job back. So like I said, if there's anything I can do to help the man . . ."

"You just did, Esther." (At least I hoped so.)

"You and Mr. Allegro are the only people who ever fought for me." She studied her combat boots. "Not many employers would have come down to this coffee cave with me bawling away in it."

"I was glad to. Now get some rest. Things will feel better in the morning. And if they don't, please remember—what Matt said was right. We're family. We care about you, so don't be afraid to reach out for help."

"Easy for you to say. Not so easy for me to do."

"I know. But there's a life truth here, Esther, and you might as well accept it."

"What?"

How did Quinn put it? "At one time or another, even the toughest of us needs backup."

THIRTY-SIX

I found Mike in my apartment's kitchen. He put down his cell so quickly I assumed he was checking messages. But the pinched look around his blue eyes told me he was irritated by what he'd seen there.

"What's wrong?" I asked.

"Nothing."

His tone was clipped. Something *was* wrong. He simply didn't want to talk about it.

"You tired?" he asked instead, slipping his suit jacket off my shoulders.

"You'd think I would be. My leg is aching, my jaw hurts, but my mind is racing, and I'm still wide awake."

"It's the adrenaline," he said, peeling off his shoulder holster. "Getting shot at will do that to you. I feel it, too."

He bent close, but (unfortunately) not for a kiss. Instead, he coolly took hold of my chin and examined my jaw, where a nasty-looking bruise was beginning to show.

Below us, Java and Frothy circled our legs and made their way to the royal buffet I'd left for them (before our weekend travel plans went kaput).

As my furry girls consumed their crunchy feast, I told Mike about the Goth Cinderella crying in our basement—and her tenuous connection to a friend of Anya's. In the middle of my update, Mike tugged me over to a kitchen chair.

"Sit, will you? Get off that leg already."

I did, and he agreed that "Red in the 'Hood" was a good lead.

"Well, she'll be here for tomorrow night's Poetry Slam, and she wants to see Matt. I'm sure he'll get something useful out of her."

"Tell him to be careful. He shouldn't try to bait her. She could use what he says to burn him."

"Then I'll feel her out first. Maybe she'll agree to speak with Franco."

As Mike nodded his approval, his attention strayed—first to my empty cookie jar, then to my nearly empty fridge.

"What are you looking for?"

"Snacks. Your cats are having them. We can, too."

"Mike, you ate *four* hot dogs three hours ago."

"Ah, yes, but no *dessert*."

"And your ex-wife called *me* the pastry pusher."

"Push away, sweetheart. Dealing with scumbags always makes me hungry. Case in point—those amazing meltaway cookies you baked for me last week, the ones with chopped hazelnuts around the edges? Got any of those around?"

"I'm sorry, but Mother Hubbard's cupboard is bare. I was supposed to spend the weekend with you, and Esther was going to look after these two."

In reply, Java began licking her coffee-bean-colored paw. Frothy plumed her tail, and slipped her long-haired body around Mike's leg, leaving a white fur trail on his charcoal pants as he tried to detect what was in my freezer.

"Not even any ice cream?" he whined, reaching down to scratch the ears of a purring Frothy.

"Check the fridge again. What's in there, remind me?"

"A jar of olives, a bottle of champagne, a carton of almond milk, three eggs, and one lemon."

My culinary gray cells started spinning. "Get out the last three ingredients."

"Why?"

"We're going make something that's even better than ice cream on a chilly night like this."

"Okay, I'm officially curious. What else do we need?"

"A medium saucepan—" I started to get up, but Mike pushed me back in the chair and dropped Frothy on my lap.

"You sit. I'll cook."

With my sore leg, I didn't argue. Frothy appeared happy with the arrangement and settled in for the show—and some chin rubbing.

"Go on," Mike prompted. "What else do we need?"

"Cornstarch, vanilla, and a little salt . . ."

Watching this formidable man obey my every directive was surprisingly enjoyable, and I couldn't help thinking up a few more commands for Detective Lieutenant Mike Quinn. But I'd have to hold off on those, because they had *nothing* to do with cooking.

TEN minutes later, Quinn had followed my foolproof steps for stirring up Almond Milk Custard.

"Holy cow, Cosi, this is amazing."

I watched his eyes roll back in ecstasy and laughed. "I told you it was better than ice cream."

"It's official. You're a kitchen witch."

"Thanks, but my spells are limited by my ingredients."

"Maybe, but the proof is in the pudding."

"Ouch, there's a hoary saying."

"Believe it or not, when I was a young rookie, one of my field training officers did his best to pound that little ditty into my skull."

"Why?"

"Two reasons—*one*, the guy was obsessed with pudding: chocolate, vanilla, mousse, flan, custard pie, you name it, he sampled it, wherever we stopped for coffee."

"And reason number two?"

"The proof really is in the pudding. As he used to put it:

'Evidence and facts are the ingredients we gather to make cases. But we can only serve a DA what we can cook up from it, a proof that a court of law will swallow.'"

While Mike continued to enjoy silky spoonfuls of warm custard, I digested those words.

"Okay, given our situation, how do I *prove* that Matt didn't do anything wrong?"

"You can't prove a negative, not without a solid alibi. Allegro was there, and he was paired with Anya for most of the day. If you want Endicott off Matt's case, you're going to have to do better than just claim he's not guilty. You'll need to serve him up another suspect—or scenario. Do you have a theory? Can you tell me what happened to Anya in those woods?"

I thought it over. "This Red sounds like a party girl. Maybe she gave Anya the overdose by accident and is freaking out now. Maybe she wants to speak with Matt to find out what the cops know."

"Maybe, but like I said, Anya wasn't a drug user. She was a happy mother's helper. How likely was it that she went into the woods with her friend, during a children's festival, to get high? And if she overdosed, why would Anya's *friend* leave her in the woods? What's Red's story? What's her motive? What kind of drug did she use on Anya? And how did Anya ingest it?"

"I don't have answers. Not yet."

"Then get some rest."

"But—"

"Sweetheart, I've learned a few things doing this kind of work. The mind is a black box. Solutions come when you're *not* looking for them."

"I get it. But I don't feel like going to sleep yet."

Quinn's eyes lit up. "Then why don't you go upstairs, take a nice, hot bath, and I'll make things . . . *cozy* for us."

THIRTY-SEVEN

In the upstairs bathroom, I stripped down and sank into the tub as prescribed. An ugly bruise formed on my thigh where that *Cuckoo* nurse had stomped me, but the hot water felt good, and I attempted to "chill-ax" (to borrow a phrase from my baristas) by focusing on the swishing of branches outside my bathroom window.

A minute later, the chill became real.

Though the window was sealed tight, an icy breeze touched my shoulders. At the same time, the water in my bath grew hotter.

How was that possible?

In the blink of an eye, I found out—

My apartment's walls melted away, and I was outside in some kind of hot tub. Looking around, I realized the "tub" was black iron, shaped like an antique pot, and propped over an open fire.

Paralyzed, I rubbed my eyes, but the vision was still there. Then the heat of the fire increased. "Help!" I cried. "Someone help me!"

Cackling laughter was the only reply.

I drew breath to scream—but didn't have to. In another eye blink, I was back inside my bathroom. The black cauldron was gone, the water harmlessly tepid. Instead of a scream, I blew out air.

What in heaven's name just happened?

Sanity dictated one answer—I had dozed off. Yet what I experienced wasn't a dream. It felt far too real. My heart was beating double time; my brow was damp with sweat.

It must be the coffee . . .

Matt's crazy African coffee was still affecting me. I stepped out of the tub, splashed cold water on my face. Then I threw on my short terry robe and hurried down the hall to find the master bedroom empty.

Where did Mike go?

His suit jacket was draped over a chair and his holstered gun sat on the dresser. The sight of both eased my mind. While most nights I was fine with my solitude, tonight I really needed Quinn's comfort.

In the hearth, a fire now crackled. I was glad he'd kindled it. With the lights low, the flames cast an almost magical glow across the room's antiques—from the stained glass of the Tiffany lamps to the Italian marble of the century-old mantle and the polished mahogany of the four-poster bed.

The radiant light continued up the French mirror and across the high walls, gilding the hundreds of paintings, etchings, and doodles that helped make this landmark home so special to me. Over the years, Madame had cheered these artists on—and up—even sobered them up with her pots of French roast. In return, they'd given her these works.

I may have been an art school dropout, but I was the *de facto* curator of this precious coffeehouse collection, in sole charge of selecting what to rotate down to the shop or lend to museums—like Basquiat's *Dreadlocks and the Three Bears*, a mixed-media collage that I'd proudly delivered to the Museum of Modern Art for the upcoming Brothers Grimm exhibition.

If I *were* to move to Washington, caring for these treasured pieces was one of the many things I'd miss.

My gaze caught on another of my favorites, a small oil-on-canvas titled *Café Corner.* The artist had conceived it right downstairs. The subject of the piece was a golden-haired young woman, sitting alone among a sea of empty tables.

Like Edward Hopper's much more famous *Automat*, the girl was more than alone. She seemed completely isolated (a common enough irony of city life, being alone in a crowd). And the cup she stared into didn't exactly runneth over. It was full once, but she'd drained the contents, and now sat contemplating the emptiness.

The city was full of girls like this. They came to New York with golden dreams for fairy-tale futures, dreams drained by all the bad choices and wrong turns, by dark intentions rooted here long before they arrived. And though the afternoon sunlight was strong in the painting, it cast equally strong shadows.

I'd never noticed it before but the crossbars of our French doors looked almost like prison bars. It made me reconsider Hopper's title for the work.

Was the girl in *Café Corner* doing more than sitting in a corner of a corner café? Perhaps she was feeling cornered, like all those fairy-tale characters, trapped by a choice she'd made. Or couldn't make.

Or was I reading too much into it because of my own situation?

Out the window, the storm was getting worse. Raindrops pelted the glass, and the bushy top of a sidewalk tree swayed heavily in the wind, back and forth, back and forth.

For weeks now, I'd felt like that battered tree, swinging between two wishes: Being here. Being with Mike. In the morning, he would expect an answer. He deserved one. But which choice was right? Which would I regret?

Catching my reflection in the window, I saw the same troubled expression as the girl in the painting. To confirm it, I glanced again at the canvas—and froze.

What in the world?

The painting had changed. The golden-haired girl was replaced by a fortyish woman with shoulder-length hair the color of Italian roast. I stepped closer.

It's me. I'm the subject of the painting!

I rubbed my eyes and looked again, but my image was still there.

"You know, you look adorable in that robe, Cosi. But it's got nothing on that peasant dress."

Mike had returned to the room. I could hear his deep voice, yet it sounded miles away.

"I didn't want to mention it at the hospital, but I especially liked the sopping wet, button-free version . . ."

What's happening to me? I felt disoriented, woozy, and unable to tear my gaze away from the canvas.

Should I tell Mike what I'm seeing? And if I do, will he believe me? Or drag me out of this asylum and into a real one?

THIRTY-EIGHT

MIKE crossed the room and pressed a warm cup into my hands. "Drink this. You'll feel better."

I took a few gulps, hardly tasted it.

"Is something wrong? You look a little confused."

"I'm fine," I croaked and gulped down more of the hot liquid.

"The coffee's good, isn't it? I made it myself." He put his lips close to my ear. "Of course I had a great teacher."

When I failed to reply, he touched my cheek, pressing me to face him.

He'd changed into his old NYPD sweatpants and a worn Rangers tee. His light brown hair was mussed and he looked more human, more huggable. His typically icy gaze was alive now and flickering with the warmth of blue fire. He looked ready for bed, for me.

I watched him sample the coffee he'd made for us. I joined him, slowing down and sipping this time, so I could actually taste what was in my cup.

The notes of flavor were enjoyable—chocolate, plum wine, cloves. Then came that familiar hint of exotic spice, the one I couldn't identify.

That's when I panicked.

"Mike, what is this coffee?"

"Why? Is something wrong?"

"Just tell me."

"I don't know exactly. I got the beans from a shiny green bag in your cupboard."

Oh, God. Matt sent that bag up from the roasting room two days ago, but I'd been too busy to sample it!

"I admit I was curious about the *M* written on there with black marker. Is the *M* for Mike?"

"Only if you're *Magic* Mike."

"That would require a striptease, wouldn't it?" An impish smile appeared. "I'm not averse to that, if it's just you and me—and I get one in return." He waggled his eyebrows.

"What's gotten into you?" I asked and knew the answer was right in front of me: *the coffee!*

"Mike, listen to me, these beans aren't meant for drinking casually. They're for ritual fortune telling. My ex-husband sourced them in Africa, and his mother used them at the festival today. The beans are supposed to be . . ."

"Be what?"

I felt silly saying it, but—"I wasn't kidding about the *M*."

"You mean I'm drinking *magic* beans?"

"Yes!"

"You're serious?"

"All I can tell you is these beans are having a peculiar effect on me. I believe they're inducing . . . well, *visions*, for lack of a better word. I better not drink any more. And you shouldn't, either."

He took a few more sips. "I don't taste or feel anything out of the ordinary—except excellent coffee. Look, I think you're overwrought. You need to take it easy. Why don't you try some more? You'll see your imagination is getting the better of you."

"How do I get through to you? Fine, I'll show you." I pointed to the wall. "See anything strange?"

Mike frowned at the work. "What should I be seeing?"

"Me!"

"You're in it? Really?" Mike stepped closer. "Where? Behind the counter?"

I gawked and looked again. No more Clare Cosi in the corner.

The golden-haired girl was back in her seat, contemplating an empty cup.

"I do think someone should paint you," Mike said as he set our own cups aside. "But not like this, more like . . ." Behind me now, he curled his arms around my waist, fumbled with my robe's belt.

"Mike, I swear, I saw myself in this painting—"

"Mmm, yes, like this." His fingers finished their work and my robe fell open. "It's time to relax."

"I can't."

"You can. And I'll help. After all, I've been dreaming of these curves all week."

"You have?"

"Oh, yeah." I felt his lips on my neck, his hands on my body. "And don't you want to make a guy's dream come true?"

"It's my dream, too," I whispered.

"Good. We can dream together."

Then Mike's mouth found mine and my robe found the floor.

Thirty-nine

BEEP-BEEP! *Beep-beep!*

Car horns?

Stirring from a deep sleep, I rubbed my eyes. Mike's large body lay beside me, sinking the mattress. I was a happy victim of gravity, tight against his snoring form.

Unsure of the time, I glanced at the bedside clock.

Seven PM*? That can't be right . . .*

Lifting Mike's heavy arm from around my waist, I slipped free of the covers and went to the window. Laughter drifted up from the sidewalk crowd as taxis snarled traffic, dropping off fares at my coffeehouse.

If the clock was right, then we'd slept all day, and this mob was here for Esther's Poetry Slam—the thought of which made me slam my forehead.

If I don't get a move on, I'll miss my chance to question Red!

Letting Mike sleep, I threw on jeans and a sweater. Then I dashed down the service staircase and burst into our shop's second-floor lounge.

The mass of bodies was thick, merry, and loud. As I plowed my way through, Esther grabbed a microphone and announced—

"Attention, everyone! She's here!"

Applause and cheers rang out. A bright light swung and I was blinded. *Is that spotlight on me?!* Confused, I lifted my arm to shield the glare and saw a broad-shouldered silhouette approach. *Matt?*

My ex-husband was back to his Prince Charming act—literally. He wore the same costume he had at the festival.

"Allow me to escort you," he said, offering his arm.

As we walked forward, I saw our queen. Matt's mother wore a flowing gown of royal purple and a golden crown on her silver head. When I stepped up on the stage, she opened her arms—

"Welcome, my dear princess!"

"But I'm not a princess," I said. "And I certainly don't look like one."

Madame waved her diamond wand and my jeans and sweater transformed into a pink gossamer gown, its filmy fabric sparkling in the spotlight.

"You see? You are a princess," Madame insisted. "But you cannot have two kingdoms. You must choose one."

"No, I can't choose. Please don't make me!"

"You must choose by morning, dear, or the choice will be made for you."

"We came here to dance!" cried a young woman from the crowd.

"Yes, we want to dance!" another shouted.

"Dance, dance, dance!" more girls chanted.

"And so you shall!" Madame replied. "Ladies, come up to the stage!"

Out of the crowd, twelve young women stepped forward, wearing a rainbow of sparkly gowns. They formed a circle around me and began to dance, sing, and *float*—because each had a pair of translucent fairy wings.

Then thunder cracked and a lightning bolt shot through the room. When the flash was over, a dark silhouette stood in the middle of the gasping crowd. The figure wore a long black robe with a large hood.

I peered into the raised hood and saw a pitch-black void

where a face should have been. Everyone in the room quaked—except our queen. She was furious. Madame rose from her throne and pointed a finger.

"You were not invited!"

Ignoring the accusation, the hooded figure floated toward the circle of twelve princesses. "Show me your keys," the specter commanded.

Each of the twelve quivering fairy princesses pulled out a golden key, hanging on a chain beneath her gown. I touched the chain around my own neck, pulled it free, but there was no key attached.

"Show me your key!" the specter demanded.

"But I have no key," I squeaked

A hideous howl sounded and everyone fell back.

"She is a princess," Madame warned the specter. "You must bow to her."

The hooded figure stooped in front of me. I could feel its dark pride and murderous anger as it went down on one knee—but not to bow. An animal paw shot out of the robe. A single claw stabbed my leg. Blood poured out, but there was no pain, only wooziness.

"Sleep!" the figure commanded, and I collapsed on the stage.

I woke abruptly. The crowd was gone and so were my clothes.

Stripped naked, I sat in a giant cauldron of hot water. Dark woods surrounded me and an open fire burned underneath. The sound of cackling filled my ears—Fletcher Endicott stood laughing at me.

A black pointed hat covered his receding hairline, and a velvet cape hung from the shoulders of his hound's-tooth sport jacket. His nose had grown long and crooked, and warts freckled his newly pronounced chin.

"You're in hot water now, my pretty!" he cried.

Equal parts embarrassed and enraged, I sank lower in the water, folding my arms over my breasts.

"What do you want?" I demanded.

He pointed to something in the distance—a large snow-covered hill. Two figures were skiing down the slope toward us. One was Matt in his Prince Charming costume. The other was Endicott's heavyset partner, wearing his flapping raincoat.

As they skied up to the fire, Endicott's partner pulled out his gun and waved it at Matt.

"Get in, Your Royal Pain-ness!"

"That's right!" Endicott cried. "You two should be in it together!"

Matt said nothing. Head hanging low, he pulled off his boots and climbed into the hot water with me. But he didn't float. He sank.

"Matt, no! Don't give up!"

As I lunged to save him, Endicott's partner used his ski pole to stir the pot. Then the two men chanted—

"Double, double toil and trouble; Fire burn, and caldron bubble!"

The flames beneath us rose higher and the water began to spin. The bubbling whirlpool was pulling me under!

All sound stopped as the water enveloped me, washed me down a giant pipe. With a splash, I landed in an immense rectangular pool. The woods were gone, along with Endicott and his partner. I looked around for Matt, but there was no sign of him.

"Ma'am? Would you like a hand?"

I looked up to find two linebackers in blue suits. They stood next to a horse-drawn carriage.

In the distance, I saw the rounded dome and fluttering flag of a grand castle. Closer to me stood an immense obelisk. In the opposite direction, a stone giant sat on his throne, gazing into the pool I'd landed in.

As I waded out of the water, one of the blue-suited men held up a bath sheet. I wrapped myself in it and climbed into the carriage, where my towel transformed into a ball gown and my wet hair dried into a stunning French twist laced with flowers and pearls.

One of the men talked into his suit sleeve while another tapped an earbud.

Then the horses began to trot and we were on our way, rolling along a lengthy strip of manicured lawn and towering trees. Finally, the carriage pulled up to my destination—a neo-Palladian palace of painted sandstone.

The carriage door opened to a red carpet flowing down a staircase between grand columns. On the carpet stood a rugged man in formalwear, light brown hair in military trim, cobalt eyes blue enough to steal the breath from my lungs.

"Hi, Clare."

"Hi, Mike."

"Welcome to the White House."

He escorted me inside, where a large party was under way. Men and women waltzed on a ballroom floor. Mike took me in his arms and we danced together. He spun me so fast that I felt drunk, dizzy with happiness.

"Choose me," he whispered.

"I do," I said, and my words released a glittering whirlwind around us.

Then the ballroom dissolved.

Forty

"GOOD morning, sleepy head . . ."

The edge of the mattress sank a little as Mike sat. The man was grinning, ear to ear.

"You never grin." I reached out and pinched his arm—hard.

"Ouch! What's the idea?"

"I needed to make sure you were real."

"Is that so? Then I guess I better prove it—" Pushing me back against the pillows, his mouth took over mine. When the sweetly aggressive kiss was done, he was grinning again.

"Real enough for you?"

Still catching my breath, I nodded.

"Good," he said, "because I made us some *real* coffee and it's getting cold." He gestured to a silver tray with a French press and two cups.

Oh, God, not again . . .

"Don't worry. I checked the bag this time. Go on, try it."

With trepidation, I took a small sip and recognized the sparkling citrus of the Ethiopian, silky body of the Colombian, and floral fruitiness of the Guatemalan. They all added up to one thing—my *Sunshine Breakfast Blend.*

"It's delicious," I said with relief, "but it doesn't explain the grin."

"Come on, Cosi, you know why. I'm happy about your decision."

I blinked, confused. "You're happy I—"

"Don't worry. I know you need time to put things in order. You still have to give notice to Allegro and his mother, right? But I'm overjoyed you're going to be moving to Washington."

I nearly spit out my coffee. "Refresh my memory. What did I say exactly?"

"I asked you to choose me. You said 'I do.'"

"Mike, I *dreamed* that."

"I know. It's my dream, too—having you in my life every morning and every night. And speaking of dreams. I had a few crazy ones last night, including Endicott as the Wicked Witch of the West."

"Wait, back up. *What* did you dream?"

"Endicott and his fat partner were trying to boil you alive in a big cauldron out in the woods—you and Allegro. After that, you went skinny-dipping in the Lincoln Memorial reflecting pool; I enjoyed that part. Then you joined me at the White House for a state dinner. Funny, huh?"

No, I thought, *not funny—disturbing. How in heaven's name could we have had the same dream?!*

"—then I woke up and you were gazing at me so lovingly from your pillow. That's when I asked you for your decision. And you said yes, you're moving to Washington. You won't regret it, Clare, I promise."

He glanced at the bedside clock. "I better get a move on. My kids are expecting me for brunch. You're joining us, right?"

"Ah . . . right."

"Good. Shall we tell the kids about your big move?"

"No! I mean, it's like you said, I still have things to work out."

"You're right. We won't tell them yet. After all, I have to break the news to Molly and Jeremy about Anya. I'm sure they'll be upset." He paused a moment, met my eyes. "I'm glad you're coming, Clare. I really need you there."

His choice of words surprised me. "You never say that."

"What?"

"That you *need* me."

"That's because I don't like to need anyone." His gaze held mine. "But I need you."

I touched his cheek. "Why don't you take the shower first? I have to make a phone call . . ."

As Mike whistled his way to the bathroom, I threw off the covers, found my cell, and speed-dialed my ex-husband.

Forty-one

"Matt, we need to talk," I whispered.
"About my case?"
"About your beans! Your crazy magic beans!"
"Why? What happened?"
"I had more visions, that's what happened. Then Mike and I drank the coffee before we made love, and we had the *same dream*."
"That's a new one."
"It gets worse. Mike said I woke up and told him I was moving to Washington."
"You what?!"
"I don't *remember* telling him, but he says I did."
"Well, tell him you made a mistake!"
"I can't."
"Why not?"
"Wait, I hear him coming—"
I listened and realized he was still in the bathroom. What I heard sounded like singing. *Singing? Mike Quinn was singing in the shower!*
"My God," I whispered. "How am I going to tell him I didn't mean what I said? The man is floating. I have to let him down easy. What is happening to me? Am I going insane?"
"Clare, you're perfectly sane. It's my coffee that's

affecting you. I knew it last night. That's why I contacted Dr. Pepper."

"The soft drink company?"

"No, this Dr. Pepper has an MD and a PhD, actually he has a few doctorates—biochemistry, anthropology—anyway, he's an expert on the chemistry of coffee and he's intensely interested in these beans, which have a pretty incredible history behind them."

"Well, get over here this afternoon and tell it to me because I need to get control over this! And you need to cancel any plans you have for tonight."

"But Bree wants me to take her—"

"Listen to me. Your coffee has made a mess of my head *and* my personal life. And you are *still* a person of interest in a reckless endangerment case that could turn into homicide, which means you are not taking Bree anywhere tonight, you're coming to Esther's Poetry Slam."

"I don't follow. What does Esther's Poetry Slam have to do with—"

"I'll explain this afternoon—"

"Clare, sweetheart," Mike sang, "the shower's free!"

"Thanks!" I cooed sweetly into the hallway then ended my call with a threatening hiss. "Just get over here!"

FOR the next few hours, I tried my best to focus fully on Mike Quinn and his kids—*especially* his kids.

Molly and Jeremy were upset about Anya's condition, but in different ways. Jeremy was shocked at first and then he began to act like his father, grilling me about where I'd found her, how she'd looked, how long she'd been like that.

"Why didn't you tell us last night?!"

"That's enough," Mike said, shutting down his queries, but it didn't stop the boy from stewing, and I could understand why. At thirteen, he was old enough to take on a complex mix of feelings over what happened to Anya—anger, frustration, even guilt over being so close to her in the woods yet failing to keep her from harm.

Mike sensed his son's distress and said a few words, but I could tell they didn't help.

Molly didn't become angry or frustrated. The little girl just cried.

As I hugged her sobbing form, she insisted we visit her "Annie" at the hospital.

Once there, Jeremy remained stoic at Anya's bedside, but I could see the questions in his gaze. He wanted answers.

"Your dad and I are working to find out what happened," I told the boy.

"But I want to help."

Quinn overheard. "There's nothing for you to do, son. And I don't want you involving yourself. Understand?"

Jeremy didn't argue, but his jaw was set and I wondered if the boy had something specific in mind.

When we finally dropped off the kids at Leila's apartment, Quinn asked me to wait in a lobby chair while he informed his ex-wife of Anya's condition—which was (sadly) no better.

"How did she take it?" I asked when he came back down. "Was she emotional?"

"No, not really. She looked a little . . ."

"What?"

"Well, a little scared actually."

"Scared? Of what?"

"I asked her what was wrong, but she clammed up."

"I wish you would let me talk to her." I started for the elevator, but he yanked me back.

"The last time you two spoke, Leila nearly clawed your eyes out. She's in a state."

"But I still have questions."

"Next time." He tapped his watch. "See me off?"

We grabbed a cab, and by the time we reached Penn Station, his train was already boarding.

"I'm going to miss you," he said.

"I'll miss you, too."

"Stay out of trouble, okay?"

He threw me a wink before turning to go. He also

promised that Franco would keep me informed of any developments in Anya's case.

Though I had no evidence, I was pretty sure the newest development was about to happen tonight—and in my own coffeehouse.

I just prayed my ex-husband would be waiting there for me when I got back.

Forty-two

For once, my prayers were answered.

When I returned to the Village Blend, I found Matt at our espresso bar, hunched over his smartphone, munching one after another of our new Peanut Butter Chews. (My special recipe gave a sophisticated spin to the traditional peanut butter cookie, making them, as Matt discovered—and he would know—dangerously addictive.)

I pulled us a couple of doubles, and then I pulled him to a corner table, far away from the prying ears of Esther and Nancy.

"So?" Matt began the moment we sat down. "Did you tell the flatfoot?"

"Tell him what?"

Matt scowled. "That you're *not* moving to Washington."

"I told you, I have to let him down easy."

"Why? Because you're afraid he'll dump you?"

"No, because I love him, and I don't want to hurt him. And I don't want to talk about this now—I want to know about your crazy coffee. Am I going insane? Or did you spike those beans with LSD?"

"You're perfectly sane, Clare. And my coffee is unadulterated. If it's inducing visions and dreams, then *pay attention* because they're real."

"What is that supposed to mean?"

"It means what it means."

"Matt, my dream last night was not *real*. It was a Fellini movie! Endicott in a witch's hat? His partner on snow skis? Dancing fairies and an angry intruder with a poisoned animal claw?"

"You have to look at it like a fortune teller. When you read coffee grinds, you decipher the symbols formed in the grounds, right?"

"Right."

"It's the same with these visions. You have to *interpret* what you see. Apply it to the present and the future."

"Are you having visions, too?"

"No." He resolutely shook his head. "I've never gotten them."

"Then why are you so sure these coffee-induced hallucinations have any validity for me?"

"Personal experience."

"I need more."

Matt shifted and expelled a breath. "Over in Africa, these beans saved my life."

"They *what*?!"

A few customers looked our way.

"Matt, you never told me your life was in danger!"

"Lower your voice, will you? I'm fine now. But what happened in Africa convinced me there is something to this 'magic coffee.' The beans themselves are extremely rare."

"I know they're rare. That tells me *nothing*."

"Fine, I'll start at the beginning." He paused for a hit of espresso and leaned across the table. "Last year, in Addis Ababa, I met with the Patriarch of the Ethiopian Christian Church. During my audience, he told me about a sacred coffee that once grew wild in the forests around Lake Tana."

"Sacred?"

Matt nodded. "Three thousand years ago Hebrew tribes carried the Ark of the Covenant to Lake Tana and hid it on an island. You've heard of the Ark of the Covenant, haven't you? That holy relic from the *Indiana Jones* movie?"

Oh, for heaven's sake. "You mean that holy relic from the *Old Testament*. Yes, I've 'heard of it.' Go on."

"The Patriarch claimed that proximity with the Ark had infused nearby wild coffee plants with mystical power. Naturally I expressed an interest in tasting the stuff, but he explained that the region was so heavily deforested that the beans were nearly extinct."

"Nearly?"

Matt nodded, a glimmer of pride in his gaze. "But I found some."

Forty-three

I stared at my ex-husband. "You actually went to Lake Tana?"

"I did, and I was pretty nervous about it, too . . ."

That didn't surprise me.

For years, my bean-hunting partner has been traveling to Harar, Sidamo, Yirgacheffe, and Limu—all of them traditional growing regions in Ethiopia. Lake Tana, however, was on the other side of the country. Matt had no connections there, no guide, and no clue where to look for coffee.

"But after a week of searching, I located a tribe on the Zega Peninsula," he confided. "They still harvest wild, forest-grown coffee on a small stretch of protected land. I can't say I was greeted with open arms, but I hung around a few days, tried to help out, and I finally managed to charm my way in."

"There must have been a woman involved."

"As a matter of fact, Adina supervised the harvest for the tribe. She also happened to be the village shaman. She spoke Greek and French and a little bit of English, so we managed to communicate. When I told her I wanted to sample the sacred coffee, she nodded and sent me back to my tent to wait."

"How long did you—"

"Three days. I was about to give up when an old man woke me at midnight. He led me through the forest. Under a full moon, we climbed to the top of a cliff that overlooked

Lake Tana. Adina was there, along with many others, including an Orthodox priest wearing old, worn robes. I joined the circle, and while prayers were chanted, we were served pan-roasted coffee around the ritual fire."

Matt paused. "The coffee was exceptional. After we drank it, the old man led me back to my tent while the rest stayed behind to meditate or pray."

"And did you experience any visions? Weird dreams?"

Matt shook his head. "Nothing. At the time, I figured it was all bunk, a good story to tell when selling the beans for an upmarket price. And when I saw Adina again, I offered to buy what the tribe was willing to sell—two fifty-pound bags. Then, as I was packing the rented Rover, Adina showed up with the coffee and a *warning* . . ."

"Matt, are you okay? You look pale."

He nodded and shifted again. "She said the coffee gave her a vision. She told me to avoid 'the blue goose.' She insisted the blue goose would destroy me if I got too close."

"I didn't even know they had geese in Ethiopia."

"Around Lake Tana blue geese are about as common as pigeons in Manhattan. Anyway, I didn't know what to make of her warning until three days later. I was boarding a ferry to cross the lake when I noticed a blue goose painted on the ship's bow. I got a sick feeling seeing it. I remembered what Adina said and decided to postpone my trip for one more day. Take the ferry in the next town."

"That doesn't sound too bad."

Matt's expression darkened. "That night I found out the blue goose ferry capsized. Everyone was lost."

Despite our cozy surroundings, Matt shivered—and so did I.

"It could have been a coincidence," I said.

"You really think that?"

"No, but I don't have any other rational answer. And right now I need rational answers. I mean why did Adina see your future after drinking the coffee? But you saw nothing? And why am I having visions—while you're experiencing nothing?"

"At first, I thought maybe it was gender. You had to be a woman. Then I thought it had something to do with being psychic. You know, Clare, I always thought you were a little psychic. When we were married, there were times when I could never get anything past you."

"I wasn't psychic. You were predictable."

Matt drained his espresso cup. "Look, I told you already, if you want rational answers, the man to see is Dr. Pepper."

"And who is he exactly?"

"We met on a transatlantic flight and talked coffee for like eighteen hours straight. He's a biochemist and medical doctor, and he's had a lifelong passion for our favorite beverage—consuming it and studying it."

"And how is he supposed to help me?"

"I sent him the Lake Tana beans for testing. After I texted him about your vision, he got very excited. He wants you to visit him in Columbia."

"Colombia, South America?!"

"No! Dr. Pepper isn't South American. He's East Indian. And he's teaching at Columbia *University*. He wants you to come uptown to his lab."

"Why his lab?"

"He's going to wire you up to some machine and test your brain functions after you drink the Lake Tana coffee."

"Matt, I am not drinking that coffee—not ever again."

"Suit yourself. But the fact is, you already drank it, more than once, and it gave you visions. So why not use them?"

"Because I've sworn off fortune telling."

"What harm can it do?"

"Plenty."

Matt sat back and studied the tin ceiling. "How can I convince you?" Pushing away his empty cup, he leaned forward.

"If you don't want to believe this coffee saved my life, then don't. But you have to admit it helped us find Quinn's kids. Remember? Back in Central Park?"

"The Oak Bridge," I whispered. "You're right."

"Remember how we figured that out?"

"Actually, you're the one who figured that out."

"Yeah, after I heard the clues in your vision. And we can do it again. Come on, what do you say?"

I closed my eyes and considered my (far too limited) options.

"Fine. Where do we start?"

Forty-Four

"We need to interpret what you saw under the coffee's influence," Matt said, "which means I'll need to know more about your dream. Tell me what you remember."

I began with the surreal Poetry Slam—how I was treated as the guest of honor and young women with fairy wings danced around me until a dark figure intruded, ruining the party.

"That sounds a lot like the Sleeping Beauty story, doesn't it?" Matt observed. "All the fairies are invited to a royal party for a beloved princess, all but one. The one who's not invited shows up and curses the princess with a sleeping spell."

"How do you know about the Sleeping Beauty story?"

"How do you think? Our daughter."

"You read it to her?"

"I took her to the animated movie. Before her Hello Kitty and vampire phases, Joy went through a Disney Princess obsession, don't you remember?"

"Of course I remember. I didn't think you did."

"Are you kidding?" Matt shivered. "That evil Disney fairy gave me nightmares for days."

"*Maleficent* gave you nightmares? She's a fictional character."

"Let's just say she reminded me of a few not-to-pleasant romantic entanglements."

"That I believe."

"Back to your caffeinated dream: So there you are on stage, dressed in a pink gown like Anya's, and this hooded figure pricks you in the leg with its animal-clawed hand and puts you to sleep, which means it did the same thing to Anya, right?"

"It's possible something like that happened. She has no history of using drugs. So it makes sense that someone injected her without her consent. This dark figure also wanted to see everyone's golden key. But I didn't have one—and there wasn't a key on Anya when they found her, either."

Matt frowned. "What are the keys for anyway?"

"From what I can tell, they're pass keys to an exclusive club on the Upper East Side. And get this—Mike Quinn's ex-wife has one."

"Wait a second, isn't Anya *working* for Quinn's ex?"

"Yeah, it seems suspicious to me, too. Leila was also acting strangely at the festival yesterday, but I can't point to any rational reason she'd want to silence Anya."

"Let's go back to the hooded intruder. If this figure wanted to see your key, then he or she must be connected to that exclusive club."

"Matt, I think it's *all* connected to that club. I had a very sick vision outside its door. I felt the same heavy darkness in Central Park that night. That figure in my dream was the source, a dark soul willing to kill for what it wants."

"Okay, but what *person* does this dark soul inhabit?" We sat in silence a moment. "Maybe we should approach it like we did the clue to the Oak Bridge. Let's try being literal. Who do you know that wears a hood?"

Of course. "Red!"

"The hood in your dream was red?"

"No. It was black. But remember Anya's friend, the Red Princess? According to Esther, she raps around town as Red in the 'Hood. She's also coming to the Poetry Slam tonight, and she expects to meet with you."

"Me? Why?"

"I don't know, but Quinn thinks you should be careful—"

"I think I can handle myself, Clare."

"No, listen, she could be dangerous."

"What's the big deal?"

"Esther described Red as a party girl. So if she gave Anya drugs and the girl accidentally overdosed, then Red might be panicking now. She could have heard about the police questioning you and might want to set you up in some way, plant drugs on you, and turn you in to avoid blame herself—especially if Anya dies."

"So am I meeting with her or not?"

"You're waiting upstairs in my apartment until I call you down. I want to talk with her first."

"About what?"

"About Anya—I need to see how Red reacts when I bring up her friend."

"What are you looking for?"

"The real story between them." I leaned across the table and lowered my voice. "I can't stop thinking about Anya's golden key. Mike's daughter claimed she had one, yet it wasn't on Anya when I found her—and her necklace chain was broken. What if Red wanted Anya's golden key to get into that exclusive Upper East Side club? What if Anya refused to give it up? Red might have hatched a plan to drug her friend, steal the key, and leave Anya unconscious in the woods, making it look like a drug overdose."

"If that's true, then the clawed hand you saw shooting out of that black robe makes perfect sense."

"Why?"

"The Red Riding Hood story isn't complete without the ruthless wolf. Maybe Red is the wolf. In her story, they could be one and the same."

"Or we could be wrong. That's the trouble with fortune telling. Interpreting signs is tricky business. Red could be innocent. After all, the hood in my dream was black, not red."

"Then why does she want to see me?"

"If she's innocent, then maybe she simply wants to question you. After all, for most of the day you were paired with Anya as her Prince Charming."

"She's either a suspect or a witness, Clare, make up your mind."

"I can't. Not without more to go on. And I've got to figure it out fast, or you could be in real trouble."

"I'm already in real trouble."

"Then I guess we've got nothing to lose."

Forty-Five

A few hours later, Esther's Fairy Tale Invitational Poetry Slam was under way, and I was front and center when Red strutted onto our temporary stage.

Smart and sexy in a tight, red leather dress with a sequined hood half covering her scarlet-streaked dark hair, Red's saucy poses easily netted male attention. But her tarty act was broad, self-aware, and so funny it brought the females along, too.

Sticking to the fairy-tale theme, she rapped out a story about Jack and Jill's journey up the hill. Her version was a ribald tale about two runaways in the big city. Her slam was sharp and clever, her voice melodious, but Red's real talent was her remarkable skill at connecting with the audience.

I watched from a front row table, sitting among members of Esther's *Poetry in Motion* urban outreach program. Esther's teenage students were enthralled by Red's rapid-fire rap, which was more than I could say for my zaftig barista.

"My puppies are killing me," Esther whispered as she untied her shoelaces.

All evening, Esther had been jumpy, awaiting the arrival of her boyfriend. Thus far, he was a no-show. And she became distracted by a more down-to-earth matter—her feet.

I glanced at her combat boots. "Why didn't you wear your comfy Keds?"

"Comfort is out the window, boss. Tonight Boris is going

to break up with me, and I have to be prepared." Esther slipped her feet out of the shoes and wiggled her toes inside her tights. "It's part of my female survival manual. If a woman's going into battle, she's got to have the proper footwear."

The boots worked well for her own rap, too—*Gretel's Revenge*, another urban retelling of a Grimm tale in which a tough girl frees her younger brother from the clutches of a female crime boss who wants to fry him for stealing hallucinogenic candy.

The crowd loved Esther (as usual), but I could tell she wasn't enjoying the evening. Not with Boris expected to show up for their scheduled "discussion." Though Esther was convinced he was going to dump her, I wasn't so sure.

Despite their disagreements, Boris and Esther truly were made for each other, and I was hoping they could work out whatever was wrong. On the other hand, I was glad he'd stayed away tonight—for Esther's sake as well as mine. She didn't relish a public quarrel, and I needed all the help I could get handling Red.

The Girl in the 'Hood was now winding up for her finish. Esther noticed, and slipped her feet back into the boots, though she didn't bother with the laces.

Red ended her slam to wild applause, which she acknowledged with a smile. But the second she exited the stage, the girl's people-pleasing persona left, too.

Before I even had a chance to stand, she jumped down from the stage and confronted Esther with a scowl.

"Where is Matteo Allegro?" she demanded. "I don't see him, and you promised he would be here. Did I waste my time?"

"Matt's here," I said, rising. "You can talk to him. But first you have to talk to me."

Forty-six

RED stared in silence, clearly taken aback.

Thank goodness, Esther jumped in. "Talk to her," she firmly advised. Then without bothering to tie her boots, she clomped to the stage to thank the audience and announce a short intermission.

As members of the crowd began milling around, stretching their legs, Red moved to the chair where her scarlet backpack sat. I shadowed her.

"So who are you?" she asked, fishing around her pack.

"My name is Clare. I'm Mr. Allegro's business partner. Why do you want to see him?"

"My business with Matteo Allegro is none of your business, *business partner*."

"You're wrong about that. His business is my business. And we're both wondering if you heard about the business involving your friend Anya?"

"You mean my *stupid* friend? The *stupid* girl lying in that *stupid* hospital? Do you think I'm stupid? Of course I heard what happened to Anya!"

In a dazzling blur of motion, Red's right hand opened a silver case, flipped a cigarette into her mouth, and lit it.

"Yesterday morning in Central Park, you were looking for her. What was the reason? Did you need something from her? A key maybe?"

"What is this? Shakedown? Maybe *you* are looking for key of your own?"

"I don't want anything from you but the truth."

"You can trust her," Esther broke in, returning to her seat. "And you're not allowed to smoke in here."

"Why should I trust her?" Red snapped, ignoring the smoking ban. "And why should *she* care about Anya?"

I stepped closer and lowered my voice. "Because I'm a friend of the two children Anya helped care for. I promised them I'd find out what happened to her. And right now I think it's connected to her missing key."

Red pursed her lips, as if reevaluating me. Then her tone changed from defensive to curious. "You think I took her key?"

"Did you?"

"No." She took a long drag on her cigarette and blew a smoke stream toward the ceiling. "Why would I need Anya's key? I have my own key."

"So . . . you're a *member*?" I said, unconvinced.

"You don't believe me? Who do you think helped that stupid girl get her stupid key? Was me!" Then she surprised me by showing me proof. Her right hand angrily stamped out the cigarette, yanked off her sequined hood, reached down her neckline, and pulled out a golden key.

The key itself didn't convince me, but the chain did. That signature chain made of silver and gold links in little diamond shapes couldn't have been Anya's because Molly had it.

"You see. I am not lying. I did not want Anya's key. And I did not hurt her. Anya was my friend. But she would not listen to me. I *tried* to tell her—once you say *da* to these people, you do not say *nyet*!"

"Who? What people?"

But Red wouldn't tell me, simply ranted in Russian. Though I understood nothing, I did recognize the phrase Esther mentioned last night—

"Ya budu ryadom! Ya budu ryadom!"

She repeated it several times. When I asked her what it meant, she shook her head. "I told you enough. Now let me see Matteo Allegro or I am leaving."

"If you're really Anya's friend, then you should care about what happened to her."

"Are you stupid? Of course I care!"

"Then prove it. Come back here tomorrow morning. Matt will be here to talk to you—along with a friend of ours."

"What friend?"

"He'll listen to your whole story, off the record. We'll all put our heads together and figure out the next step."

"Who is this off-the-record man? Reporter?"

"No . . ." I leaned close, whispered in her ear. "His name is Emmanuel Franco. He's a cop, you can trust him."

That did it. The mention of police spooked Red completely. She shook her head hard, pulled her hood back up, and turned to gather up her raincoat and bag.

"Wait—" I grabbed her arm.

"You get one last chance," she hissed, shaking me off. "Matteo Allegro comes to get me in five minutes or I am going. And I am never coming back."

I didn't like Red, but I did believe her about the key and the club, and I wanted to know more about both, along with "these people" to whom Anya had first said *yes* and then said *no*.

Matt, who could charm the pantyhose off most women, was now my only hope for getting more out of this edgy girl.

At the moment, my ex was ensconced upstairs, in the kitchen of my duplex, munching cookies, playing smartphone games, and catching up on international calls.

He'd already agreed to my rules about speaking with Red. (No leaving our coffeehouse. No touching. And he had to let me hover like a mother hen, close enough to witness their conversation.) Given those parameters, even Quinn would have agreed it was worth the risk.

"I'll ask Matt to come down," I promised.

"Clock is ticking," Red warned then turned on her sharp heels and clicked toward the back of the room.

I pulled out my cell, speed-dialed Matt, and got his voice mail.

"Okay, you're on—" I began when the rest of my sentence

was drowned out by the deafening sound of electronic feedback.

I knew something was happening behind me on stage, but I was more concerned with getting my ex down here, so I switched to text messaging. And that's when I heard Esther's agonizing groan.

Glancing up from my typing, I was alarmed to see the shock and horror crossing my barista's face.

"Esther, what's wrong?"

A second later, I knew, as the familiar male voice boomed out of our speakers—

I am Man with a Purpose, as you will soon see
And tonight you will all stand Witness for me—

Esther's boyfriend, Boris, part-time recording artist and full-time baker had finally shown up, which meant the moment Esther was dreading had come.

My life has been up and it has been down.
Just like a window, pain is all around . . .

In alarmed disbelief, Esther pointed at the stage. "He's doing it, boss. He's actually doing it! Boris is turning the end of our relationship into performance art!"

Forty-seven

As the audience cheered, I faced the stage and saw the reason for the excitement.

Boris had gelled his short blond hair into its usual defiant spikes, but the wiry Russian émigré had exchanged his typical baggy jeans, backward baseball cap, and Eminem T-shirt for a tight black evening jacket and leg-hugging pants that ended, Buddy Holly–style, above his ankles. His open-necked shirt was starched white, but not as bright as his close-set gray eyes, now shining with the electricity of an energized performer.

He'd even thrown some sharp new dance moves into his usual hip-hop strut, including a few Michael Jackson–inspired spins and moonwalks. What surprised me more than his choreography was the reason for this transformation—

You said let's live together
And you offered your hand.
But I don't want to roll
with a temporary plan.

Our love is deep, our passion strong.
And the two of us actually get along!
With a love like that, you don't just play.
So my sweet czarina, please make my day . . .

Skidding to the end of the low stage, Boris dropped to his knees, coming face-to-face with a slack-jawed Esther.

The audience members jumped to their feet as Boris pulled something from his back pocket. Esther gasped at the sight of the tiny jewel box. Boris flipped it open with his thumb. Inside a diamond engagement ring was cradled on a bed of red velvet.

Offering Esther the ring with one hand, he touched his chest with the other.

My pumping heart awaits your reply
Please say yes or I think I'll die.
Marry me, Esther, and share my life
And we will live together as man and wife.

I was so overjoyed by Boris's proposal that I cheered and applauded along with everyone else. Esther thought her life with him was over. Instead, to paraphrase the popular wedding song refrain, *It's only just begun.* (Not that Karen Carpenter's tune had a snowball's chance of turning up on Esther and Boris's nuptial playlist.)

I couldn't wait to hug Esther and congratulate them both. Of course, Esther had to answer Boris first. I assumed she would rap it. Then he would surely hand her up on stage, where they would embrace and live happily ever after.

Dozens of camera phones were poised to capture the anticipated, once-in-a-lifetime scene.

But it never came.

For a surreal minute, the pair remained frozen: Esther staring at Boris, eyes wider than an anime Bambi in a Hummer's headlights; and Boris waiting on his knees, hand to heart, holding out his ring.

Finally, the cheers died down and everyone leaned forward to hear the bride's reply.

Well, she gave one.

In a fair imitation of Edvard Munch's most famous painting, Esther Best covered her ears, and let out a bloodcurdling scream. Then she jumped up, pushed through the crowd, and headed for the exit.

At the back of the room, near the spiral staircase, Red was still waiting for Matt's arrival. Esther saw her and shouted—

"Get me out of here!"

Grabbing Esther's hand, Red pulled her onto the staircase. Halfway down, Esther stumbled, slowing them both, but like Alice's White Rabbit, they kept going.

"Esther, wait!" I called. "Please don't go!"

My words were drowned out by Boris's amplified voice shouting the very same thing.

I tried to elbow my way to the front of the mob, but the audience was madly waving camera phones, convinced this was contrived entertainment, and not a dreadfully conflicted moment in a young woman's life.

Then Boris shot off the low stage, and the sea of bodies finally parted.

"Czarina! Come back!" he wailed.

But Esther ignored her wannabe fiancé and hit the sidewalk with Red.

I bolted down the staircase, hopping over the object Esther had left behind. Outside I heard a driver gun his engine, and watched a Lincoln Town Car speed away with Red and Esther huddled in the backseat. The man behind the wheel had long wavy hair topped by a bowler hat—it was the same driver who'd picked up Red the night before.

I tried to get the plate number but the street was too busy and a van cut off my view. The only thing I glimpsed was a flash of that flag bumper sticker I'd seen last night.

Hearing fast footsteps behind me, I spun to find a stricken Boris clutching something in his hands.

In his black formalwear, he had the look of a dumbfounded Prince Charming grasping Cinderella's slipper—only this shoe wasn't glass. It was an unlaced combat boot. Esther had lost it on the stairs.

"My czarina . . . where is she?" he asked.

"I'm sorry, Boris. She's gone."

Forty-eight

Still clinging to Esther's boot, Boris sent his "czarina" a heartfelt text message. When she failed to reply, I led the distraught young man back inside, sat him down at my espresso bar, and began making him a comfort drink.

Matt approached me behind the counter. "Where's Red? And what was all that commotion about?"

I filled in the details and asked him to oversee the exiting of the Poetry Slam audience. "After that, I'd like you to stick around."

"Why? Red's gone, isn't she?"

"Yes, but I may need your help looking for Esther."

"You sound worried."

I lowered my voice. "She's with Red, and I don't trust that girl."

Matt glanced at Boris and then back to me. "What are you planning?"

"Boris knew Red pretty well," I whispered. "If I can talk him out of this funk, maybe he'll tell me more about the girl. Either way, I'm hoping he and I can track down Esther tonight."

"Good idea," he said. "When you need me, call me . . ." And on that Diana Ross note, my ex-husband headed up to our second-floor lounge.

I finished Boris's drink and slid the brimming latte glass across the counter.

"*Nyet*," he said, pushing it away. "Coffee will make me jittery."

"This is our special Dream Steamer. No espresso. Just steamed milk and our homemade orange, vanilla, and caramel cream syrups. Drink up. It'll calm your nerves."

He sampled it. "Is very good . . . *spasibo*."

"You're welcome."

While Boris sipped and sulked, I moved to the pantry area to phone Esther myself—and heard a muffled ringtone in the staff closet. That's where I found her coat hanging, along with her purse and her smartphone still inside it.

Boris nearly lost his mind when I brought the items up front. I wasn't thrilled with the discovery, either. The phone was locked. I couldn't see her contacts or get Red's number. And since Esther had no landline in her apartment, I suggested we take a ride over to her East Village building ASAP.

"Maybe Red gave her a ride home," I said with crossed fingers. "The only snag might come at her front door. What if she refuses to answer?"

"I have key," Boris said.

"Then let's go."

THE yellow cab dropped us at Avenue C, a tar-patched thoroughfare in Alphabet City, which was not, in fact, an invention of *Sesame Street* (as my youngest barista once thought), but a residential neighborhood located between the East Village and the East River.

In the late nineteenth century, this area had been a densely populated tenement ghetto where immigrants lived short, hard lives. By the mid-twentieth century, an influx of Puerto Ricans gave birth to the "Nuyorican" Art Movement, and struggling artists and musicians began flocking to the neighborhood for its low rents as much as its Bohemian atmosphere.

As Mike Quinn often noted, this time period brought high levels of crime and illegal drug activity, but it also spawned the world's first break dancers, rappers, and DJs. And in 1988, the city's very first poetry slam was held at the Nuyorican Poets Café—an avant-garde enclave only a few blocks from Esther's address.

We now stood before the battered entry door of her six-story walk-up, a former tenement building that once had no running water. These days, most of the East Village had gone through gentrification. Trendy restaurants, bars, and clothing boutiques occupied many of the storefronts, and old apartment houses had undergone multimillion-dollar renovations. But this one, not so much.

We rang the bell several times. No one answered, so Boris used his key. Actually, three keys: first the street door, then the front door, and finally the dead bolt.

Bolt was the word of the day because inside there was no sign of Esther.

I'd never been to her place. The one-bedroom flat was small yet cozy. We entered into a brightly lit kitchen with potted plants on the fire escape. Her roommate had occupied the sitting area to the right, which Japanese screens had turned into a private room. The space was emptied of personal items—the roomie had already moved out.

Esther's bedroom was on the other side of the kitchen, through a proper door, which stood half open.

I moved inside for a look around. Framed photos from her life covered one wall, and not one of them was a perfect, posed shot. Like Esther herself, the pictures were offbeat and honest: her Poetry Slam kids horsing around; her fellow baristas doing a kick line; her married sister in Westchester, struggling to wash the dog with her kids; Boris wearing a milk mustache in front of a half-eaten birthday cake; even Matt and me at the Village Blend counter, sticking our tongues out at the camera.

Her ceiling had been wallpapered with the night sky, and the rest of her walls were a fascinating collage of images and words. But the most interesting thing in the room hung above her cluttered desk—a large black magnetic board filled with movable white letters.

"Looks like she never came back here at all," I said, and read with interest the last words she'd put together on her poetry board. "*Like otiose vacillating enemies stuck together in neverending krappy situations.*"

I frowned. "What does that mean? And why did she spell crap with a *K*?"

Boris stared at the board and groaned.

"What is it?" I asked.

"Is acrostic," he said.

"Is that Russian?"

"Acrostic is word play. Like code—" He pointed at the board. "Read words down, first letters only . . ."

Like	**S**tuck
Otiose	**T**ogether
Vacillating	**I**n
Enemies	**N**everending
	Krappy
	Situations

I cringed when I read it, and was truly sorry I'd asked.

Boris sank to her mattress as the meaning of her coded poem sank in—

"Love Stinks."

Forty-nine

"TELL me, Clare Cosi. Am I cursed?"

With his spiked blond hair, tight-fitting tux, and crushed expression, Boris looked like a hopeful young recording artist who'd been passed over at the Grammys. Feeling his pain, I sank down next to him.

"Try to understand. Your girlfriend convinced herself that you no longer loved her."

"But how could she think this? We were happy! Our love does not stink!"

"Yes, but when Esther asked you to move in with her, you took so long to answer her offer that you . . . how do I put this? You opened up a void, a black space in her mind without answers. And to someone like Esther, a void is a dangerous thing. She automatically fills it with worst-case scenarios."

Boris shook his head. "You know the difference between a half truth and a whole truth?"

"What?"

"All the difference in the world." He pointed at the night sky wallpaper on Esther's ceiling. "When we look at space, we see black, so much black. But that is not the whole of it. There are bright points of light—*so many!*—between the dark places. This is what's important. This is where life is."

"Do you have a whole truth, Boris? One that Esther needs to hear?"

With a sigh, he hung his head and slowly nodded. "When my czarina asked to me to live with her, I was flattered, but it did trouble me. That much is true. And then it troubled me that I was troubled. After all, I love her. She loves me. I thought and thought and finally the reason was clear: I do not want to be Esther's *roommate*. I want to be Esther's *husband*. So excited I was by this discovery that I planned surprise proposal."

"But, Boris, you said it yourself—you 'thought and thought'—you had time to think through your feelings. Until Esther heard you propose on stage, she thought you were going to break up with her. Now she's very confused."

"Tell me something I don't know!"

"She may not be ready for marriage. And that may be something she never resolves, but she does love you. Give her time and she'll come around—" (I hoped she would, anyway.) "Unfortunately, that's not what truly worries me tonight. And if you knew the whole truth, I'm sure you'd feel the same."

"What whole truth?"

"About Red—the young woman Esther ran off with . . ."

Boris hadn't yet heard what happened to Red's friend, Anya, so I explained everything I knew, ending with a simple conclusion—

"I think Anya and Red got themselves involved with the wrong people. One of those people put Anya in a coma. Red knows more about this crime than she's telling. That's why I want to see Esther back here, safe."

"Is that all you know?"

"I'm afraid so. Red ranted more of the story to me in Russian, but I only remember one phrase. She used it over and over."

"What was it?"

"*Ya budu ryadom! Ya budu ryadom!*"

At those words, Boris's pale skin went ghostly white.

"What is it? What's wrong?"

He didn't waste time explaining. Instead, he jumped up, moved to the kitchen table, and began making phone calls.

While he spoke to a dozen people—all in Russian—I

found Esther's French press and made us coffee. This time Boris didn't push it away.

"Another pot, please," he said after quickly downing two cups.

I stood to make it. "Before you place another call, will you *please* tell me what you're doing?"

"I am contacting my friends in Brighton Beach. They say Roz moved out of neighborhood months ago. No one knows where she lives now. I sent text messages to my contacts."

"You called her Roz?" *Esther had used that name, too.* "What's her real name?"

"Rozalina Krasny."

"Will you please tell me all you know about her?"

Boris shrugged out of his suit jacket and draped it on his chair. "She came to America as young girl, never knew her father. Her mother died in Russian prison."

"So her mother was a criminal?"

"Russian government called her that. You would call her 'political prisoner.'"

"What did she do?"

"She joined radical group. Was like *Voina*. You know *Voina, da*?"

"No."

He studied the ceiling. "You know Pussy Riot?"

"Sorry."

"These are artists and performers who demand freedom of expression."

"Wait. I have heard of Pussy Riot . . ." They'd been in the news—a group of Russian women outspoken about repressive restrictions and antigay laws imposed under Vladimir Putin.

"You must understand," Boris said, rolling up his shirtsleeves. "Here in America, poets can go to neighborhood café and rap about president, government, laws that they do not like. Nothing will happen to them. But twenty-five years ago, Russia was in chaos. Freedom was new idea. Not everyone was comfortable with it. The old guard, the *nomenklatura*, they hated the new way."

"And Red's mother?"

"She was watched because she was outspoken. They convicted her of vandalism against the state when she took part in demonstration where others set fire to police van in Moscow. Punishment for artists and radicals is harsh. Red's mother could not take strain of this. She died of influenza in prison."

"Who got her daughter out of Russia?"

"Group dedicated to freeing victims of government oppression. Many of these men suffered at the gulags of the old Soviet Union. Here they formed local business collectives. You know some of these men, Clare Cosi. They are friends of mine. I introduced you not long ago."

"Yes, I remember . . ." (How could I forget a meeting wearing nothing but a towel and a smile in a Brighton Beach bath house?) As I poured hot water over the ground coffee in the press, Boris went on—

"Red has relatives in America. Older couple owned little pharmacy in Brighton Beach. Red was raised by them. They were not nice people—the kind who hit children instead of talk, you know? They sent her to school, told her she must be pharmacist and work for them. But she broke away, was like her mother, wanted artistic expression."

"And Anya?"

Boris shrugged. "Anya has not been here long—two years maybe. No one knows much about her. Some say Anya's mother and Red's mother were friends. That's all I can find out."

"Well, Red is the only one with answers because right now Anya is lying unconscious in a hospital. And she may die."

"That's why I am scared—for Red and for my Esther. We must find them."

"You agree then. They're in trouble?"

"The Russian phrase Red used when speaking of Anya: *Ya budu ryadom! Ya budu ryadom!* You know what phrase means?"

I shook my head.

"I will be next."

Fifty

AFTER our second pot of coffee, Boris headed into the streets of Alphabet City to check places in the neighborhood where Esther sometimes hung out.

I returned to the Village Blend with a list he'd scribbled of other possible places she might have gone.

Nancy and Dante checked addresses around NYU. Matt volunteered to take a cab to Astoria, Queens, where Esther sometimes worked with a documentary filmmaker. And I remained behind to hold the fort, coordinate the search, and send out text messages to the rest of my staff.

I even texted Harrison Van Loon.

The festival's lawyer texted me back an address for Red, but it was her adopted family's house in Brighton Beach, and Boris had already told me that she no longer lived there.

Then I *finally* heard from Tucker:

> No sign of Goth Queen. Will watch 4 her. Am crazy busy w/ so many shows this week. Will drop by 2 CU soon.

Esther's married sister in Westchester replied next. She said she hadn't heard from Esther in over a week.

"Is everything all right?" she asked.

"Fine," I texted back—seeing no reason to alarm the

woman (yet). *"She's been out of touch and I'm trying to reach her."*

Secretly, I hoped Esther would return to the coffeehouse, so we could have a heart-to-heart. For her sake and (to be honest) for mine.

My discussion with Boris about love and misunderstanding, dark spaces and disappointment, had unnerved me. But I had no one to talk to about my conflicted feelings, certainly not Matt, who was apoplectic about the possibility of my moving to Washington.

But the more I considered Boris's crushed expression, and Quinn's elated singing in the shower, the more I worried about losing the heart of a man I cherished. Maybe not all at once, but little by little, like grains of sand washing out to sea until the softest parts were eroded away and nothing was left but stone.

I didn't like being alone with these thoughts, but Esther never came back. Nancy and Dante returned with nothing but sleepy frowns. And an hour later, Boris called to report that he'd had no luck with his local search.

Finally, Matt fired off a text message. The Astoria filmmaker was out of town, but a neighbor knew about Red, who performed in the area often. So he was heading off to check a few Astoria nightclubs.

I wished Matt luck, closed the shop, and went up to my duplex.

On the way, I got a call from (of all people) Gardner Evans.

"Hey, boss, what's up?"

Hearing my night manager's friendly voice cheered me immensely. He'd spent his day off performing at jazz clubs around town with his group. When they finished their last set, he checked his phone and saw my text message.

"Why are you looking for Esther? Is anything wrong?"

"Lots. I can't explain now. Just let me know if you see her."

"Will do," he said. "Me and the guys are heading up to Harlem for fried chicken and waffles. You want to come?"

"Amy Ruth's?"

"You know it."

Gardner had taken me there a few times. It was a homey little place with a soul food menu, and the best Belgian waffles and honey-dipped fried chicken I'd ever tasted.

Gardner laughed. "I still remember the night you asked Sister Janet how she makes everything so good."

Sister Janet was the head chef at Amy Ruth's. And her answer impressed us all. She told us there was one simple secret to her soul food—she *prayed* before she cooked. I smiled at the memory, and couldn't help thinking of Boris and his points of light in the dark.

"Thanks for calling, Gardner."

"No problem. Text me if you want a take-out bag."

Signing off, I sat down at my kitchen table and drummed my fingers, wondering what else I could do to help find Esther. That's when I noticed the shiny green bag with the *M*, sitting exactly where Quinn left it.

Matt's Magic Beans . . .

I told my ex-husband I'd never drink his Lake Tana coffee again. Just thinking about it sent me into a cold sweat.

If I drank this coffee one more time, would it help me find Esther? Or simply mess with my head? Was there really something to this stuff? Or was it all coincidence and superstition?

I couldn't help thinking of Sister Janet at Amy Ruth's, praying in her kitchen. Was that superstition? Or could an act of faith better focus the mind?

I wonder what Matt's friend "Dr. Pepper" would say about it . . .

Whatever the answer, I didn't have time for lab experiments or religious debates. A young woman I thought of as a daughter could be in danger. She was lost and needed to be found. That meant I needed to try anything and everything within my power, namely—

A little prayer, which was why I recited one as I walked to the counter and put on the kettle.

And a little magic, which was why, with shaking hands, I measured out Matt's special beans and ground them.

Fifty-one

"Out of bed, sleepyhead! Your coach awaits!"

I opened my eyes.

I was no longer in my kitchen, where I'd bolted down a pot of Lake Tana coffee. I was lying on a dirt floor, dressed in a gossamer pink gown.

Rising, I looked for the promised waiting coach, but saw only earth-covered stone walls and prison bars.

"Am I in jail?"

"You're in the queen's dungeon." The familiar voice came from the next cell.

"Gardner? Is that you?"

Dressed as a Renaissance troubadour, with an English bowler on his head, my jazz musician night manager began strumming a lute.

"Is there a way out?" I asked.

His only reply was a jazzy rendition of a children's song: *"Frère Jacques, Frère Jacques, dormez-vous? Dormez-vous?"*

I went to the iron bars and shook the cell door. It wouldn't budge.

"Aunt Clare! Are you there?"

"She's down there. I see her!"

Far up the high stone wall, the innocent faces of Jeremy and Molly Quinn were pressed against the iron bars of a tiny window.

Mike's kids! "What are you doing here?" I shouted.

"We're here to help," Jeremy told me firmly.

"How?"

Bark! Bark!

"Penny!" The little collie poked her head through a narrow gap in the dungeon wall. Squeezing through, she raced up to me. As I bent down to pet her soft head, she barked in greeting then set to work, digging a hole in the dirt.

"What are you looking for, girl?"

She dipped her head into the hole, and her teeth brought out something shiny. *The key—Anya's golden key!*

When I tried the door, it opened, and Gardner's serenade finally stopped.

"Free me, too!" he called. "I'll show you a way out!"

I tried the lock on Gardner's cell. The door swung wide. He grabbed my hand, and we raced down a shadowy, torch-lit corridor, Penny at our heels.

When we turned the corner, fluorescent lights nearly blinded me. The dirt floor changed to linoleum, and we were running down a ground-floor hallway at St. Luke's–Roosevelt.

"There's the exit!" Gardner cried, tugging me toward glass doors. But before we reached them, they opened and a heavyset man with a ski mask stepped through. He aimed his gun and fired.

I was hit. Shocked at the blood seeping out of my lower left leg, I collapsed to the floor.

"Wake up, boss!" Esther called. "Wake up! Wake up!"

She's come back to us, I thought groggily. *Esther's back! Thank goodness!*

I lifted my head from the kitchen table and realized I wasn't in my kitchen. I was lying on a cold slab of pavement outside that creepy Upper East Side club.

"Are you there, boss?"

"Esther? Where are you?"

"In here!"

I rose from the ground and shuffled over to the recessed brick wall. The diamond-shaped mirror was talking with

Esther's voice. But I couldn't see her face. The glass looked cloudy, as if filled with smoke.

When the smoke cleared, I saw Red dancing like she had at the Poetry Slam, but not in her red leather dress. She was dressed in Anya's Pink Princess gown. Unlike my own gossamer gown, her fragile garment had lost its sparkle. It was dirty and ripped, and sadly soiled—the way I'd found it on Anya in the park.

As music played and Red rapped, waving flags appeared in a framed border around the picture.

I tried the door, but it wouldn't open. Then I stumbled backward, falling into a chair at a café table. I was in my coffeehouse. The tables around me were empty—and so was the cup before me. Coffee grinds showed my future, and I refused to look.

Then the cup turned into a laptop computer. The lid flipped open to show me a scene. It was the very same scene I'd glimpsed in the magic mirror.

I stared, mesmerized, at Red dancing in Anya's pink gown, UN flags around her. Then she stopped dancing and the laptop screen went black.

"Help! Please, someone! Help me!"

Red was calling out. Her voice was small, like a little girl's. She sounded scared.

I tried to move my arms, but couldn't. I was frozen in place. Looking up, I saw my master bedroom from a high vantage through a strange wood-lined window.

Not a window, a *picture frame*. I was trapped inside the *Café Corner*, the painting in my own bedroom.

I could see a fire blazing in the hearth, two bodies making love under the covers of the four-poster bed. I closed my eyes, hating the paralysis, wishing for freedom.

"Let me go! Please! Let me out of here! Help me! Someone, help me!"

"Clare?! What's wrong?"

"Let me out! Let me go!"

"Wake up, Clare! Wake up!"

I opened my eyes to find a frantic Matteo Allegro shaking my arm. I felt groggy and a little dizzy. When he saw that I was conscious, he peered into my face.

"You were raving like a madwoman. What's wrong? Did something happen?"

I spoke, my own voice sounding distant—

"I drank your coffee."

Fifty-two

"WHY did you do that, Clare?! And all alone?! You told me you were never going to drink it again!"

Matt looked less than steady himself as he ranted at me. His cheeks were ruddy from the cold, his brown eyes filled with fearful confusion.

"I'm okay," I told him, "give me a minute to get my head straight."

Matt shrugged out of his suede jacket and began to pace. "How do you sober someone up from *coffee*?" He stopped, took my hand, and patted it. "Do you want an aspirin? An antacid? How about some ice cream? Chocolate? A pickle and chipped ham sandwich?"

"I'm not pregnant, Matt, I'm disoriented. But it's nice you remembered."

"Of course I remembered! I made enough trips to all-night delis. And I had to learn what *chipped ham* was."

"I appreciated it. If our daughter were here, she'd concur."

"You sound better. More lucid."

"You can stop patting my hand now—I need it back. Thanks."

I rubbed my eyes and tried to stand. Seeing me wobble, Matt grabbed my waist. But after a glass of cold water, and a few minutes on my feet, I felt back to normal.

"What time is it?"

"Four in the morning. I just got back from Astoria, Queens."

"Any luck?"

"Very little. People knew about Red. She performs in clubs there, but they had no idea where she lived or how to reach her." He looked defeated. "Come on," he said, putting an arm around me again. "Let's go to bed."

"Whoa, there, Charming, I'm not that disoriented. I still remember the divorce—and your remarriage."

"I didn't mean we should go to bed together . . . unless you *want* company?"

I flashed on that scene at the end of my vision: two bodies making love under the four-poster's covers. *No, no, no!*

"Joy's room is open," I told my ex. "If you want to crash here tonight, that's my best—*and only*—offer."

THE next morning, Matt shocked me by sneaking into my bedroom very early. (No, not for that reason.) He turned off my alarm, went down to the shop, and opened the Village Blend.

"I wanted you to get some rest," he confessed a few hours later. "You really worried me last night."

"You don't need to worry."

"Yes, I do."

Yawning, I sat up in bed. Before I could say another word, Matt pressed a freshly made cappuccino into my hands.

"I didn't know what you'd want to eat, so I brought up a couple of choices: the Corn Muffins with Caramelized Bacon. We're almost sold out, but I snagged one along with that low-fat chocolate muffin you're always eating during your afternoon break, the one with ricotta and virgin coconut oil, what do you call it at the shop?"

"Chocolate Ricotta Muffins."

"You want that one?" He held it out.

"That's really sweet, but I don't have an appetite yet. I'll just sip the capp. Have you heard anything?"

Matt's shoulders slumped. "I'm sorry. No word yet."

Silence fell between us, and then he met my gaze. "So? Do you want to tell me about it?"

"I don't know."

"There could be something in it, Clare, something that could help us."

With a sigh, I slid over a little to make room on the mattress.

"It was so bizarre," I began as Matt sat down and tucked into the corn muffin.

"Another Fellini movie?"

"More like David Lynch. Near the end of it, I was trapped in your mother's Hopper painting and before that Esther spoke to me through a mirror."

"Was Red in the dream?"

"She was the star of it, dancing and rapping to music, but wearing Anya's pink gown. And all these flags appeared around her—"

"Flags? What sort of flags?"

"National flags from dozens of countries. Like the flags on my scarf—"

"The one Joy gave you."

"Then the magic mirror changed into a laptop screen."

"That's funny," said Matt.

"What's funny?"

He shrugged. "Sounds like you were looking at an amateur music video, something Red's fans might edit with an app, throwing on some hokey flag border before uploading it to YouTube."

YouTube, I thought. *Of course!*

"Where's my laptop?"

"I'll get it."

Ten minutes later, Matt was looking over my shoulder as I searched online for videos tagged with *Red in the 'Hood*.

"There are too many. Pages and pages of them!"

"You need another search filter."

"Let's narrow it by date." I typed in the parameters. "Okay, now the list has Red's most recent appearances on top. Before Esther's Fairy Tale Slam last night, she appeared in Brighton Beach twice."

"Yeah, but look at the next five." Matt pointed. "They're all in Queens. I was at a few of these Astoria clubs last night."

Many of the videos were too long to view fully, so I sampled. And then I saw it—the *bowler.* Red was wearing the hat in one of the videos, dancing around tables at a restaurant. A party was going on, and when the camera panned the room, I recognized the flag hanging on a wall: a yellow triangle on a field of blue with a line of white stars.

"There's something here."

Matt read the video's title. "Eldar's Birthday." He looked at me. "Who's Eldar? Do you recognize the name?"

"No, but Red was very friendly with the livery driver who drove her and Esther away last night. He wore a bowler. The same man picked up Red here the night before."

"Who uploaded this video?"

"A car service company: Zenica Limousine—and I'll bet if we can find this bowler-wearing driver, he'll tell us where he drove Red and Esther last night."

Matt agreed. "Search for the address of the car service."

"I'm doing it—oh my God, Bosnia!"

"Bosnia?"

I pointed at the screen. "It's the first entry that came up."

Matt read the screen. "Zenica is a city located about seventy kilometers north of Sarajevo and is situated on the Bosna River. I don't get it—why are you so excited?"

"That's why I didn't recognize the flag!"

"What are you talking about?"

I typed in another search. "Look!"

"The Bosnian flag?" Matt stared at the yellow triangle on a field of blue with a line of stars.

"I memorized every flag on Joy's UN scarf. This one wasn't there, and it was driving me crazy. Now I know why. When Joy was in grade school, Bosnia didn't have a flag! It wasn't adopted until 1998!"

"Are you going to call these people?"

"No. I don't want to risk spooking Red's driver." I threw

off the bedcovers and headed for the shower. "I'm going to Queens myself."

"You need backup, Clare. I'm coming with you."

"No, Matt. These guys are Eastern European. They're more likely to trust me if I have a young male émigré with me. I'm calling Boris. He'll come with me. You keep the coffeehouse going, okay? That's the biggest favor you can do for us all right now."

Fifty-three

Zenica Limousine Service was in an area of Astoria packed with hookah bars, Turkish coffee shops, and Arab restaurants unofficially dubbed Little Egypt.

I'd arrived early enough to loiter across the street. I watched Lincoln Town Cars come and go, but there was no sign of the driver with the bowler.

There was no sign of Boris, either.

I paced impatiently until he finally called. He'd rented a car to widen his search for Esther, but it had broken down. Now he was miles away, on the shoulder of the expressway between Manhattan and Queens, awaiting a replacement car. He couldn't possibly be here before noon.

I saw no point in delaying. The car service seemed benign enough, so I pushed through its creaking wooden door.

Inside, the sun gleamed through a streaked window. Once upon a time these walls were white. A bulletin board overflowed with dog-eared notices and schedules. A yellowing poster depicted Bauhaus buildings beside a river, the word *Zenica* emblazoned across the top.

Behind the counter, a balding man in shirtsleeves listened patiently as I regaled him with the story I'd prepared.

"I took a ride in one of your cars last night and I left something in the backseat. I don't know the driver's name, but he had longish dark hair and wore a bowler."

"You're looking for Eldar. He's around the corner at the Queen Catherine."

"What's that?"

"Queen Catherine Café is Bosnian diner."

He scribbled something on the back of a business card and slid it across the countertop. It was the café's address.

TWO things struck me as I approached the Queen Catherine: the mouthwatering scent of grilled lamb, beef, and exotic spices wafting through the open door; and the gang of rough-looking men crowding the outdoor tables.

Despite the latter, I refused to slow my pace.

A lot of women in this city—and probably as many men—would have been intimidated by the undisguised male stares. But I'd grown up in a factory town in Western Pennsylvania, more specifically, in my nonna's Italian grocery. While cozy out front, our store had a back door where my dad ran numbers and sports betting for a group of . . . let's just say *local businessmen.*

Consequently, I spent many happy years around bulldog faces and Popeye forearms. Stubbly chins chewing stumps of cigars said "home sweet home" to me. Besides, I was too worried about my missing barista to be deterred.

Veering off the sidewalk, I walked through the open door, surprising more than a few of those bulldog faces. But once inside the tiny restaurant, it was my turn to be astonished.

I expected an unsanitary little hole-in-the-wall packed with more dour, wary men, dented Formica tabletops, a television blaring some sporting event, perhaps a forest of dusty plastic plants.

Instead the interior of the Queen Catherine was neat, charming, and practically empty. There was the now-familiar Bosnian flag mounted on the wall. Beside it a framed medieval portrait of "Blessed Catherine of Bosnia."

Of the six little tables, each covered by a woven cloth and twin place settings, only one was occupied. I recognized the customer by his long, wavy hair and the bowler on the chair beside him.

More than a little impatient, I charged across the polished hardwood floor and right up to the man.

"Excuse me, I need your help," I said, looming over him. "You picked up two women in front of my Greenwich Village coffeehouse last night. I need to know where you took them."

The hat man looked close to forty, maybe a little younger, with weary eyes. His hand rubbed a prominent jaw, then he shrugged stocky shoulders.

"It's not every day an attractive woman approaches me, so I will make allowances for your brusqueness."

"I'm sorry, I didn't mean—"

"You ask questions about a friend. You don't introduce yourself. You don't say, 'Hello, Eldar, how is your day?' You don't even ask to share coffee with me."

He shook his head as if he were contemplating the decline of civilization.

"Please sit," he said at last. "We will talk. Perhaps I can be of help."

Dialing down my inner cop, I politely nodded.

If I were going to get any information from this man, I would have to accept some hospitality, suppress all urges to go "manic Manhattan," and call on the manners my nonna taught me.

And so I did.

Fifty-Four

Taking a seat, I started over. "Allow me to introduce myself. My name is Clare Cosi and I manage the Village Blend."

"Ha! That's how I know you! You make the most wonderful coffees."

This, I realized, would carry weight. Matt once trekked through the Balkan Peninsula. He told me sharing coffee was a cherished ritual in that part of the world, a beloved custom for cementing bonds between friends and family. Now Eldar leaned across the tiny table and extended a very large hand.

"I am honored to meet you, Clare Cosi. You like coffee, yes? Then you will love Bosnian coffee!"

Eldar called to the woman at the register. "Bosnian coffee for two!"

I was passingly familiar with this method of preparing coffee—a single-boil variation of Turkish brew—but Eldar took such pleasure in introducing me to his native beverage that I happily played the naïf as he explained the brewing process.

The waitress soon arrived with an ornate copper tray, *Sarajevo* embossed around one edge. Each of us was given a small, intricately decorated *džezva*, a bell-shaped pot with a long handle designed to keep coffee grounds out of the cup.

Mimicking Eldar, I dropped a sugar cube into my demitasse, and slowly tilted my *džezva*, pouring the thick, black brew over the sweet square.

The coffee was superb: rich and strong like Turkish, but with a body and taste all its own. After sighs of satisfaction, I decided enough friendly pleasantries had been exchanged that I could now explain my problem.

"One of my baristas left my coffeehouse in a distressed state last night. I think of her as a daughter, Eldar, and I'm very concerned. She was with one of your regular customers, and I'm sure she got into your car. It's important that I find this young woman. A lot of people are worried about her."

Eldar drained his cup and nodded. "Your friend is a big, bosomy girl, eh? I remember because she was not one of Red's usual friends."

"You mean my barista isn't a party girl?"

"No. I mean she isn't a man."

Okay, that answer was frank and honest. Good start. "So you're saying Red is popular with the opposite sex?"

He shrugged. "I'm not saying anything about Red."

"But you just did. And since she's a friend of my friend, I'd like to know a little more about her. I'm concerned—"

Eldar cut me off with a gesture toward the approaching waitress. "You will join me for lunch," he said. It was not a question.

The tantalizing scent of sizzling meat dominated the restaurant from the moment I'd entered (and I *had* skipped breakfast), so I nodded my thanks, which was even more genuine once I saw what we'd be eating.

"Is that a hamburger?" I asked, dumbfounded. It was the largest one I'd ever seen, about the size of a Frisbee.

"Is Bosnian burger," he said with pride. "Much better than Mr. Mack Donald's." He smiled and explained the dish was called *pljeskavica*. And the fresh-baked bun, which looked like a thicker and fluffier version of a pita, he called *lepinja*.

He pointed to the three copper bowls that came with our meal, which contained traditional Bosnian condiments: raw onions, *kajmak* (a slightly fermented cheese butter), and a delicious roasted red pepper and eggplant spread called *ajvar.*

"I know this spread," I was happy to inform him. "Russians make something close to this, don't they?"

"Ah, yes." He nodded. "They call it 'poor man's caviar.'"

Eldar sliced the burger in quarters and dug in. I followed his lead by spreading on the cheese-butter and *ajvar* and sprinkling on the raw onions. The juicy, charcoal-grilled lamb-and-beef patty made a spectacular base for the riotous flourish of bright, tangy, salty-creamy Bosnian condiments; and for a few minutes, my interview was forgotten in a foodie haze.

With lunch so pleasantly under way, Eldar now seemed more willing to open up, which shouldn't have surprised me. As my nonna said: *"Breaking bread helps break the ice."*

"Before you judge Red," he began, "you should know she had a hard childhood. Is not easy for a child to lose her mother and be sent away to live in another country with strict, cold relatives. So I do not blame her for her wish."

"What wish is that?"

"A wish to find her prince. After so many hard years, Red wants a rich husband who will make the rest of her life easy. What is wrong with that?"

"I'm not judging," I said between my final few bites of Bosnian burger. "I'm only asking. And given your comment about the number of her male companions, I assume she's putting the fairy-tale theory in play."

"Excuse me?"

"For a girl to find her prince, she must kiss a lot of frogs."

Eldar laughed. "That is one way to look at it. But there is a place she's found recently that does not admit frogs. Red calls it the Prince Charming Club. Is special spot for matchmaking. Rich men go there, men from other parts of the world who find themselves in New York—for work or politics or pleasure. They want pretty wives or girlfriends who can help them know this country."

"Is that where you took Red and Esther last night?"

"Oh, no. That club is too exclusive. Your friend has no

key to get in. I took the girls to Red's apartment, not far from here."

Eldar set money on the table and rose. He adjusted his navy sport jacket, placed the bowler on his head, and gestured to the door.

"Come, Clare Cosi. I will take you there."

Fifty-five

Eldar insisted I ride in the front seat. To make room, he moved several blocks of unfinished wood, and a rough carving of a leaping deer. Wooden figures were affixed to the dashboard: a tiny frog, a snarling wolf, and an old woman.

"Your carvings are beautiful. Did you study art?"

"My grandfather was carpenter. My father was forester. When I could hold knife, I began to carve."

"When did you come to New York?"

"Eight years ago. Before that, I lived in London. I moved there from Bosnia."

"Why did you leave?"

"War was bad, Ms. Cosi, many left. I lost much of my family."

"I'm so sorry."

"I was just a boy, but I grew up quick. In London, I drove cab but didn't own. Here in America, car is mine. I own part of company, too."

"Well, thank you for taking me to see Red."

"You are lucky. I have order to pick her up at noon. If your friend is with her, your luck continues. If not, you speak with Red."

I paused, studying Eldar's profile, then took a chance. "I know another friend of Red's. A Russian girl with blond hair named Anya. Do you know her?"

"Oh, yes." Eldar nodded. "Very pretty girl, Anya. Very pretty. Have not seen her for some time. Red said she got into trouble with a woman on Upper East Side." He shot me a sideways glance. "You know the kind."

"What do you mean?"

Eldar raised one hand and rubbed his thumb and forefinger together in the universal sign for loot.

"Can you tell me the name of this woman?"

Instead of a reply, Eldar made a sudden swerve that threw me against the shoulder strap. We landed in an illegal parking spot in front of a fire hydrant.

"We're here," he announced, adjusting his bowler. "Talk to Red about her business. Is not for me to say."

On the opposite end of Astoria, we'd halted in front of a neat two-story brick house. A calico cat was perched in the bay window, observing our arrival with curiosity. A statue of the Virgin Mary presided over a small flower garden out front.

"Red lives here?" I asked, surprised.

"Basement apartment in back," Eldar replied. "But she usually waits for me on sidewalk."

He produced a smartphone and speed-dialed. After a moment he frowned and cut the engine.

"Not like her. Red had important meeting. Told me I must come *on time*."

"What kind of meeting?"

Concerned, Eldar told me more. "That problem with Anya? Red is trying to fix it."

"With who? Where are you taking Red?"

"I don't know. Better to ask her. Is her business."

We exited the car and circled the house to the back. A small concrete patio led to a narrow yard of grass that stretched to a tall wooden fence. We took five steps down to the sunken door of a basement apartment. Eldar knocked once, and the door swung open.

"Žabica!" he called. "Out of bed, sleepyhead! Your coach awaits!"

Eldar's choice of words sent shivers through me. I'd heard those very words in the dead of night, during my fitful vision.

Now sunlight arched into a tiny, crowded room, and I stifled a scream when I saw a scarlet stain spread out on the animal print carpet.

Moving closer, I realized I was only seeing the edge of a wine-colored nightdress, not a puddle of blood and gore.

Then I spied tiny pink feet with bright red toenails mingled with the lace, and I pushed past the stunned driver, into the batik-walled apartment.

Red was lying on the floor, soot black hair splayed around her head. I didn't have to touch her to know she was dead. Rigor mortis had already set in. Her eyes were half open and unfocused. Her scarlet lips were parted like a fish gasping for air. And there was a hypodermic needle sticking out of the vein of her left forearm.

"*Žabica!* Oh, my *Žabica!*"

Eldar rushed into the room, but I pushed him back. "Don't touch anything," I warned. "This is a crime scene!"

"But *Žabica* . . ."

"She's gone," I rasped, clutching his arms. "Go outside and wait for me."

Square shoulders hunched, he allowed me to guide him onto the patio.

I cautiously looked around. The apartment consisted of two rooms and a bath, all empty. There was no sign of Esther, no indication she'd been there.

Except for a resin-stained bong, there was no sign of other drugs.

Exhaling a breath I didn't realize I'd been holding, I stepped outside again. Eldar was leaning against the house, tears staining his face.

"What do we do?" he asked.

"We call the police."

He shook his head hard. "I don't like police."

Another Matt, I thought. "Don't worry. I'll call them."

Sergeant Emmanuel Franco answered my speed dial on the first ring.

"Hey, Coffee Lady. What's up?"

"How soon can you get to Astoria, Queens?"

"Why?"

I told him.

"Be there in twenty. Don't contact the borough cops. I need to see the crime scene first."

"Can't we get into trouble? Failure to report a crime to the proper authorities?"

"You just did. Leave the rest to me."

Fifty-six

"I'VE got a New York State driver's license issued to Rozalina Krasny, a Visa, a Bank of America debit card, and four hundred and twenty-two dollars cash."

Sergeant Emmanuel Franco dropped Red's wallet into a plastic evidence bag and tugged off his crime scene gloves.

"The jewelry in the bedroom was untouched, and there's some electronics in there, too." He shrugged his broad shoulders. "I don't know what happened here, but it wasn't a robbery."

Franco and I stood on the small concrete patio outside Red's apartment. As soon as the detective arrived, he put on gloves and a pair of paper booties. Then he went in to check the scene. He didn't come out again for fifteen maddening minutes.

Eldar, too upset to wait on the patio, strode into the yard and paced the back fence. It was clear he didn't trust the police, so I wasn't surprised when he refused to join us.

"I didn't see a note," Franco said, "so barring a tearful pronouncement on some social media site, I'm guessing this wasn't a suicide, either."

"It looked like a drug overdose. Do you think it was accidental?"

Franco scratched the top of his shaved head. "That's what someone wants us to believe."

He fished around inside the deep pockets of his leather bomber and produced a second evidence bag. This one contained a tiny plastic vial.

"I found this under the body, and you saw the needle stuck in the crook of Red's left arm, where you'd expect a right-handed junkie to shoot up." Franco paused. "What I found next is thanks to you, Coffee Lady."

"Me?"

"Yeah, I discovered a second needle mark on her other arm, and I wouldn't have bothered looking, but I remembered what you told my loo."

"Lieutenant Quinn?"

"He said you had some kind of hunch. You wanted the docs to check Anya's left leg again, so they did. Among all those scratches from the park brush, they found the puncture point where the drug entered her system."

I flashed back to my vision of Anya with a bleeding leg.

"How did you find out about that? I assumed Endicott would keep the OD Squad at arm's length because of Quinn's relationship with me."

"They tried. But when preliminary toxicology report arrived, Endicott had to cut OD in."

"Why? What did the report say?"

"The drug injected into Anya's system is something different—and a brand-new street drug means a new threat to the public safety. But what I found interesting is how this drug was administered. Anya received what's called a Goldilocks dose."

"Goldilocks? Are you kidding?"

"No. The Goldilocks Principle is scientific shorthand for something that falls within certain margins, as opposed to reaching extremes. You know, the porridge that isn't too hot or too cold? The bed that isn't too hard or too soft—"

"I get it."

"Anya didn't receive enough of this Sleeping Beauty drug to kill her. Yet she received so much that the docs are unable to snap her out of her coma without an antidote. The toxicologist said it was a one in a million chance—that's because she thinks it's a coincidence."

"You don't?"

"For a Goldilocks dose to work, the perp would need to know the victim's weight and height in advance. I think someone knew that, and I don't think it's a coincidence."

"Then someone wanted Anya out of the picture—*silenced* but not dead. Why?"

Franco had no answer. Not even a theory.

I mentioned the lawsuit Anya was involved with, but we both agreed it didn't add up. (Why drug a plaintiff in a secluded area of a park only to track her down hours later, in a much more public hospital room, to coerce her into signing a legal release?)

With both of us confounded, I focused on something I hoped was finally resolved, the issue of Matt's culpability. "If they confirmed the drug is not cocaine, that gets Matt off the hook, doesn't it?"

Franco grimaced. "Sorry, Coffee Lady. Endicott is the lead detective. He and his partner, Ned Plesky, know your ex-husband is a world traveler. They're convinced he picked up something new and exotic during his coffee-hunting expeditions and smuggled it back here. It's the most obvious solution to the case, and that's the angle they're pursuing."

A chill went through me—and it was only partly due to the fall breeze blowing across the patio. I regarded Franco.

"Given your continued involvement with the case, I take it Endicott and Plesky don't know about your personal connection?"

"You mean my relationship with your daughter?"

"She's not only my daughter. She's Matt's, too."

Which posed more than one problem for the young sergeant.

Once upon a time, Franco had arrested my ex-husband. Though I was locked up during the same incident, I'd long since gotten over it. Matt never did. He and Franco nearly came to blows in that interrogation room; and when he first caught wind of Joy and Franco together, he blew a gasket.

After my ex-husband's years dealing with corrupt police officials in banana republics—not to mention his own rocky past as a former cocaine user—he'd put officers of the law at the top of his despise list. It had taken quite a while for Matt to accept Quinn, but that was nothing compared to Franco.

The idea of his little girl marrying any cop, let alone this streetwise "mook," was a situation he would not tolerate. And while daughters defied their daddies all the time, Joy loved her father dearly. I knew it would break her heart to break his—and so did Franco.

Of course, with the Atlantic Ocean separating the young lovers, Matt believed one or both would lose interest, and the sparks would fizzle and die.

I knew it was possible, too, maybe even probable. Now I wondered if that was the reason Franco didn't recuse himself from involvement in this case. Was he done with Joy?

His next words set me straight—

"Endicott and Plesky have no idea I have a conflict of interest here. Over the last few years on the job, I've learned to keep my private life . . ." He shrugged. "You know, *private*."

"But you could get into trouble for keeping the truth from them."

"I'll take my chances."

"You'd do that for Joy?"

"I'd do that for family."

I was speechless. His relationship with Joy hadn't fizzled out in the least. It had grown more serious—so serious that Franco was willing to risk his career to change Matt's mind about him; to prove that he could be trusted, that he could be family.

Given the disastrous romantic choices in my daughter's past, I was elated by this news. I actually flashed on Joy in a wedding gown, bells pealing, birds singing—then a heart-rending sob from across the small yard burst my mother-of-the-bride fantasy.

Eldar stood some distance away from us, slumped against the back fence, bowler askew, face buried in his hands. His good friend had dreamed of a white wedding, too. But fate had delivered a black body bag.

As my spirits sank, my anger rose. This crime scene was made to look like the result of a party girl who'd partied too much. But something more sinister had happened here. Franco knew it, and so did I—

"You said you found a second needle mark on her body?"

"Here . . ." Franco touched the inside of his right arm, a few inches above his wrist.

"Her right arm?"

"Other than that first, obvious injection site on her upper left arm, she had no other needle marks on her body so Red probably wasn't a junkie. And if the victim was right-handed—"

"She *was* right-handed . . ." I recounted her deftness last night in lighting her cigarette. "That makes it unlikely she used a hypodermic on herself with her left hand, doesn't it?"

Franco nodded.

I faced him. "Let's shake."

"And make up? I didn't know we'd had a tiff."

"I'm not kidding. Shake my hand."

Franco extended his right arm. Instead of shaking it, I grabbed his hand, rotated his arm, and pretended to stab the inside of his forearm with an imaginary needle clutched in my left fist.

"Smooth move, Coffee Lady. That could be how it was done."

"Do you think Red and Anya were injected with the same drug?"

"It's likely," Franco replied, checking his watch. "But for Rozalina Krasny, there's no wake-up kiss. I'm sorry to say, this Sleeping Beauty is DOA."

Fifty-seven

ASSUMING we were done, Franco raised his phone to call in his colleagues. I pushed it back down. Red might be DOA, but I had no leads, and Esther was still missing.

"Didn't you find anything else in Red's apartment?" I pressed. "There *must* be something more we can go on. Was her smartphone there or was it taken?"

"I've got it. What do you want to know?"

"What was the last call she placed?"

"Metro-North Information, shortly before midnight . . ."

Why would she want train info at that hour? I wondered. And the answer quickly occurred to me—one that involved Esther. I prayed it would pan out.

"Other than that," Franco went on, "there were a few calls to take-out joints in the area. The rest of her phone and text messaging history was erased."

"That's it?"

"Yeah, her apps are password protected."

"How soon will Endicott be able to retrieve this phone's data?"

"An expert on file system extraction can download the data on almost any phone in fifteen or twenty minutes. Doesn't matter if that info is password protected, locked, or even deleted. A trained tech can grab it all."

"Then you should have a lead fairly fast, right?"

"We already have one. I was able to access her day timer—she left it open—but most of it's in code. I'll give you an example: Eldar said something about an appointment Red had on the Upper East Side this afternoon, right?"

Franco pulled another evidence pouch from his leather bomber. It contained Red's smartphone. He didn't don gloves again. Instead he activated the phone through the clear plastic bag.

"There's no name on today's meeting, only a time and address."

I half expected to hear the number for Leila Quinn Reynolds's apartment building. But the address Franco read wasn't hers, so I jotted it down.

"Red has a second appointment scheduled for ten o'clock tonight. No name or location, only someone's initials."

"Can I see?"

"Here it is." Franco pointed. "The initials are *PCC*. Beside it she typed *free*."

"Are there any more entries like that?"

Franco's finger swept across the screen. "I've got two from last week. Tuesday and Friday. And two from the week before, same days. We need to find this individual."

I called to Eldar, still slumped against the back fence, and he sullenly approached.

"Did you drive Red to the Upper East Side last week?" I asked.

Eldar nodded. "Two days she went. Tuesday and Friday, like the week before."

"There's your answer," I told Franco. "PCC isn't a person. It's Red's code for the *Prince Charming Club*. That's what she called the place. And guess what? Anya was a member, too."

I told Franco what I knew about this uptown speakeasy, the limousines and well-dressed couples coming out of its battered black door with a diamond-shaped talking mirror, one that threatened me when I tried to enter without a key.

"It looks like Red's been going there for a few months," Franco said as he paged through screens of her day timer. "Most entries say *free*, but a few say *match*."

"Maybe Red had a special date on those nights."

"You should look for one of those men," Eldar declared, stabbing the air above the smartphone.

"Why do you say that?" Franco asked. "I mean, Red may have been a member of some secret Playboy Club, but she was also a rap artist, wasn't she? In that world, violence and rivalries are way more common than in the land of day spas and Dom Pérignon."

"Violence might be more common in the rap world, but not rivalries," I pointed out. "They're just as fierce at the better addresses. And this death wasn't violent—monstrous, yes, but coldly and cleverly done. It points *uptown*, not down."

Eldar nodded. "One of her men will know something."

Franco fixed his stare on the driver. "Red did seem to know a lot of men, didn't she? How did *you* feel about that? Did it bother you?"

Eldar stiffened. "Sure, it bothered."

"Enough to want to do something about it?"

"What would I do about it?" Eldar said. "Stubborn girl. There was no talking sense to her."

"Maybe talk wasn't enough," Franco pressed. "Maybe you had to take action. Stop her from making a mistake."

Eldar took a horrified step back. "I would never hurt Red. She was good friend. Good person—"

Franco stepped forward. "You have an alibi for last night?"

"Check my log, Mr. Officer. Check GPS in car and phone. I have nothing to hide! I dropped Red and her friend here last night and never saw either girl again. Not alive."

"Believe me, I'll check." Franco deactivated Red's phone and turned to me. "Time's up on this little discussion, Coffee Lady. Now I have to call in the local *gendarmes*."

"How are you going to explain your presence? You're an awful long way from the Sixth Precinct."

"No problem . . ."

When Franco joined the investigation, Endicott's partner handed him a list of Anya's known associates for follow-up interviews. It was busywork to keep him out of the way, but one of the names on that list was Rozalina Krasny.

"I'll say that you two came on the scene before I did. I was here to question Miss Krasny about Anya. And you two were searching for the young woman she was last seen with. I have your statements, and if the other detectives want to question you further, you'll have to speak with them, okay?"

Eldar and I emphatically nodded.

"Just find the man who did this," Eldar said. "Find him and put him in ground."

As Eldar and I returned to his car, I asked him for another ride and he readily agreed. On the way to our destination, I came clean and told him the truth about Anya and her comatose state. This came as a shock to him.

"Red never mentioned any of this to you?"

"Red was nervous last couple of days, but I thought it was because of her problem with 'East Side' woman. Now I know better. Tell me, Miss Cosi, will your policeman friend find the man who did this to my *Žabica*?"

I took in his sad expression and remembered my vision from last night: Red's little girl voice calling for someone to help her, someone to care.

"If Franco doesn't find her killer, I will. I promise . . ." The words seemed to buoy Eldar and I was glad. I was also curious. "Why did you call Red *Žabica*?"

Eldar shrugged. "It means 'Little Frog.'"

"She reminded you of a frog?"

"Was joke between us."

"I don't understand."

"When Red found Prince Charming Club, I told her she was like story of Princess and Frog but in reverse . . ."

Eldar swiped at new tears that filled his eyes. "She was like frog—cold sometimes, and she had tough skin, you know? But if just one of those Prince Charmings kissed my Red with love in his heart, he would have found beautiful person hiding inside."

Fifty-eight

I felt for Eldar. He was a kind man with a sweet spirit, which was why I trusted him to drive me to the best lead we had on Red—the address of her appointment on the Upper East Side. Unfortunately, bumper-to-bumper bridge traffic stalled our progress (no surprise, this was New York), and like most inhabitants of this manic city, I shifted into multitask mode.

Behind the wheel, Eldar noticed me pulling out my phone. "Who are you calling, Coffee Lady?"

"Remember my friend, Esther? She was the reason I came to you in the first place. Well, Sergeant Franco gave me a clue to where she might be."

"And where is this?"

"Westchester. Esther's sister lives there, and it's along the Metro-North commuter train line—where Red called for information last night."

He nodded. "Very smart, Coffee Lady."

"Only if I'm right," I said, dialing.

Eldar regarded me. "I hope you do not mind that I call you Coffee Lady. Is term of endearment, yes?"

"I don't mind," I said, listening to the line ring. *Come on, Hattie, pick up!*

"This young police officer Franco is sweet on you?"

"On *me*? No. On my daughter."

Eldar frowned. "And you approve of this?"

"I know he seems rough around the edges, but Franco is an amazing person. And he's backed me up more than once. He and my daughter are very much in love."

"But your daughter—" He looked me up and down. "She cannot be more than thirteen, fourteen. Is this not too young for such a man?"

"Bless your bad eyes, Eldar. My daughter is in her *mid-twenties*."

"Nothing wrong with eyes." He gave me a little smile. "Nothing wrong with you, either, Coffee Lady."

"Thank you, but I should tell you that I have a boyfriend."

"Oh." Eldar's shoulders slumped a little. "Too bad."

"I appreciate the compliment. It's very flattering."

"Is okay. Pretty lady like you should have boyfriend."

"And a nice man like you should have a girlfriend."

He didn't smile again, but he did sit up a little straighter. "Is kind for you to say, *hvala*."

"You're welcome," I said then gritted my teeth because my call to Esther's sister went to voice mail. I left a message.

As traffic began to move, Eldar zipped us from lane to lane until the low-rise buildings and attached houses of Queens were a river away. Now we were smack in the middle of mid-Manhattan's towering skyscrapers.

Eldar slalomed around cars, vans, and delivery trucks like a bowler-wearing Nascar driver, moving us past slick office buildings, designer shoe stores, and high-end restaurants. Soon he was pulling into a parking space across the street from our destination.

I gawked. "*That's* where Red was going? Are you sure?"

"Am sure."

I thought we'd be heading to an apartment building or business address. But Eldar was pointing to the twilight purple awning of Babka's, one of the most storied restaurants on the city's cultural map.

"Elaine's South" was how Tom Wolfe once referred to the eatery—ironically, since it was hardly more than twenty blocks down from the famous literary watering hole. After

Elaine Kaufman's death, however, her titular restaurant closed its doors while Babka's remained standing.

The restaurant's footprint was expansive, taking half the city block with sidewalk seating and an attached bakery. While the dining room served a menu of upscale comfort food, the bakery specialized in babkas of all kinds: Russian, Ukrainian, Polish, Hungarian, Lithuanian.

There were traditional chocolate babkas (the favorite), as well as cinnamon (not bad, either), and inventive new flavors like Nutella and Key Lime Crunch. They even featured seasonal babkas like Vermont Maple in early spring; Glazed Maine Blueberry for summer; and a fall bounty of Pumpkin-Spice; Harvest Apple; and Sugared Cranberry.

Famous movie scenes had been filmed inside Babka's, authors had celebrated it, and now tourists flocked to it. On weekends, there were lines around the block.

"We're in luck," I said.

"Why?"

"My boss is an old friend of the restaurant's owner, which means she might let me have a look at the reservation list."

"You wish to find out who Red was to meet here."

"You got it."

Eldar studied the restaurant. "You know *babka* is not only pastry. Is also word for *grandmother*."

"I know."

"Is owner Barbara like grandmother, too? Nice little old woman?"

How to answer? "She's a *business*woman."

Eldar glanced at me. "You are businesswoman, no?"

"True. But I'm not in her league."

"Sorry?"

"Let me put it to you this way: You don't build a babka empire by being a 'nice' little anything. Listen, will you stay here and wait for me?"

"Sure," Eldar said with a shrug. "For once, I parked legal."

"Thanks. I'll be right back."

I popped the door, dodged traffic, and hurried into the restaurant.

Avoiding the hostess, I quickly scanned tables for anyone dining alone. But couples and groups were all I saw. Then I noticed one empty chair at a primo table by the window.

A large group of diners sat around the table, all of them members of the Fairy Tale Fall Committee. I recognized the Committee's bearded lawyer, Harrison Van Loon. And at the table's center (and center of attention) was the legendary Barbara "Babka" Baum. The elderly restaurateur appeared to be commanding the conversation the same way she ruled her restaurant—with a forceful attitude and a very loud voice.

To Babka's right was Madame, my employer. To her left sat Samantha Peel. Our festival's commanding general was dressed much softer today in a V-neck cashmere sweater and pencil thin skirt as black as her lustrous hair. No tight ponytail today. Samantha's long locks were down, ends curled with care.

I yanked the phone from my purse to quietly contact Madame, but stopped when I saw Sam rising, her high-heeled fashion boots heading for the restroom. I quietly followed her into the paneled hallway.

"Excuse me, Sam?"

"Clare! How are you? Are you here to join us?"

"Sorry, no. I came to keep an appointment for someone else, only I don't know who I'm supposed to meet."

Sam's dark eyebrow rose with gossipy interest. "A blind date?"

"No." I pointed back toward the dining room. "Your group wasn't expecting a no-show, were they? Maybe one of the festival's Princesses?"

"Heavens no. This is a meeting about the next FTF event, the Brothers Grimm MOMA exhibit."

"Then I better explain why I'm here—"

I pulled Sam into the women's room and whispered the news about finding Red's body. Sam's complexion went whiter than her creamy cashmere sweater.

"Oh, my god, Clare. Are you sure she's—"

"Yes, she's gone. The police are at her place now."

"I think we should tell Harrison, don't you?" Sam started for the door.

"Wait." I pulled her back. "Mr. Van Loon can't help us. But Babka can. Red had a date to meet someone here."

"You want to see the reservation list."

I nodded.

"Come on—" This time Sam was pulling *me*. She quickly found the restaurant's hostess and crisply pointed to the FTF committee table. "Barbara asked us to check on a reservation in the system. You'll help us, won't you?"

The hostess immediately hopped to it, taking us to the reservation desk and punching in the exact time we asked for. As she stepped back from the screen, we both reviewed the list—and gasped.

"Matt Allegro?" I whispered in shock. "I don't believe it!"

"Neither do I," Sam replied. "The Committee's meeting is into its third hour. My chair gave me a view of the restaurant's entrance. I never saw Matt come in." She pointed at the screen. "And look, Allegro is listed as a no-show."

"That only makes him look more guilty," I whispered. "The police might think Matt didn't show because he knew Red was already dead!"

Sam looked as horrified as I felt. "Something's wrong here."

I nodded. "I think Matt is being set up."

"I think you're right."

"You do?"

Sam glanced back to the Committee's table. *Who was she looking at? Babka? Van Loon?*

"What's wrong?" I whispered. "Sam, talk to me."

"Not here. I better get back—"

Before she could bolt, I caught her arm. "I want to know what you know. *Please.*"

She nervously met my gaze. "I'll call you tonight, okay? We'll talk on the phone. But right now, I have to get back to that table, and you should get out of here."

OUTSIDE again, I climbed back into Eldar's car.

"Did you get a name?"

"Dead end," I said, regretting my words when Eldar winced. "But I may have a new lead. Someone is going to call me with—"

Just then, my phone vibrated, I thought it might be Sam, or even Esther's sister. But I was wrong on both counts. On the other end of the line was the last person I expected—Mike Quinn's son.

"Aunt Clare, I need you to meet me," the little boy's voice commanded. "It's important."

I tensed. "Jeremy, what is going on? Is anything wrong?"

"Yes, there's lots wrong. But I can't tell you about it on the phone."

"Where are you?"

"Central Park."

"Who's with you?"

"Penny."

At the sound of her name, the little collie barked.

"Who *else* is with you, Jeremy?"

"Nobody."

"Young man, you *know* you're not allowed in the park without an adult!"

"Tag, Aunt Clare. You're it."

Fifty-nine

"Okay, Jeremy, I'm here. Now tell me why *you* are."

Afternoon sunlight streamed through overhead branches, and ducks splashed around the craggy stone base of the Oak Bridge. The pretty park scene was a picture of serenity. Not so Jeremy. I found Mike's son pacing in the middle of the span, phone in one hand, Penny's leash in the other.

When he spotted me, Jeremy's chin stuck out and his brilliant blue eyes flashed with defiance, as if he knew his actions were correct even if no one else could see it. In other words, he was behaving exactly like his father.

"I need you to *show me* where you found Anya."

Now I was in a pickle.

I knew Mike would not want his son involved in a criminal case, but the boy was obviously determined, and he was a tad big for me to throw into a stroller and wheel down Park Avenue.

"I might be able to help you, Jeremy. But you have to tell me why you want to see this place."

"I just have to."

"That's not good enough."

He shook his head. "Aunt Clare, you're not going to understand."

"Try me."

"I've been lying awake in bed, going over and over it. I was *here* in the Ramble on the night Anya overdosed. Penny found her. If I'd just kept looking, I would have found her, too—"

"There was nothing you could have done," I assured him. "When I got to Anya, she was already unconscious—"

"But if I had found her, she might have gotten help in time. I looked it up on the Internet. Doctors can save a person with an overdose, but only if they get immediate treatment."

How could I explain to the boy that Anya didn't overdose, that she was drugged? That the substance used was as mysterious as the identity of the person who administered it? Or that Anya's friend was now dead, probably poisoned by the same stuff?

The simple answer was I couldn't. These facts were even more disturbing than the ones keeping him up at night.

On the other hand, if I could prove to Jeremy that there was absolutely nothing he could have done to help Anya, maybe I could relieve some of his anguish.

"All right, Jeremy, I'll take you there—"

"Great!"

"If I can find the spot again."

"We can do it, Aunt Clare. I'm sure we'll find it."

I led Jeremy through the Ramble Arch and up the hill, retracing my twisted path from two nights ago. It wasn't easy, and I wished Officer Daleki were here with his trusty horse, O'Brian. Daleki had rattled off the precise GPS location when he reported in.

"By the way," I said as we walked, "how did you get out of the apartment without your mother knowing?"

"Mom's not home. She went shopping to buy a new dress, and then she has an appointment at the salon. She said an invitation came for her, and she's going to meet someone important tonight. She seemed really happy about it."

An invitation? I flashed on the card that came with her golden key. *Invitations to come.* "Is Leila going alone, do you know?"

"If you mean without my stepfather, yes. He hasn't been home in nearly two weeks."

I checked my watch. "Where's Molly?"

"Ballet lessons. A babysitter's going to watch us tonight—even though I *keep* telling Mom I'm old enough to watch Molly."

"She's probably still rattled by you two getting lost the other day, and I don't blame her. It shook me up, too . . ."

We were halfway up the hill when I paused beside a boulder. Penny happily left her mark on yet another tree trunk while I scanned the area.

"This place looks familiar . . ."

Despite the fallen leaves, the colorful fall foliage was still fairly thick. I searched for some clue, and then I saw it. A fresh cobweb had been woven between two low-hanging branches, its delicate threads beautifully illuminated by a beam of sunlight.

"Over there—" I pointed. "I remember running through a spiderweb and getting the strands all over my face."

"Yuck," Jeremy murmured.

"Let's duck under it this time, so the spider won't have to build it again."

"And we don't have to get it all over our faces," Jeremy added sensibly.

We wandered around until I found the wall of shrubbery that had separated me from the lost Penny. I pushed aside the brush.

"This is it . . ."

No police tape had been left behind, but I could see where the undergrowth had been trampled by EMS and the Crime Scene Unit. Penny recognized the spot, too. As she began to bark and strain at her leash, I faced Jeremy.

"Now I want you to look around and realize how impossible it is to find this spot from the path. Anya was on the ground, practically invisible. I only found her because Penny knocked me down and I could see through the shrubs."

Jeremy frowned with disappointment. He thought he would make a discovery here or remember something that could help Anya's case. But there was nothing.

I touched his shoulder. "I know you want to help, but—"

Suddenly Penny yanked the leash so hard it threw Jeremy off balance. The dog dragged him to the base of an old elm and began digging frantically with her front paws.

For some reason, the sight of this suddenly rocked *me* off balance.

Tunnel vision overtook me and I felt eerily detached, as if I were experiencing déjà vu. Then I recalled where I'd last seen Penny digging. *My crazy dream!* I had been locked in a dungeon and she helped free me—

"Bad dog," Jeremy said.

"No, let Penny dig!" I cried. "Don't pull her back."

The little collie continued digging. When her frantic paws stopped, she stuck her brown muzzle into the hole, lifted her head, and deposited a shiny object at Jeremy's feet.

I stared, stunned at the sight of Anya's golden key.

"Penny must have buried it that night," Jeremy said excitedly. "She buries things all the time. Last month she tried to bury Molly's sunglasses in Riverside Park!"

I hesitated then plucked the key off the ground. Between the mud and doggie spit, I doubted there was significant evidence left to corrupt.

Wiping the dirt away, I found the key in good shape.

Meanwhile, Jeremy was beaming with pride. "Did I help, Aunt Clare? Did I?"

"You helped, Jeremy. More than I can explain . . ."

With Anya's key in my hand, I could appease the Magic Mirror and open that mysterious door to the Prince Charming Club. It was a risky plan, but it could yield some real answers.

"Is there anything else I can do?" he asked.

"One small favor. Go to Molly's room and find Anya's chain, the one she lost in the park."

"You want to put her key back on the chain?"

"That's right. Can you do that for me—and for Anya?"

"That's easy. No sweat!" he said.

Unfortunately, I couldn't say the same. Given my plans for this key and its special chain, I was sweating already.

Sixty

In the dim light of the parked Town Car—borrowed from one of Franco's informants—I put on the first earring and examined the short, thin wires and tiny earbud attached to the back of the other.

"Did you get these from the police equipment locker?"

"Naw," Franco said, "that means paperwork. I bought this stuff at the Spy Shop in Queens. Nice and discreet, no questions asked."

We were a few blocks from the Prince Charming Club, making final preparations for my attempt to enter with Anya's key.

"They look kind of cheap," I pointed out, "and they don't go very well with the dress."

"Style should be the least of your concerns tonight, Coffee Lady. If you get caught in that private club wearing this transmitter, they won't care whether the gold is real. But they will care about your snooping—and who knows what they'll do to you."

"I'm going in, okay? You can't scare me, so stop trying."

"Right. Then let's get you ready . . ."

Leaning across the front seat, Franco held the second earring next to my lobe while I slipped the listening bud firmly into my ear canal. Then I slipped on the earring with the transmitter and checked my reflection in the rearview mirror.

The cheap earrings looked fine—*after* I unclipped my hair to partially cover them. At least the electric blue Fen gown was top quality, a gift from Madame for a charity event at Otto Visser's gallery. The neckline was perfect, daring enough for me to pass for one of the women who frequented the club, but not so risqué that I'd draw too much male attention. The gown itself was exquisitely forgiving, hugging my curves attractively.

Matt had taken care of the shop all day—thank goodness—which gave me the time to get ready. Like Leila, I'd gone to a salon for highlights and a mani-pedi, and bought a sturdy pair of Spanx. (Okay, so *she* didn't need the Spanx.)

What I was about to do was risky, but Franco's update a few hours ago had made up my mind.

Red's death hadn't dissuaded Endicott and his partner from focusing on Matt as their favorite suspect. In fact, the data they retrieved from Red's smartphone provided a gold mine of circumstantial evidence, and they were determined to use it.

"I tried to talk them out of their theory," Franco had explained, "but the evidence, I'm sorry to say, is pretty damning . . ."

There were text messages about Red's plan to meet Matt the night before she died. And the cops canvassing her neighborhood found witnesses who stated Matt was aggressively asking for Red at several Astoria nightclubs.

In other words, my ex-husband's earnest desire to make sure our distraught barista was safe would be used against him in the worst possible way. As early as tomorrow, he could be charged with murder.

The least I could do was a little undercover work tonight.

With luck, I'd find a lead on the real killer, hand the evidence over to Franco, and bury Endicott's plan to destroy Matt, break my daughter's heart, and devastate my beloved employer.

I was about to test my earring transmitter when my smartphone vibrated. I checked the caller ID.

"It's Esther's sister. I better take this . . ."

Hattie Best-Margolis spoke as fast and loud as her little sister: "Clare, I'm sorry I didn't call you back earlier, but Esther is beside herself—"

"Then she's in Westchester? With you?"

"Yes, but she wouldn't let me call you back! She doesn't want Boris to know where she is. She told me all about what happened with that awful public marriage proposal—"

"It wasn't awful. Boris took great pains to make it special. He simply didn't realize what was going on in Esther's head. But listen, Hattie, I really do need to speak with Esther—"

"When I *think* of the men I've served up to that girl over the years! Doctors. Lawyers. College professors. Accountants. Even a city planner. And who does she pick? A Brooklyn rapper who bakes bread!"

"She hasn't picked him yet," I pointed out.

"True. And I hate to admit it, but those two belong together."

"I agree."

"I'll work on my sister at this end, try to straighten her out—not that she's ever taken my advice, mind you. But you better tell Boris to stay away. If he comes up here, she'll feel pressured and you know what happens to things under pressure. They blow!"

"I'll make Boris understand. But I *still need to speak with your sister.* It's imperative, and it's not about Boris."

"Esther's not here. She took my kids to the Cheesecake Factory, something about drowning her sorrows in Oreo cheesecake."

I closed my eyes. *Do I call the restaurant?* "Wait. Your teenage daughter must have a cell phone. Give me her number. I'll ask her to hand the phone to Esther."

"Okay," Hattie said, "but don't blame me if my sister hangs up on you!"

A few minutes later, I was finally speaking with Esther—

and yes, like her sister, it took some fast talking to get her to *listen*.

"I'm sorry to break this to you over the phone, Esther, but . . ."

I explained the very bad news about Red. Esther was shocked and promised to come back to the city tomorrow. Unfortunately, nothing she said exonerated Matt or nailed another killer.

"I left Red a little after midnight. She gave me plenty of money for the trip. I caught a green boro taxi and went to Grand Central. That's all I know. And BTW, she didn't sound like she planned on any company . . ."

I ended the call and turned to Franco. "Esther doesn't know anything. She can't help our case, which means I've *got* to go in there."

He tapped the phone's top. "Then you shouldn't have anything on you that identifies you. Hand it over."

"Here."

"Now pay attention." He took my hand and placed the tip of my index finger on the cubic zirconia in the center of the right earring. "That's the on-off switch. Try it . . ."

I pressed, and the next voice I heard was coming from inside my head.

"Say something—nice and low so I can test the amplifier."

"I'm hungry. I can't stop thinking about Oreo cheesecake. And these Spanx are too tight."

"Good, it's working. Now turn the transmitter off and keep it off until you get past front door security."

Franco paused, fingers gripping the steering wheel. "You're *really* sure you want to go through with this?"

"What choice do I have? You said yourself, the only theory Endicott will entertain is the one that says Matt's guilty. The person I need to confront is going to be here tonight, and we both agreed it's the best source of information we have."

Franco met my gaze. "You may be crossing paths with a murderer. And not your run-of-the-mill killer, either. This individual has the means to kill with a pinprick."

"I know, but look at it logically. The killer could have struck in a crowded place, but didn't. Anya was attacked in a secluded area of the park, and Red in the privacy of her apartment. The last place a killer is going to hurt me is in that club."

"You could still be opening yourself up as a future target. And if anything happens to you, Mike Quinn would never forgive me. Neither would Joy—and FYI—I wouldn't be too happy about it, either."

"With you watching my back, what could happen?" I smiled.

Franco blew out air.

"Try not to worry," I said, patting his big shoulder. "I can handle myself."

"I know. I've seen it."

"Then wish me luck."

"I do. Just be careful in there . . ."

While I moved to the backseat, Franco slid his listening device under an open *New York Daily News*. Three minutes later, we were rolling up to the ominous black door.

"I'll monitor things in front of that hot dog joint down the block," Franco said. "If there's trouble, get the hell out. If we lose communication, get the hell out. The charge on the device only lasts about an hour so when midnight rolls around—"

"I know, scram before my Spy Shop transmitter turns back into a cheap earring."

Franco wished me luck one last time. Then, like a swimmer diving into uncharted waters, I took three deep breaths and exited the Town Car.

Sixty-one

THE street was quiet and full of shadows, and the dingy building was as bleak as I remembered. The recessed doorway took me a few feet off the sidewalk, and I automatically looked for a handle on the battered metal door. Then I remembered, there was no handle, only that talking mirror with the ominous male voice—

"Show me your key . . ."

Parroting the attitude of Leila's crowd, I rolled my eyes, as if I'd done this *dozens* of times and was *so* very bored with it. Then I pulled up the long chain of silver and gold that Molly had found and revealed Anya's key.

A blast of bright red laser light startled me. I let the beam scan the key and (presumably) me. Then it shut off, plunging the recessed area back into blackness.

For a few seconds, I held my breath, until a loud click sounded and the heavy door cracked open. I nearly shouted, "Thank you!" Instead, I pushed the thick slab of metal.

"Welcome—" No more threatening male voice. Now a sweet and sultry female was addressing me. "Please step all the way inside . . ."

The space was dimly lit, and I saw no one. Then the door shut itself behind me, clanging and locking with frightening finality. Bright lights came up to reveal a cinderblock room with all the charm of Sing Sing solitary.

My heart began beating faster as the voice instructed me to: "Please wait a moment . . ."

There was no beam this time, but I saw eyes in the sky—twin security cameras in opposite corners of the cell, moving to and fro to check me out.

"Please step into the elevator . . ."

Before I could ask, "What elevator?!" one of the stone walls lifted like a Broadway curtain. Elevator doors slid wide and I stepped into a mirrored square. The doors shut (more mirrors) and I watched myself attempting to count how many levels we were descending—five, maybe six floors?

The doors opened on a darkly paneled lobby with a cloak room window, and I finally saw a human being. A young blonde in a little black dress approached with crisp steps.

"Good evening," she said.

"Good evening," I replied.

She stood and waited, blinking at me, as if I were slow on the uptake.

Great. What am I missing?

"Your bag, please."

"Oh, yes, of course . . ." I handed it over. She held it out and a large olive-skinned man in an evening jacket stepped out of the shadows on my left side. As the well-dressed line-backer pawed through my lipstick, compact, and hairbrush, a hard-faced woman in a pantsuit appeared on my right.

The woman wanded me with an electronic scanner from top to toe then she receded again. Back to the netherworld—or a passenger terminal at JFK.

"Free or match tonight?" the blond hostess asked.

"Free," I said with a wave of my French manicure.

"Tips?" she asked.

"Oh, no," I assured her, "these are my nails."

For a tense second, the hostess stared blankly into my face. Then she burst out laughing. "Good one!" She glanced up to see if the towering security guard was laughing, too. He wasn't. With a shrug, she focused back on me.

"Diamond can really use some of that life-of-the-party joviality tonight—if you're up for that." She smiled, warming to me as she handed back my bag. "What are your languages?"

"Italian," I said because *English* was obvious, wasn't it? "And French. *Passable* French."

"Passable is good enough here, as you know." She glanced at the two guards again and they melted back into the shadows. Then she pulled a smartphone from her pocket, activated an app, and began scanning a text scroll while strolling toward a grand arched doorway trimmed in gold leaf.

I quickly caught up.

"We have a Saudi prince in Silver tonight," she conveyed in quiet conspiracy. "French is one of his languages. As for Italian, there's a baron in Diamond, he races Formula Ones and summers in Olbia-Tempio. And we have a Venezuelan import-export heir in there, too. He didn't care for his match tonight, so if you're up for that, he's ready . . ."

Obviously, "tips" here had nothing to do with nails.

The club's hostess ran down a few more gentlemen profiles—executives, politicians, aristocrats. None were American. And she never once showed me a photo or used a name. No one had asked me my name, either, and I got the distinct impression that would be a *faux pas*.

What I really needed was a tip about how this place worked. The hostess continually referred to Silver, Gold, and Diamond. I had no idea why, but with those guards looming, I feared too many questions would get my Spanx-firmed rear thrown back into that selfie-ready elevator.

Once I started mingling, I'd look for someone who could tell me more without giving me away as an intruder. (A bartender maybe? Or a conveniently inebriated guest?) Until then, I'd have to smile and nod and keep my mouth shut.

"Enjoy your evening," the hostess sang then tapped her smartphone again and swiped it over a scanner in the wall. Double doors slid open, and with a snappy turn of her heel, she left me at the gilded archway.

Another giant keyhole . . .

Holding my head high, I steeled my soul and stepped through.

Sixty-two

THE space was cavernous and absolutely stunning.

The archway opened on a railing-rimmed gallery. Thirty feet below me stretched the carpeted main floor of the club, an elegant expanse of marble columns, sumptuous draperies, and live flowering trees. Fifteen feet above me, large stained glass leaves, hundreds of them, were suspended from the ceiling.

The lighting in here was ingenious. The upper perimeter looked like a pinkish-blue twilight sky, which made it feel more like a piazza in Europe than an underground garage (which was what I suspected it once was). The *action* on the main floor below, however, was clearly that of a casino, with posh couples laughing and drinking around dozens of gaming tables.

Now I knew why the club's owners had hung those colorful glass sculptures. They were attempting to re-create Dale Chihuly's *Fiori di Como*, the chandelier of handblown glass blossoms that famously adorned the Bellagio.

As casually as possible, I touched my earring.

"Hello?" I quietly said then listened hard.

"Signal's good," Franco buzzed in my ear. "What do you see?"

Pretending to scratch my nose, I covered my mouth and said: "Las Vegas meets Monte Carlo in an underground parking garage."

"Oh, man. Watch your back."

"I'll keep you posted."

Lowering my hand, I moved toward a grand staircase and noticed men in evening jackets and women in slinky gowns making their way to the very same descent. I scanned the gallery and saw another archway at the far end. Clearly, the street door I'd used was not the most popular entrance to this place. I let Franco know.

"So where is the other entrance?" he asked. "On the street? Inside a building?"

"I have no idea."

"See if you can find out."

"I have a few other things to do first!"

"Yeah, I know, but—"

"Fine, when I exit, I'll go through the *other* archway."

"Copy that."

Down on the main floor, I strolled around fragrant flowering potted trees, abstract sculptures, and gaming tables, mostly card games with one crowded roulette wheel and a raucous craps table.

The far end displayed a wide doorway to a quietly elegant baccarat room, which clearly had much higher stakes. Security guards flanked that entrance, and I steered clear of it. I noticed a billiard room, also flanked by guards, and at least three games of serious poker going on in there. Mostly men—and cigar smoke.

As I walked along, pretending to mingle, I heard a few different languages—French, Japanese, broken English, and a lot of Russian along with some Mandarin (that or Cantonese, I wasn't sure). The looks I was getting, however, needed no translation. Men openly raked my curves, some giving me nods and smiles—the kind a chef would give a butcher showing off a fresh cut of meat. Some of the women gave me the once-over, too, but no smiles.

I continued searching.

"She's not on the gaming floor," I whispered to Franco. "I'm going to check out the lounges."

"How many are there?"

"Three . . ."

Each was set off by a wide decorative archway with different motifs: one glistening in metallic silver, one sparkling with LED diamonds, and another with gold leaf.

Eeny, meeny, miny . . .

I entered the closest one, which was also the loudest and most crowded of the three. Machine-age silver was the clear theme here—everything was Art Deco, including the railings wrapping around the dance floor, the metal sculptures, and mirrored chandeliers.

As I pushed into the crowded space, another theme stuck me that had nothing to do with art movements.

"Are you in the lounge?" Franco asked. "What's it like?"

"An international frat boy party . . ."

Amid a deafening pounding of French disco music, shrieks of laughter erupted all over the room. Men of every race were behaving badly with beautiful party girls riotously amused by their shenanigans.

An Italian soccer star squeezed two young women to him while his forgotten buddy was passed out on his chair. A man I recognized as a deputy police commissioner was groping his female companion, who was most definitely not his wife.

In one corner two Japanese businessmen had drunkenly stripped down to underwear bunched up to look like Sumo pants. Tables were moved and they wrestled to cheers from the others.

At a corner booth a girl was dancing suggestively on the table, with a pair of Middle Eastern men puffing on a hookah and politely clapping.

A long, mirrored bar stretched across one side of the room. Caught in the rocky sea of laughing, dancing, *groping* men—*ouch!*—and mostly inebriated women, I lunged for an empty barstool like a lifeline from the Coast Guard.

Wishing I were back in Queens, sharing Bosnian coffee with a poor but civilized livery driver, I ordered champagne and asked the young male model of a bartender an innocent question—

"What's up with these Silver, Gold, and Diamond lounges?"

His plastic smile fell. "You don't know?"

I shrugged. "I'm new here."

The frowned deepened into a look of hard suspicion. "Wait right there," he said. "Don't move."

But when he moved away, so did I—and fast. On my bumpy way to the exit, I downed my expensive champagne (for courage) and set the empty flute on one of the tables ringing the dance floor. Bad move. The man sitting there thought I was making an overture.

"Ciao, bella!" the red-faced Romeo exclaimed, grabbing me around the waist and pulling me onto his lap. "Dance with me!"

The crowded dance floor was steps away, but he didn't bother getting up. The type of dancing he wanted was the kind you do sitting down.

"No, thanks!" I insisted—in three languages. He pretended not to understand. Then his big hands began moving north of my Mason-Dixon Line, and I threw civility to the wind, along with the contents of the glass on a passing waiter's tray.

Romeo was not pleased to have his martini shaken (not stirred) right into his face, and he let me know it. Jumping to his feet, he called me the most vulgar things in Italian. We were both standing now, but I couldn't get away. He was gripping my wrist during this tongue-lashing, hard enough for me to prepare a good swift kick when the waiter swept in with a linen napkin.

"My fault, sir, my fault," he gallantly insisted as he patted the man down.

The move was smooth, breaking Romeo's grip. Now the big man focused his abuse on the poor waiter, a baby-faced Latino man no more than an inch or so taller than I, but head and shoulders above his abuser in dignity.

After Romeo stormed off, I thanked the waiter sincerely for the rescue.

He blinked at me, practically in shock. "You are quite welcome," he said, as if no one had ever bothered to thank him before, at least not in this club.

As we spoke, a pair of German businessmen traded beer shots while a colleague entertained their dates by juggling cocktail glasses. Then someone's fedora whizzed by us like a Frisbee.

The waiter leaned close. "Forgive me, but are you sure Silver is the right room for you?"

At last, a compadre!

"Silver is for hookups," he explained in my ear. "It's a big party. Men and women here are looking for short-term fun. If they hit it off, they move to Diamond."

"And what is Diamond?"

"Diamonds are a girl's best friend." He shrugged. "Men in the Diamond Room are usually older. They are looking for a longer-term girlfriend experience but not necessarily marriage. You know . . ."

"Mistresses?"

He nodded. "And Gold—"

"Gold bands of marriage?"

"That's right. Gold is for matches. Men and women who are wanting a partner in marriage."

After thanking the waiter again and asking for directions to the restroom, I moved back onto the main floor and took another look at those handblown glass leaves suspended above me.

Whoever put this club together wasn't just making a metaphor about love and marriage. They were re-creating Anya's favorite folktale, *The Secret Ball*—

Twelve princesses wishing to dance all night slip away through a trap door in their bedroom floor, passing through an enchanted grove with trees of silver, gold, and diamonds.

I took a deep breath and moved with anxiety toward the restroom.

While the ball sounded glorious enough, the secret kept by those fairy-tale princesses ended up costing lives; and if I was found out before I found Leila Quinn Reynolds, this little masquerade could very well cost me mine.

Sixty-three

Posh potties were nothing new in this town, but I'd never seen a restroom like this. While the perfumed stalls were as elegant as the Waldorf's, the adjacent mirrored area looked less like a ladies' lounge than the communal dressing room of a Fashion Week runway show.

Wingless fairy godmothers in pink smocks worked on a half-dozen female club members who needed stains removed, buttons resewn, or hair demussed. When one of the smocked godmothers gestured for me to take a padded chair in front of a floor-to-ceiling mirror, I gratefully sat.

Lying low for fifteen minutes was a smart idea. That Gestapo bartender was clearly suspicious of my membership status; and besides, Romeo's lap dancing had left my hair a fright and my nose in need of serious fairy dusting.

I tried eavesdropping on the multilingual "chatter" around me but didn't hear more than global anxieties over running stockings and broken nail tips.

"Did I miss something?" Franco buzzed in my ear. "Sounds like you left the club and dropped into a hair salon."

"I'm reglamming."

"Clock's ticking," he reminded me, but needn't have bothered.

As my beauty godmother redid my makeup and hot-curled my locks into cover girl smoothness, I spied my target coming through the restroom door.

Catwalking like the lingerie model she once was, Mike Quinn's ex-wife sashayed her chic figure toward the bathroom stalls.

"Well, well, well," I whispered, "of all the powder rooms in all the towns, in all the world, it looks like she just walked into mine . . ."

"Guess you were right," Franco admitted. "Good hunch. And good luck . . ."

Counting the minutes, I waited until Leila's off-the-bony-shoulder gown glided into the lounge area. Her money green skirt was slit high to show off her brand-new pedicure in designer stiletto sandals, and her auburn locks were tightly slicked into a cheek-lift-worthy twist. Gazing into the mirror, she studied her dominatrix 'do then inspected every line and curve of her delicately sculpted face for the crime of imperfection.

Disdainfully waving off a pink-smocked lady, she began the delicate task of touching up her own expertly applied makeup—until she saw my reflection looming in the glass.

"Good evening," I said. "I have a few questions . . ."

The woman whipped her head toward me so fast she streaked her entire right cheek with lipstick. Quietly cursing, she clawed for a nearby box of tissues and began furiously swiping off the high-end war paint.

"What are you doing here?" she hissed.

"I told you. I need a few questions answered."

"You're not a member. I'll have you thrown out!"

"This is Anya's key," I calmly replied. "If you turn me in, I'll tell them you sold it to me. Then they'll throw you out, too. Is that what you want?"

Like an overtaxed computer, Leila froze. This was my chance. Grabbing her arm, I yanked the bewildered beauty queen toward a corner of the lounge. The branches of a potted tree gave us cover, its tart lemons hanging down. Rebooting her disdain, Leila crossed her slender arms and glared at me as if she'd sucked on one.

"You have five minutes," she spat. "What do you want to know?"

"How do you know Anya? Did you meet her through this club?"

"Oh, please. I only recently rejoined. And Anya was too naïve for this place. She wanted out."

"Why?"

"She thought she'd find her Prince Charming here, but girls from her background don't get princes, they get sugar daddies. She played the game for a little while, but she got disillusioned and decided to cash in her chips."

"Until someone did it for her. Who drugged her?"

"I have no idea."

"Because it was *you*?"

"Me?! Absolutely not! Why would I drug that poor girl?"

"I've had a look around. These women aren't Girl Scouts. They're hard rivals for men with money. Maybe Anya and you were after the same sugar daddy."

"That's ridiculous for more reasons than I can list."

"Well, you better list a few because I'm prepared to give you up to the police."

(Okay, so I was bluffing, but rattling the woman appeared to work.)

"Anya was never my rival," Leila quickly insisted. "I'm here strictly for Gold while Anya wanted money without matrimony. She was a Diamond girl. Not me. In the circles I travel in, I need a legit husband."

"Don't you have one?"

"Had." Leila glanced away. "Humphrey's become enamored with some tarty business associate." She waved her French tips. "Whatever. I'm done with him, too. Unfortunately, the prenuptial agreement he made me sign is a joke." She quoted me the arrangement. "So I'm in the market for a new match, one that will make life as easy as possible for me and my children."

"You make it sound like a transaction."

"Oh, please. When you get down to it, that's all relationships are."

I didn't agree, but I wasn't here to debate her personal philosophy—except in one matter. "Most of the men in this club appear to be foreign nationals."

"So?"

"So if you marry one of them, at some point in the future, he may take you and Mike's children to another country. You can't do that to him."

"I'll do what I must for my needs."

Her needs? It took some control on my part not to laugh in her face. Leila's prearranged split settlement left her an annual figure that was twice my salary. Then again "needs" had a flexible definition for a woman who was raised with money and wished to maintain a "respectable address" with a regimen of day spa beauty treatments, lavish vacations, and a closet full of designer togs.

"Like I said, Anya was a Silver and Diamond girl, and I'm here only when I have an invitation for a match date in the Gold Room. Tonight I'm meeting with a very polite older gentleman from Abu Dhabi."

I couldn't believe my ears. "You want Jeremy and Molly to grow up in the Arab Emirates?! Mike would never agree to that!"

"When and if it comes to that, *Mike and I* will deal with it. Not *you.* As for Anya, it's clear enough who drugged her, and you can tell the police that."

"Oh, really? Then you better tell me first."

Sixty-Four

"THE football player," Leila whispered with a self-righteous glare. "That's who you should be ambushing. Not me."

"What football player? Give me a name."

"Dwayne Galloway."

Even without the listening device in my ear, I could have heard Franco's "Holy crap!" in that Town Car parked six stories north. Unfortunately, I didn't have the sports knowledge he did.

"Who exactly is Dwayne Galloway?"

"He's a former New York Giant, Clare, an ex-running back with two huge Super Bowl rings. He hooked up with Anya here a few months ago. The man was obsessed with her. It didn't work out, and they broke up. Then he started up with her friend—she goes by Red, I think. Anyway, Galloway never got over Anya. He was practically stalking her at the festival last weekend."

"Galloway was there? In Central Park?"

"He was dressed as a knight, just like his cast."

"Cast?"

"After he left football, Galloway bought a warehouse near the old Giants Stadium and converted it into one of those awful theme restaurants. Jeremy keeps bugging me to go there, but—sorry—not in *this* lifetime." She checked her watch. "Okay, I'm done now. My date is waiting."

She turned to go, but I yanked her back. "Why didn't you tell the police what you knew?"

"You're kidding, right?"

I pointed to Anya's key around my neck. "Does it look like I'm kidding? I'm here for answers."

"Well, you're not going to like *this* answer." Leila leaned close. "My friend Samantha *tried* to tell the police what was up—"

"You mean Samantha Peel? The festival director? You two are friends?"

"She's a member here, too—we had the same divorce lawyer. She saw Galloway stalking Anya. Ask her. She gave the police her statement, but they buried it."

Oh, God, I thought. *Leila's right . . .*

I flashed back on that "man in medieval garb" mix-up with Endicott and Plesky on the night they arrested Matt. *Or was it a mix-up?*

"Don't you see?" Leila smirked. "Mike's precious brethren in blue are protecting the Giant because he's a sports celebrity. He gives half the Mounted Unit moonlighting jobs at that awful *Meat*-dieval Tournament and Feast; even hands out free family passes to the NYPD brass." She shook her head. "I shudder to think what Galloway was going to do to Anya in those woods with that date rape drug of his, but the detectives involved are obviously going to look the other way. They'll probably pin it on some innocent dupe."

I cringed.

"That's all I know," she snapped. "Now I'm going back to the Gold Room. And don't you dare follow me."

As Leila moved to the door, I counted to ten then checked in with the man upstairs (the one with the badge and Spy Shop receiver)—

"Did you get all that?"

"Got it."

"Good. With luck, you might even have a second witness to Galloway's stalking of Anya."

"Who?"

"Me. The morning of the festival, I was working at our

coffee truck. Two knights in armor stopped by the window. One of them was big enough to be a former football player. I saw him watching Anya's every move, like he was some kind of predator."

"Would you recognize him if you saw him again?"

"I think so. Can you scare up a photo of Galloway? I haven't followed football since the Curtain came down."

"The Iron Curtain?"

"The Pittsburgh Steel Curtain—Mean Joe Greene and his defensive crew."

"Given Leila's statement, what worries me now is the Blue Curtain. We need to find out who exactly brought it down to protect Galloway."

I thought about that. "Listen, I know someone who can help us. When I found Anya's body, a mounted cop in armor galloped to the scene. He moonlights for Galloway, and he was very upset when he saw what was done to our Sleeping Beauty."

"Good. Come back up and we'll talk about our next move."

"Okay, I'll just take one last look around."

"Copy that—and remember, don't leave the same way you came in. I want to know where that second entrance is located."

"No sweat."

Back on the main floor, I checked my watch and scanned the table games. There was still plenty of time left on my trusty transmitter's charge.

One more roll of the dice might be worth the gamble, I decided; and despite Leila's little warning, I headed straight for the Gold Room.

Sixty-Five

The romantic, getting-to-know-you vibe of the Gold Room was the polar opposite of Silver's perpetual party.

Candlelit tables ringed a gilded fountain, gurgling with a liquid that resembled melted-down bullion. Mosaics with gold-flecked tiles sparkled on the walls beside replicas of Gustav Klimt, the gold leaf master. And along the rear wall, a marble bar, trimmed in gold, was hosting a gold medal wine tasting for several couples.

I spotted Leila's slender figure rejoining the wine-tasting group. An olive-skinned man in his fifties gallantly stood to welcome her back. But before I could take another step in their direction, a golden-haired hostess approached me with a pointed—

"Good evening."

"Good evening," I parroted.

"May I see your invitation?"

"Oh, I'm free tonight," I said, projecting Leila-like aloofness as I moved away. "I'm only here to mingle . . ."

My voice trailed off in the face of twin white-gloved waiters passing me to the left and right with jaw-dropping confections.

One looked like Bloomsbury Café's Golden Phoenix Cupcake Plate, an internationally famous dessert served under glass on an Empire Morning Cake Stand. Perched beside it was a small bowl of American Golden Caviar, a salt-free caviar often sweetened with infusions like passion fruit and Armagnac.

The other waiter appeared to be carrying a Golden Opulence Sundae, a signature dessert at New York's Serendipity restaurant, home of the frozen "haute" chocolate. (Five scoops of ice cream, infused with Madagascar vanilla, were covered in edible gold leaf, drizzled with syrup made from one of the world's most expensive chocolates and garnished with gold-dipped French Dragées Longuettes direct from Paris. The cost? Like that golden cupcake, around one thousand US dollars.)

"Had a little too much champagne, have we?"

My flight of golden foodie fancy was interrupted by the hostess, who'd popped in front of me again.

"Excuse me?" I said.

She leaned close and lowered her voice. "When a club member reviews your profile and wishes to meet you, you'll receive an invitation to this room. Until then, you'll want to mingle in Diamond or Silver. Good evening." She gestured toward the exit.

Oh, well. Craps on that throw . . .

Back on the main floor, I was about to call it a night when I noticed another familiar face—a furry one.

Strolling around the table games in a tailored evening jacket was Harrison Van Loon, Esquire, the Fairy Tale Fall Committee's bearded attorney. The man appeared quite comfortable in his fashionably tie-less state. Drink in hand, he stopped every few feet to chat with a male or a female club member.

I shouldn't have been surprised to see Van Loon here. After all, he was an uptown big shot from a Dutch family whose roots in this burg went back to its earliest immigrants. Rubbing elbows with obscenely wealthy new arrivals was shrewd networking, although I did wonder why he'd risk any connection with an illegal gambling establishment—unless he knew something I didn't.

Whatever his reasons for being here, I was eager to say

hello. He'd helped Matt get free of police custody once. Maybe he'd consider working his legal magic again.

But before I could reach him, his head of salt-and-pepper hair moved off the casino floor and through the LED Diamond archway.

This gave me pause.

Should I be following a man I knew directly into the "mistress meet" room? Or was that meat?

One glimpse through the glittering archway confirmed a plausible reason to enter.

"What are you doing?" asked my earring.

"I've decided to investigate the catering."

"There's a spread?"

"Oh, yes . . ." (And after spying that costly cupcake and haute chocolate sundae, I was now exceedingly curious about the kitchen.) "The food here could give me a clue to who's providing the catering, which could give us a connection to the club's owner."

"Then let the culinary inspection begin," Franco declared, "and while you're at it, grab me a cannoli."

"I'll see what I can do."

Sixty-six

As I moved toward the buffet, I couldn't help applying Franco's Goldilocks Principle. The Silver Room had been too loud, the Gold too quiet. But this Diamond Room—with its smooth jazz, ballroom dancing, and tempting table of tapas—was shaping up to be *just right.*

Keeping one eye on Van Loon, I studied the stunning buffet. But the spread gave me little in the way of clues as to who was catering this private party.

The small plates offered tastings of signature menu items found all over this city—from Buddakan's tender tea-smoked chicken with a scallion and ginger chutney to the 21 Club's gourmet chicken hash in béchamel. There was Spice Market's Cilantro Lime Steak; Café Boulud's Sugar Cane Grilled Shrimp with Peanut Sauce; and Le Bernardin's Roast Monkfish on Savoy Cabbage with a bacon-butter reduction.

Forget Goldilocks! I felt like Gretel in front of the witch's house, greedily sampling little plates of Aquavit's Glazed Salmon with Wasabi Sabayon; Jean-Georges's Peppery Green Beans; and a creamy-spicy Buffalo Chicken Salad with Gorgonzola dressing—I had no idea who created the latter, but I made a note to copycat it.

After inhaling Babbo's Mint Love Letters (ravioli filled with pureed peas, ricotta, and fresh mint in a lamb ragout), I crunched down Babka's Shrimp Kiev, making sure to tilt back my head (as Matt once taught me) to catch every drop of the delectable herb butter inside.

Finally I was ready to look over the table's sweeter offerings.

No cannoli for Franco, but there were mini Cronuts à la Dominique Ansel and Chef Thomas Keller's famous version of the Oreo.

"I haven't seen you here before, have I?"

Tearing my eyes from the amazing "Inside-Out" Chocolate Cream Coffee Cake (a fluffy cloud of mocha whipped cream tucked between layers of devil's food), I glanced up to find Harrison Van Loon raking my Fen-hugging curves with the same hungry interest I'd been giving the dessert display.

"Oh, hello there," I said, feigning surprise. "I'm new here. This is my first night, Mr.—"

"Call me Harry."

Van Loon's horn-rimmed glasses were gone, replaced by contact lenses that intensified the green of his hazel eyes. He stepped closer—a little too close for comfort actually—and out came the toothy smile I remembered from Central Park. Only this time it had a decidedly wolfish edge to it.

"I'm very pleased to meet you," he said in a tone that sounded more like *And what's in your basket, little girl?* Then he held out his hand.

As we shook, I reminded him—"We already know each other."

"Oh?" His head tilted and his grip tightened. "You must be one of my firm's clients?"

"Close. You helped me out with your legal expertise this past weekend."

When he drew a blank, I lowered my voice. "I'm Clare, from the Village Blend."

"The coffee lady?" Van Loon simultaneously dropped his smile and his hand before taking a giant step back.

"I hope I'm not giving you the wrong impression. I mean about being in this room."

"No. In fact, I shouldn't have been surprised to see you here, given your employer—"

My employer? "What do you mean?"

Ignoring the question, he continued babbling, "I must say, you're very well spoken." He looked me up and down again, less like a wolf this time than one of those pink-smocked fairy godmothers in the ladies' lounge. "Yes, you *have* fixed yourself up quite nicely."

Gee, thanks. "Listen, I won't keep you, but I do have a quick question, if you don't mind?"

"What's that?"

"You lent a legal hand to my business partner when he was questioned by the police. You remember, don't you, after the Central Park Festival?"

"Yes. A most unfortunate business."

"It's about to become even more unfortunate, and he may need your help again. Would you be willing to—" I took a step closer.

"I'm sorry." He held up his hand. "I must stop you . . . *Clare*, wasn't it? I was happy to make a call on behalf of my work with the festival committee, but I am not a criminal attorney."

"Can't someone in your firm handle—"

"No." He lowered his voice. "We're primarily divorce lawyers."

"You don't do anything else?"

"We draw up prenuptial agreements. But that's about it."

I glanced around, getting it. "Fish in a barrel here, I suppose?"

"You could say that. Actually . . ." He leaned closer and let himself share an insider's smile—one entrepreneur to another. "I often advise my female clients to join the club, so to speak."

I recalled Leila's comment about meeting Samantha through the club and their shared divorce lawyer. Was it Van Loon? I took a chance—

"Oh, I'm not surprised"—I casually waved a hand—"you handled Samantha Peel's divorce and Leila Quinn Reynolds's, didn't you?"

"Yes, two of many. And my firm does handle some civil

actions for our clients, as well, but not criminal. Tell you what. Call my office in the morning. My assistant will provide a short list of referrals, in accordance with your . . . well, your *resources,* as limited as they no doubt are. Now if you'll excuse me . . ."

And that was that. The furry-faced lawyer was off to sniff out more lucrative prey. I tracked his movements past the espresso bar to a table of two gentlemen and two ladies—the latter dripping in a girl's best friend.

But the diamonds weren't as interesting to me as that coffee station he'd breezed by, and I couldn't help wondering—

Whose coffee are they serving anyway?

My professional curiosity piqued, I headed over and ordered a double. The taste seemed strangely familiar.

"This coffee is quite good," I told the barista.

"Thank you, ma'am."

"Would you mind telling me who supplies it?"

"The Village Blend."

Sixty-seven

FLABBERGASTED, I stared at the barista. "Did you say Village Blend?"

"Yes, ma'am, they're an excellent coffeehouse. They source and roast their own beans."

"You don't say?" I was about to pepper the man with questions when a small group approached with orders. Drumming my manicure on the counter, I checked my watch. Still fifteen minutes to go on the transmitter charge.

"You there?" Franco asked.

"I'm waiting for the barista to get back to me," I whispered. "The club is serving my coffee. Can you believe it?!"

No reply.

"Franco? Do you copy?" I tapped the cubic zirconia switch a few times. Though the transmitter was broadcasting, the signal didn't seem to be reaching him. As more customers arrived at the coffee bar, I reluctantly gave up.

Better get out of here.

Not an easy task. The lounge was now packed with bodies. As a jazzy rendition of "Amapola" began, I felt someone grip my arm.

"Care to dance?"

Before I could react, a white-haired gentleman stepped in front of me, hooked his hand around my waist, and practically lifted me off the carpeting and onto the hardwood.

This guy was solidly built, in his mid-to late sixties, and tall. Even in my highest heels, I had to crane my neck to meet his gaze; otherwise I'd be staring straight into a red silk tie and crisp white shirt.

"I'm sorry," I said, trying to pull away, "but I was just leaving."

"That's the point," he whispered in my ear. "You may not get out of here without some trouble."

My eyes widened. "I don't know what you—"

"Your earrings are the problem. If I were you, I'd tap that right one again. They're jamming you now. But you're still broadcasting a signal, which means they can follow it to the source."

I quickly switched off the transmitter. "How did you know?"

"Because I have my own listening devices planted in this place, but I'm not trying to broadcast beyond its walls, which means—at the moment—*you* have a very big problem." He tilted his white head, indicating the two big security guards who'd entered the room. "They have staff waiting for you at both exits. Do you have an emergency escape route planned?"

No, I thought—and then I remembered that friendly waiter. "Yes, I think so."

"Take this." He slipped a business card out of his lapel. "It will confirm my identity. There's a bit of a riddle to it." He smiled. "But I think you can handle it."

Without glancing at the card, I tucked it down my neckline.

"The song's about to end," he whispered. "When it does, leave immediately."

As the final strains of the Spanish love song faded, I thanked the mystery man and attached myself to a small group of couples leaving the Diamond Room.

I hated the idea of returning to that awful Silver lounge to find my helpful waiter, but luck was with me in this subterranean casino: I spied him serving drinks to a couple playing roulette.

"I need your help again," I whispered. "Another masher

is after me. He won't leave me alone. I lost him, but he and his friend are waiting at the doors to catch me."

"Oh, Chiquita, you're not having a very good night, are you?"

"I'm afraid not."

He leaned close. "Don't worry. I've done this before. See that curtain behind those potted coconut trees? Slip through there and make sure no one sees you. I'll meet you there in a few minutes."

Everyone was watching the gaming tables, so I easily slipped behind the coconut curtain. After five excruciating minutes, I began to wonder if I could trust my waiter—not that I had any choice.

That was when a wheeled cart bumped my rear. Pushed by my waiter, the stainless steel wagon was draped in a tablecloth, and piled high with empty tapas dishes.

The waiter pulled the white cloth aside and pointed to a crawlspace.

"Your carriage awaits."

I ducked inside, sitting with my knees under my chin.

"Here we go," he said, dropping the cloth. "Keep quiet and you'll be fine."

After a bumpy ride, the cart halted. I held my breath as the waiter spoke quickly in Spanish to a man with a gruff voice (security, no doubt).

Deep male laughter ensued. I heard the security guard mumble "clear" and then came the sound of elevator doors opening—not the clean swish of the uptown doors but the awkward, industrial clanking of a large service elevator.

(I may not have had much experience as a superspy, but I did cater enough private parties in this town to know "the help" always had its own exit.)

"Almost out, Chiquita," he whispered after the doors closed. "Stay quiet."

When we cleared the elevator car, I heard the shouts, hisses, and banging of a busy commercial kitchen, which faded as we rolled down another hall. Finally the cart lurched to a stop.

"When I leave, please count to twenty so I can get clear.

Then exit through the closest door. You'll see the ladies room to your left. Take your time, freshen up, and exit through the restaurant's dining room."

"Thank you."

"No hay problema," he said. "But if you don't mind my saying, are you sure our club is for you? There are plenty of other ways to meet a man, you know? Ever try Match.com? How about Christian Mingle? Or JDate?"

"Thanks, I'll consider it."

The waiter's footsteps receded. As soon as I counted to twenty, I was out from under and through a swinging door. I found myself in a strangely familiar paneled hallway with a rare public telephone.

Should I call Franco? No. Better get out now!

I found my way out to the main dining room, and stood stunned for a long moment. I may have failed to pick up a cannoli for Franco, but I did find him that second club entrance.

It appeared the Prince Charming Club was directly under one of New York City's most iconic eateries—Babka's, the restaurant owned by that little old grandmother Barbara Baum.

I thought back to my snooping in the entryway of Leila's apartment. That box with the golden key included a note card. *"Invitations to come,"* it read with a signature of two initials. *"BB."*

BB . . . Barbara Baum. Holy cow!

Sixty-eight

On the car ride down to the Village Blend, I gave Franco back his Spy Shop costume jewelry and filled him in on the Mystery Man, my service elevator escape, and the Babka connection.

Still swathed in electric blue Fen, I unlocked my small office on the second floor of the coffeehouse, settled in behind my battered wooden desk, and fired up my computer. Franco took the chair opposite and wasted no time popping the strings on the pastry box. (Yes, since I was already at Babka's, I figured why not stop by its famous bakery counter?)

As Franco tore off pieces of their most popular babka, the heady scents of chocolate and cinnamon filled the cramped space, along with similar aromas from our steaming cups of Sumatra Sunset.

"I should have suspected something," I said, staring at the twilight purple box. "Babka's is located right around the block from that black mystery door. And Leila's club key came in a box the same shade of purple as the awning over Barbara's restaurant—and her bakery boxes."

"Matchmaker, make me a match," Franco said between bites. He licked his fingers and smiled.

"Very funny," I said, but we were both thinking the same thing. Madame's old friend had brought much more than Lower East Side comfort food and courtship rituals to her uptown address. "It's hard to beat a Silver disco, Diamond gourmet buffet, Gold-flowing fountain, and gambling floor, complete with pink-smocked fairy godmothers in the women's room."

"Sounds like *Hello Dolly* does Vegas in a storybook speakeasy," Franco declared. "And what happens in her underground parking garage *stays* in her underground parking garage."

I pointed to my computer screen. "According to this news article I'm skimming, Dwayne Galloway is in her league—he can afford to buy silence. The man is one of the richest NFL players in the history of the game. How did he manage that?"

"Hatchet for Men is my guess."

"Excuse me?"

"Galloway used to make commercials for men's body wash, shampoo, and deodorant. They posed him with a sexy woman on each arm while he delivered the tag line 'Slay them with Hatchet.'"

"He also owns a ranch and raises Angus beef in Wyoming. That explains the Meat part of this Meat-dieval Tournament and Feast, I guess."

"Dwayne Galloway was a major player, Clare. Sportswriters called his time with the Giants 'The Reign of Dwayne.'"

"I can see that. But, hey, look at this!"

I pointed to my screen again. ESPN archives had a clip of Galloway horseback riding on his Wyoming ranch, and a much older clip of him practicing on a parallel bar. The narrator noted—

"In college, Galloway studied gymnastics under Olympic coach and Soviet defector Rolf Tamerov . . ."

"Gymnastics," Franco said, scratching his shaved head. "That explains it."

"Explains what?"

"Galloway was famous for jumping incredibly high over tacklers. And after making a goal, he'd somersault in the air and land on his feet."

"The Russian connection is what intrigues me. Is that why he went for Anya and Red?"

"Probably has a thing for Russian girls."

"I wonder if he speaks Russian, too . . ."

I studied the most recent photo of Dwayne Galloway. He had dark brown eyes, and I was fairly sure he was the same predatory knight I'd seen in Central Park, staring at Anya.

My phone rang. I checked the caller ID and quickly told Franco to stay quiet while I answered on speaker mode—

"Hello, Samantha, I've been waiting for your call."

"Sorry it came so late, Clare. Committee work kept me busy all evening."

Not everyone on the committee was busy, I mused. *Harrison Van Loon went clubbing.*

"It's okay," I replied. "We're still working here."

An awkward pause followed. "You know, I used to hear that *exact* phrase from my disaster of an ex-husband." Sam expelled air. "Mr. Wall Street was working, all right, on getting interns into bed . . ."

Oh, good grief, has she been drinking? I tensed. This was no time for 1-800-therapy, especially with Franco listening. *Better keep her on topic—*

"I'm sorry, Sam, but I'm so worried. You said you'd talk to me about my business partner's situation. Why do you think Matt is being set up to take the blame for Red's death?"

"That's easy. Do you know about Dwayne Galloway and his connection to Red?"

"Now I do. I ran into Leila Reynolds tonight at . . . a social gathering and got the story out of her."

Sam sighed again. "You must think all I do is gossip. But I was frantic, Clare, I had to talk to someone, so I told Leila. She was *supposed* to keep it a secret—"

"It's okay. She didn't want to tell me. I more or less dragged the truth out of her."

"Well, not even Leila knows *everything.* Did she tell you the police are protecting Galloway? Because they are."

"Is that why you fingered Matt when you spoke with Endicott's partner?"

"Fingered Matt? Where in the world did you get that idea?!"

"Detective Plesky said you told him that Anya was last seen with a man wearing medieval garb—"

Sam cursed. "I said 'armor,' Clare. I told that chubby detective that the man with Anya was wearing armor, which meant he was dressed as a knight, and guess what? The only people dressed as knights at the festival were Galloway, his football buddies, and—"

"The officers from the NYPD Mounted Unit."

"Listen, I'm sorry. I feel bad about what happened to Red, but I'm only a volunteer trying to help the city organize a few events. What I'm telling you is in the strictest confidence. I'm in no position to go up against bad cops trying to protect their celebrity football hero."

Franco's frown deepened.

"Okay, Sam, I understand," I said. "Thanks for your help."

By the time the call ended, I'd come up with a plan of action.

"Are you free for dinner tomorrow night, Franco?"

"At ye olde Meat-dieval Tournament and Feast?"

I nodded. Both Samantha and Leila said the police were protecting Galloway. Well, there was one member of the Mounted Unit moonlighting for Galloway that I knew by name: Troy Dalecki. I didn't know if I could trust Troy; but since I still had his knight's cape, I had a perfectly innocent excuse to drop in on the young officer—not something I wanted to attempt alone.

"You're on, Coffee Lady. I want to get to the bottom of this as much as you. And I've always wanted to see that place."

"Bring your badge. You'll be out of jurisdiction in New Jersey, but we're going medieval, so you might need *ye olde* NYPD shield."

"I don't leave home without it. And I'm glad you're taking backup, especially after what you allowed to happen tonight—"

"Not that lecture again."

"That guy you danced with could have had a needle full of poison. With one stick, he could have killed you and walked away."

"But he didn't, all right? Let it go. Besides, he seemed like a nice guy."

Franco rose. "I've heard that before, usually from victims of sexual assault."

"It wasn't like that. Without his help, security would have caught me in there."

"Maybe. Maybe not. Con men use that ploy all the time. Before they fleece suckers, they 'help' them to gain their trust."

"Does my daughter know you're this cynical?"

"I call it *careful*. And the next time you run into this guy, you better be careful, too."

Franco tucked the purple bakery box under his arm and headed for the door. "Pick you up at seven. Dinner's on me, and bring your appetite. I hear the portions are huge."

"How huge?"

"Their biggest seller is the Brontosaurus Rib."

Note to self. Bring ye olde wheelbarrow to cart home ye olde leftovers.

As Franco's footsteps clanged down our spiral stairs, I studied the business card my white-haired dance partner had left with me.

He claimed it contained a "riddle" that explained who he was, but I couldn't figure it out and neither could Franco. The card displayed no address. Not even a web address. Simply the name *Wilson* and a phone number with far too many digits.

Maybe it's a phone number plus an extension number, I thought and tried to dial it again. As before, all I got was a busy signal. For the umpteenth time I read the card:

RED, BLACK & AEGEAN
INTERNATIONAL
AUDITORS

I ran several Internet searches, but there was no corporation or institution with that name.

I remembered the acrostic that Esther used to spell out LOVE STINKS, but the only thing that key unlocked was RIA—an Italian television network.

Is Wilson a European television producer? If he was, why would he hand me such an obscure business card?

The words themselves didn't help. I couldn't even find a definition for an "international auditor," and Red and Black were both colors, while Aegean was a sea—

Hold on, I thought, *Red, Black, and Aegean are all seas.*

I literally smacked myself. Change the word *sea* to the letter *C* and the acrostic suddenly made sense, along with Mystery Man's ability to locate a rudimentary transmitter—

CIA. Central Intelligence Agency!

"No way. It can't be . . ."

Letting the card game go, I removed Anya's key necklace and tucked it into my evening bag. Then I closed my computer and called it a night.

As I locked the door, I noticed my cell phone vibrating. It was Gardner, calling from downstairs.

"Hey, boss. Nancy had to go, and it's time to close."

"I'm coming."

Gardner met me at the bottom of the spiral staircase, loaded down with a tray of used cups and saucers. "There's an older gent in back," he said. "I'll dump this stuff and tell him we're locking up."

"I'll do it," I said.

"In electric blue Fen?" Gardner laughed. "That makes you the best dressed bouncer I ever saw."

I headed for the table near the hearth, where a white-haired man in a black jacket sat with his back to me. *That can't be him*, I told myself. But when he moved his head, I caught a glimpse of his profile and tensed.

The Mystery Man had followed me to my place of business.

Remembering Franco's warning, I hurried behind the counter to find my favorite club—and it wasn't silver, diamond, or gold. This club was aluminum with a rubber grip.

"Gardner, stay here. If that man takes one step toward me, you hit the speed dial, and—" I raised my Louisville Slugger. "I'll hit him."

Sixty-nine

GARDNER grabbed my arm. "Boss, maybe we should call 911 now."

"No. Not yet. I want a word with him first."

"You know this guy?"

"I know his name," I whispered. "It's Wilson. What I don't know is whether he's friend or foe."

While my night manager watched and waited, I moved toward the white-haired intruder. He looked harmless enough, sitting there, calmly sipping his espresso while he tapped his smartphone.

I was a few steps behind him, and getting closer, when he suddenly said—

"Hello, Ms. Cosi."

I stopped moving. "You know my name?"

He turned, smiling. He was still in evening clothes—though his tie was gone and his collar open—and he didn't bat an eye at the sight of my metal bat.

"Now that we're properly introduced, may I call you Clare?"

"That's the problem. We haven't been properly introduced."

He feigned disappointment, and then rose to protest. "I did give you my card."

"Not another step, buster!"

He spread his arms. "I'm not here to harm you. I'm here to talk. Believe me, if I were going to prick you with a poisoned needle, you wouldn't have seen it coming."

"I'm dialing!" Gardner called from behind the counter.

"No, don't!" I shouted when I realized Wilson was simply standing there, patiently waiting out our panicked reaction.

"I can't prove a negative," he quietly told me. "But I can assure you that I had nothing to do with the poisonings of Anya Kravchenko or Rozalina Krasny. And I can prove my credentials are real. Will you sit down and let me do that?"

"How are you going to *prove* your credentials are real, short of introducing me to the director of the CIA?"

He smiled again. "Very good, Ms. Cosi. I would have been disappointed if you hadn't figured out the riddle. Tell you what. If Michael Ryan Francis Quinn confirmed my credentials, would you believe me then?"

I stiffened at his mention of Mike. "It's after midnight. I shouldn't bother him."

"You talk to Lieutenant Quinn every other night of the week. Why should tonight be any different?"

I cringed, remembering Esther's NSA joke. *Edward Snowden warned us there'd be days like this.*

"Fine, sit!" I commanded—and like Penny on a good day, he sat.

Eyeing him warily, I shifted the bat from one hand to the other before tensely perching myself on the chair across from him.

"Don't move." I placed my phone on the tabletop, set it to speaker, and pressed speed dial.

"Hi, sweetheart—" Quinn answered on the first ring. "You're calling early. But I'm glad, because I wanted to talk to you about something important—"

"I want to talk, too, Mike, but I need your help first."

"Help with what?"

Wilson put an index finger to his lips, and slid a second business card across the polished marble. I recognized that number again, the one that wasn't a phone number. He pointed to it.

"I'm going to read a number to you. Would you mind telling me what it is?"

"I'm listening."

I rattled it off.

"That's a cross-agency protocol number," Quinn said.

"What does that mean exactly?"

"It's from an ID database. When federal law enforcement agents are in the field, they use it to verify officers from other agencies or operatives working undercover."

"Like a Yellow Pages for spies?"

"More like a driver's license. Sometimes agents can be compromised if they carry a government badge on them. This number is a way to confirm their identity. Now, sweetheart, while I'm logging on to the office computer to confirm what's probably semiclassified information—*you* can tell me how you came across this code."

I gave Quinn a highly truncated version of my sleuthing with Franco, telling him "a source" gave me a lead on our case. (And yes, I left out the fact that his ex-wife was the source and his son helped me find the key to corner her because, frankly, I didn't need more drama tonight.)

Needless to say, Quinn was less than thrilled about my underground adventure—even the truncated version. On the other hand, Wilson appeared to be thoroughly entertained, so much so that it wasn't a stretch to believe the guy's true vocation was glorified eavesdropping.

"Okay, that's a real number," Quinn confirmed. "For someone in the CIA."

"What can you tell me about this person?"

"Caucasian male, age sixty-two. He's an expert on the former Soviet Union and Eastern Bloc. In the field, he goes by the name *Wilson*."

Across the table, Wilson gave me a gallant little half bow.

"Listen, Clare," Quinn continued, voice hard. "The next time this guy shows up, I want you to let Franco deal with him. Promise me, okay?"

I let out a breath. "Okay, Mike. I promise. The *next time* Wilson shows up, I'll do that."

Wilson's eyebrow arched.

"Good," Quinn said. "That makes me feel better. But you sound tired." His voice turned softer. "I wish I was there to tuck you in. Or you were here."

"Me too."

"Of course, if we were together, sleep's not something I'd imagine we'd be doing—"

I felt my cheeks begin to flame. "Er, Mike, I'm still in the coffeehouse. Can I call you in an hour?"

"Only if we continue where we left off. Fun on the phone is better than no fun at all."

"Sure," I hurriedly replied, ignoring Wilson's silent chuckle.

"Oh, wait! Before you hang up, I wanted to know how things were going, with the move to DC. Have you told Allegro yet?"

"I'm still . . . in the process, you know?"

"Well, I have good news, something that might speed up your transition. I found this great coffeehouse near the Federal Triangle. They're looking for a master roaster. If it works out, we'll be working within walking distance, like we did in Manhattan. Maybe you and I can even heat up the roasting room on my lunch break, just like the old da—"

"Gotta go!"

I ended the call and locked eyes with the far-too-amused Wilson.

"Okay, I believe you. Now why are you here?"

"In New York City or in your coffeehouse?"

"Both."

"I'm in New York because I received an anonymous tip about a cold case that's grown suddenly hot. I'm in your coffeehouse because I think we can help one another. Perhaps share intelligence."

"About?"

Wilson leaned across the table. He wasn't smiling anymore.

"About the person who poisoned those poor Russian girls, Ms. Cosi. About the cold-blooded murderer I've been hunting for over twenty years."

Seventy

WHILE Wilson and I talked, Gardner locked the front door and brought over two Americanos and a plate of the shop's new Silver Dollar Chocolate Chip Cookies—my thin-and-crispy recipe, perfect for late-night snacking.

"You claim an anonymous tip brought you here," I said after Gardner returned to the counter (with my Louisville Slugger). "What tip was that?"

"The drug was the tip, Ms. Cosi. The drug that put Anya Kravchenko into a coma and killed Rozalina Krasny is extremely rare, but not unheard of. It was used exactly once before on US soil. Twenty-five years ago it killed one of my agents, right here in New York City."

"Okay, you've got my attention. Why exactly was your agent killed, Mr.—"

"Wilson. Just Wilson. Most people think the Soviet Union crumbled when the Berlin Wall fell in 1989. But it really didn't end until the August Coup in the 1990s."

"Were you there? In Russia?"

"For most of the eighties." Wilson paused to sip his coffee. "Then I was brought stateside for a delicate mission—to find and follow the activities of a Russian Intelligence officer who had set up shop in the place you call the Prince Charming Club."

"You're joking."

"Not at all. To get a lead on him, I planted three of my own agents in the club. Tonight you visited one of the front lines of the Cold War. It may not be the kind of battleground with a memorial or souvenir shop, but it's historic nonetheless."

"I thought the CIA wasn't permitted to operate on US soil."

"It's not. But that unmarked black door you used to enter is on a building that also houses an annex to the Consulate General of the Kingdom of Morocco. Technically it's foreign soil."

"And part of the Prince Charming Club is underneath that address?"

"That's the way we got around our domestic restrictions—with select members of Congress anyway . . ." He dunked a crisp little cookie into his cup, popped it in his mouth, and reached for two more. "The club was a lucrative field for counterintelligence, in close proximity to the United Nations, packed with foreign nationals—and not your average tourists and immigrants. These were well-heeled, well-connected businesspeople, cultural leaders, politicians, even military officers."

"Then it really was Casablanca down there."

"Actually, that's the op name we used to reference the club. And we weren't the only ones placing agents in there. The British, French, and—as I mentioned—the Russians were as busy as we were. Sexpionage mostly—"

"Sexpionage?" I suppressed a shudder. "Is that what it sounds like?"

"If it sounds like the seduction of targets to elicit classified or restricted information, then yes, sexpionage is what it sounds like. We were all chasing trade secrets, government intel, defense plans—"

"All those spies must have been tripping over one another."

"As I said, it was a Cold War. No violence, no exposure of assets. It was simply about collecting intelligence—knowing where the other players were planning to move their pieces. Nobody likes surprises about the future, especially not heads of state."

"Sounds like you were doing the same thing as my nonna back then."

"Excuse me?"

"My grandmother read the future with coffee grinds."

"And I'll bet we would have used her, too. Anyway, things changed with the Soviet's August Coup."

"I don't remember much about that."

"I'm not surprised. It was the 1990s. The Berlin Wall was gone, and in the Soviet Union *glasnost* was the order of the day—"

"I do remember *glasnost*. It means openness, doesn't it?"

"That's right, Ms. Cosi. It was a blanket term to describe reforms that led to personal freedom in the Soviet Union. *Glasnost* also meant establishing ties with Western democracies, including the USA."

He shrugged. "Those new freedoms didn't sit well with the communist hardliners. So one August morning, the Committee staged a coup in Moscow."

"What Committee?"

"The Committee for State Security, Ms. Cosi. You probably know them better by their acronym—the KGB."

Seventy-one

"Of course I've heard of the KGB! It's the Soviet counterpart to the CIA."

"*Was* our counterpart," Wilson said. "The KGB doesn't exist anymore. After two violent days, the coup fell apart, the conspirators were arrested, and the KGB dissolved, eventually replaced by the FSK, then the FSB and SVR. But within a year of the KGB dissolving, the Soviet Union dissolved, too."

"Excuse me, but what does all this have to do with the Prince Charming Club?"

"I'll tell you. Once upon a time, there was a KGB operative named Petrov, who went by many names, spoke perfect English, and was easy to trust. He was handsome, charming, and highly intelligent. Those virtues helped him recruit several agents here in New York. He placed them in the underground club."

"For sexpionage?"

Wilson nodded. "I was tasked with finding out who his agents were—and who they were compromising. If those targets involved US citizens, I had an FBI contact ready to assist. To accomplish my mission, I ran my own agents. My very best was a young American woman."

Wilson sounded almost wistful. "Her name was Faith. Newly graduated from Brown. Whip smart. Spoke three languages. She was very beautiful and very good at her chosen profession."

"What happened to her?"

"One of Petrov's agents murdered her. A cold-blooded execution, using the very same drug that was used on Anya."

Wilson's anguished expression said it all.

"You cared for Faith, didn't you?"

He laughed, but there was no humor there. "I loved her, Ms. Cosi, from the day I met her—and through every one of the four hundred and forty-nine days she lingered in that coma before she finally let go. I still love her today."

"You must have wanted to catch her killer?"

"There's an understatement."

"Why didn't you?"

"After the coup in Moscow failed, a lot of hardliners with connections to the conspirators were called on the carpet. Petrov was summoned back to Russia for questioning—and possibly trial. After that, the Agency closed the file on Faith, blaming Petrov for her murder."

"But you don't think Petrov was guilty?"

He leaned forward. "Petrov was guilty of turning young Americans against their country. He was guilty of teaching them tradecraft, of making them ruthless. But he did not drug Faith. One of his agent's did that, which means he or she got away with it."

"If the CIA doesn't agree, why are you so sure?"

"Faith successfully uncovered the identity of two of Petrov's agents and she was working on a third. She was poisoned because this third American feared exposure and prosecution as a traitor."

"If the murderer was a member of that club, why didn't you have the place shut down? There's unlawful activity going on down there. Illegal gambling, for one."

He shook his head. "Technically the club is running a perfectly legal gambling *school* for members who want to become better gamblers. High-stakes games do take place in the side rooms, but those are private matters. The house takes no share of the winnings."

"Okay, but there must be other things going on that aren't entirely—"

"The club is a useful asset to the intelligence community, Ms. Cosi. We didn't want to shut it down then, and we don't want it compromised today."

Wilson leaned across the table. "Until now, Faith's was the only murder connected to that club. Rozalina Krasny is the second. The Agency would like this case wrapped up as quickly and quietly as possible."

"That's what the Agency wants. But what do you want?"

"Call it closure. Or vengeance. After Faith's murder, my superiors sent me back to Eastern Europe. They said I was too close to Faith's case. Well, I still am."

"I can see that."

He drained his cup and set it aside. "Then see this—Faith's death was officially recorded as a drug overdose. Her family never knew the truth: She didn't die a junkie. She died a hero. And the use of that drug on two young women connected to that club is not a coincidence. I want to find Rozalina's killer because I'm sure—in my bones—it will help me finally resolve the murder of my Faith."

"Okay," I said on an exhale. "How can I help?"

"Tell me everything you know, Ms. Cosi."

"If we're going to work together, you better call me Clare."

He extended his hand, and I shook it.

Then I told Wilson everything I knew—about Anya and her connection to Red; about how the police were trying to pin the crime on Matt. Lastly, I revealed how Leila fingered Dwayne Galloway for murdering Red and drugging Anya, and that Franco and I were planning to pay the former pro-football player a visit.

"But does Galloway hold up as a suspect?" I asked. "Given your theory on the killer's Cold War activity, does that make sense?"

He nodded. "After you spoke with Leila, I did a little research on Mr. Galloway—"

"But I *just* told you about Leila. How did you have time

to do any—wait, you were eavesdropping on my conversation in the club, weren't you?"

"What I picked up from your little broadcast was certainly more interesting than the conversations on my own listening devices." The man was back to smiling.

"You know what, Wilson? I think you enjoy being a snoop."

"Well, it takes one to know one, Clare, and from what I've seen so far, you would make a fine intelligence agent—"

"Let's talk about Galloway," I said, cutting off any windup for a CIA recruitment pitch. "Could he be involved?"

"It's possible. He started out like many spies do, growing up wealthy, confident, and capable. In his case, he was raised by a horse-breeding family in Hunterdon County, New Jersey—"

"Wait! I read online that Galloway took gymnastics in college, taught by some famous Russian defector."

"Rolf Tamerov," Wilson said with a nod. "And here's something you won't read online. Tamerov defected for show. He was really here to recruit young Americans to the Communist cause."

"Then Galloway might have been turned?"

Wilson nodded. "Not only that. Galloway attended school in upstate New York, but he spent his summers in and around New York City, including the summer of the August Coup."

"And we know Galloway is a member of the Prince Charming Club. Leila told me so. Was he a member back then, too?"

"That I can't confirm, although Galloway certainly could have joined. He was wealthy enough to afford it, even then."

"But we don't know for sure?"

"No, we don't, but I think you and that young detective Franco are the perfect pair to find out."

Seventy-two

"WOW," Franco said. "Even Ye Olde Parking Lot is a party."

The Meat-dieval Tournament and Feast was a massive faux-castle the size of the biggest big box store you could imagine, but with parapets, crenelated walls, a moat, and four towers beaming spotlights into the night sky.

Ye Olde Parking Lot (so identified by the neon signs along the entrance road) was expansive, too, and required "squires" with incandescent "laser" swords to guide us to the next spot. Medieval-ish music emanated from speakers, and a "Prince and Princess" tent was manned by more squires hawking souvenirs.

"Let's remember where we parked," Franco said, eyeing the sign. "We're in the Domain of Richard the Lionheart."

I grabbed the plastic-wrapped cape from the backseat (since Dalecki was kind enough to lend it to me, it was only fair to have it dry-cleaned). Then Franco and I followed an exuberant horde of diners to the front gate.

But when we crossed the wide wooden bridge over the moat, Franco steered me away from the box office to a double door marked *Employees Only*. There was a buzzer, but before he pressed it, Franco drew his shield.

The door was opened by a sour-faced security guard clutching a smartphone. Franco flashed his police badge.

"We're looking for Officer Troy Dalecki."

"Sir Leg of Lamb? He's probably in the dressing area. Second door to the right."

"Sir Leg of Lamb?" Franco shot me an amused look. I shrugged and we headed down a wide hallway, toward an odd scent combination of disinfectant and horse manure.

The antiseptic smell came from the "dressing area," which more resembled a high school gymnasium's locker room, with steel doors along one wall, benches in the middle, and a dozen athletic men in various states of undress. There was one difference, however. These guys were donning aluminum armor, not team uniforms.

I spied Dalecki the moment he spotted me, and we met in the middle of the room.

"A nurse told me I just missed you at the hospital on Sunday," he said.

"You visited Anya?"

Dalecki nodded. "A couple of times. I feel bad about what happened."

I'd seen his anguished expression before—on Mike's son, Jeremy. *Did I do enough to save her?*

I couldn't answer that. So I simply smiled and held out the dry-cleaned cape. "I came to return this and thank you again."

"You're welcome, Ms. Cosi," Dalecki replied. "And you should stay for the show. The Lord and Ladies Parade begins in twenty minutes."

I introduced Franco while Dalecki tore through the plastic to reveal his cape. The back featured some elaborate embroidery. I hadn't done more than glance at it. Now I realized what it was—two lamb shanks crossed over a plate of cheese fries.

Good lord, he really is Sir Leg of Lamb!

Franco suppressed a laugh. "That's some coat-of-arms there, Troy."

"Yes, we knights joust for the honor of our designated main course," Officer Dalecki said without a trace of irony. Then he turned and pointed out the other Sirs, most still in their skivvies—

"There's Sir Drumstick of Turkey. That's Sir Loin of Beef. There's Sir Barbecue of Chicken talking with Sir Ham of Burger, and over there is our newbie, Sir Salad and Sides."

Franco elbowed me, too close to tears to speak.

I cleared my throat. "I gather the fans root for their favorite dish?"

"That's exactly right, Ms. Cosi, When they place their order, they're given flags to wave. Of course, the winners are decided before we hit the field. The most popular main course of the day is always the victor. Dwayne wants as many folks as possible to leave here feeling like a winner."

Franco finally found his voice. "I'm guessing Sir Salad and Sides doesn't win much?"

Dalecki nodded with sad resignation. "Sir Loin of Beef is the reigning champ. He wins practically every night."

"You mentioned Dwayne," I said. "That's Dwayne Galloway, right? Is he here tonight?"

"He's here most nights. This is his kingdom, after all."

Franco winked. "Any chance we could meet and greet? We're big fans."

Dalecki shook his head. "Nobody gets an audience with the King."

The King?!

"Come on, man," Franco pressed, "not even fans of his gridiron days with the Giants?"

"He's done with all that," Dalecki assured us.

"What if I flash my shield and call it official business? Can I see him then?"

"This is New Jersey, Sergeant Franco. Galloway will have his bodyguards toss you out, and his good friends in the township police will be waiting in the parking lot to arrest you for harassment."

"So Galloway does have police protecting him," I said. "I've heard rumors to that effect."

"Nobody's protecting Dwayne." Dalecki replied. "He's just a guy who likes his privacy and is willing to throw his weight around to keep it."

Galloway's fanatical quest for privacy made him seem guiltier than ever—and despite Dalecki's assurances, I was starting to believe the police *were* protecting him—probably because Galloway gave so many cops lucrative moonlighting jobs.

Franco's ploy of being a big Giants' fan wasn't working. His New York shield had no weight, either. *I have to get Dalecki on our side. But he's obviously enamored of his boss, so how do I do it?*

As he turned his back on us to finish dressing, my gaze caught sight of that coat-of-arms again. To me and Franco, it seemed ridiculous, but to Dalecki, it was deadly serious.

I remembered my college reading of *Roman de le Rose*. With the rise of courtly love came that old chivalric code—a knight believed in a moral and honorable system, vowing to protect others who could not protect themselves.

It was a code worth believing in. *And for a true knight, something does trump the love of King.*

I tapped Dalecki's shoulder. "This is really about Anya," I revealed. "Franco and I both think that Galloway may know something that will help solve the case. We only want to ask him a couple of questions—"

And nail King Creep if he's guilty, I silently added.

"Dwayne knew Anya?" Dalecki appeared disturbed by this revelation, which didn't surprise me since he had to know about his boss's reputation as a playboy.

"Dwayne Galloway was even better acquainted with a friend of Anya's," I carefully added, "a girl who called herself Red in the 'Hood. Red's and Anya's cases are connected, we think."

"I'm sorry, I *would* like to help. But even I can't walk up to him and talk. Dwayne's always surrounded by his Men-at-Arms. If you have questions, you'll have to go through his lawyer."

"There's no time for that," I said. "Come on, Officer, *think*. There's must be some way. Anya's life may depend on it."

Dalecki studied his boots. Finally, he glanced up, a light in his eyes.

"There is a way," he said as the sound of heralding trumpeters echoed from the arena. "It's unorthodox, but it's the only thing I can come up with."

"We're ready for anything," I assured him. "Tell us."

Dalecki faced Franco. "You'll have to volunteer for the gauntlet, challenge the Black Knight, and vanquish him."

Seventy-three

Officer Dalecki quickly explained how the Meat-dieval Tournament and Feast's most popular spectacle worked.

"Every night a volunteer from the audience is selected by lottery to face the Black Knight in Galloway's Gauntlet."

"What kind of gauntlet are we talking about?" Franco asked.

"It's an obstacle course," Dalecki explained. "Balance bar, rope climb and swing, hand-over-hand ladder, then down a sliding board. At the bottom is the Wheel of Fortune, a spinning platform that tosses you like a mechanical bull when you don't approach it the right way. *If* you get that far, you have to complete a running jump from one platform to another."

"Does the challenger have to beat the Black Knight to the finish line?"

"It's not a race. If you finish the course, without falling, or being knocked off, you win. On the other hand, if the Black Knight stops the challenger from succeeding, he wins."

"How does this help us with Galloway?" I asked.

"The prize for vanquishing the Black Knight is a free dinner with the King in his private box. That means two hours sitting at a table with Dwayne Galloway."

"We have to try," I said.

Franco actually grinned. "I'm game."

"It's not as easy as you think," Dalecki warned. "I can fix the lottery for you to win the chance. The Monk owes me—"

"The Monk?" I asked.

"You'll see," Dalecki said. "But the problem isn't winning the chance, it's the course itself. The Black Knight will try to trip Franco up. He can do the same to the Black Knight, of course. Nobody will get hurt. If you fall, you land in 'the moat'—six feet of water."

"Doesn't sound bad," Franco said.

"We all learn the course in case we have to sub for the Black Knight."

Franco eyed the men in the locker room. "Who plays the big villain?"

"Sir Loin of Beef," Dalecki replied, frowning.

We all looked in his direction. The guy was clearly an accomplished athlete. He was also big. His muscles had muscles.

Franco's confidence faltered and so did mine.

"Can't you ask Sir Beefcake there to give Franco a pass?" I whispered. "As a favor?"

Dalecki shook his head. "Sorry, he's not the kind of guy who does anyone a favor. Last year, he let a little kid win, and Galloway nearly fired him, so he's *very* serious about winning. He's also a little full of himself because he wins *all* the time. I wish you could beat him. It might bring his ego down to size."

Dalecki pulled us close and lowered his voice. "Here's the big trick—the platform is rigged. If you don't make a running leap from the right spot, the final jump is nearly impossible."

"What are my chances without practice?" Franco asked.

"In the five years this place has been in business, two people have made it through—the first was that little boy I mentioned, the one the Black Knight took pity on."

"And the second?" I asked.

"A Navy SEAL."

Franco blinked. "Okay, so it's difficult. But it's not impossible, right? I mean, *you* learned."

"It took me a week. And that's not all. You have to wear armor."

"Armor?!"

"It's no heavier than a Kevlar vest, but it restricts movement. And the helmet doesn't help, either."

"Helmet?" I echoed. "Hmm . . ." My little gray cells started working. "Does this helmet have a visor?"

"Yeah, it does."

I stepped back to size up the two muscular policemen. Dalecki was a little taller, Franco a little heavier, but—

Yes, I decided. *It might work.*

"Listen up, boys. I have a plan . . ."

Seventy-Four

"HEAR ye! Here ye! Before his Majesty's jousting commences, the moment has come for *one* among you to challenge the Black Knight on *Gallowaaaay's* Gauntlet!"

The monk-robed announcer began his speech in faux Middle English but finished like a World Wrestling Federation barker. The cheering, whooping audience didn't appear to mind the mash-up.

We'd already watched the King enter his box to great fanfare. Former Giant Dwayne Galloway sat on a high throne, contemplating his kingdom from the canvas-topped executive section in the top tier of the arena.

Franco and I were seated on the first tier, on backless benches before a rough wooden table. But at least we had a nice view of the Lord and Ladies Parade as knights; beautiful, spirited Spanish horses; and a bevy of princesses marched around the circular arena.

We'd placed our order. Franco cast a vote for Sir Loin of Beef. I gave poor Sir Salad and Sides a much-needed boost. Now, my pea green veggie flag in hand, I waited impatiently for the lottery, which the monk-robed announcer had agreed to rig in our favor. (I understand a forgiven sports bet was involved.)

Meanwhile, Franco tore into my pile of "Fryer Tuck's Ale-Battered Onion Rings"—one of my Sir Sides.

They were crunchy, hot, and delicious, but I was too nervous to eat more than two and settled for sipping my "Gingered" Ale from an ornate plastic goblet.

After more verbal theatrics, the Monk finally made a show of drawing a card from a wooden bucket. Then he spoke into the microphone.

"The poor, unfortunate wretch who will face the Black Knight's wrath is . . . Mr. Manny Franco of Brooklyn, New York!"

As rehearsed, Franco and I jumped off our benches and hopped around excitedly. A pair of Princesses in coned hats arrived, to escort us to a stage entrance masked by purple curtains. Dalecki escorted Franco to the dressing room, while I waited on an uncomfortable throne facing the obstacle course.

It was an impressive stage, thirty feet high, with all the animated features Dalecki described and more. What the young cop failed to mention were the spinning lights, the disco ball, and blaring music.

Soon a confident Black Knight strutted into the arena to booming "medieval" hard rock. Clearly the favorite, the audience chanted his name as he climbed the ladder to the top of the platform.

Finally the armored and helmeted challenger emerged from behind the curtain. A spotlight hit him as the house lights dimmed.

"And here he is, Sir Franco! Step forward, noble knight . . . like a *lamb* to the *slaaaaaaughter!*"

Laughter followed.

"Salute your Lady, Sir Franco, and enter the Gauntlet!"

Sir Franco faced me, bowed once. I could barely see his eyes behind the visor, but I swore he winked. Then he turned and raced to the ladder.

"Good luck, my prince," I muttered and silently prayed. *Dear God, if you've got a minute, give him a hand!*

A moment later, champion and challenger stood side by side on a platform above the watery moat, which bubbled and smoked like a boiling cauldron.

"Commence!" The Monk's command was followed by an explosion of light and sound, as the hard rock intensified.

The contestants got off to a pretty even start before things turned ugly. As the pair hit the side-by-side balancing bars, the Black Knight deliberately jabbed Sir Franco, throwing him off balance.

The underhanded move was greeted by *oohs* and boos.

"Watch out!" warned the Monk. "Black Knights don't play fair!"

Regaining his footing, Sir Franco caught up with his foe at the rope climb.

When they reached the second tier, champ and challenger both swung easily across the abyss. But at the hand-over-hand ladder, the Black Knight tried to entangle Sir Franco's legs with his own.

More boos erupted as the audience began to warm to the underdog.

The Black Knight was first onto the sliding board, and when Sir Franco hit the slippery steel slope behind him, they began to wrestle.

They were fast approaching that "Wheel of Fortune," the spinning platform that would toss you off if you didn't approach it the right way.

Knowing you had to land on your feet to survive, the Black Knight turned on the slide to aim his legs at the wheel. Sir Franco, behind him, placed his boots on the Black Knight's helmet to steady himself, then nudged his foe sideways.

The Black Knight twisted on the slide, hit the wheel on his derrière—and was immediately shot into space. Plunging through clouds of dry-ice vapor, he back flopped into the bubbling moat.

The audience rose to its feet when Sir Franco hit the wheel, teetered, and jumped onto the stationary platform.

But it wasn't over yet.

There was still a wide leap over an open section of the bubbling "cauldron" to the finish line. Without hesitation, Sir Franco took a running start and leaped—to land safely on the opposite side. He thrust his arms into the sky and ripped through the tape at the finish line.

The Monk, who'd been speechless since the Black Knight turned Frisbee, found his voice at last.

"And ye winner is, Sir Francooooo of Brooklyynnnn!"

As planned, my champion hurried down the ladder and raced to his Lady's open arms. We hugged and spun around—right through the purple curtains behind us.

On the other side "Sir Franco" tore off his helmet with a relieved breath and passed it to the real Sergeant Franco, who waited, clad in identical armor.

"Great job, Dalecki." Franco was grinning as he slipped the helmet over his head and closed the visor. "Now for the switch!"

I took Franco's hand and we raced back through the purple curtains, free arms high, into an arena full of wild applause.

A blaring fanfare thundered the auditorium. It went on a little too long, but it gave the pointy-hatted Princesses enough time to surround us.

Ringed by what had to look like a rainbow of traffic cones, the "Princesses" stripped Franco of his armor and draped both of us in fake-fur-lined capes.

Finally, the Monk stepped forward to greet us with a bow.

"Sir Franco and his Lady Fair, prepare yourselves for an audience with the King!"

Seventy-Five

"Congratulations," gushed the doe-eyed head Princess as she led us up the special guarded stairs to Galloway's table. "You are so incredibly lucky to have an audience with the King. We all envy you."

Franco and I glanced at each other. Crowd and crew alike appeared to be in awe of this chance we'd won.

Franco leaned toward me. "Is this dinner theater or cult?"

Given Dalecki's stories about the Black Knight nearly being fired for losing, I wondered if Galloway would be petulant or hostile because Franco had bested his champion. But the laughing King who stood to greet us was neither.

"Whoa," mumbled an awed Franco. "The New York Giant really is a giant."

Now when you're as low to the ground as I am, an Internet profile stat like "six feet nine inches" doesn't begin to prepare you for the intimidating mass of muscle and armor that was former New York Giant Dwayne Galloway.

The curly-haired Giant howled and slapped Franco on the back—a blow that might have fallen a lesser man.

"What a show!" he roared. "I'm using the footage for our next commercial!"

Galloway certainly looked regal enough in a (real) fur-trimmed tunic over gleaming chain mail, a bejeweled sword belt girding his size 40 waist. Only one anachronism—the

Super Bowl ring on his finger—and the open expression of almost boyish excitement undercut the illusion of the tough medieval warrior king he clearly fancied himself to be.

I felt the Giant's eyes on me next—starting with my knee-high boots, running up my black tights, casual skirt, and nothing-special sweater beneath the fake ermine cape.

"I am so pleased to meet the Lady . . ."

"Clare."

He bent low—really low, given my five-two height—and swept his eyes over my sweater again as he kissed my hand. "Sir Franco is fortunate to have such a curvaceous little Queen."

"Princess," I corrected. "We're not married."

Galloway's dark eyes narrowed like a wolf on the hunt. The reaction was practically autonomic and gave me absolute assurance: This was the predatory knight I'd seen in Central Park.

"Please sit, and we shall feast!"

He led us to the massive table (and yes, it was a round table) set with silver and pewter goblets. Seating was arranged to provide an excellent view of the arena below, where the knights' parade of horses had begun.

The gargantuan Giant held my chair—not a bench, which was apparently only suitable for the peasants on the lower tier. I noticed he also made sure his chair legs were very close to mine.

Good, I thought. *All the better to trip you with . . .*

Serving wenches appeared bearing a decidedly off-menu meal fit for a king: hickory-smoked deep-fried turkey; stuffed pork chops baked with pears and Stilton; beef bourguignon; and a farro salad with arugula, edamame, and a sweet-and-sour vinaigrette.

As we feasted, the King chatted amicably with Franco, and we all watched the knights jousting below. Finally, the King leaned close to me.

"So, Lady Clare," he rumbled sweetly in my ear, "what brings you to my domain?"

I swallowed hard. *Franco ran his gauntlet. Now it's my turn . . .*

"Actually, Dwayne," I softly replied. "I came to ask you about two women you've spent time with recently—Rozalina Krasny and Anya Kravchenko."

The former Giant sat back and stared at me, as if I'd slapped his face.

"What is this," he hissed, "a shakedown?"

The King immediately raised his arm high and snapped his fingers, summoning a pair of his dreaded "Men-at-Arms," who were not in amusing period costumes. These bodyguards looked more like a Secret Service detail, complete with grim black suits and holstered (so far) Glocks.

Instinctively, Franco reached for the weapon he'd left locked up in his car. Then he cursed and put up his hands.

Seventy-six

"YOUR Majesty," I quickly said. "Look around you. We are sitting in an *open box*, in front of hundreds of your fans. If you throw us out, you're going to look like the sorest of sore losers. How courtly is that?"

"I won't tolerate a shakedown," Galloway growled.

"This isn't a shakedown."

"My partner's right," Franco said. "It's an off-the-record homicide investigation that's ready to go *on* the record if you don't cooperate."

Galloway's jaw dropped. "Homicide?"

I nodded. "How many families would bring their kids here if they found out you, the noble King, are suspected of drugging one girl and killing another?"

Galloway's dark eyes widened in shock. "What happened? Tell me? Is Anya okay?"

The reaction looked real. *Are we on the wrong track? Or is he simply a good actor?*

"Anya was drugged at the Central Park Festival, and she's still in a coma," I told him. "Don't deny you were stalking her. I saw you watching Anya come out of the fortune teller's tent. Later you spoke to her, too."

Now I was using the evidence Plesky presented against Matt—which was (admittedly) circumstantial. "Anya was seen speaking to a man in medieval garb at around four o'clock. That was you, wasn't it?"

Galloway dismissed his Men-at-Arms with a gesture. Then he turned back to me and nodded.

"Yeah, I spoke to her. I saw Anya crying at the fortune teller's tent. But I didn't catch up to her until the afternoon."

"That makes you the last person we know of who saw Anya before she was drugged."

He frowned. "I didn't touch Anya, and I don't touch drugs."

"Then why did you seek Anya out?"

"We broke up, but I still cared about her. I wanted to know why she was crying. But when I asked her, she told me to go away. She said she had important business." He shook his head. "Anya was the most beautiful girl I ever . . ." He sighed. "It doesn't matter. Anya was trouble, and I don't need trouble."

"How was she trouble?"

"Look, we started out great, had lots of fun together. We became friends. She was really my type, you know? But then I found out something about her that I could not have in my life."

"What was that?" I asked.

"She was paying off mobsters in Brooklyn."

"Mobsters? For what reason?"

"I never found out why, but she asked me for a loan of ten thousand, said it was really important but wouldn't tell me why. She was nervous, upset. I gave her the money—and I had her followed. She went straight to the bank, then to a Russian mob hangout in Brighton Beach. I knew it had to end when I heard that."

I met his eyes. "So you threw Anya over, just like that?"

"Hell, yeah. I liked her a lot, but I couldn't trust her, not after that. I've got a family-friendly dinner theater here. I don't need the mob shaking me down. Anya was beautiful, a real Diamond girl, but there are always other girls—"

"Like Red? She's the one who's dead, by the way—"

Galloway cursed.

"I noticed you didn't ask about her."

"Look, I'm sorry she's dead, but Red was a Silver Room girl. We had a few good times, nothing special. There are plenty of girls just like her—"

"You mentioned the Silver Room from the underground club. Is that why you go there? To meet women?"

In a flash, the bristling predatory knight reappeared. "Look, I shouldn't have said that—about the Silver Room. On the record, I don't know what club you're talking about. Off the record, that's precisely why I go."

The King's giant fist thumped the table. "I'm a multimillionaire, a former star athlete, and a celebrity. Do you think I can just go to some bar or dance club and party with a sweet young thing without risking everything? Early in my career I learned the hard way—phony paternity suits, fake assault charges, I've dealt with enough of them to make my membership dues well worth it."

Galloway gulped loudly from his goblet. "That's what the club is for, Clare—if that's even your name. That's why I go. For a man like me, it's the safest place to be, next to this kingdom."

"You've been a member a long time, haven't you? Even before you were a New York Giant."

"Where did you get that bit of misinformation?"

"Is it? I thought you were going to the club during your college years, when you spent summers in New York City."

"I wish," Galloway said. "But no. I was in college then. I didn't join the club until my second season with the Giants."

"But in college, you did study gymnastics under a Russian defector, didn't you?"

"Rolf? Yeah, so? Rolf was a great teacher and a good guy."

"You're still friends?"

"No, I messed up our friendship. Rolf introduced me to his niece. Svetlana was her name. I think she was his niece. Anyway, he said they were related . . ."

"Svetlana?" Given Rolf's CIA dossier, Wilson's sexpionage stories sprang to mind.

"Yeah, Svetlana," he repeated wistfully. "Killer figure. Cute Russian accent. Long blond hair and big blue eyes, exactly like Anya's. Man, I really fell for her."

"The relationship didn't last?"

"I wasn't ready to settle down. And Svetlana got bored with me. She resented the hours I spent gaming."

"Football?" Franco assumed.

"No, she was okay with football. What she didn't like was my off-season *gaming*. Role-playing games. I was Dragon Master in the Knights and Wizards Club at my university."

Now I had a clue where the Meat-dieval Tournament and Feast came from.

"Like I said, I didn't join the underground club until my second season with the Giants—after all the crap I got from women my rookie year."

"Define 'crap,'" I demanded.

"Aren't you listening? Sports celebrity begets con artists in skirts. I slept with enough of them on the road. Live and learn, they say, and I did. Someone tipped me about an underground club—a safe place to play because everyone knows the rules. I ponied up the dues and asked to be let in."

"If you didn't drug those women, who do you think did?" Franco asked.

"I don't have a clue, but there's someone who probably does. The lady running the club—BB."

"You mean Barbara Baum, Babka?" After my friendly neighborhood CIA agent's claim about the club's official address being under an annex to the Moroccan consulate, I wasn't sure how heavily involved Babka actually was. But Galloway made things clear. In fact, he snorted at the mention of her.

"She's more like *Baba*. You know? *Baba Yaga*, the Russian devil woman. If Babka doesn't know, nobody does."

Suddenly the Giant loomed over me. "And you didn't hear *any* of this from me. Got it? That old bag carries a lot of clout. If I get tossed from the club, I'm coming after you."

Galloway snapped his fingers again. The Men-at-Arms reappeared.

"Escort them to their car. If they give you any trouble, call the township cops and have them both arrested." Galloway's smile was villainous. "I'll be happy to press charges."

Seventy-seven

SERGEANT Franco kept a cooler head than I did as we were "escorted" to the parking lot—and not very gently.

When one of the guards took his manhandling too far, I kicked him in the shin. He yowled and called me a difficult wench. (Okay, so his choice of words wasn't nearly so quaint.) I spat back a Mother Hen lecture about a decent gentleman's manners that left him gawking.

Before he or his partner could phone the local constabulary, Franco grabbed my arm, hustled me into his SUV, and peeled out of the lot. On our way to the Pulaski Skyway, he shot me a hard look.

"What got into you back there, Coffee Lady? Why did you kick that goon?"

"I was pissed, okay? The one I really wanted to kick was King Giant Jackass."

"Listen, I've spent years dealing with scumbags in suits and in slums. You can't let guys like Galloway get to you. You have to treat police business as business. Not personal."

"I'm not angry for *me*! I couldn't care less that Galloway insulted us and threw us out. What I'm angry about is his *disgusting* attitude."

"Dwayne had a lousy attitude about a lot of things. I need more."

"His attitude toward women in general and his reaction to Rozalina's death in particular."

"Yeah, it was pretty cold."

"That puffed-up sports legend pretends to be a master of knights in armor, but he knows next to nothing about the true code of chivalry . . ."

I couldn't help comparing Galloway with another man in Red's life—Eldar.

The Bosnian car service driver might have been a humble man, but he would have walked through fire for the woman he loved. I could still hear his heartbroken sobs as the tears fell for his lifeless friend, a stark contrast to the football hero's ghoulishly indifferent response.

As Franco turned his attention back to the steering wheel, I thought about that "Wheel of Fortune" in Galloway's Gauntlet, a circus version of an ancient idea—

Rota fortunae, the wheel of fate.

There were so many young women like Red in the big city, anxious to present themselves as worldly, tough, clever. Yet they were woefully naïve where it really mattered.

What a shame it was. What a terrible shame . . .

Red had traveled all over—even under—New York to find her prince, and all along he'd been literally in front of her, a man so determined to make her happy that he was willing to endure heartache by turning the Wheel, night after night, toward lesser men.

By the time Franco dropped me at the Village Blend, I was feeling pretty low. Now that we'd spoken with Galloway, the theory of his guilt was shakier than his plywood throne.

Feeling a sudden need for caffeine, I went straight to the espresso bar.

At this late hour, Matt was gone and Gardner had taken over the shop's evening management. Things appeared to be running smoothly with customers enjoying the jazzy playlist and my youngest barista, Nancy Kelly, laughing with three tables full of NYU students near the fireplace.

I sat at the counter, and Gardner slid over a freshly pulled double. But despite draining my demitasse, I couldn't relax.

A prickly feeling tickled my back, as if eyes were on me.

Fearing another CIA ambush, I spun on my stool to find Boris standing there, arms folded.

The last time I saw Esther's champion, he'd been in his marriage-proposal tuxedo. Not tonight. The baggy jeans had returned, along with the high-top sneakers, Eminem tee, and black leather jacket to ward of the fall's chill.

"Boris? What are you doing here?"

With his gray eyes narrowed and his chin set, the Russian baker cum rapper answered with four words—

"Take me to her."

Seventy-eight

"Boris, I told you, I don't know where—"

He held up his hand. "Do not lie to me, Coffee Lady. You are harboring my czarina in your apartment upstairs!" He tipped his spikey blond head toward the fireplace. "Nancy let slip the dogs of truth!"

Oh, for heaven's sake. "Look, Boris, I'm sorry I lied to you. But Esther needed time and space to think things through, and she didn't want to sleep on her sister's couch for a week. I offered her my guest bedroom, and she made me vow to keep it a secret."

Boris shook his head with despairing heaviness. "'When in disgrace with fortune and men's eyes, I all alone be-weep my outcast state—'"

"Please try to understand—"

"'And trouble deaf heaven with my useless cries.'" He thumped his chest. "'And look upon myself, and *curse* my fate!'"

"Don't curse it yet—"

"'And in these thoughts myself nearly despising, happily I think on *she*—'" With puppy-dog longing, he gazed at the ceiling. "'And then my state . . . like a bird at break of day arising, from gloomy earth sings hymns at heaven's gate!'"

Half the coffeehouse fell silent and stared. A few customers lightly applauded.

I blinked. "That's not Eminem, is it?"

He sighed and shook his head.

"Look, I feel for your outcast state. But Esther is confused. She won't even talk to me. If you'll stay away a little longer, give her more time—"

"Nyet!"

I jumped in my seat, along with a few customers.

"Love does not wait for fate! And men of action do not leave things to chance. Esther must be reminded how much we love each other!"

"She knows, Boris. She heard your marriage proposal—"

"*Da*, two days ago! Two very long days. But if I give my czarina more time, she will fill her empty head with blackness!"

"Okay, you've got me there . . ." Given how this whole thing started—with a vague coffee reading and that morbid-running void in Esther's head—I saw no reason to argue the point.

"You must help me," Boris pleaded. "For absence does not make the heart grow fonder. Absence is the enemy of love."

"Now *that* my nonna used to say."

"Is Italian proverb, *da*?"

"*Da*. I mean, *yes*."

"And Italian is *romance* language!" Boris declared. "You see! You think as I do!"

"But I'm not your problem. Listen, I'm willing to go upstairs and tell Esther her cover is blown and you're down here waiting to speak with her."

"Spasibo!"

"Don't thank me yet." I rose and leveled with him. "If she doesn't come down in fifteen minutes, she's decided not to. So let her sleep on it. She has a shift late tomorrow, and you can try to speak with her then, okay?"

"I will wait here."

"All right, then. Good night, and good luck—and if you value Nancy's life, do not tell Esther how you found her."

Turning, I headed for the back stairs. "By the way, I really liked your poem."

"Is not my poem," he called after me. "Is sonnet by William Shakespeare. But English is not best way to enjoy his work. You must read him in the original Russian!"

Seventy-nine

"No, boss. I do not want to see Boris."

I found Esther in front of my living room hearth, a quilt tucked around her legs, a book in one hand, a cup of cocoa in the other.

"He's down there waiting for you. Won't you put him out of his misery?"

Esther frowned. "How did he find out I was here?"

How to answer? Gardner already gave me two weeks' notice. If Esther kills Nancy, I'll have very little staff left—

"I think he saw you through the window."

"Well, I'm not ready."

I sat next to her on the sofa. "Are you really confused? Or are you angry with him?"

"I don't know." She gazed at the fireplace flames. "Yes. I think I am angry with him."

"Why don't you talk your feelings over with me?"

"If I do, will you stop bugging me?"

"Maybe."

"Fine." She slammed her book shut. "Number one. I'm angry that he put me through hell after I asked him to live with me—"

"Is that why you're torturing him now? Payback? You want him to suffer without an answer like you did?"

"No, I just . . ." She studied the ceiling. "Okay, maybe a

little. Number two. I'm angry that he made a *spectacle* of our love life. It was mortifying!"

"I understand that reaction. But isn't that what poets do? Share their lives with an audience? Didn't you tell me that's what you do—turn your misery into art?"

"Well . . . when you put it like that, it's hard to argue."

"Then don't. Put yourself in Boris's basketball shoes. You know what he told me? He said he didn't want to be your roommate. He wanted to be your husband."

"Three! I'm angry that he proposed marriage. Marriage!" Esther violently shook her head.

"Marriage is a problem, I take it?"

"So? It's a problem for *you* these days. Isn't it?"

"We're not talking about me. We're talking about you and Boris. Don't you want to talk about it?"

"Spare me. That's why I came back to the city. My sister wouldn't stop talking about it. 'I want to see my little sister married, in a white dress, cutting the cake, moving to the suburbs, having children . . .'"

"Whoa, back up. Is that what you think marriage has to be? White dress, children, suburbs?"

"That's what my sister thinks it has to be."

"Only because those things are her happily ever after—and she thinks they'll make you happy, too. But you're not your sister, Esther, and marriage doesn't have to be some dark forest where you lose who you really are."

"What is it then?"

"A promise, a solemn promise by two people to be there for each other—to go into those dark places and bring each other out again. I'm sure that's all Boris wants for you both. But you won't know for sure until you let go of your anger and your fears and *talk* to him."

Esther fell silent, finished her cocoa, and set down the cup. "He's really down there, just waiting for me?"

"Yes."

"I have to say, it's nice that he didn't try to barge in, or pressure me. It's good that he's willing to give me my space."

"Yes, it is—"

"'With love's light wings I would fly over these walls!'"

"What's that?" Esther frowned. "It sounds like Boris."

I rose and went to the balcony doors. Boris was standing beneath us, under a West Village streetlamp.

"'For stony limits cannot hold love out! And what love can do, that dares love attempt . . .'"

I cleared my throat. "I think he's reciting Shakespeare—"

"'Therefore thy employer is no stop to me!'"

"Translated from the 'original' Russian."

A few more lines and he turned on a boom box and lifted it over his head. The music pulsing out wasn't hip-hop. It sounded more like the opening strains of an old love song from the seventies.

Boris began to sing, karaoke style. *"You . . ."*

I scratched my head. "Is that . . ?"

"You Light Up My Life!" Esther screamed and ran up to the guest room.

I sighed, hearing neighbors complain. "Knock it off, Romeo!" A minute later came the red flashing lights and *whoop-whoop!* siren bursts of our local constabulary.

As I watched from above, Officers Langley and Demetrios tried to convince Boris to close his one-man street cabaret and move along. He refused—several times—and they invited him into their nice, clean patrol car.

"'Alack, there lies more peril in thine eye than twenty of their swords!'"

That I believed.

"'Good night, good night, my Esther! Parting is such sweet sorrow. That I shall say good night till it be morrow . . .'"

Whoop-whoop! As the police car carried Boris away, I closed the balcony doors, climbed the steps, and checked on Esther.

Her head was under a pillow. "Did they arrest him?" asked her muffled voice.

"They'll give him a bench warrant and let him go. Get some sleep. I'm sure things will look better in the morning."

Actually, I wasn't so sure. But I knew she needed to hear it.

Heading for the master bedroom, I felt my cell phone

vibrating in my skirt pocket. Checking the caller ID, I suddenly knew how Esther felt.

Though I dearly loved Mike Quinn, he was turning up the pressure on getting me to move to Washington, and it was hard to take. With a tense hello, I answered his call, but after the night I'd had, all I wanted to do was put *my* head under a pillow.

Eighty

"What's wrong?" Mike asked.

"All I said was *hello*."

"It's the way you said it. I repeat. What's wrong?"

"Mike, I'm putting you on speaker so I can undress . . ."

"In that case, how about putting us on video chat?"

For the first time since my switcheroo plan sent the Black Knight's derriere flying, I smiled. Despite conquering Galloway's Gauntlet, I'd come back to Manhattan a loser.

With a sigh I unzipped my knee-high boots, and then my skirt. Finally, I peeled off my tights.

"Are you going to talk to me, Clare? Or should I just listen to you torture me with zipper sounds?"

"I'm sorry. I'm not in the mood to talk tonight."

"Well, I wish I were there to help. But since I'm not, I'm going to have to insist you tell me why you're upset—and if you don't, I'll be getting on the next express to Penn Station."

Okay, now he's starting to sound as pushy as Boris.

"Fine, I'll tell you. Just don't start quoting Shakespeare."

"What?"

"Never mind. Listen, I'm upset because Franco and I drove all the way to Jersey, but we didn't get anywhere with this awful case. And if I don't get somewhere soon, my business partner and the father of my daughter is going to prison for putting Sleeping Beauty in a coma and murdering Red in the 'Hood."

"You know what, Detective Cosi? I've hit plenty of roadblocks working cases, and so have every one of the officers under me. Frustration is part of the process."

"The lousy part."

"Don't whine. It's a waste of energy. The only way to *guarantee* you lose any case is to give up."

"I'm not giving up. I'm just at a dead end."

"No, Cosi. The *victim* is at a dead end. You're still breathing."

I sank down on the bed. Quinn had a point. He also had effective tactics as a police lieutenant. Franco often sang his praises as a supervisor. Now I knew why.

"Okay, loo, what do you think I should do?"

"Other than continue to let me listen to you taking off your clothes?"

I smiled again. "Yes."

"Every witness, every suspect, even the evidence tells a story—one part of the truth. The investigator's job is to find the whole truth."

"Go on."

"You spoke with a suspect tonight, correct? One who was close to both victims?"

"For almost an hour."

"Maybe you did get somewhere and you don't know it. Talk to me about the interview . . ."

I did, including possible reasons Anya might have gone to a Brighton Beach Russian mob hangout with ten thousand dead presidents. Loan sharking? Blackmail? Intimidation? Extortion?

Was Dwayne Galloway even telling the truth about that?

I couldn't confirm it, although I could corroborate his story about the underground speakeasy. And he certainly confirmed Barbara Baum was no sidelines player. According to him, she ran the place.

"That's valuable intel, Cosi. You can do something with that."

"Like?"

"Like confront Barbara Baum."

"Threaten her?"

"Persuade her. If Galloway gave you the information, and you saw the club, she can't deny it. Get her to see that cooperating with you and clearing up Anya's case is in her best interest."

"Unless she's involved with drugging the girl."

"If she is, watch her closely—and listen hard. She'll give something away. Take what she gives you and build on it."

"By all accounts, she's a shrewd lady. Getting her to talk won't be easy."

"She's a friend of your employer, isn't she? Use that connection."

"Believe me, I'd like to . . ." With Madame Blanche Dreyfus Allegro Dubois sitting next to me, I'd be dealing with Babka, the kind old granny—and not Baba Yaga, the devilish trickster witch. "I'll have to persuade Madame to help me ambush her old friend. I don't know if she'll do it."

"Ask her."

I put Mike on hold and texted Madame: *Urgent. Must question Barbara B. Could get sticky. If UR OK with this, call me in AM to set up lunch at Babka's.*

Given the late hour, I was surprised (and relieved) when her reply came almost instantly: *Understand. The game is afoot! Leave it to me!*

Madame always did like a good mystery. But this time it was more than a game. She didn't know it yet, but her son's freedom depended on it. And if Franco's warning was true, then a killer was out there somewhere with a needle full of poison for anyone who got in the way—me included.

"I hope that helped," Mike said.

"You know it did. Thanks."

"Anytime."

We said our good nights and ended the call. Then I climbed into bed and realized something: For the first time in weeks, Mike hadn't pressured me to move to DC.

Strangely, a part of me now wished he had.

Turning off the light, I snuggled down under the covers and yawned. Silver moonlight spilled in from the window, illuminating the emptiness beside me.

I turned over.

Now that Mike and I had talked, I no longer wanted to put my head under a pillow. What I truly wanted was his head on the pillow next to mine.

"HERE you go, sleepyhead."

Matt slid a demitasse across the counter.

"I'm sorry I slept through the alarm."

My ex-husband smiled. "You had a big night—*and* you're currently living with Esther. Master roaster, amateur investigator, and premarriage counselor. That's a lot to manage in one week."

I shook my head. "Between Esther's drama and Tucker's vacation—"

"Hey, I told you I'd be here for you. And apart from what happened to Anya and her friend, it's been great. I'm loving being in the shop again . . ."

Like the captain of a smooth-sailing vessel, Matt flattened his palms on the counter and proudly scanned the busy shop.

"I've spent so many years sourcing beans and wheeling and dealing them on the international market, I almost forgot what coffee is all about." He opened his arms. "It's this. The place we've got here, where people can gather, relax, in company or in solitude, share something warm and rejuvenating . . ."

Matt was quoting his grandfather now, part of an inscription on an old photograph of the Village Blend's interior, circa 1936.

After knocking on the counter for good luck, he threw me a wink and left to greet an approaching group of office workers.

As I continued sipping my perfect espresso, I watched Matt laugh with the customers and recommend beans he'd brought back from half a world away.

It started me thinking . . .

Would Matt be willing to consider pulling back on his constant globe-trotting? Maybe drop anchor to manage the shop for a year or so?

If he was, could a temporary move to Washington be such a crazy dream, after all?

FIFTEEN minutes and two espressos later, the bell above the front door jangled, and I heard a familiar voice.

"Tucker Burton, center stage!"

As customers hooted and applauded, I turned to take in a happy sight, my long-lost (and much-loved) assistant manager. "Enjoying your vacation?"

"Hardly a vay-cay, CC." Tuck plopped on the barstool next to me and tossed his floppy hair. "Between my off-off Broadway cabaret and FTF *Storytime* kiddy shows, I'm missing sleep."

"You're missing messages, too. If you recall, I asked you to do a little spying on Mike's ex-wife at the Central Park Festival. You *never* told me what you saw."

Tuck leaned close and lowered his voice. "What I saw isn't something I wanted to commit to a text message."

"It's early Tuck, and I had a hard night. Just tell me what happened."

Tuck began to speak, but when Matt came over to serve him an espresso, he clammed up. Suddenly he was wearing the same fearful expression he'd worn in Madame Tesla's tent.

I thanked Matt and moved Tuck and I to a corner table for privacy.

"Come on, Tuck, since when do you avoid gossip?"

He glanced around and whispered: "Since it involves one of the most powerful women in this town." He paused to sip some caffeinated courage. "Look, you wanted the scoop on Leila, here it is, and you *did not* get this from me: While I was working with my cast at the Delacorte, I saw Leila talking to Babka Baum. I didn't hear a word between them, but I did see Babka give Leila a small purple box. They talked quietly for a long time, and then they hugged."

I already knew about that little box and what it contained. But there was still a mystery here, and it had nothing to do with Leila.

"What was Babka doing at the theater?"

"She's our *Storytime* kiddie show's main sponsor for Fairy Tale Fall week."

"And *that's* why you were afraid of telling tales on her?"

"Let me put this in perspective for you, CC, remember that VIP I went to meet the night of the Central Park Festival? Well, he's a big producer, and he wants to take my cabaret show, *Goosed,* to a larger venue, a place on Eighth Avenue that's right off the Theater District. The run will be limited, but it's great exposure—for me and especially for Punch."

"That's amazing for you both, Tuck, congratulations."

"Thanks, but listen up . . ." He leaned closer. "*Babka* is the one who made that happen. She loved my work for the FTF's kiddie shows, so she made a few phone calls—and suddenly I've arrived."

"I get it. Babka likes you."

"Yes, but here's the rub—when Babka *doesn't* like you, ugly things happen."

Tuck told me the show business legend about a young actor who went from the hottest commodity on Broadway to a weatherman's job at a public access station in Pahrump, all because he took a few jabs at Babka's "old fashioned" menu on a popular talk show.

"Babka ruined the man. He went from a potential starring role in a Hollywood feature to the Fourth Ring of Thespian Hell. Let me tell you, there's more to Babka than yeast cake. If you want to survive in this town, you don't mess with Baba Yaga."

Eighty-one

By the time I arrived for lunch at Babka's, the restaurant was packed with a line out the door.

The famous dining room was an immense open rectangle with a wall of high windows facing the avenue. Despite its size, large furniture pieces were artfully used as room dividers, making things intimate, and several marble fireplaces—each culled from some elegant old Manhattan mansion before demolition—filled the area with warmth and a lively crackle.

The décor was over-the-top Victorian. There was so much bric-a-brac that I was afraid to wave my arm for fear I'd break something. Among this homey clutter were framed photos of Babka herself posing with actors, musicians, artists, writers, and politicians from the 1960s to the present.

"Barbara likes to say she's friends with 'everybody who's anybody,'" Madame once told me, "and she rules her dining room like the Queen of Hearts." So-called "nobodies" were stashed in one area while select guests were ushered into another.

Oh, sure, you could eat Babka's Shrimp Kiev and her Gourmet Knishes of roasted truffled potatoes pureed with mascarpone in the same dining room as a blockbuster film director and millionaire pop singer, but thanks to the huge room dividers, you wouldn't be seated anywhere near them.

And if you happened to "casually stray" into the exclusive area to snap a quick cell photo or ask for an autograph? *Off with you head!* You would be ejected immediately and forever.

I counted on Madame's longtime friendship with Barbara to skirt the velvet rope. Favored customers (and celebrities) were usually placed in one of the reserved areas, and I figured Madame would be among The Elect.

Sure enough, my employer had been given a treasured spot by the window, and a hostess dressed as a Victorian housemaid escorted me to her cozy booth.

Tea had already arrived, in the kitschy "Mother Hen" service Babka's was renowned for. And I noticed Madame couldn't resist ordering the restaurant's mini tribute to a classic strawberry dessert from Leo Lindermann's original Lindy's (a favorite old eatery of Milton Berle, Damon Runyon, and the Jewish mobster Arnold Rothstein).

Me? Well, if my employer was starting lunch with a freshly baked white cupcake filled with glacéed strawberries and served with a drizzling shot of fresh strawberry syrup, why not join her?

I ordered and in mere minutes was also enjoying Babka's famous Twinkie Baba Rum—modern comfort food meets old world classic in forkfuls of guilty pleasure.

"You said you wished to speak with Barbara?" Madame dabbed a bit of strawberry syrup from her chin and leaned with bright eyes across the gingham tablecloth. She was looking as flamboyantly elegant as ever in a chartreuse shift and silk scarf printed with Van Gogh's *Green Wheat Fields, Auvers.*

"I take it this is part of your investigation? Matt filled me in on some of it—finding a Sleeping Beauty in Central Park . . ."

Over cups of the strong black tea, I told Madame the rest of the tale, including the not-so-pretty chapter of Anya's friend, Red, dead on her basement apartment's floor; and how both young Russian women were associated with the speakeasy six floors below our feet, which was why I investigated the place myself.

I noticed she tensed at the mention of the Prince Charming Club.

"That secret club is secret for a reason, dear. Be sure to tread lightly when you speak with Babka."

"She's been your friend for years, hasn't she?"

"Yes, but . . ." Madame's smile was enigmatic. "She holds a lot of clout and can be punishingly direct. That does not mean you can be equally honest with her. Babka takes offense as easily as she offends."

"You mean you don't want me to ask her about the secret club?"

"Find a way to ask without asking."

We were interrupted by a raucous cry that nearly shook the low rafters.

"Clare, baby! Stand up and let these tired old peepers get a look at you!"

I was hardly on my feet before I was enfolded by the arms of the legend herself, Barbara "Babka" Baum.

Eighty-two

A petite, birdlike woman in her early eighties, Babka continued to present the image of the stylish New York businesswoman she'd been for decades.

Still chicly thin, she wore a tailored designer suit with a pair of diamond-studded glasses on a chain around her neck. Through her perfect makeup, her senior skin showed gentle wrinkling along with a few cosmetic enhancements (all tastefully done, of course) while her short, wavy hair was maintained with a bitter-almond rinse tempered with salon-perfect highlights of burnished gold.

As her restaurant's name suggested, Barbara thought of herself as everyone's grandmother, and behaved accordingly. When the energetic hug ended, she pinched my cheek between her thumb and forefinger. The sting made me flash back on those terrible slaps the unconscious young Anya received in her hospital room.

"Where have you been keeping yourself, Clare? Madame tells me you still haven't married that detective. You've found your prince. What are you're waiting for?"

"So my love life is what you discuss at those Fairy Tale Fall committee meetings?"

My employer raised a plucked eyebrow. "I'm afraid we do nothing but chinwag, my dear. That committee is a hotbed of steamy gossip."

Babka gently nudged Madame. "Scoot over, Blanche, and I'll join you."

At tables around us people tried not to stare at the boisterous display, and largely failed.

While Babka was famous for stopping by a customer's table for a greeting and a chitchat, an actual sit-down with the celebrated restaurateur was a rare privilege. A few customers—among them a sitcom star and a major cable news personality—shot us envious glances.

"I really love what you've done to build your coffeehouse into an international brand, Clare. Your Billionaire Blend is the talk of the trade." Babka tapped the side of her head. "Smart to cater to the upmarket, too. The rich are the only ones with 'doe-ray-mi' these days."

Madame grinned like a proud parent at Babka's compliment.

"Well, I can't take all the credit," I replied, "Matt sourced the—"

"*Feh!* Take credit where credit is due, kiddo. You've earned it."

Babka shot Madame a sidelong glance. "You know Blanche could have made that old coffeehouse into a franchise long before the *bucks* was added to *Star*, but she chose to marry that little Frenchman and slip quietly into retirement."

Madame pursed her lips. "Let's not go down *that* road again."

"Come on, Blanche! Years ago, I told you to think big. I did and you didn't. Next month I'm flying to Nevada for the opening of Babka's at the MGM."

She counted with her fingers. "I've got the restaurant downtown, and one in Chicago. There's a Babka's in LA—which makes the Vegas opening my fourth location since you took up knitting or Mahjong or whatever old people do."

"Madame was hardly playing Mahjong," I shot back.

My employer's "retirement" consisted of overseeing Pierre Dubois's four homes and two estates in three countries; staging his business and social gatherings; and as Pierre's health waned, running her husband's import-export business.

I was about to say as much, but Madame silenced me with a gesture and replied to Babka herself.

"Not all of us want that sort of life, you know. There are other things of value. Gracious living. The love and companionship of a good man—"

Babka dismissed that line with a wave. "I was married once. It's not all it's cracked up to be."

"Let's not speak ill of the dead," Madame cautioned.

"Why not? Marvin thought your late husband was a supercilious lout."

Madame made a face. "Well, maybe just this once."

Late husband disposed of, Babka jumped to a new topic.

"Truthfully, Clare. I do know a smart cookie when I spot one, and you're smarter than most. If you ever get tired of living in New York City, I'll open a franchise anyplace you like, and you can be my manager. Name your town. Boston. Memphis . . ." She paused and winked—

"How about *Washington, DC*?"

I tensed. *How can she possibly know my plans, when I hardly even know if they are my plans?!*

Before I could reply, Madame's violet eyes flashed. "That will be quite enough of that!" She gripped my hand. "Clare is not an employee to be stolen away. She's family to be cherished, and she always will be, no matter what she decides for her future."

Whatever my future, it was certainly not the topic I'd come here to discuss, and I quickly attempted to steer the conversation to other subjects—like purple jewel boxes and key necklaces.

"What other endeavors have you undertaken, Babka? Have you ever opened a club? Something very exclusive, perhaps?"

Babka didn't blink an eye. "Five restaurants are *endeavors* enough for anyone, sweetie. And pretty good for a girl who started as a humble tea lady."

"Tea lady?"

Madame was close to rolling her eyes. It was clear she'd heard this story before.

"I pushed a tea service cart at one of those elegant old law firms here in Manhattan," Barbara said with a shrewd smile. "You know the kind? Full of blue bloods with country club memberships. Back in those days they had teatime in the afternoon. It was all very civilized.

"Anyway, in the little spare time I had, I baked babkas in my Bowery tenement. Everybody on the Lower East Side knew babkas, but the stuffy lawyers I worked for never heard of them. When I started serving babkas on my tea cart, those waspy farts went crazy for it!"

Madame sighed heavily, but said nothing.

"It was my sweet old boss and a couple of other partners who lent me the cash to start a bakery and restaurant. The rest is history."

Unable to hold her tongue any longer, Madame cleared her throat.

"Everyone tweaks their résumé, Barb, but you should never leave out the juicy parts. Intrigue is good PR."

"Intrigue?" My ears perked up.

"Barbara was indeed a tea lady at a white-shoe law firm," Madame said. "But she neglected to mention that 'sweet old boss' of hers was 'Wild Bill' Donovan, the Father of the Central Intelligence Agency. He was officially out of the CIA by the time Barbara met him at the firm, but I do wonder if anyone really retires from a life of espionage . . ."

I thought of the white-haired Wilson and his spy story involving the underground club. But the bragging Babka was suddenly (suspiciously?) dismissive of this intrigue idea.

"Don't exaggerate, Blanche!" she cried. "Mr. Donovan was simply a lawyer, that's all."

Madame cocked an eyebrow. "And yet Babs found herself at the center of an international incident during the Cold War, didn't you, dear?"

This must be it, I thought. *The story Wilson told me about all the sexpionage going on in Babka's club and the murder of his agent Faith!*

But the story Babka told wasn't about any of that.

"Years ago, when the Iron Curtain was still welded

closed, I hid a Bolshoi Ballet star who wanted to defect." She laughed. "I hid her in plain sight, too. The girl wore a wig, worked as a waitress right here, and slept in my office until everything blew over. A marvelous waitress. With her balance, she never dropped a tray."

Babka faced me. "Dancers make great waitresses, and mariachi players are good cooks. But never hire a writer, they're too damn moody! Remember, Clare, good employees are one of the keys to success—"

Keys! Finally an opening! "Speaking of keys, Babka, I wanted to ask—"

Just then, my phone went off—the *urgent* ring.

I apologized and checked the screen. Franco was calling. I was hoping for good news, but he started with: "I have an update on Matt. I'm sorry, Clare . . ."

My heart nearly stopped. "Hold the line, Sergeant."

Excusing myself from the table, I stepped outside.

Eighty-three

On the chilly East Side street, Franco laid out the cold, hard facts.

"Matt's been arrested. We scooped him up at the Village Blend."

"We?"

"Yeah." Franco paused. "I had no idea it was going to happen. Endicott and Plesky ordered me to come with them, and things turned pretty ugly."

"Matt wasn't hurt, was he?"

"No, but he resisted arrest when Endicott demanded that I cuff him—"

"Oh, Franco, no!"

"Yeah, I felt pretty bad, Coffee Lady. All I could think about was Joy and how heartbroken she's going to be when she hears about this. And, of course, your ex-husband wasn't too happy about it, either." Franco paused. "In the process, he struck a police officer. Matt could be charged with assault. He could go to jail for that alone."

"Is the officer okay?"

"I'm fine. Thanks for asking."

"Matt hit you?!"

"Couldn't be helped—and I have to admit your ex packs quite a wallop."

"What's next?"

"I'm calling from the precinct bathroom. When I leave this stall, it's back to the interrogation room where they're holding him. I don't know what Endicott has up his sleeve, but I'll keep you in the loop."

Franco ended the call, and I found myself staring at the restaurant's purple twilight awning and pondering my next move. Red was dead, Anya in a coma, and now Matt was under arrest.

Enough with the verbal sparring, I decided. *It was time to shoot from the hip.*

Boris once told me that Russians had two faces, a public one, and another that was secret. That certainly fit Barbara Baum. Despite her public face as a kindly old lady who baked cake, there was a snarling Baba Yaga lurking behind the façade.

But I can be formidable, too—especially when my family is threatened.

My mind made up, I marched back to our table.

"THERE'S our girl," Babka said when I sat down. "Now what were we talking about?"

"Keys," I said. "Like the keys you hand out to pretty girls and beautiful women. Those special key necklaces that get them admission into your private club downstairs."

In a flash, the jovial Babka was gone, a serious, sharp-eyed Baba Yaga in her place.

"Honey, I don't know what you're talking—"

"No more lies. Rozalina Krasny is dead, murdered. Anya has been drugged, and Madame's son, Matt, was arrested this afternoon for both crimes."

"Heavens!" Madame cried.

"I'm sorry you have to hear the news this way," I told Madame, "but Barbara needs to hear it, too. An innocent man, the son of your friend, is being framed for crimes connected to the club downstairs."

"You're wrong," Babka insisted.

"Am I? Anya had a key. So did Red."

"You're wrong about the *club*, Clare."

"I saw the rooms of Silver, Diamond, and Gold, right out of *The Secret Ball*, Anya's favorite fairy tale. Was that your intent? To create a fantasy for hungry men and willing women?"

Babka shook her head. "I started the club to help all the poor, pretty girls who worked for me as waitresses, and the lonely women who came to my restaurant for a meal. You're a businesswoman, Clare, you know the score."

Babka touched my arm. "You can only do so much charity before you're broke. My girls hit me up for money all the time. 'I can't pay my rent. I need this, my kid needs that.' For a while, I was a soft touch, but things got so bad I had to start saying no. That's when I got the idea to introduce the pretty girls to fat cats who were good at making money—but not so smart about meeting women."

"Like a dating service," Madame put in.

"An *exclusive* dating service. The club started small and got bigger. Madame knows—she was a member once."

I did a double take.

"Don't look so shocked, dear. I wasn't searching for a sugar daddy or even a rich husband. Remember, I'd lost Matt's father far too soon, and that tragic affair with the police detective left me bereft. I was lonely. The continental men at the club were quite accomplished and interesting."

"Eventually Blanche met Pierre," Babka added. "I was there that day. It was like lightning. He was instantly smitten."

I gawked at Madame. "But you told me a friend introduced you to your second husband."

"A white lie," Madame confessed. "A friend convinced me to join the club, and that's how I met Pierre."

"But the gambling," I pressed. "Surely that's criminal."

Babka shrugged. "I brought in overseas investors. You know how it goes. They sold me on the 'casino school' idea. There's nothing technically illegal about it, and we have a certain amount of protection, given our clientele and connections."

"I guessed as much when I saw the deputy police commissioner down there."

"Really, Clare, it's just a matchmaking club, and I keep things on the up-and-up. I even have a lawyer who works hard to protect my members."

"Harrison Van Loon?"

"Oh, you are good," Babka replied. "Yeah, that's my guy."

I got the picture real fast. Like Hansel and Gretel's witch, Babka used eye candy to lure men in, but many of them must have gotten burned because she made sure to bring in a legal eagle to pass out guarantees, in the form of flame-retardant prenuptial agreements.

But I still had a problem with Babka's story.

"If Van Loon is supposed to look out for your girls, how did Anya get stuck paying off Russian mobsters in Brighton Beach?"

I waited for an outraged reaction, but Babka didn't appear upset in the least by this line of questioning.

"They're not mobsters," she calmly told me. "Not technically anyway. These men are more like facilitators. They live in America, but they have ties to the government in Russia. Anya was paying them to get her mother out of jail."

"Jail?"

"Anya's mother is an artist and political dissident. She spoke up for human rights, a little too loudly as it turned out. She was imprisoned under the same crackdown that snared other artists."

I remembered my talk with Boris. "Like the rock group Pussy Riot?"

Babka nodded. "The facilitators in Brighton Beach have done this before. It's a lengthy process, getting individuals freed from custody over there, and it's costly. Anya needed money fast. Her friend Rozalina sponsored Anya, and she quickly attracted a big-catch sugar daddy—"

"Dwayne Galloway, the former New York Giant."

"I thought Anya was doing well, but then she was assaulted on a modeling job by some *pig* who was *not* a member of our club." Now Babka's eyes flashed with fury. "I don't tolerate that sort of behavior and the men downstairs know it. The ones who don't get a reminder from my staff."

I thought about the helpful waiter who intervened between me and that masher in the Silver Room and realized he'd stepped in to help me for a very good reason. As part of Barbara's staff, he'd been taught to police bad behavior.

"If you want to know the details, you'll have to speak with Anya's lawyer. Lucky for you, Harrison Van Loon is having lunch right here in the restaurant."

"Point the way," I said, rising.

Eighty-Four

Harrison Van Loon was in preppie mode today. His staid wool suit was accompanied by a sprightly vest of red plaid, his salt-and-pepper hair and beard were nicely styled. But what really gave the lawyer his Ivy League patina were the bifocals perched on the end of his nose.

"Are we dining alone today?" I asked.

Not waiting for an answer, or an invitation, I plopped down across from Anya's lawyer. This time Van Loon recognized me. He closed the blue-covered legal document he'd been scanning and clasped his hands over it.

"Ms. Cosi, what can I do for you?" he replied with patient irritation.

"You can tell me about the lawsuit filed by Anya Krevchenko."

Now Van Loon looked as if he'd swallowed a rock. He reached for his wineglass and took a lengthy gulp before replying.

"I'm not at liberty to discuss an ongoing suit."

"You can discuss it with me, or you can speak to Detective Emmanuel Franco of the NYPD. I'm sure he'd be interested in what you have to say, because it is surely pertinent to Anya's case."

"How did you find out about the suit?"

"Barbara Baum told me. But don't fault the woman, I forced it out of her."

Van Loon stared over his bifocals. "So you forced the truth out of Babka." The disdain in his eyes changed to respect. He dipped his head. "I'm impressed. What do you want to know?"

"Who is Anya suing?"

"Two days ago I never would have told you. But I've heard from the man's lawyers. He plans to go to trial so it will all be public soon anyway."

"His name, please?"

"Stuart Packer of Price and Packer, LLC. He's one of the top hedge fund managers out there, I'm told. In some circles he's known as the Wall Street Wolf. The reference is valid to his business and personal life."

"He's a lothario?"

"I plan to use his reputation against him in a civil court. That, and the evidence we have, will surely win the day."

"What kind of evidence? An eyewitness?"

"Physical evidence, Ms. Cosi. Let's leave it at that."

"So where is this Wolf's lair?"

"Packer has business interests all over the world, but most of his time is spent commuting between New York and Moscow."

Van Loon removed his bifocals. "The man is in town now. He's invited to tonight's opening of that Brothers Grimm exhibit."

"At MoMA? How did you know?"

"As a member of the Fairy Tale Fall Committee, I had a hand in moderating the guest list. Mr. Packer is a very generous donor to the Museum of Modern Art."

In the tensions of the past few days, I'd completely forgotten about the black-tie grand opening. I'd received an invitation but decided not to go. Now I changed my mind.

Here was my chance to confront this "Wolf" man who'd assaulted Anya and had the gall to challenge her in civil court.

I'd be going in unarmed and without backup. Even

worse, I had no leverage and no angle. No way to intimidate the man.

How would Wilson do it? I wondered. *A kidnapping? A seduction? Some sort of* Mission Impossible*–style ruse?*

Then it hit me.

How about all three?

Eighty-Five

In a Midtown Manhattan building not much different than the office skyscrapers around it, the Museum of Modern Art housed the most comprehensive collection of modern and contemporary art in the world.

Architecture and design, painting and sculpture, photography and film, even prints and illustrated books were represented. Tonight *The Brothers Grimm: Art of the Fairy Tale* exhibition was celebrating its grand opening.

For "Madame Tesla" and her motley entourage, *performance art* was the order of the day. Our little group planned a private theatrical presentation meant for an audience of only one.

The stakes were incredibly high. What happened here tonight could decide Matt's fate, and my own future as well.

Arriving by limo, a gypsy-robed Madame (with me clad in somber black) met up with the other members of our "infiltration team"—a trio of costumed characters out of *Red Riding Hood* who'd spent the past hour entertaining partygoers waiting for admission.

"The Woodsman" (Eldar, the Bosnian car service driver) sported a fake beard and lumberjack gear. He was tasked with carving tiny animals out of perfumed soap and handing them out to the ladies.

"Red Riding Hood" (Nancy, my youngest barista) tossed gourmet cookies and other treats from her picnic basket.

And "The Wolf" (Boris, the Russian baker) delivered fairy-tale-inspired raps at a rapid-fire pace through an elaborate fur mask with snapping jaws and animated eyes.

Among the invited guests were patrons of the arts, critics, celebrities, and the press. When the museum doors finally opened, Red, her Woodsman, and the Wolf joined the high-toned crowd filing into the gleaming lobby.

The loan of the Basquiat work, *Dreadlocks and the Three Bears*, from our coffeehouse collection, had gotten me an official invitation to tonight's bash.

Madame had scored one, too, as a member of the Fairy Tale Fall Committee. In her guise tonight as "Madame Tesla, Mistress of Palmistry," my employer was ready to fast-talk the guards into believing the costumed trio out front was her entourage.

Luckily, she didn't have to.

Years ago, Gus, that poor Greek immigrant who became the Papaya King, had placed hula girls in front of his tropical juice stand to hand out samples. The ploy had saved his business—and it appeared to save ours.

The guards assumed Red, Wolf, and the Woodsman were part of the entertainment and waved them right through.

"We're in," I said, expelling a breath—and silently thanking those two immigrant restaurateurs, Gus and his frankfurter-loving Birdie.

Now we need a base of operations.

Fortunately, I'd catered at this venue many times, and was familiar with the back halls and hidden rooms. We were now headed to a small storeroom a few doors down from the party area. There was a combination lock under the doorknob, but I remembered the code from my last visit.

As we raced through the museum, Madame's eyes were bright with excitement. "I haven't had this much fun since I smuggled coffee into Matteo's seventh grade summer camp!"

Nancy was aghast. "You allowed Matt . . . I mean, Mr. Boss, to drink coffee in the seventh grade?"

"Of course," Madame replied. "What could I do? The poor boy needed some respite from the camp's constant diet of orange juice and chocolate milk."

"Please," Boris groaned, voice muffled by the Wolf mask. "I must escape fur suit before I perish!"

"It's around the next corner," I said, praying the staff hadn't changed the code. "Then you can shed your old costumes and put on your new ones."

"But I really like this cape," Nancy whined.

"Sorry," I said, "but the hood's got to go. The Wolf we're hunting needs another kind of bait."

I addressed my other coconspirator. "How are you holding up, Eldar?"

"I feel silly." He tugged the suspenders on his neo-pioneer denim overalls.

"You shouldn't," Nancy said, patting his shoulder. "You're a lumberjack, but you're okay."

"I know that joke!" Eldar exclaimed. "Montgomery Python, right?"

We hurried past a marquee listing the fairy-tale movie screenings.

Madame pointed. "Look, they're playing Jean Cocteau's *Beauty and the Beast*." She sighed. "I've loved that film since I was a girl."

"You can love it *later*. Now come on!"

I located the door and punched in the code. The lock clicked and we were in. The space was crammed with stacked boxes and supplies. Elbow room was limited, but there was a mirror and a sink.

And it's probably more space than poor Matt has in his jail cell.

"Let's get to work."

With a relieved grunt, Boris tugged the gigantic mask off his head.

"Careful with that prop," I cautioned. "Tuck needs it back for a Saturday matinee."

Boris fished around inside the mask until he found Franco's transmitter. While he stripped off his fur suit and washed the sweat from his brow, I fitted Madame with the Spy Shop earrings.

"They're positively ghastly," she complained.

"With those gypsy robes and veil, who's going to notice? Here, I'll show you how they work."

Meanwhile Nancy dumped a leather jacket, two black phone cords, and a collection of high-priced war paint from Grandma's basket of goodies. Cosmetics in hand, she went to the mirror and began to unravel her blond braids.

Eldar lost the overalls and flannel shirt, to reveal a form-fitting (and hopefully intimidating) black tee and matching chinos. He slipped the black leather jacket over his shoulders, finally remembering to tug off his fake lumberjack beard.

"Now we trap this wolf," he said.

Clad in black, sans the comical bowler, Eldar looked fairly intimidating. And his determination to catch Red's killer only added to his credibility.

"Ready, boss lady," Boris declared, looking equally scary in a black commando sweater with leather patches and tight black denims.

I sized them both up. "One more thing."

I stuck a phone cord in Eldar's ear, tucking the other end into his jacket. I did the same for Boris, running the wire down the back of his sweater.

"Now you both look like you're wired."

"Okay, I think I'm ready," Nancy said in a trembling voice.

The girl's makeup had been applied perfectly. Tasteful, obviously expensive, and just on the edge of tarty. Tucker had schooled her well.

"Take off the hood," I insisted.

A blushing Nancy let the long cloak slip to the floor, to reveal my Fen gown, now tailored to fit curves I never knew the girl possessed.

"Hubba, hubba," Eldar said with a wink.

"Little Nancy is all grown up," Boris declared.

"Oh, to be so young again," Madame said wistfully.

Satisfied the cast was ready, I pulled the smartphone from my purse and called up my intelligence on our prey, beginning with a recent photograph.

"Remember this face," I said. "Our target is the CEO of hedge fund Parker and Price, LLC. His name is Stuart Packer, but he's known in the trade as the big, bad Wall Street Wolf."

Eighty-six

The Brothers Grimm gala was an hour old and I was starting to panic. I'd circled the exhibition space twice, hovered around the splendid buffet, and even scouted the screening room. But I could not find hide nor hair of the Wolf.

Has he chosen to remain in his lair tonight? Bad news if he has . . .

The uncertainty was galling, but it gave Madame Tesla time to move through the crowd, establish her cover by reading the palms of manicured ladies, well-heeled celebrities, high-toned literati—even a grinning Mayor Stanton.

I ended my second circuit at a section devoted to Taschen's illustrated volume of *The Brothers Grimm.* Many original works reproduced in the book were displayed, including nineteenth-century German illustrations by Gustav Sus, and Arthur Rackham's *The Brave Little Tailor Meets the Giant.*

I was proud to see the Village Blend's mixed media Basquiat given a place of honor among illustrations by Haitian artists Edouard Duval-Carrié and Frankétienne.

Finally, I went back to the buffet table. For tonight's showcase event, dishes were contributed by a few notable chefs from around the city, and they all had fun with the fairy-tale theme.

Del Posto provided splendid little squares of their famous

hundred-layer lasagna—originally inspired by the bedding in *The Princess and the Pea.*

Fat Witch Bakery contributed delicious brownies with your choice of Snow Witch (white chocolate) or Red Witch (cherry). And my pastry chef friend Janelle had baked up trays of her special Fairy Bread Cookies, inspired by the classic "fairy bread," a staple of Australian children's parties.

Nancy took pity on Eldar and Boris stuck in the storeroom, and sweet-talked an entire "Poisoned-Apple" Sharlotka from a server.

Ever the good egg, she delivered it on a tray with silver, dishes, a big carving knife, cups, and a pot of tea.

As a baker, Boris skeptically sampled this so-called "poisoned" version of a classic Russian apple cake. With one bite, he determined the "poison" was cinnamon schnapps, and he suspected apple vodka was used in the crumb, as well.

"Not traditional," he said, "but I approve!"

Back at the party, I enjoyed a second helping of Three Little Pigs (I could have huffed and puffed and inhaled a whole tray of those prosciutto-wrapped mini franks in bourbon-bacon-laced pastry), when Nancy appeared.

"The Wolf is here," she whispered.

I turned and there he was.

Taller than his photo suggested, Stuart Packer wore evening clothes worth more than I earned per annum. With a square jaw and blond business pompadour, the Wolf was conventionally handsome. But the hungry green eyes from his photos were now unfocused, probably due to the pair of cocktails he'd inhaled while chatting with another businessman.

There was a third man in the mix. A tall, dark-haired bodyguard silently hovered behind Packer's shoulder. He seemed familiar somehow, but I could not place him.

"It's show time. Tell Madame to activate her earrings."

"Roger," Nancy replied.

I took another glance at the Wolf. He snagged a third cocktail from a passing waiter, ignoring a lovely woman who stood close, clearly interested.

I panicked. *Is this going to work?*

"Look, Nancy. I feel like a hypocrite after the things I thought about the 'agents of sexpionage,' but I'm relying on your beauty and charm to get Madame close to the Wolf."

Nancy glanced nervously over her shoulder then nodded. "I can do it."

I hurried back to the storeroom and my transmitter, while Nancy alerted Madame.

The stage was set, the curtain about to rise. But would there be a happy ending?

Eighty-seven

"Can you hear me, Madame?"

"Loud and clear, my dear."

"What's happening?"

"Nancy and I are circling our mark, and—oh, excellent."

"What?"

"Mr. Packer took one look at our bait and his jaw dropped. In fact, I do believe the Wolf is slavering."

I was in the storeroom, headset in place, smartphone primed with my intelligence on Stuart Packer.

At my elbow, a carving knife lay beside a half-eaten Poisoned Apple Sharlotka. The cake was forgotten as Boris and Eldar eavesdropped on our transmission.

"I hope Nancy can pull this off. She's so sweet and naïve—"

"Anya was innocent, too," Madame reminded me. "Nancy's naiveté may be her appeal—that, and her daring *décolletage!*"

Suddenly I heard another voice. The Wolf, speaking to his friend.

"You remember my ex, don't you, Phil? Well, the best thing I can say about that marriage is she had the same initials as me—and the Standard and Poor's index—which means I didn't have to change monograms on the luggage and towels."

Gruff laughter was interrupted by Nancy's sweet voice, speaking in a sexy Southern drawl I'd never heard her use.

"Excuse my rudeness, Mr. Packer. Madame Tesla would like to read that cute palm of yours. We're both quite interested in your future," she added coyly—and no doubt with a toss of her flowing wheat-colored hair.

Taking the bail, the Wolf quickly dismissed his pal.

"Sure, honey child. Anything you say."

"Why, thank you, kind sir."

"Your hand, please," Madame commanded.

"No, the right hand," I heard Nancy purr. "Here . . . Let *me* help."

"What does the future hold?" Madame asked after a beat.

The Wolf replied, but his words were directed at Nancy. "Here's hoping you're a big part of my immediate future, honey child."

He loudly drained another cocktail glass.

"Oh, Mr. Packer, you are so funny."

"Mr. Packer is my daddy's name, darlin'. Call me Stuart."

More like "stewed," I thought. The Wolf was loud and his words were slurred—he'd been drinking constantly, and he probably started to party before actually arriving at the party.

A lucky break. If his little gray cells are pickled, he'll be easier to spook.

"I see a journey, Mr. Packer," Madame continued. "To a foreign capital. Ah, yes, it's Moscow. And you're leaving within the week."

"How did you know?"

An article in Forbes Business News, I silently answered. *Reporting you're a guest speaker at an international investment seminar next week.*

"But I sense danger," Madame Tesla continued ominously.

"Let me guess. A plane crash or something?"

"I see no crash in Aeroflot's future—"

"Lufthansa!" I corrected. "He flies Lufthansa!"

"Nor will a Lufthansa airplane crash," Madame amended. "Accidental death is not the threat, Mr. Packer. You have moved millions of dollars out of Europe and deposited the money in the Bank of Moscow—"

"You can't know that!"

I glanced at the smartphone. *Why not, Packer? I'm looking at a* Financial Times *article about the transfer, with a photo of you and the bank's president.*

"Madame Tesla is very good," Nancy cooed. "And she has one more message from the spirit world."

"I don't know if I want to hear it."

The Wolf was suspicious, and the alcohol was making him belligerent. Fortunately, Madame's years of experience with bad customers proved invaluable.

"The message is this," she said in a calm and even tone. "Accompany this young woman to a private meeting across the hall, or those assets will vanish."

"What the hell—"

"Overnight," Madame interrupted with a snap of her fingers.

"Nobody can do that," the Wolf declared. "I'm not going anywhere."

Did we overplay our hand? Too late to stop now. In for a kopeck, in for a ruble, I say.

"Deliver the coup de grâce, Madame," I commanded.

"Listen closely, Mr. Packer," Madame said. "You can talk to my colleagues now. Or you can hurry to Moscow to retrieve your lost assets. There you will be met by less reasonable men, who will put a bag over your head, shoot you in the heart, and leave your corpse in Sheremetyevo International Airport's parking lot."

It was quiet for so long I worried that the earring batteries had died. Finally, Madame spoke again.

"It is only a conversation, Mr. Packer. You can bring your bodyguard there if it makes you feel safe."

I didn't need visuals to sense the Wolf was wavering.

In the end, it was sheer curiosity—and young Nancy—who swayed him.

"Maybe we can clear up this silly old mess without resorting to extortion, or violence," she said in a breathy tone.

"How about it, Stuart? Let's go for a walk."

EIGHTY-EIGHT

THROUGH the crack in the door, I spied Nancy and the Wolf approaching, arm in arm. Nancy continued her charm offensive, but the increasingly wary Wolf was no longer buying it. The creepily familiar bodyguard loped sullenly and silently behind them.

I closed the door but left it unlocked. "Everyone take your places."

Eldar flattened himself against the wall, so when the door opened, he would be hidden behind it.

Boris stood beside me, the transmitter in plain sight between us. I no longer needed the device to communicate, but it was a useful prop to convince the Wolf of my "credentials."

I held my breath until the door opened and Nancy and the Wolf stepped inside, the bodyguard sticking like glue to his charge.

As soon as they were through the door, Eldar slammed it.

Wolf and bodyguard whirled, saw Eldar's intimidating stare, and faced me again. "What the hell is—"

"I do the talking here, Comrade Packer," I said, channeling Boris's heavy Russian accent.

"Who are you people?"

"I am Magda," I replied. "Man beside me is Boris. Man behind you Eldar. Now we have been introduced—"

The Wolf was flushed under a sheen of alcohol perspiration, but he was so scared he was no longer slurring his words. "Look, I don't mean names—"

"Sluzhba Vneshney Razvedki," Boris snarled.

The Wolf didn't react, but his bodyguard sure did. The man hadn't taken a drink all evening, but suddenly he was flop-sweating rivers, just like his boss.

"American rudeness is renowned," I continued. "To answer your rude question, we are from the Foreign Intelligence Service, Comrade Packer."

"The SVR?" The Wolf pointed at Nancy. "But you can't be Russian spies. This sweet young thing has a Southern accent."

"Because she went to school in your Georgia," I replied. "But was born in ours—*Republic of* Georgia."

Now the bodyguard spoke up, his tone challenging. *"Я не верю вам!"*

Boris stepped forward. *"Вы поверите мне, когда я разбить череп!"*

Whatever he said worked. The bodyguard blanched.

Wolf saw his man's fearful reaction and was suddenly in a mood to cooperate—

"Okay, okay, I believe you. What do you want with me?"

"I wish to know why you murdered one of my sexpionage agents, and put another in coma."

Wolf's knees got weak and he wavered. "You've got to be kidding! Are you talking about Anya Krevchenko?"

"And Rozalina Krasny."

"I never heard of this Krasny chick, but Anya . . ." He frowned. "I know her."

"She is suing you," I said. "For your vicious assault on her person."

"She was . . . *is* suing me, it's true. But it's extortion. I spoke with the girl for *ten minutes*, and I sure didn't assault her. If I were guilty, I wouldn't be pushing for a court date."

"You want trial?"

"Sure, if that's what it takes to clear my name."

My expression was doubtful.

"Look, if I wanted Anya out of the way, I would have

killed her," the Wolf insisted. "Girl dead, the lawsuit goes away. Alive, justice marches on, with my legal team and that bastard Van Loon getting rich off *my* misery."

"Perhaps this is misunderstanding?" I offered. "You made unwanted pass. She took it too hard."

The Wolf shook his head. "Van Loon claimed he had proof, the kind of evidence a certain White House intern had on the former President. I knew that was bull, so I let Van Loon's docs take my DNA."

His frown deepened. "They came back claiming the test proved my guilt. Now we'll see—in court."

Stuart Packer was as convinced of his innocence as he was convincing. If he was lying now, then he had to be a stone-cold sociopath with no fear of death.

Not so his bodyguard. The man had been glancing over his shoulder at Eldar, as if he expected an ice pick to plunge into the back of his neck at any moment.

When he turned this time, I got a good look at that neck—and the crescent-shaped scar that marked him!

"It's you!" I cried, dropping my accent. "You are the phony nurse who slapped Anya in the hospital. You got away because your partner took a shot at me and my boyfriend!"

With the desperate cry of a trapped animal, the bodyguard pushed his boss aside and snatched the carving knife from the Sharlotka tray. Before I could react, he wrapped a powerful arm around my throat, and held the blade aloft.

"I'll kill her!" he threatened.

Oh, no, you won't!

Channeling my inner She-Wolf, I bit down on his arm, *hard*. The man howled, releasing me enough to lunge away. That was when Eldar and Boris both jumped him. Suddenly the blade flashed, and Boris cried out.

I saw blood! Boris was badly hurt, yet still clutching at the man as Eldar struggled to hold him. I whipped around for a weapon, saw the heavy Sharlotka serving tray and dumped its contents.

As cups bounced and shattered, and the Sharlotka splattered on the floor tiles, I swung the metal disc, striking the bodyguard's head once, twice.

He was probably down for the count after two, but you can never be too careful so I whacked him again.

The Wolf, paralyzed during this entire struggle, turned with a girlish scream and ran through the door. Blond pompadour flying, he raced toward the party shouting at the top of his lungs—

"Help! Help! Russian spies are trying to kill me!"

I dropped to my knees and tried to stem the bleeding from Boris's wound. He looked up at me, eyes bright with pain.

"I'll find a doctor!" Nancy cried, racing to the party.

"I will call 911!" Eldar declared.

I pressed my hand against the wound in Boris's abdomen, but warm blood continued to seep between my fingers. Suddenly the young baker gripped my arm.

"Tell my czarina my last thoughts were of her."

Then he closed his eyes.

Eighty-nine

When I phoned Esther with the bad news, she screamed again. But this time she didn't bury her head under a pillow. Instead, she raced to the hospital to join the rest of us, crashing through the doors of the Intensive Care Unit, demanding to see "her Boris."

Eldar, Nancy, Madame, and I waited until Boris was out of danger. But when we spoke with the docs and it was time to go, Esther remained behind, waiting for her man to open his eyes.

I knew that simply seeing his "czarina" would be the best medicine for Boris, and (thank goodness) Esther's ferocious vigil was a good sign for the future of their relationship.

The clock was close to striking twelve when I finally trudged into the Village Blend. I found Franco waiting at the espresso bar. He stood to greet me—

"I heard about your rough night, and I have news."

"About Matt?"

"That, too . . ."

I pulled us fresh espressos and we took over a quiet corner table.

"Listen to this," he began. "I talked to the team who collared Packer's bodyguard. Turns out the guy was more afraid of 'Russian spies' than he was of the arresting officers. He confessed because he thought exposing foreign agents would get him pardoned."

"What did he confess to exactly?"

Franco frowned. "Not Red's murder, or Anya's drugging. He and his boss were both way out on Long Island, in the Hamptons. Ironclad alibis. Someone, probably an accomplice, tipped them about Anya landing in the hospital with what looked like a drug overdose. The bodyguard took a helicopter to Manhattan, arriving in time to pull that gender switcheroo at the hospital.

"The bodyguard also admitted to phoning Anya a few days before—and that morning. He spoke to her in Russian, trying to convince her that if she didn't drop the lawsuit against the Wall Street Wolf—who has important financial connections in Russia—her mother would be killed in prison. It was a fake threat. He said he was only trying to shake her up, get her to drop the lawsuit."

"And who's the Cuckoo nurse's accomplice?" I asked. "The fat guy who fired the gun?"

"The bodyguard is mum about that, even with a weapons charge hanging over his head."

The news was so depressing I changed the subject.

"How's Matt holding up?"

"He's still being interrogated. Plesky and Endicott are pulling an all-nighter and tag-teaming him."

"Not you?"

"They figured out I was working my own angle at Dwayne Galloway's Meat-dieval Tournament and Feast. Endicott is keeping me at arm's length now."

"How long can they hold Matt?"

"The full twenty-four hours, if Mr. DNA has his way. Or they can charge him with a crime and keep him longer. Endicott is hoping for a confession because the evidence is circumstantial."

Franco shook his head. "He and Plesky are so off the mark it's scary."

"What do you mean?"

"They're hoping Matt's hooked on this mystery drug, and if they keep him away from it long enough, he'll break down in a cold-turkey sweat and confess to his crimes to get a fix."

"Fat chance."

"No chance at all." Franco grunted. "I suggested they keep bringing Matt coffee so he'll stay alert. Endicott and Plesky are delivering cups every hour. Your ex-husband's complaining about the 'crappie cop swill,' but he's drinking it."

"Thank you, Franco!" I hugged him, smiling for the first time that evening. "As long as he gets his caffeine fix, Matt will be okay."

"I think so," he said. "We may get out of the woods yet."

"You two look chipper," a familiar voice proclaimed. "What am I missing?"

Wilson approached us, a big grin on his face. Without an invitation he pulled out a chair and sat down.

I'd promised Mike that the next time Wilson showed up, I'd let Franco deal with him.

Okay, Franco was here, and that would have to do—because I was angry and frustrated enough to "deal" with Wilson myself.

Ninety

"Listen, Mr. Government Agent, my business partner is in jail and possibly facing a murder rap. You can fix this. You need to tell the police that Red's murder is connected to a cold case from the nineties, that there is no way Matt could be involved."

Wilson scratched his chin. "Well—"

"No! Don't even try it! No hemming. No hawing. Start with Franco. Tell him what you told me."

Franco narrowed his gaze. "Who is this guy exactly, and what is he supposed to tell me?"

After a quick introduction, Wilson did as I asked. Then he explained to us why going to Endicott with this information wouldn't do us any good.

"It's only a theory. I can't prove a thing. That's why I came to you, Clare. In a few short days you've uncovered more leads than I could."

"But I'm at a dead end!"

"For now. You're also close to the principal players, closer than me, and in one case, practically a part of the family."

Part of the family? I stared at him. "You're talking about Leila, aren't you? You actually consider Mike's ex-wife a suspect in a CIA agent's murder?"

"She came to the city at seventeen as a young model. She fits the profile, and Anya Krevchenko was working for her at the time she was drugged. I can see how much this distresses you, Clare, but you have to consider every possibility. The clock is ticking."

"Clock? What clock?"

"The police are likely to release Matteo Allegro in the morning. If that happens, he'll be dead within the week."

"What?!" Franco and I cried in unison.

"That's what I came here tonight to tell you, Clare. I wasn't completely honest with you."

"Is that so?"

Wilson nodded. "Back in the nineteen nineties, when that KGB coup failed in Moscow, Petrov—also known as Vasily Petrovus—was called back to the Soviet Union."

"You told me that."

"What I didn't tell you was that he never arrived. Petrov ignored his superiors. He was preparing to flee the USA, but not for Mother Russia. He'd established a new identity for himself in Quebec. He even had a young wife and a son resettled there. And he never got to them."

"What happened?"

"Petrov was shot through the head inside his apartment. On his corpse they found a vial of the drug used to kill my agent—and my love—Faith. The murder weapon was traced back to Cuba, so the CIA concluded Vasily Petrovus was murdered by the KGB to prevent him from defecting, or as punishment for his part in the August Coup."

Franco's eyes widened. "But you don't buy that?"

"Clare knows my theory, Sergeant. I believe one of Petrov's agents killed him and framed him for Faith's murder. If I had to guess, I would say this agent felt betrayed by Petrov, and was exacting revenge on him for being abandoned."

Wilson leaned across the table.

"I also believe the pattern is about to be repeated. Once again, this clever killer will set up someone to take the fall. That someone is Matteo Allegro. Whether Allegro is released for lack of evidence or makes bail before a trial, he'll be murdered and the drug will be discovered in his possession. And just like Petrov, it will be case closed."

I felt weak. “We have to do something.”

Wilson smiled. “Good to hear you say that because I have an idea. Why not use Matt as bait?”

“What!” I cried, horrified. “No! Absolutely not. Better he gets out of town.”

“I doubt the police will allow him to leave town. They’re probably going to seize his passport. And this killer can wait weeks. Months. They’ve already waited decades.”

Franco nodded. “He’s right. Matt will never be safe.”

“What if he stays in jail?” I said.

“What?” Franco and Wilson both replied.

I turned to Franco. “You have to press charges. Matt hit you when you were cuffing him, right? That’s assaulting an officer. Charge him.”

Franco stared at me in horror. “He’ll hate me forever. Joy will be crushed!”

“But you’ll save his life.”

“There’s no guarantee of that.”

“If your charge keeps Matt in jail another day, maybe two, we can track down the real killer and keep Matt from being set up and murdered.”

Franco covered his eyes. “Oh, man. I’m sick about this.”

Now Wilson spoke up. “Clare, listen to me. This won’t stop the clock.”

“No,” I said, “but it will slow it down, give us a little more time to find the killer. We *need* it.”

“I’m going.” Franco rose. “Sleep on this, okay? If you feel the same way in the morning, call me. I’ll press charges.”

When Franco was gone, Wilson regarded me.

“What is it?”

“Something that I think I should tell you. It’s not about the case, and you may not want to hear it.”

“Of course I want to hear it. What do you know?”

“Have you spoken with that man of yours?”

“Mike? No, he’s flying to LA tonight for a meeting tomorrow.”

Wilson rose and touched my shoulder. “I have a little free advice. The next time he speaks with you about moving down to Washington, listen a little harder, okay? Listen to what he's saying, between the lines."

"What is that supposed to mean?"

"Men like Mike Quinn don't often admit to needing personal backup. But from what I've seen, you can handle it."

"Handle what?"

Wilson didn't tell me. "I'm sure we'll talk again, Clare. Good night."

And just like that, he was gone.

Ninety-one

An hour later, I was upstairs, sitting at my kitchen table, Frothy and Java circling my legs. While I absently stroked their fur, I stared at the shiny green bag containing Matt's magic beans.

If I drink the coffee again, will there be answers in my visions? Could I finally solve the case?

Wilson's cryptic words about Quinn were disturbing, to say the least, and I was desperate to know more. But tonight, the clock was ticking down for *Matt*, and none of us could be certain about who the real killer was.

Matt's Lake Tana coffee beans might give me a clue, but I absolutely loathed the idea of drinking them again. I had no control over the mind trips it gave me. And the last time I chugged it, I'd blacked out. Matt even warned me not to take it again—not on my own.

But I was alone now. And he was in some awful interrogation room with his life in danger. The least I could do was have a bad dream.

After mulling over my options, I rose and headed for the bedroom. I'd left a business card on my dresser, something Matt had given me.

Though it was close to two in the morning, I gave the man a call. Miraculously, he answered.

"Hello?"

"Good evening, Dr. Pepper, this is Clare Cosi. I'm in the coffee business with Matteo Allegro—"

"You are the Coffee Lady!" He sounded ecstatic. "You are the one with the visions from the Lake Tana beans?"

"Yes. I guess Matt told you about me?"

"Of course! And I am very pleased you called. Very pleased."

"Dr. Pepper, I would like to drink the coffee again, but not without supervision."

"Oh, my goodness! How exciting! This is perfect timing, Ms. Cosi. Perfect! I'm in my lab now. Columbia University. Come right up, and we'll get started."

Ninety-two

"ARE you comfortable?" Dr. Pepper asked.

"The bed's nice. I can't say the same for the sensors glued to my head."

"I am sorry, but we must monitor your brain functions . . ."

When I arrived at Columbia University's Sleep Studies Lab, I found an energetic, mocha-skinned man in a white lab coat, presiding over a dimly lit ward where undergrads were earning credits for continuous sleeping (something I recalled plenty of my college classmates doing without the benefit of extra credit).

After interviewing me, Dr. Pepper had two grad-level students take my vital signs, swab my mouth, and draw blood. Then I drank three cups of Matt's Lake Tana coffee, and the doctor wired me in.

"A contrast MRI would be more effective," Dr. Pepper explained, "but that is a more complex procedure that we do not have time for this evening. Please bear with me, Ms. Cosi . . ."

"If you're going to track every neuron in my head, you should call me Clare."

"And my real name is Swapnil Padmanabhan."

"Since I'm already feeling a little loopy, Doc, I hope you don't mind if I stick with the soft drink mnemonic."

Dr. Pepper smiled. "Are you having trouble relaxing?" He glanced at the polysomnography monitors. "Your heart and respiration rate indicate that you are nervous."

There's an understatement. "The last thing I wanted to do was drink Matt's crazy coffee again."

"Trust me," the doc insisted. "I will not let any harm come to you."

"Maybe if you tell me a story, I'll be able relax."

"Shall I begin with 'Once upon a time'?"

"Just tell me what you've learned about the coffee. Can you explain why it has such a strange effect on me?"

"Easily! You know coffee beans contain hundreds of chemicals?"

"I'm a master roaster, so I'd better know that. I also know the composition depends on the type of bean and how it's roasted."

"The Lake Tana cherries possess chemical substances that are similar to caffeine but much more potent, and these substances act as a powerful, natural nootropic."

"Nootropic?"

"A broad term for a substance that improves brain function. You may have heard of 'smart drugs' like memory and intelligence enhancers?"

"But this is coffee, not a drug."

"Nootropic substances can also be found in plants and foods."

"So what does this coffee do? Enhance memory or intelligence?"

"Both and more. Interestingly, your own genetics and biochemistry are as important as the nootropic substance in creating the reaction you are experiencing. For one thing, Clare, you have built up a very high tolerance for caffeine—"

"It goes with my job."

"This resistance to the stimulant in the beverage allows your unconscious mind to function even while the conscious mind sleeps. Consequently, you reach a state of lucid dreaming."

"Doc, *lucid* means awake. You're saying I'm not sleeping when I have these visions?"

"Technically, no. You said you were *conscious* when you saw the vision of the woman on the sidewalk—and again in your bedroom when you saw yourself in the painting, correct?"

"Yes, both times." I studied the doctor's kind face. "Have you known others like me? People who've experienced visions?"

"Oh, yes." He nodded emphatically. "My grandmother. She drank a special tea from Ceylon, and her visions made her a guru of sorts, as people from the village and the towns around our home sought her wisdom. She did much good, though the *karabasan* proved trying for her."

"Karabasan?"

"A Turkish word to describe a common phenomenon of lucid dreams. In your visions, Clare, have you seen a dark, frightening figure, the face invisible or obscured in some manner?"

I tensed, thinking of that dark, hooded figure I continually saw. "You're not saying everyone who has lucid dreams sees something like that?"

"The dark figure is universal. It can be male or female. In American folklore, it is called the Boogeyman. The Japanese refer to it as the *Kanashibari* demon. In Newfoundland, she is the Old Hag. In the West Indies, it is *Kokma*, a baby ghost who jumps on sleepers' chests to strangle them; and in ancient England, they called the phenomenon *witch riding* because they believed witches descended upon the helpless sleepers—oh, my, Clare, your heart rate is increasing again. Do calm yourself."

"I will if you explain what this dark figure is."

"Darkness is a part of nature, and our human nature. Darkness transcends nations and races, even time. Though the particulars of the dark one may change, the archetype is universal; consequently, so is its projection by the subconscious mind. Of course, the superstitious believe it is . . . something else."

"The 'something else' part is what worries me."

"Do not worry. Trust your mind," the doctor counseled.

"When there is no clutter of consciousness, no ego to get in the way, your subconscious is liberated to make intuitive leaps and associations that your conscious mind would be unlikely or slow to make."

"Now you sound like one of my baristas talking about artistic inspiration."

"A sound comparison—for in a lucid dream, you lose your sense of time, as artists do in their creative states. And your brain is performing faster than normal, resulting in total recall of stored memories, bits and pieces that might otherwise be filed as 'unimportant' by your conscious mind . . ."

As Dr. Pepper continued to speak, I closed my eyes, trying to will myself to sleep. Time passed, but Morpheus was a no-show.

"It's not working, Doc. I'm sorry. Maybe I need more coffee . . ."

I opened my eyes.

I was still in bed, but the lab was gone, along with its walls. Twisted trees rose up around me. Above me, a canopy of dark leaves swayed on restless gusts of wind.

I pulled off the sensors and threw back my covers. As I climbed out of bed, I saw something glowing in the brush—a pair of predatory eyes, red as blood.

Then a wolf's slathering jaws burst through the bushes, and I took off!

Ninety-three

I raced through the forest. Sharp stones cut my bare feet. Clawing branches tore my thin nightgown. With the predator behind me, I didn't dare slow my pace—until I saw a distant light.

"This way, Clare!"

Dr. Pepper?

I jogged into a small clearing. In the center of the manicured grass sat James Elliot's orange sandwich wagon with an inflatable Cheshire Cat grinning on the roof. Inside, Dr. Pepper in an English bowler was flipping portobello mushroom burgers.

But it was Rozalina Krasny who appeared in the wagon window, dressed in a white lab coat.

"Where is prescription?" Red demanded.

"I don't have one," I replied.

She frowned. "What drugs do you need?"

"I don't know."

"Give her this." Dr. Pepper handed over a mushroom burger.

"Eat it!" Red demanded. "Hurry!"

After a few bites, I felt a tingling. "What's happening to me?"

The sandwich wagon seemed to be growing bigger and bigger. So was the burger. It was bigger than Eldar's Bosnian

Frisbee! Then I realized these things weren't growing bigger. I was shrinking!

Dropping the evil mushroom Frisbee, I took off again. But the blades of grass were up to my waist. Dodging a soda can the size of a refrigerator, I tripped and fell down a rodent's hole.

Down, down, I slid, far underground until the tunnel of dirt spat me into an immense cave filled with music. The cave glowed with a beautiful pinkish light, and all around me couples danced under trees of gold, silver, and diamond.

"Where is Annie?" asked Molly Quinn, skipping up to me.

"I'm sorry, Molly, I don't know . . ."

"Annie wants to be a teacher, Aunt Clare. But first she needs money, *lots and lots* of money. Let's go find some for her!"

"Molly, no! Wait! You'll get lost!"

I ran after her, pushing through the dancing bodies, but I couldn't find Mike's daughter!

"Clare, dear, over here!"

Madame? I followed her voice through a key-shaped archway to a room with many tables. It looked like Babka's restaurant, except the tables were filled with storybook characters: The Three Little Pigs were stuffing their faces; Jack and Jill sipped sparkling water; Beauty flirted with a Beast in a suit; and Papa and Mama Bear complained to the waiter about their food being (respectively) too hot and too cold.

"Sit down and have tea with us," Madame directed from a corner table somewhere behind me.

"Yes!" cried Babka Baum. "We were just wagging our chins about you and Matt—and all of his past problems!"

I turned to face them and gasped. Madame and Barbara looked like two giant hens! Clothed in finery with scarves flung around their feathered necks, they continue to buck-buck-buck at each other and the other hens at the large round table. I moved toward the vacant chair.

"No, not *that* seat!" clucked the Babka hen. "That's Samantha's!"

"She can have it," a voice quickly replied. "I'm busy!"

I wheeled to find a harried (*human, thank goodness!*) Samantha Peel in safari jacket and knee-high boots, clipboard in hand, taking down Goldilocks's measurements.

"If you want to fit into the new costume, you better drop a few pounds," she warned the character.

Leila Quinn Reynolds suddenly appeared, looking over Sam's shoulder. "Oh, yes, I agree!"

Then both women turned to me. "We still need our Prince Charmings! Do you know where they are, Clare?"

I shook my head and they began to bicker.

"Ladies, please!" Harrison Van Loon rushed up to them, evening clothes elegant, beard neatly trimmed. "Quiet down. We don't like that sort of thing in this club."

I tapped his shoulder. "You're Anya's lawyer, aren't you?"

"I'm primarily a divorce lawyer. But I also draw up prenuptial agreements."

Leila flipped her scarlet hair and pouted. "My husband made me sign a prenup. It's a joke!"

I confronted Mike's ex-wife and gripped her bony shoulders. "Answer me: How do you know Anya? Did you meet her through this club?"

"Oh, please." She waved her hand. "I only recently rejoined. And Anya was too naïve for this place. She wanted out."

"That's not an answer! *You never answered my question!* How do you know Anya?!"

Leila rolled her eyes. "She thought she'd find her Prince Charming here, but girls from her background don't get princes—"

"FI-FIE-FO-FUM!"

The booming voice echoed from above, shaking the cave. Then a huge arm reached down the rodent hole. Giant fingers closed around my waist. "No! Let me go!"

I felt myself lifted up, up, all the way up to the clouds.

Dressed in his King's robes, Dwayne Galloway laughed, his voice splitting the air like thunder as he dropped me in a golden birdcage hanging in his castle bedroom.

"See you soon," he sang as his steps shook the floor.

When the bedroom fell quiet, I heard a tiny voice.

"Help me!" The beautiful, young Anya, was inside the cage with me, caught in a spider's web. "Free me! Please!"

I spied a letter opener on the desk below, dragged it into the cage, and cut her loose. She fell to the cage floor.

"Thank you!" She hugged me tight. "Thank you so much!"

Using the letter opener like a crowbar, we threw our weight against it and popped open the little locked door. Then we dropped to the desk, raced to the window, and climbed a vine down the castle wall.

"Look!" I pointed. "We can use that beanstalk to get back down to earth."

As fast as we could, we began to climb down.

"FI-FIE-FOE-FUM!"

Above me, the Giant leaped onto the beanstalk. But this time he wore full armor. He was too heavy! The beanstalk swayed and began to fall. I went with it, down, down, and then—

SPLASH!

I landed in a black cauldron. My clothes were gone, and the water was starting to boil! I scrambled naked over the side, horrified to find a blond male wolf standing upright in a tailored business suit, watching me.

The wolf held up a *Standard and Poor's* newsletter and it instantly changed into a plush bath sheet. The towel displayed the embroidered letters *S&P*.

"Since my divorce, I didn't have to change the monogram," the beast told me with a wink. Then he licked his slobbering maw and wrapped me in the towel. "The better to dry you off with . . ."

"Get away from her!" Matt shouted.

I looked up to find my ex-husband dressed in his Prince Charming getup, charging the wolf with his plastic sword. The animal turned into a man, Stuart Packer. He frantically looked for his bodyguard, then ran away screaming like a little girl.

"We did it!" Matt cried and we hugged.

Suddenly, he went limp in my arms. "Matt?"

He fell to the ground, blood pouring from an evil wound in his back, and I saw the dark hooded figure standing there.

As I peered into the blackness that should have been its face, the figure lifted its arm and showed me the bloodied knife, angling its blade one way then the other in a kind of pride.

"NO!" I shouted, launching myself at the figure. I wanted to tear its evil hood off, expose it for what it was. "I know who you are! I know!"

I blinked.

Dr. Pepper was standing over me in his white lab coat, looking concerned. From flat on my back, I recognized the Sleep Studies Lab at Columbia.

"How do you feel, Clare? Did you get your answers?"

My body was tingling, my mind still racing.

"Almost . . ."

Ninety-Four

After splashing water on my face and grabbing a bottle of orange juice from the lab fridge, I asked to borrow Dr. Pepper's office. There I looked up a single fact on the Internet. It confirmed my theory, and I called Mike Quinn.

He answered on the third ring. (I'd forgotten he was in Los Angeles, where it was two in the morning.) "Hey, sweetheart, is something wrong? Isn't it too early for you to be opening the shop?"

"This may sound like a crazy line of questioning—"

"From you?" Quinn yawned. "Nah."

"Sarcasm noted. Now please listen. In the last month or so, has Leila asked you what sort of evidence police looked for in a sexual assault case?"

"Yeah . . ." He paused and I heard him moving to sit up. "She asked exactly that question. It was about two months ago. After we brought Molly and Jeremy home from our camping trip."

"What did you tell her?"

"*Physical evidence*. DNA is the trump card. It establishes whatever happened was beyond casual contact."

"You're talking bodily excretions, right?"

"Ideally, yes."

"Now why would Leila grill you about something like that? You told me she couldn't stand hearing about your police work. When you two were married, she asked you not to bring it home—or even talk about it."

"She was vague, claimed she was curious, something she saw in the news." Mike paused. When he spoke again, his tone was wary. "Where are you going with this?"

I took a breath, not sure how he was going to take this development. But when I laid out my theory, he agreed with my conclusions.

"Clare, you have to go to Franco with this. He'll see it to the end"—Mike took a difficult breath—"no matter where it leads . . ."

I knew this wasn't easy for him, but lives were on the line, and we both knew it. We said our good-byes and I rang Sergeant Franco. He didn't answer right away, but at least he was awake. I heard the shower running in the background.

"Yeah?"

"It's Clare. *Do not* press assault charges against Matt!"

Even without the huff and puff, Emmanuel Franco's sigh of relief could have blown a house down. "Understood," he said. "But we still don't know who the killer is."

"Yes. We do . . ." I laid out the facts and told Franco my plan. "We're going to put Wilson's idea in play, but we'll do it right. We'll use Matt as bait with the full backing of the NYPD. If you and Quinn can sell my theory to Endicott's superiors, he'll have to go along."

"He will," Franco assured me. "The ADA is already nervous about the lack of physical evidence. And Endicott and Plesky were so certain that Matt was a drug addict, they practically promised a confession under pressure."

"And?"

"And all they got was an overcaffeinated prime suspect—and a protracted lecture on the proper maintenance of the precinct's coffee machine. Matt's warning about mold got the night guys so rattled they sent out for vinegar."

Ninety-Five

My conversations with Mike and Franco left me feeling hopeful for the first time in days.

After thanking Dr. Pepper, I left the lab and grabbed a cab back to my coffeehouse, where I pulled myself a double espresso (with *non*magical beans, thank you very much), found a chair by the French doors, and watched the predawn sky for signs of sunrise.

Over the next few hours, I dealt with the bakery delivery, opened the shop with Dante, and pulled espressos like a machine through the AM crush. By ten thirty, the October morning was cloudy with a chance of rain.

The sun looked weak and so did I.

"Boss, you okay?" Dante asked. "You seem a little wobbly."

"More than a little," Nancy seconded, tying on her apron. She put a hand on my shoulder. "Go upstairs and take a rest. Dante and I can handle lunch rush."

I smiled as I hung up my apron, grateful for my great staff. As I started for the back staircase, my cell phone vibrated. It was Franco giving me one more thing to be thankful for: Matt would be released from police custody by noon. *Yes!*

Quinn's early morning call to Endicott's lieutenant—laying out my theory and Wilson's involvement—worked magic.

Now Franco, Wilson, and members of Quinn's OD Squad

would put together an operation using a wired-up Matt as bait to entrap our murderer. There would be plenty of safeguards, according to Franco, including officers ready to shoot to kill, if necessary.

"Can I be there?" I pleaded.

"I don't know, Coffee Lady. There's loads of prep work ahead. I'll call you back."

"Okay but *please* keep me informed."

"Will do . . ."

Unfortunately, the higher I moved up the service stairs, the lower my spirits sank. The sting operation sounded like a good idea, but things could still go wrong. Whether I wanted to face it or not, Matt's life remained in jeopardy—and it was me who'd put it there.

When my cell phone vibrated again, thirty minutes later, I thought it was Franco or even Mike Quinn. Instead, it was *Jeremy* Quinn texting me.

> Home sick from school. Found something in Mom's room. Belongs to Anya. It's bad, Aunt Clare. Please come. Come right away!

I read and reread the cell phone screen. *What could he have found?*

The last time Jeremy contacted me, Penny had dug up Anya's golden key. Now he'd found something else, something in Leila's bedroom. But what?

Could it be something that would nail our killer? Something that would save Matt from having to risk his safety, maybe even his life?

With hope, I texted back—

> Coming right now. Don't leave the apartment. And don't tell your mother!

Jeremy's reply was immediate—

> Mom shopping. Will leave front door unlocked. Hurry!

* * *

My body was still bone-tired, my nerves frayed, but I was on the edge of the cab seat all the way uptown.

Thunder cracked open the sky as I raced into Leila's Park Avenue lobby. Shaking off the rain, I greeted the doorman, and hurried into the elevator.

Upstairs, I found the apartment door unlocked, as Jeremy promised. I closed it behind me and moved quietly down the hall. But as I approached the keyhole archway, I froze.

Leila was back.

I heard her voice speaking at length about a pair of shoes she was "lusting after." I waited but no other voices spoke.

Is she on the phone?

With a few more steps, I peered carefully beyond the archway.

As usual, Leila's prized vanity mirror stood on its pedestal, the ornate gold-and-silver frame reflecting part of the fashionably sparse beige room and wall of rain-streaked windows. Inside the mirror's polished glass, I saw Leila's reflection but no one else's.

Moving all the way into the room, I realized my mistake.

Samantha Peel sat in a far corner chair, back to the wall, with an imperious view of the rectangular space. She wasn't dressed for a safari today. The long-legged brunette was clad in a somber black pantsuit, flowing hair in a tight bun, her only jewelry a chunky ring. She looked ready for a funeral, and I feared it was going to be mine.

The socialite's smile seemed inviting, but that warmth did not thaw her icy stare. "Hello, Clare," she said.

Our eyes met and the charade was over.

Not so for clueless Leila. "Clare?" she spat as if the word were a vulgarity. "What in the world are *you* doing here?"

"Where are the children?" I quickly asked.

"Why?" Leila snapped. "Do you want to take them to the park and *lose* them again?"

"Answer me!"

"For heaven's sake, Molly's downstairs visiting a friend. She doesn't have school today, but Jeremy does and that's where he is—"

Which means his mobile phone is right here in this apartment because his school doesn't allow them. And that's how Samantha lured me up here.

"Leila, I need you to come with me," I said. "You have to hurry. Where's Penny?"

"At the dog groomers—" Leila began to rise.

"Sit down. You're not going anywhere. Either of you."

From her corner throne, Samantha Peel had already pulled the gun from her handbag. As lighting flashed across the New York skyline, she pointed the barrel directly at me.

Ninety-six

LEILA laughed at the sight of a gun pointed in my direction. "What are you trying to do, Sam, solve all of my headaches with one bullet?"

"Shut up." Samantha rose and gestured to the sofa. "Sit down, Clare. Beside Leila."

"Sam, really." Leila's hands went to her hips. "Stop joking around."

"Did I not tell you to SHUT UP!"

"But we're friends!" Leila's tone was confused, almost plaintive. "You told me if I hired Anya, you would help me!"

That statement certainly fit in with my theory. But there was one thing I didn't know. "Tell me the truth, Leila, were you in on this, too?"

Mike's ex-wife gawked at me. "In on what?"

"On putting Anya in a coma and framing Matt for it?"

Leila's jaw dropped. "Clare, what are you talking about?! Sam told me Dwayne Galloway slipped Anya a date rape drug. She said the police were protecting him!" Leila turned to Sam. "Right?"

Sam shook her head. "Leila, you are just too stupid to live."

Eyeing the gun, I swallowed my panic and gave reasoning a try. "You can't get away with this, Samantha. The doorman saw me come in."

"Of course he did!" Sam laughed. "That's part of my narrative. You see, Clare, *you* figured out that *Leila* was the killer. You came to confront her. You fought and in the struggle you killed each other."

"Except the doorman saw you come up here, too," I snapped back. "So the police will know you did it!"

"No, they won't, because the doorman didn't see me. What he saw was a blond maid go to another floor, the same maid who established that pattern for the last two weeks. My uniform, wig, and glasses are sitting in the stairwell. I'll be putting them on before I leave through the back service exit. And any physical evidence they find of me in this apartment can be explained quite easily because"—she smirked—"I'm such a *good friend* of Leila's."

Leila stepped toward her. "Stop this! Right now—"

Samantha's hard kick slammed Leila's stomach. With a cry of shock and pain, she doubled over and fell back onto the couch.

"Killing us won't help," I cried, shielding Leila. "The police know."

Sam's eyes narrowed. "And how do they know?"

"Because I know," I assured her. "I know *everything*."

Sam shook her head. "Bluffing won't work, Clare, you don't know shit."

"I know Stuart Packer, the Wall Street Wolf, is your ex-husband—easy enough to discover on the Internet, once I actually looked it up. I know you made a deal with Anya to entrap your ex-husband in a bogus sexual assault lawsuit. I assume, like Leila here, you had a prenuptial agreement that stuck in your craw?"

I turned to Leila. "Isn't that what Samantha promised you? If you hired Anya and made her look like a legit mother's helper, she'd help you run the same kind of sexual assault scam on your rich, soon-to-be ex-husband?"

"Yes." Leila avoided my eyes. "That's why I hired Anya. I wanted to learn from what they were doing. I wanted to do the same thing to Humphrey."

I met Samantha's stare. "But your plan wasn't working,

was it? Not after your ex-husband's bodyguard terrorized Anya. He spoke fluent Russian, which made it all very convincing when he threatened to have her mother killed. So Anya went to you in tears and said she wanted out of the bogus lawsuit."

Sam's eyes flashed with the lightning outside. "Anya was weak and stupid."

"But you couldn't kill her, right? If you killed Anya, the lawsuit would disappear. And I assume you provided her with some kind of incriminating physical evidence?"

"That's right," Sam smugly admitted. "Stuart forgot about a specimen we'd stashed in a fertility center. He stopped paying the bills from the clinic, but I didn't. I bribed a worker to get me his specimen without any paperwork, and then I closed the account to avoid scrutiny. That stupid Russian bitch used all I had!"

"Which is why Anya's backing out was devastating," I went on. "All your hard work and planning would come to nothing, until you came up with the perfect solution—the *Goldilocks* solution. You knew Anya's height and weight because you hired the models for the Central Park Festival. With that information you created a 'Goldilocks' dose of your sleeping drug. You injected Anya in the Ramble. That's why you arranged to have Matt Allegro be her Prince Charming. You needed someone to take the fall."

"With his drug history, Allegro fit the frame perfectly," Sam admitted, almost proudly. "I thought my plan was perfect, too—until you started sniffing around like a mongrel dog."

"I wasn't the only one sniffing," I told her. "A CIA agent thought it was worth his time, too."

Sam's confident expression faltered. "What do you know about that?"

"The drug you used on Anya was also used to assassinate a CIA agent named Faith years ago—and then *frame* a KGB operative named Vasily Petrovus for her murder."

"*Who* told you that?!" she demanded.

I ignored the question. "And let's not forget, you killed

Red because she knew too much. You needed drugs to remix that potion Petrovus taught you to synthesize all those years ago. So you paid Red to provide your chemistry set. Since her parents own a pharmacy, it was easy. But when Anya turned vegetable, Red figured out who did it and how—"

"Don't talk to me about that stupid Russian whore!" Sam cried. "She didn't even try to blackmail me. She just wanted the antidote so she could wake her friend. Red learned the hard way, there *is* no antidote."

"But there is *the truth*," I said evenly. "And the true narrative is out there. The police know it. The CIA knows it. So you might as well give yourself up. Killing us will only add two more murders onto your sentence."

"We'll see what the *'true narrative'* is once both of your bodies are discovered," Sam said.

That's when I saw it, the Predatory smile.

As the clouds around us rumbled their threats, I saw exactly what kind of monster lived within Sam's slick façade—the She-Wolf, a killer who relished the planning and stalking as much as she did the striking down.

"You see, Clare, I learned my tradecraft well. *Always have a backup plan.* The charges aren't sticking to Allegro? Fine. Here's another fairy tale: 'Once upon a time,' many years ago, a pretty teenaged model named Leila Carver became a member of the underground club. The authorities will declare her the killer once they find your bodies, along with more of the drug I've already hidden in Leila's bedroom and key pieces of evidence linking her to all of my crimes."

"Now . . ." Samantha waved impatiently. "Let's end this, because if one of Leila's brats comes through that door, they're dead, too—and you wouldn't want that, would you?"

I cast about looking for a weapon, *something* to fight back with. I considered rushing her, but Samantha was too far away. The second she saw me moving, I'd be eating bullets.

"You first, Clare. Hold out your arm. I promise, the drug is a less painful way to die than five bullets to the stomach—"

Suddenly, a door slammed shut and we all froze.

Someone had entered the apartment. A moment later, I

heard little feet pounding down the hallway as a young voice called out—

"Mom! I need an umbrella!" Then Mike's daughter burst happily into the living room. "Becky's mother is taking us to the museum, and I want to—"

Eyes wide, the child stopped dead as Samantha swung the handgun toward her.

Ninety-seven

No! *You are NOT hurting Molly!*

My reaction was automatic. I shot off the sofa, body slamming the brunette witch to the floor. An ear-splitting blast filled the living room as the gun discharged, firing a bullet through a window.

As the glass shattered, Molly screamed in terror.

"Run, Molly!" I shouted over a deafening thunder crack. "Get out!"

But Molly didn't run for the front door—as I hoped she would—the little girl ran for the "safety" of her bedroom with Leila racing after her.

Letting them go, Sam punched me in the face and scrambled toward her fallen gun. Like the storm outside, I was raging now, angry enough to fight with everything I had. As Sam moved toward her gun, I body slammed her again and my hands closed around her throat.

Choking, Sam struggled in place, but not to fight me. A moment later, I realized why. A sharp needle prick stung my arm. I looked down, but didn't see a hypodermic.

The ring!

Sam had slid back a large jewel on her chunky ring to reveal a retractable needle. I stopped choking the woman to knock away her lethal hand. A bead of blood appeared on my skin. In minutes, or maybe seconds, I would not be able to fight anymore—but I refused to stop.

As Sam lunged for the gun again, I began to pummel her. But my adrenaline-fueled strength didn't last long. My muscles began to spasm and my vision grew hazy. Now Sam easily broke from my grip, pushing me away like a bored child with a worn-out toy. She stood to her full height and brutally kicked me in the ribs.

"You lose, bitch!" she spat as pain ripped through my body.

Sucking air, I watched helplessly as she gripped the gun.

"Time to clean up your mess," she said, pushing back loose strands of hair.

I couldn't fight. I couldn't even rise. Tears streamed down my face as I watched her start for the bedroom where Leila and Molly ran to hide.

Except Leila wasn't hiding. Not anymore.

In the haze of my weakening vision, I saw the slight figure of Leila Carver Quinn Reynolds standing her ground in front of her daughter's bedroom. In her manicured hands was something big and shiny. It wasn't a bat, though she held it like one.

Sam was so cocky she laughed in Leila's face. "And what are you going to do with *that*?"

On a jungle roar, the Mother Lioness showed her and swung her prized antique vanity mirror like my Louisville Slugger.

Shocked, Samantha pulled the trigger—and missed.

Leila didn't.

Staggering backward, the stunned She-Wolf raised her gun again. And the Mother Lioness hit her again. With the third blow the mirror shattered, raining shards of gold, silver, and diamonds over them both.

After that, my vision flickered in and out.

I saw Samantha Peel on the floor, out cold; Leila calling 911 while she hugged a crying Molly close.

As the last image of mother and daughter faded, I smiled.

There were sirens, I think, and men shouting, the movement of a stretcher on wheels.

"Aunt Clare, can you hear me? Aunt Clare!"

I felt Molly's hot tears hitting my cheek, then the freezing rain. Finally, the light went out of me completely and the world faded to black.

Ninety-eight

FOR a long time, I saw nothing but darkness. Then I saw lights, dimly at first, trembling little points that slowly grew stronger. Next came the voices . . .

"Can she hear us? Clare, dear?"

". . . her brain activity . . ."

"Every witness, every suspect has a story . . ."

"I don't give a damn. Try something. Anything!"

"Black, so much black."

". . . and I came to read to you today, Aunt Clare. Are you listening?"

"Experimental doses may or may not be . . ."

". . . between the dark places . . ."

"Once upon a time . . ."

"Wake up, Sweetheart! You can do it. COME BACK TO ME!"

MIKE? I couldn't seem to move or speak or even see, but for the first time in what felt like an eternity, a voice wasn't vague or distant or part of some past memory, but loud and clear and real.

It was Mike Quinn's voice.

"Sensory stimulation will help, Detective Quinn." *(And that was Dr. Pepper's voice!)*

"What do you want me to do?"

"Touch her."

"Oh, I can do better than that, Doctor . . ."

Warm lips brushed mine. The kiss felt soft but urgent. I concentrated on that delightful sensory stimulation, and soon my own lips began to move.

Finally, I opened my eyes—and recoiled from the brilliant brightness.

"Draw the curtains!" Dr. Pepper directed. "It has been eighteen days since her eyes have functioned."

Everything went dark again and I nearly panicked. "Mike! Where are you?"

I struggled against the sheets until I felt his strong arms around me. "I thought I'd lost you," he whispered.

"No such luck," I replied, my voice raw and hoarse from disuse.

As a pair of nurses swung into action, Mike reluctantly released me.

"Soon she will be right as rain, Detective Quinn."

Even the room's dim artificial lights were too much and I shut my eyes against them. In the darkness, Samantha Peel's words came back to me: *"There is no antidote,"* and I had to ask—

"How did you wake me, Doctor?"

"Thanks to Detective Quinn here, I was able to obtain a small sample of Ms. Peel's 'Sleeping Beauty' drug. After careful analysis, I synthesized a genetic-specific remedy."

"Genetic-specific?"

"Yes, remember the DNA sample we took when you visited my lab? Well, I used it to tailor a multiphase drug therapy. For laymen's ears, I call it the Keppra-based Intravenous Sensory Stimulator, though the nursing staff has taken to using its acronym—KISS."

"You're kidding?"

"I'm quite serious," Dr. Pepper assured me. "It was my KISS that woke you."

Mike grunted. "I beg to differ."

"Well, Detective, I certainly won't argue the point. After

all, given the choice, I do believe Ms. Cosi preferred waking up to *your* kiss."

OVER the next few hours, Mike delivered many more of those charming kisses (to my delight). He was less forthcoming about what transpired during the two-and-a-half weeks I'd been unconscious; and by the time the hospital staff served dinner that evening, this patient was out of patience.

"Okay, Mike, I'm sitting up with my first solid food—"

"If you call watery broth, cherry gelatin, and weak tea 'solid,'" he quipped between bites of his warm pastrami sandwich, deli pickle, and kettle chips.

Normally I'd be salivating for a bite of Mike's meal, but today I could barely handle the bland chow on my tray. "I should slip into a coma more often. I can't believe how much weight I lost. I may need to borrow clothes from Leila—"

"Bite your tongue," Mike said. "As soon as the docs here cut you loose, I'm taking you for a prime rib dinner at Smith and Wollensky, followed by a trip to Junior's for a slab of New York cheesecake. In the meantime"—he pointed to the meager offerings on my tray—"pretend you're feasting on a Per Se tasting menu because I want to see meat on those bones."

Envisioning Thomas Keller's consommé, I sipped the soup. I even downed the gelatin and tea. "All done," I said, locking on to Mike's gaze. "I think I can stomach the truth now, so *please* talk to me. And tell me everything, starting with Samantha Peel. Did she survive the thrashing Leila gave her?"

"Three days in the hospital and straight into custody."

I sighed with relief. "Thank goodness for Dr. Pepper. He not only saved my life, he gave me a lucid dream that solved the case."

"No, Clare, you're the one who solved it, and the good doctor agrees. He told me he felt like the Wizard of Oz, handing Dorothy's friends what they had already."

According to Mike, the evidence against Sam was easy

to find and overwhelming. "We got the vial of the Sleeping Beauty drug planted in Leila's bedroom; found her maid disguise in the stairwell. And Leila's testimony, with Molly's statement, ended the debate. The grand jury indicted Ms. Peel last week."

"Sounds like she's in more hot water than the boiling cauldron from my visions."

"And that water is getting hotter. A DA in Connecticut and another in Jersey are now looking at a pair of suspicious deaths—one five years ago and the other seven. Causes of death were attributed to side effects of prescription drugs. But both victims were former financial rivals of Sam's Wall Street whiz ex-husband. Now that they know the composition of the Sleeping Beauty drug, they can look for evidence of it. More charges may soon be filed."

"Did the Wolf know?"

"He denies any knowledge of his ex-wife's crimes, but we're looking hard at him."

"And what about Leila and the kids? Are they okay?"

Mike's eyes flashed at the mention of his ex-wife. He expelled a hard breath. "The kids are fine, but sometimes I think my little Molly is more mature than her mother . . ."

Mike said he nearly lost it when he heard the details of what went down in Leila's apartment. After he got over the violence of Sam's assault—and the jeopardy Leila had put Molly and me in, as well as herself—he focused on Leila's stupendously bad judgment.

His ex-wife had set herself up as an accessory to the fraud scheme that Samantha and Anya had perpetuated on Stuart Packer. Even worse, she was planning on running the same con on her own ex-husband.

Luckily for Leila, her testimony was badly needed by the Manhattan District Attorney's Office and immunity from her crimes was granted.

But she received no such immunity from Mike Quinn.

"I read her the riot act," he said. "As far as I'm concerned, she's on probation. One more screwup, and I'm going for full custody of Molly and Jeremy. I told her she's now part of Sam Peel's criminal history while I'm a decorated cop who works for the Justice Department. In other words, if I sued for custody of the kids, who do you think would win?"

The reality check left Leila genuinely cowed, according to Mike. Tears in her eyes, she vowed to turn her life around, settle for the terms of her husband's prenuptial agreement, and give up her key to the Prince Charming Club.

"I also suggested she find a job," Mike said. "Not only to help pay the bills, but to keep her out of trouble. Idle hands and all that."

I raised an eyebrow. "How did she take your suggestion?"

"Surprisingly well. She says there are plenty of jobs for older models, catalog and commercial work, so she'll be looking up her former agent . . ."

I considered the fall Leila was about to have—from the clouds of Park Avenue down, down, down, to a humble apartment address; from Gold Room caviar to middle-class meals and multiplex movies.

But then I remembered the difference between Dwayne Galloway and Eldar, the Bosnian car service driver; and it seemed to me, wealth and worth were two very different things. In the end, no amount of money could make a true prince.

Mike regarded me. "What are you smiling about?"

"Poor Man's Caviar."

"I never heard of it."

"It's something I discovered at a little Queens café. It's very good."

"What is it exactly?"

"For me? The key to happiness." Touching Mike's cheek, I leaned in for another kiss. "Tell Leila, when she's ready, I have the recipe."

Epilogue

"HAVE you told her yet?" Matt asked, delivering fresh espressos to our table.

"Not yet," Madame said.

I eyed them suspiciously. "Told me what?"

"You'll see," she said then made a shooing motion to her son. "Come back later. Clare and I are still catching up . . ."

As I sipped the sweet crema on my warm *doppio*, Madame briefed me on what I'd missed while I was sleeping.

"Babka's closing her speakeasy," she announced.

"Why?"

"Oh, my dear, you haven't seen the headlines, have you?"

Apparently, the public story of Samantha Peel's apprehension blew the lid off the Prince Charming Club. Everything came out, including dozens of local, national, and international celebrities who suddenly admitted they knew all about the subterranean hookup party.

"But there is a silver lining," Madame noted. "Lots of silver, as it turns out. All that publicity helped Babka's aboveground business triple. So she's turning the underground space into a 'family-friendly theme eatery.' That's how she described it to me anyway."

"Sounds a little like the cleaned-up Vegas Strip." I shook my head. "So ends an era."

"Not quite. You see, Las Vegas was what Babka had her

eye on for years. Her foreign investors have finally agreed to break ground on a Vegas resort hotel called *The Secret Ball*, this time with an actual casino inside."

"Do you think it will work?"

"Oh, yes. To keep the public's interest piqued, Barbara is writing her memoirs. She's going to reveal how she accepted money from her old boss, Wild Bill Donovan, to open the underground club as a place where US intelligence agencies could easily spy on foreign nationals."

"Has she hired a ghost writer? Or is her 'writers are moody' rule still in effect?"

"As I understand it, her cowriter is a CIA agent who's about to retire, the very man she contacted for help when she heard about Anya's drugging."

Stunned, I sat back in my chair. If memory served, Wilson had claimed an "anonymous tip" had brought him back into the underground club. Clearly, Babka had been the tip—and she'd wanted the cold case solved as much as he did.

Madame raised an eyebrow at my reaction. "Clare, do you know who this CIA man is?"

With a clueless shrug, I sipped my espresso—though I certainly knew. Wilson had even made a late-night visit to my hospital room three days before, bearing gifts of yellow roses and Belgian chocolates . . .

"I would have brought champagne," he'd said, "but I heard you needed fattening up . . ."

Pulling his chair close to my bed, Wilson quietly confided that he'd made quick work of breaking Samantha Peel. Now he was returning to Washington with an official report—and an unofficial feeling of vindication: Faith's true killer was caught, at last, and her heroic story was public, because during his interrogation Samantha had spilled everything she knew about Vasily Petrovus.

"Samantha had been young and vulnerable," he told me. "The handsome Russian operative had thoroughly enchanted her. In her fairy-tale delusion, the crimes she committed weren't crimes at all, but acts of devotion. The rude awakening came with the revelation that Petrov had a family in Canada. When Petrov mocked her, she snapped, ending his life and framing him for the murder of my Faith . . ."

When I asked about Anya, Wilson informed me that a genetic-specific KISS had awakened her, too.

"Will she face any charges?"

"No," Wilson assured me, and I was relieved to hear it.

Apparently, Anya Kravchenko deeply regretted her part in Samantha Peel's fraud scheme. The DA's office believed the girl's remorse, and they had no desire to prosecute. Instead, they granted her immunity in exchange for her full cooperation.

For one thing, she was able to clear Harrison Van Loon, Esquire, of any wrongdoing, confirming his claim that he had no idea her story was false. Neither did he know that Samantha Peel was behind the scheme. Anya even produced paperwork that Sam pressured her to sign, making Sam the executor of her will and any trust that resulted from the legal settlement.

"But there won't be any settlement money now," I pointed out.

"Not from the Wolf," Wilson acknowledged. "But I'm happy to report Barbara Baum stepped up to help Anya. She's providing funds to secure the release of the girl's mother from custody in Russia. By the way, Anya told me she's looking forward to hugging you in person when she's out of the hospital. And I do believe her mother will want to thank you, too, when her freedom is secured."

"A happy ending," I said, though not for everyone.

Rozalina and Faith were two Sleeping Beauties who would never awaken, and their princes-in-waiting would forever mourn them.

But I was awake—and grateful. Given the Wheel of Fortune's turn, I was lucky to be alive, and even luckier to have the family and friends I did . . .

Now, sitting in my coffeehouse across from my beloved employer, I waved good-bye to departing guests. My surprise welcome-home party was winding down, and I appreciated the chance to spend a happy afternoon with my staff and well-wishing neighborhood regulars.

Our shop's baker, Janelle, had made a beautiful iced coffee cake, and Gardner had brought in Four on the Floor to fill the Village Blend with live jazz music.

Esther and Boris, who'd come to the party arm in arm, were now *officially* engaged. True, Boris felt he and his czarina should not cohabit before marriage, but Esther did find a new roommate to share the rent—my youngest barista, Nancy Kelly.

Now *that* was a surprise.

An even bigger surprise was my adult daughter. When she'd heard the news of my coma, Joy had taken emergency leave from her restaurant duties in Paris and flown home. When she wasn't sitting vigil at my bedside, Joy was helping her father run the Village Blend.

Unfortunately, there was no happy ending for Emmanuel Franco. Matt refused to forgive the young sergeant for arresting him. No amount of explaining could persuade my ex that Franco was a hero and not a villain.

"Your father can be pigheaded," I told a tearful Joy. "Let some time pass. He'll come around . . ." At least I hoped he would. Until then, Joy was back to seeing the love of her life in secret while Franco was downing energy drinks and avoiding the Village Blend.

That was why I saved the good sergeant a very big piece of Janelle's cake. Joy would be taking it to him this evening—along with my heartfelt thanks.

My own shield-toting boyfriend was already back in DC, patient as ever with our situation. How long that would last, I had no idea, which was why it surprised me to hear my employer say—

"When I saw you in that hospital bed, dear, that's when I made up my mind."

"About what?"

"Your future . . ."

Madame reached into her purse and placed a plastic bag on the table between us. Inside was an espresso cup—the very demitasse I'd drunk from that night in Central Park.

"I saved it, Clare. And I insist you look at it now."

With trepidation, I read the grinds. They foretold *difficulties, danger, a secret enemy, travel,* and *a big change.*

"While you were sleeping, I had a dream," Madame confessed. "I saw you locked in a dungeon, my dungeon. Gardner was in a cell, too. And all you wanted was a key to be released. My dear, today, Matt and I are giving that key to you."

"What are you talking about?!"

"Your devotion and loyalty to me and my son and this wonderful coffeehouse have kept you from the man you truly love—"

Travel and a big change. "You want me to leave you?"

"No, and that's the beauty of it, you won't be leaving us at all." She smiled. "Remember how Babka taunted me at our lunch? Well, I've decided she was right, and we're going to start expanding our business. I'd like you to help Gardner Evans open a second Village Blend shop in Washington, DC."

"But I thought he was opening a jazz club with his cousin in Baltimore?"

Madame waved Matt over. "My boy and I had a long talk with Gardner. It seems his cousin was content to let Gardner shoulder all the management duties—food, beverage, staffing, bookings. And Gardner realized that if he went into business with his cousin, it would give him no time to devote to his music."

"That's right," Matt said. "We talked it over, and agreed that our partnership was better for him . . ." As Matt explained it, I would co-manage the DC coffeehouse with Gardner. I would also be roasting the beans in New York and transporting them down to DC. It would be a reverse commute with me living down there as long as I wanted.

"Matt will take care of the shop in New York for the time being."

"Seven months tops," he warned. "Then you'll have to come back or hire a new manager."

"What about the location?" I asked.

"Gardner's found a few places we can lease in Georgetown, one near Blues Alley," Matt said. "He wants the Village Blend, DC, to host live jazz in the evenings and serve a light dinner menu. But he needs your help getting the place up and running—like you did in the Hamptons a few years back for David Mintzer. So what do you say, Clare, are you up for it?"

Overwhelmed, I brushed away a tear. "You two need to turn around."

Matt and his mother shared confused glances. "Why?"

"I want to see your fairy godmother wings." They both laughed, but it wasn't funny to me. "While I was sleeping, you made my dream come true."

Of course, Quinn was over the moon when I told him. And I was excited, too. But I hadn't forgotten Wilson's cryptic warning—

"The next time Mike Quinn speaks with you about moving down to Washington, listen a little harder, okay? Men like him don't often admit to needing personal backup."

In Wilson's view, Mike was in some kind of trouble—trouble he either refused to talk about or didn't fully understand. Oh, I'd find out more soon enough. But whatever was wrong, I knew one thing. Mike had taken big risks to be in my corner. Now it was my turn to be in his.

This wouldn't be easy. But then neither were fairy tales. Forests could be perilous; mirrors treacherous; and candy-coated houses built to burn you. In the end, life and its choices were hard, and no matter where we stood on this fast-spinning planet, nightfall would routinely blacken our bluest skies.

But then I considered the heart of a young cop like Franco; the devotion of a boy like Boris; the kindness of strangers like Eldar; even my own deep affection for a blue knight, hardened and weary yet still guided by chivalry; and the words of Esther's favorite Russian poet came back to me—

Blackness was not the whole of it.

"There are bright points of light—so many!—between the dark places. This is what's important. This is where life is."

When, in disgrace with fortune and men's eyes,
I all alone beweep my outcast state,
And trouble deaf heaven with my bootless cries,
And look upon myself, and curse my fate,
Wishing me like to one more rich in hope,
Featur'd like him, like him with friends possess'd,
Desiring this man's art and that man's scope,
With what I most enjoy contented least;
Yet in these thoughts myself almost despising,
Haply I think on thee, and then my state,
Like to the lark at break of day arising
From sullen earth, sings hymns at heaven's gate;
For thy sweet love remember'd such wealth brings
That then I scorn to change my state with kings.

—WILLIAM SHAKESPEARE, SONNET 29
(Translated from the original Russian)

Recipes & Tips from the Village Blend

Visit Cleo Coyle's virtual Village Blend at
CoffeehouseMystery.com
for even more recipes, including:

* "Poisoned" Apple Sharlotka *(Spiked Russian Apple Cake)*
* Fairy Bread and Fairy Bread Cookies
* Chocolate Babka
* BBQ Chipped Ham Sandwich
* Glacéed Strawberry Cupcakes with Strawberry Syrup Shots
* Chocolate Ricotta Muffins
* Twinkie Baba Rum
* Clare's "Welcome Back!" Iced Coffee Cake
* Gingered Ale and more . . .

Madame Tesla's Guide to Coffee Tasseography

Coffee tasseography is the art of seeing the future through coffee grinds, and a serious art it is. The ritual was born in the culture of Turkish coffee drinking, which reaches back to the sixteenth century. In the seventeenth century, the ritual arrived in Europe and became fashionable in Paris. No, I didn't learn it then—I'm not *that* old, my dears! I was taught by my Turkish friend Yasmina, just as Clare learned the art from her beloved Italian nonna in Western Pennsylvania.

Coffee reading is an oral tradition, you see, and not something you'll learn about in books. That said, I have set down this quick guide to help budding seers, using the techniques and interpretations I learned.

Your Coffee Reading: To start, you must brew coffee. Coffee readers have traditionally used a Turkish-style method of brewing. The Bosnian method also works well, and you'll find recipes for both following my little guide.

Why must you make the coffee this way? Because these very old brewing methods will leave grinds at the bottom of your cup. It is these grinds that you will use to read fortunes.

Although there are different styles of reading coffee grinds, all require the beverage to be consumed by the person seeking his or her fortune. As the reader, you should provide a relaxing, cordial atmosphere while the seeker imbibes. When the cup is nearly drained, the reading begins.

Ask the seeker to slowly turn the cup in his or her hands for a few moments while contemplating a question or problem. When the seeker is finished, he or she should cover the cup with the saucer and turn them both upside down. With this method, the coffee grinds spread and move, leaving symbols on the walls and bottom of the cup. Allow the grounds to cool and dry for a few minutes before turning the cup over and beginning the reading.

How to Read the Cup: Visually divide the cup into horizontal halves, top and bottom. The symbols seen on the bottom half are messages regarding the past. The symbols near the top are messages about the future. This would be the *immediate* future. Like Tarot, a coffee reading cannot predict events beyond forty days. The reader must also divide the cup into vertical halves—right and left. This division helps the reader determine positive or negative answers or outcomes. Right is positive, or "yes." Left is negative, or "no."

For Example: You may see the shape of an airplane in the coffee grinds, which predicts a journey:

* If the plane is on the *top* half of the cup, this journey is in the *future*.

* If the plane is on the top *right* side of the cup, this future journey will have a *positive* outcome. However, if the plane is on the top *left* side of the cup, this future journey will have a *negative* outcome.

* If the plane is on the *bottom* half of the cup, this journey was in the *past*.

* If the plane is on the bottom *right* side of the cup, the events from this past journey will have a *positive* influence on the future. However, if the plane is on the bottom *left* side of the cup, the events from this past journey will have a *negative* impact on the future.

Your Mental Powers: As the reader, gazing into the cup, let your imagination run free. Coffee reading is not unlike cloud gazing. One must discern the shapes by using both *imagination* and *intuition*.

A Quick Guide to Symbols: There are literally hundreds of symbols found in coffee grinds. While there is not enough space here to cover every possible symbol, I have listed a hundred of the most common, along with widely held interpretations. Please note that these are not the only interpretations. As I mentioned, this is an oral tradition that will vary among readers. With time and practice, you will hone your skills and arrive at your own interpretations.

The Magic and Power of Story: Remember that the coffee reader must tell the seeker a *story* to help make sense of the symbols seen and interpreted. And telling stories is a magical thing. For when you engage imagination and intuition, you awaken the very mental powers that have shaped our world—and hold the power to reshape your own.

—Madame Tesla,
New York City

The Symbols

Acorn—Success. Financial success if found at the top of the cup. Good health if found at the bottom.

Airplane—A journey. A broken wing indicates an interrupted trip or an accident.

Anchor—Success in business or romance. A blurry anchor means problems.

Angel—Good news.

Arch—A wedding.

Arrow—Sudden bad news.

Axe—Troubles that will be overcome by great effort.

Bag—If open, a trap you can escape. If closed, you will be trapped.

Barrel—A party, feast, or celebration.

Basket—An **empty basket** implies financial woes. A **full basket** promises a gift.

Bat—False or untrustworthy friends.

Bee—Social success, or praise at work.

Beehive—Prosperity or riches. The sweet life.

Beetle—A difficult undertaking.

Bell—Surprising news. On the right of the cup, good news. On the left, sad tidings. **More than one bell** indicates a wedding.

Bird—Freedom from worry.

Birdcage—Quarrels.

Bird's nest—A loving home.

Boat—A visit from a distant friend or relative, safe refuge.

Branch—**With leaves** is a birth or new prospects. **Without leaves** is a setback.

Bridge—An opportunity.

Butterfly—Frivolity.

Car—Luck or good fortune.

Cherry—A love affair.

Claw—Hidden enemies who seek to do you harm.

Clouds—A storm brewing, trouble ahead.

Clover—Prosperity.

Coffin—Very bad news.

Comet—An unexpected visitor or sudden opportunity, not without risk.

Crescent—A pleasant journey.

Cross—Sacrifice, ill health. Conversely, **two crosses** predict a long life. **Three crosses** signify longevity *and* a great achievement.

Dagger—Impetuous actions that lead to danger.

Daisy—Romantic love and happiness.

Dancer—Shame or disappointment.

Door—Strange or mysterious occurrences.

Dove—Peace, tranquility, good fortune.

Dragon—Unpredictable changes, trouble.

Drum—Scandal, gossip.

Duck—Money is coming.

Egg—Prosperity, success—the more eggs the better.

Eye—Vigilance needed to overcome difficulties.

Fairy—Joy, enchantment.

Fan—Inappropriate flirtation, indiscretion.

Feather—Lack of concentration.

Feet—An important decision must soon be made.

Finger—This symbol emphasizes the symbol it points to.

Fish—Good fortune in all things.

Fist—Argument.

Fruit—Prosperity, fertility.

Gun—Trouble, quarrels, danger.

Hammer—Overcoming obstacles, hard, unpleasant work.

Hand—Friendship. If fingers are missing, selfish or deceitful friends.

Hat—New job or home, a change.

Hawk—Jealousy.

Horn—Generosity, abundance.

Horse—A **galloping horse** indicates good news from a lover. A **horse head** means romance.

Horseshoe—Good luck.

Hourglass—Quick action is required. Time is running out.

Iceberg—Hidden hazards ahead.

Kettle—Minor accident or illness.

Key—Unlocking new success. **Two keys** means a robbery.

Ladder—A job promotion.

Lightning bolt—Swift resolution to a vexing problem.

Mouse or **Rat**—A theft.

Mushroom—Growth after setbacks.

Musical note—Celebration of good fortune.

Nail—Physical pain.

Number—Time, usually the number of days before an event.

Oak leaf—Good fortune.

Oar—Help in difficulties.

Owl—Scandal, failure.

Pitchfork—Quarrels.

Pyramid—Success in all stages of life.

Question mark—Doubt, hesitancy, overcaution.

Ring—Closure, completion. A **broken ring** could indicate the end of a romance or marriage. **Two rings** mean plans are working out.

Rose—Approval, popularity, fame.

Saw—Outside interference.

Scales—A lawsuit. **Balanced scales** suggest justice. **Unbalanced scales** hint at an injustice.

Scissors—Domestic strife, separation.

Shamrock—Wishes granted.

Sheep—Fortune.

Skeleton—Loss of money, ill health.

Skull—Death.

Spoon—Generosity to others.

Square—Protection, peace.

Star—Health and happiness.

Sun—Status, power.

Toad—Distrust all flattery.

Torch—Turn for the better in business.

Tree—Ambition fulfilled.

Turtle—Harsh criticism.

Umbrella—Need for safety or safe shelter.

Unicorn—Secret romance or wedding.

Whale—Career or business success.

Wheel—A **complete wheel** means earned success. A **broken wheel** means toil without reward.

Wolf—Beware a jealous or selfish person.

Woman—Sensual pleasure.

Worm—Scandal. The more worms, the worse the scandal will become.

Madame Tesla's Turkish Coffee

Turkish coffee is one of the oldest of all brewing methods. Coffee is so significant in Turkish culture that their word for *breakfast* (*kahvaltı*), literally means "before coffee." The ritual of coffee drinking is endowed with friendship, affection, and sharing—an idea beautifully illustrated in the meaning of their famous proverb: "A single cup of coffee can create a friendship that lasts forty years."

Because Turkish coffee refers to the *process* of coffee making, almost any good-quality beans can be used to make it. What's tricky to get right is the grind. Turkish coffee must be made with coffee that is very finely ground, so fine that it's close to a powder. When you press your finger into it, you should be able leave a fingerprint mark. (Clare's friends from the Sixth Precinct are especially fond of that description.)

Traditionally, coffee beans were pounded down in a mortar. In our modern kitchens, home "burr grinders" are the best choice for properly grinding our daily coffee; but most electric grinders cannot grind coffee fine enough to be called Turkish; and (unfortunately) the friction and heat produced by the blade of a typical spice grinder will burn the coffee before the proper texture is achieved. The best remedy is to either purchase a Turkish hand grinder or buy coffee that is preground for the Turkish method. (See suggestions at the end of this section.)

Once you have the proper grind of coffee, you can move to the stage of making it. Turkish coffee is boiled in a long-handled pot (*cezve*) made specifically for coffee brewing. The pot is traditionally made of copper or brass. Its narrow neck and wide bottom are designed to hold back most of the grounds when the coffee is poured. Sizes of these Turkish coffeepots range from extra-small (6-ounce capacity) for making 1 to 2 servings to larger sizes: 7-, 10-, 12-, 14-, 16-, and even 24-ounce capacities.

Madame Tesla's instructions for brewing coffee in the Turkish manner are outlined in the following steps:

Step 1—Prep the pot. Into your *cezve*, measure about 1 heaping teaspoon of Turkish coffee per serving (5 to 7 grams). Add 1 teaspoon of sugar per serving—this is considered "medium sweet," but you can adjust to taste or leave out entirely. Add the water, roughly 3 ounces (about 6 tablespoons) of water per demitasse serving. Stir well to dissolve the coffee and sugar—a fork works well for this; just pretend you're beating an egg. Place the pot over *low* heat. The low heat is important to infuse the water slowly.

Step 2—Simmer, stir, repeat. This step must be monitored closely to prevent the coffee from fully boiling or boiling over your pot. When you see the coffee thicken and froth up, remove it from the heat, allowing the simmering coffee to settle back down. Do not stir. Return the pot to the heat and repeat the simmering and cooling process. Repeat this process once more, for a total of three simmers. The reason for this repeated cooking and cooling is to infuse the water fully with the beautiful coffee flavor—but without prolonged boiling, which would impart a burnt taste. For the third and final simmer, you are watching for the coffee froth to rise up to the very top of the pot. Remove the pot from the heat and pour, offering it to guests with a glass of water, which is traditional for service. Before drinking, wait a few moments to allow the grinds to settle in the cup.

A frothy tip: Serving the coffee with a thick foam or froth (*köpük*) is an important part of the art of Turkish coffee making. You can spoon a bit of froth from the pot into each demitasse as it forms during the infusion process. Or you can pour the coffee very slowly from the pot and lift the pot higher and higher as you pour, which helps to produce more froth. The cup with the most froth is considered the best, but if you are a lover of coffee, every cup of properly made Turkish coffee will smell amazing and taste divine.

A note on buying Turkish coffee: When you buy "Turkish coffee" in a can or a pouch, this is coffee that has been preground extremely fine for the purposes of brewing coffee the Turkish way. You can even purchase Turkish coffee from Turkish roasters. Two of the biggest and oldest brands to look for are *Kurukahveci Mehmet Efendi* and *Kurukahveci Nuri Toplar.*

Bosnian Coffee

In Bosnia, coffee drinking is a daily tradition, and Bosnian coffee plays an important social and cultural role. Clare discovered this for herself when she rudely attempted to question Eldar at the Queen Catherine Café. In response, she received a polite but firm lesson in Eastern European etiquette. Happily, Eldar invited Clare to join him over a hot *džezva* of Bosnian coffee, and they quickly became friends.

The coffee-brewing process in Bosnia and Herzegovina is close to that of Turkish coffee, but there are differences. Bosnian coffee is brewed from a number of Bosnian coffee brands—*Sabah*, *Zlatna Džezva*, and *Saraj Kafa*, to name a few. These brands are roasted and ground specifically for this type of preparation.

Unlike Turkish coffee's triple boiling, Bosnian coffee has only one boil, and the coffee is not sweetened in the pot. Bosnians serve it black with sugar cubes provided in a separate bowl. (Usually cream is offered only to children.) The coffeepot's shape is similar to the Turkish *cezve*, but in Bosnia and Herzegovina, as well as Serbia and Croatia, it is known as a *džezva*.

Method

Step 1—Boil water. Boil water in a saucepan. While the water is reaching its boiling point, warm the empty *džezva* over another heat source. Remove it and measure in the (very finely ground) Bosnian coffee, about 2 heaping teaspoons per demitasse.

Step 2—Pour and boil again. When the water is at a rolling boil, remove it from the heat source. To prevent the coffee from burning, allow the roiling to calm down before pouring the very hot water over your coffee grinds, filling the pot about halfway (or a little more). Stir the coffee in the *džezva*, and then immediately transfer the pot back to a heat source that is set to low. Stop stirring and watch carefully. Within a minute or so the coffee will begin to rise, crowned with a thick, foamy head that looks like molten chocolate. Do not allow the coffee to boil over the pot. Remove it quickly from the heat, and allow the risen coffee to sink down again. Finally, add a little more hot water and let the pot rest a minute to allow the grinds to settle before serving. Bosnian coffee is usually enjoyed black. Serve on a tray with sugar cubes in a separate bowl and small spoons for stirring.

Recipes

Life is a combination of magic and pasta.
—FEDERICO FELLINI

Snow White Chocolate Mocha

This marvelous mocha tastes like a warm, sweet, coffee-infused milkshake. The shop's coffee truck menu renamed this popular Village Blend drink in honor of the New York Fairy Tale Festival. And if your name's Snow White, you can rest easy—there are no apples in the ingredient list.

Makes 2 servings

1 cup milk
½ cup white chocolate, chopped, or white chocolate chips
½ teaspoon pure vanilla extract
*4 shots (about 12 tablespoons) hot espresso or double-strength coffee**
whipped cream to finish
white chocolate curls for garnish†

Step 1. Combine the milk and white chocolate in a heatproof bowl and place the bowl over a saucepan that's about one-third full of boiling water. (You are creating a double boiler.) Stir constantly until the chocolate is melted.

Step 2. Whip in the vanilla using a whisk, hand blender, or electric mixer. Continue to whip about a minute until the warm mixture is loosely frothy.

Step 3. Divide the espresso (or strong coffee) between two large mugs. Add the steamed white chocolate milk and stir to blend the flavors. You can top with whipped cream and white chocolate shavings, but it's just as delicious without.

***Double-strength coffee:** For double-strength coffee, simply make a strong version of your regular cup. For instance, in a drip coffeemaker, instead of using 1½ to 2 tablespoons of ground coffee for every 6 ounces of water, use 3 to 4 tablespoons.

†Chocolate curls: To create chocolate curls, start with a block of room temperature chocolate (white, milk, bittersweet, or dark). Using a vegetable peeler, scrape the block and you'll see curls of chocolate peel away.

"The Great Pumpkin" Spice Latte

Another fall favorite, this home version of the popular Village Blend latte brings the harvest season to your taste buds. As fans of the beloved Charlie Brown "Peanuts" gang, the Village Blend crew got a kick out of renaming their drink in honor of Charlie's friend, Linus, a sweet boy who never stopped believing that one day the Great Pumpkin would come. Until he does, however, this tasty pumpkin spice latte will have to do.

Makes 1 serving

2 teaspoons pumpkin purée (canned is fine)
*¼ teaspoon pumpkin pie spice**
¼ teaspoon pure vanilla extract

1½ teaspoons granulated sugar
1 shot (3 tablespoons) hot espresso or double-strength coffee†
⅔ cup cold milk
cinnamon stick
whipped cream

Step 1. In an 8-ounce mug, combine the pumpkin purée, pumpkin pie spice, vanilla extract, and sugar. Pour the hot espresso (or double-strength coffee†) into the mug. Stir well to blend the flavors.

Step 2. Froth up the milk using an espresso machine steam wand, *or* simply warm the milk in a saucepan over very low heat (do not allow the milk to boil or you'll get a scorched taste), and then froth with a whisk, hand blender, or electric mixer.

Step 3. Using a spoon, hold back the foam in your pitcher or saucepan as you pour the steamed milk into the hot espresso. Add a cinnamon stick and stir to mix the flavors. Top with foamed milk and whipped cream. Finish with a light sprinkling of pumpkin pie spice.

***Homemade pumpkin pie spice:** To make 1 teaspoon of pumpkin pie spice, mix together ½ teaspoon cinnamon, ¼ teaspoon ginger, ⅛ teaspoon ground allspice or ground cloves, and ⅛ teaspoon ground nutmeg.

†Double-strength coffee: To make double-strength coffee in an automatic drip coffeemaker, French press, or pour-over cone, double the amount of ground coffee that you would normally use. For example, instead of 2 tablespoons of ground coffee per 6 ounces of water, use 4 tablespoons and . . . drink with joy!

Clare Cosi's Cinderella Pumpkin Cake (Dairy-Free)

Clare's cute little coffee cake may look as humble as Cinderella's pumpkin, but the moist texture and delicious flavor will make you the belle of any ball where you serve it. The pumpkin in the cake adds nutrition and fiber, and the batter can be easily stirred together. Bake it small in an 8-inch-square pan or double it for a festive 9 × 13-inch sheet cake. One final note: This cake recipe uses no dairy. To finish it in a dairy-free fashion, simply dust with powdered sugar, or use Dairy-Free Whipped Cream (more on that in the recipe below). If dairy is not a problem for you, then use Clare's Silky Cream Cheese Frosting recipe, which pairs beautifully not only with this pumpkin cake but with other spice cakes and muffins.

Makes one 8-inch-square pan cut into 16 petite servings or 9 large squares

For one 9 × 13-inch sheet cake, double this recipe

Dry Ingredients

1 cup all-purpose flour
½ cup light brown sugar, packed
½ cup granulated white sugar
1 teaspoon baking powder
1 teaspoon baking soda
*½ teaspoon pumpkin pie spice**
¼ teaspoon table salt (or ½ teaspoon Kosher salt)

Wet Ingredients

2 large eggs
½ cup vegetable or canola oil
1 cup cooked and pureed pumpkin†

***Homemade pumpkin pie spice:** To make 1 teaspoon of pumpkin pie spice, mix together ½ teaspoon cinnamon, ¼ teaspoon ginger, ⅛ teaspoon allspice or ground cloves, and ⅛ teaspoon ground nutmeg.

†A note on pumpkin: Canned pumpkin works well in this recipe, but be sure to use 100% pumpkin and not pumpkin pie filling.

Step 1—Prep the oven and pan. First preheat the oven to 325°F. Make a parchment paper sling for your pan by allowing the paper to hang over two edges. Use nonstick cooking spray to lightly coat the paper as well as the pan sides without paper.

Step 2—Mix using the one-bowl method. Measure the dry ingredients into a large bowl. Whisk them together. Make a well in the center. Break the eggs into the well, and whisk to blend. Add the oil and blend again. Add the pumpkin puree. Switch to a large spoon or rubber spatula. Gently stir and fold until the dry mixture is completely blended into a smooth batter—but be careful not to overmix the batter or you will develop the gluten in the flour and your cake will be tough instead of tender.

Step 3—Bake. Pour the batter into your prepared pan and bang the filled pan on a flat surface to release any bubbles and even out the batter. Bake in your well-preheated oven for 35 to 45 minutes; the time will depend on your oven. The cake is done when the center is no longer jiggling and springs back when lightly touched. A toothpick inserted into the center of the cake should come out with no wet batter clinging to it. Otherwise, return to the oven in 5-minute increments. When done, remove from the oven and allow to cool for a few minutes, then run a butter knife along the sides of the pan that are not papered (to loosen if sticking). Gently lift the cake out of the pan and onto a cooling rack. When completely cool, dust with powdered sugar or try one of the frosting options that follow.

Dairy-free frosting: Clare's pumpkin cake recipe is dairy-free. If you'd like a dairy-free option for the frosting, try making Dairy-Free Whipped Cream with a well-chilled can of full-fat coconut milk. For instructions, visit CoffeehouseMystery.com, where you can download an illustrated printable PDF of the recipe. Or if dairy is not a problem for you, try . . .

Clare's Silky Cream Cheese Frosting

Makes enough to cover an 8- or 9-inch square cake

For a 9 × 13-inch sheet cake, double this recipe

4 ounces cream cheese (half of an 8-ounce block)
2 teaspoons whole milk
½ to 1 teaspoon pure vanilla extract
2¼ cups powdered sugar

Place the cream cheese into a large bowl. Using an electric mixer, beat until creamy. Add the milk and vanilla and beat again until blended. Add about half of the powdered sugar and beat until fully incorporated. Add the remaining sugar to finish. If you find the frosting too loose, add more powdered sugar. If you find it too dry, add a tiny bit more milk.

Clare Cosi's Cappuccino Blondies

After a long day playing Charming at the Central Park Fairy Tale Festival, Prince Matt was desperate for one of these. "They're like brownies," he frantically explained, "but flavored with vanilla and cinnamon and you swirl some kind of chocolate-coffee liqueur into them." Yes, Matt was describing this amazing specialty of the Village Blend coffeehouse, created by his ex-wife and current business partner, Clare Cosi. As the shop's manager, Clare is always on the lookout for tasty new menu items. As an occasional amateur sleuth, Clare finds a good mystery even harder to resist. As for your own enjoyment of this recipe, here's a final clue: You don't have to use alcohol. Clare's recipe suggests easy substitutions for the rum-based Mexican coffee liqueur known as Kahlúa. (On the other hand, to make your own Kahlúa, see Clare's recipe in the back of the Coffeehouse Mystery Billionaire Blend.*)*

Makes one 9 × 13-inch pan of blondies (24 squares)

For the Batter

10 tablespoons (1 stick + 2T) unsalted butter, softened
1 cup packed light brown sugar
½ cup white, granulated sugar
2 eggs, room temperature
¼ cup Kahlúa (or espresso or strong coffee or cream)
1 tablespoon vanilla
½ teaspoon cinnamon
¼ teaspoon espresso powder
½ teaspoon table salt (or finely ground sea salt)
1 teaspoon baking powder
¼ teaspoon baking soda
1-¾ cups all-purpose flour

For the Chocolate-Coffee Swirl

⅓ cup chocolate chips (semi-sweet or dark/bittersweet)
1 tablespoon Kahlúa (or coffee, espresso, or cream)
½ tablespoon butter

Step 1—Prep the oven and pan. First preheat your oven to 350°F. Butter a 9 × 13-inch baking pan and line it with parchment paper, allowing the excess to hang over the two long ends. This allows you to lift your final baked product out of the pan to cool and easily slice into squares.

Step 2—Mix the blondie batter. Using an electric mixer, cream the softened butter and brown and white sugars. Add eggs, Kahlúa, vanilla, cinnamon, espresso powder, salt, baking powder, and baking soda. Beat well until the batter is smooth. Finally blend in the flour, but do not overmix. Batter will be thick, like cake frosting, pour into pan and use the back of a spoon to spread it evenly and smooth the top. Set aside.

Step 3—Make the chocolate-coffee swirl. Place the chocolate chips in a microwave-safe bowl. Toss chips well with 1 tablespoon Kahlúa (or coffee, espresso, or cream). Chop in a small amount of butter (½ tablespoon). Stir again. Now zap in a microwave for 15 seconds. Stir. Zap again. This method ensures you will not burn the chocolate, which cannot be saved once ruined. You can also melt it all in a double-boiler.

Step 4—Finish and bake. Using a spoon, dollop *very small mounds* of the warm chocolate-coffee ganache (in polka dot fashion) over the entire top surface of the blondie batter. Using a wooden skewer, chopstick, or knife, swirl these dollops through the batter well, creating your own Jackson Pollock–esque mocha masterpiece. Bake until a toothpick inserted comes out clean, about 20–23 minutes. Do not overbake. Remove and allow to cool in the pan for at least 30 minutes. The blondies will deflate and ridges will appear. Finished Cappuccino Blondies will not be crunchy or cakelike but moist and chewy like fudge brownies, but with the amazing flavors of a coffeehouse cappuccino. The cooler they become, the easier they will be to handle. When completely cool, slice into squares, and eat with java joy!

Clare Cosi's Black Forest Brownies

Waldeinsamkeit *is the German term for the peaceful and harmonious feeling of being alone in the forest. Once Clare Cosi ventures into the wooded maze of the Central Park Ramble, however, her* Waldeinsamkeit *more resembles a Black Forest.*

The real Black Forest is located in Southwest Germany. While food historians aren't entirely sure who invented the famous Black Forest Cake, many believe the culinary roots lie in the soaking of the region's famous sour cherries in Kirschwasser *(a cherry brandy) and serving them with whipped cream. Because chocolate is popular in Germany, these flavors were eventually combined into a much beloved torte of chocolate sponge cake, kirsch-soaked cherries, and whipped cream. Clare's brownies are loosely based on the flavors in that wonderful German cake. May you enjoy them—in or out of the woods.*

Makes one 9 × 13-inch pan of brownies (24 squares)

For the Cherries

2 heaping cups fresh or frozen cherries (about 40) or Maraschino cherries
⅓ cup kirsch or white rum
2 tablespoons sugar

For the Brownies

Your favorite recipe or boxed mix for a 13 x 9-inch pan.

Step 1—Infuse the cherries. Destem, pit, and roughly chop fresh or frozen cherries. Place in a bowl or small plastic container, toss with sugar, and cover with kirsch (or white rum). Cover the bowl with plastic wrap or seal the plastic container and allow to macerate in the refrigerator for *at least* 8 hours. When ready to use, *drain them very well.*

Step 2—Make your brownies. Use your favorite recipe or a mix. Be sure it's a 9 × 13-inch pan recipe. Bake them and allow them to completely cool. Do not cut or remove from pan.

Step 3—Create the Black Forest topping. Prepare Clare's Whipped Cream and Marscapone Frosting (see the recipe below). Now use the infused and *drained* cherries that you created in Step 1. Set aside a small amount for a garnish and fold the rest into the frosting. Ice the top of the cooled pan of brownies. Garnish with chocolate curls* and cut into squares.

***Chocolate curls:** Start with a block of room temperature dark, milk, or white chocolate. Using a vegetable peeler, scrape the block and you'll see curls of chocolate peel away.

Clare's Whipped Cream and Mascarpone Frosting

¾ cup heavy cream, well chilled
½ cup Italian mascarpone (or cream cheese)
1¼ cups powdered sugar
1 teaspoon pure vanilla extract (for a whiter look, use clear vanilla)
2 tablespoons kirsch, white rum, or cream

Using an electric mixer, whip the very cold heavy cream until it forms stiff peaks. Set aside in the refrigerator. Meanwhile, in another bowl, beat the mascarpone (or cream cheese), powdered sugar, vanilla extract, and kirsch (or rum or cream) until combined. Take out your whipped cream and fold it gently into the bowl of mascarpone, sugar, and vanilla.

Chocolate Cream "Inside-Out" Coffee Cake

After falling down a six-story rabbit hole, Clare Cosi discovered an underground club full of temptations worthy of the "Hansel and Gretel" gingerbread cottage. Clare couldn't pass up a slice of this cake, which she recognized as one of her favorites from the legendary Babka's dessert menu. A heavenly cloud of mocha whipped cream is tucked between layers of devil's food and topped by a fudgy layer of chocolate ganache infused with espresso. It's outrageously good and sinfully delicious—but is it worth risking a run-in with Baba Yaga? Clare will get back to you on that one.

See step-by-step photos of this recipe at coffeehouse mystery.com.

For the Cake*

10 tablespoons unsalted butter, softened to room temperature
½ cup vegetable, canola, or extra-virgin coconut oil
1½ cups white granulated sugar
1 teaspoon pure vanilla extract
3 large eggs, lightly beaten with fork
1 cup + 2 tablespoons whole milk
2¼ cups all-purpose flour
¾ teaspoon baking soda
¼ teaspoon baking powder
¼ teaspoon table salt
½ cup unsweetened cocoa powder

For the Mocha Cream Filling

2 cups cold heavy cream
12 ounces cream cheese, softened
½ cup sugar
2 tablespoons unsweetened cocoa powder

1 teaspoon pure vanilla extract
1 teaspoon instant espresso powder dissolved into
¼ cup Kahlúa or brewed coffee or espresso

For the Glaze

1 tablespoon unsalted butter
⅓ cup brewed coffee (or espresso)
½ teaspoon instant espresso powder†
5 ounces semisweet block chocolate, chopped into uniform pieces
1 teaspoon pure vanilla extract

***A note on using a cake mix:** To save time, you can certainly use a devil's food cake mix, but follow the directions in Step 1 regarding (a) pan size and (b) preparing the pan to prevent the cake from sticking.

†A note on espresso powder: Espresso powder is made from freeze-dried espresso. It dissolves in water to create instant espresso. While Clare would never recommend drinking espresso made from freeze-dried powder, she highly recommends using good-quality espresso powder (rather than freeze-dried instant coffee) to add coffee flavor to your baking and cooking. Look for espresso powder in the instant coffee section of your grocery store or search online.

Step 1—Make the cake batter. First preheat the oven to 350°F. Butter a rimmed baking sheet measuring around 18 by 12 (to 13) inches and line the bottom with parchment paper. Butter the paper and dust with unsweetened cocoa powder, tapping out any excess. Use a devil's food cake mix or these directions to create the batter: Using an electric mixer, cream the butter and sugar until light and fluffy. Add the oil, vanilla, eggs, and milk. Blend until smooth. In a separate bowl, sift together the remaining dry ingredients. Add this dry mixture, a little at a time, to the mixing bowl, beating between additions until a smooth batter forms. Do not overmix. Spread the batter evenly on the prepared baking sheet.

Step 2—Bake and chill the cake. Bake for about 20 minutes, or until the cake has risen, is slightly springy, and a toothpick inserted into the center comes out with no batter clinging to it. Transfer the pan to a rack to cool. Gently invert the cooled cake and peel away the parchment paper. Slice the cake down the middle, crosswise, to form two even rectangles. Slip these into the fridge to chill while you prepare the filling.

Step 3—Make the mocha cream filling. Using an electric mixer on low speed, beat the cream cheese with the sugar, unsweetened cocoa powder, vanilla, and espresso powder dissolved into the Kahlúa (or brewed coffee or espresso). Once blended smooth, add the heavy cream and whip vigorously until the cream forms firm peaks.

Step 4—Assemble the cake. Invert one of your cake rectangles so the flat bottom is facing up. Spread the cream filling evenly. Now cover it with the second cake rectangle (again with the flat bottom facing up). Lightly press down on the top layer. Run an offset spatula (or wide flat knife) around all of the edges to smooth them. Chill the cake while preparing the topping.

Step 5—Make the chocolate-coffee ganache topping. In a small saucepan, over medium heat, bring the butter, granulated sugar, instant espresso powder, and brewed coffee (or espresso) to a simmer (do not boil). Take the pan off the heat and stir in the chocolate. When the chocolate is melted, stir in the vanilla. Let the glaze cool for about 15 minutes. It should become slightly thick. Pour the glaze onto the center of the cake and gently spread it—ideally with an offset spatula (or in a pinch, the back of a spoon)—until it evenly covers the top of the cake. Chill the cake for several hours (or overnight). Slice into squares and eat with joy!

The Village Blend's Silver Dollar Chocolate Chip Cookies

The crispy edges and chewy center of these thin cookies combined with their little silver dollar size and rich flavor notes of buttery caramel with sea salt make for a light yet blissfully satisfying snack, perfect when sharing afternoon coffee breaks or late-night secrets. The latter is why Clare Cosi chose to serve these to her new friend Wilson, the man with the mysterious business card and shocking story of a cold case Cold War murder.

Makes about 75 mini cookies

8 tablespoons (1 stick) unsalted butter
½ cup white granulated sugar
¾ cup light brown sugar, packed
3 tablespoons brewed coffee or espresso (or milk)
1 large egg
2 teaspoons pure vanilla extract
1 ¼ cups all-purpose flour
½ teaspoon coarse sea salt
½ teaspoon baking soda
1 cup mini semisweet chocolate chips
(or standard chips chopped small)

Step 1—Mix the dough. Melt the butter in a small saucepan. Do not brown or burn. Allow to cool a bit and transfer to a mixing bowl. Using an electric mixer, blend in the white and brown sugars, coffee, egg, vanilla, salt, and baking soda. Add the flour and blend again, but do not overmix. The dough will be loose and sticky. Gently fold in the mini chips.

(For the small cookie size to work, be sure to use *mini* chips or chop standard chips into bits.)

Step 2—Bake. Preheat the oven well to 375°F. Drop dough by *half-teaspoons* onto an ungreased or lined cookie sheet. Be sure to allow room between cookies for spreading. For these small cookies, only bake 6 to 6 ½ minutes. The cookies should come out of the oven a little *unbaked*. Allow the cookies to continue cooking and cooling on the hot baking sheet for 10 minutes before handling. The cooler they get, the crisper the edges become!

Clare Cosi's Insanely Easy Peanut Butter Chews

These cookies are out of this world. As Matt Allegro can attest (and he would know), they are "dangerously addictive." Thin and crispy yet chewy and full of mouthwatering flavor, they take the typical peanut butter cookie to a whole new level of sophistication, yet they're easy to make, using just one bowl and a single fork. Clare Cosi developed the recipe during her years raising her daughter, Joy, in New Jersey, when she wrote the "In the Kitchen with Clare" column for a local paper. Now her Greenwich Village coffeehouse customers love them, and Clare hopes you will, too.

Makes about 2 dozen large cookies

1 large egg
1 tablespoon maple syrup
1 teaspoon pure vanilla extract
⅛ teaspoon baking soda
½ cup peanut butter
¾ cup white granulated sugar

Break the egg into a bowl and whisk well with a fork. Whisk in the maple syrup, vanilla, and baking soda. Measure in the peanut butter and sugar, and whisk well with a fork until completely blended and smooth. The mixture will be very loose. For big coffeehouse-style cookies, drop by large spoonfuls into mounds on baking sheet lined with parchment paper. Allow plenty of room for spreading. Bake in a well-preheated 350°F oven for 10 to 14 minutes (the time will depend on your oven). The cookies will spread and puff up, but sink down as they cool into chewy, delightful treats. Be careful *not to scorch the bottoms* of these babies or they will taste terrible. To test for doneness, take a spatula and remove one cookie from the oven. Gently flip it onto a paper towel and check the bottom. If it is golden brown, the cookies are done! Otherwise, continue to cook for another few minutes and check again.

Clare's Coffeehouse Caramel-Dipped Hazelnut Meltaways

It's no wonder Detective Mike Quinn flipped for these. The cookies marry the joy of tender, meltaway shortbread with the buttery sweetness of caramel and the crunchy earthiness of hazelnuts. Caramel and hazelnut are two of the most popular flavors for coffeehouse lattes, which is how Clare came to develop this recipe. Alas, her cupboard was bare the night Mike pined for these, but she came up with ingredients for another dessert that evening. If you'd like to sample the dessert Mike and Clare made, turn to the next recipe.

Makes 3 to 4 dozen cookies, depending on thickness

1 cup (2 sticks) unsweetened butter, softened to room temperature
½ cup powdered sugar
¼ cup light brown sugar, firmly packed

1 large egg (separated)
½ teaspoon baking powder
½ teaspoon table salt
2¼ cups all-purpose flour

For Dipping

50 soft caramels or 2 cups Caramel Bits
2 tablespoons hazelnut milk or half-and-half
½ cup finely chopped hazelnuts

Step 1—Make the dough. Using an electric mixer, cream the softened butter, powdered sugar, and brown sugar. Add the egg yolk and blend until smooth. Add the baking powder and salt and beat again until incorporated. Finally, add the flour and mix on low speed until blended.

Step 2—Form log and chill. Use your hands to squeeze together dough pieces. Knead a little, working with the dough until it is smooth and form it into a ball. Turn the dough onto a parchment paper–covered surface and shape it into a thick, long log about 2 inches in diameter. Wrap the log in the parchment paper, using the paper to finish shaping and smoothing the log. Chill the wrapped log in the fridge for at least 1 hour. If you are going to chill it longer (overnight or up to 2 days), wrap the log tightly in plastic to keep it from drying out.

Step 3—Bake. Preheat the oven to 300°F. Line a baking sheet with parchment paper. Slice the chilled dough log into thin cookies. Bake 10 to 12 minutes. The centers should still be creamy and the edges golden brown. The cookies are tender when warm. Allow to cool before handling or dipping.

Step 4—Dip the cooled cookies in caramel and nuts. Place the finely chopped hazelnuts into a shallow bowl and set aside. Place the unwrapped caramel candies (or Caramel

Bits) and hazelnut milk (or half-and-half) in a nonstick saucepan. Continually stir over low heat until the candies melt. If the melted caramels are still too thick for dipping, add in a bit more milk or half-and-half. When the consistency is right, turn heat to low. Gently dip half of each cooled cookie into the saucepan of melted caramels, allowing excess caramel to drain off. Now dip each cookie into your bowl of chopped hazelnuts. Gently rest on a wax paper–lined pan until set and eat with joy!

Clare's Easy Almond Milk Custard (With or Without Roasted Blueberries)

"The proof really is in the pudding," Detective Mike Quinn told Clare after flipping for this amazing custard. The long night they spent together was fraught with dangers and difficulties. Even on the foodie front, Mike was distraught to find cupboards in Clare's duplex as bare as Mother Hubbard's. Good thing Clare is a kitchen witch. After pointing out a few meager ingredients, she guided Mike through the incredibly easy process of making this delicious homemade custard. Now she'll guide you.

Sweet, smooth, and silky, this custard can be served warm on a cold night—or chilled for a refreshingly cold summer dessert. Roasted blueberries make an elegant addition to both warm and cold versions, and Clare's instructions for adding them can be found at the end of this recipe.

Makes 4 servings

¼ cup white granulated sugar (or equivalent of sugar substitute)
2 tablespoons cornstarch
1 teaspoon lemon zest
⅛ teaspoon kosher salt (or generous pinch of table salt)

2 cups unsweetened almond milk (or any nut milk or low-fat cow's milk)
3 large egg yolks
1 teaspoon vanilla
(See roasted blueberries option at the end of this recipe.)

Step 1—Mix the custard liquid. First note that you are *not* cooking in this step. At the bottom of a nonstick saucepan (*off* the heat!), stir together these dry ingredients: sugar, cornstarch, lemon zest, and salt. Now slowly add the milk, whisking to prevent any lumps from forming. Set aside. In a separate bowl, whisk the egg yolks until light and fluffy. Add the egg yolks to the milk in your saucepan. (Do not add the vanilla yet!)

Step 2—Cook the custard. Place your saucepan over medium heat; *do not boil*. Bring the mixture to a *simmer* and begin to stir and cook for about 10 minutes. You are watching for the mixture to thicken. Remove from heat and stir in the vanilla. Allow this hot mixture to cool off for 10 minutes, until lukewarm (to prevent breaking glassware). Divide the mixture up into 4 serving containers. Clare suggests stemless wineglasses. Serve warm or chilled. To chill, cover tops with plastic wrap to prevent skin from forming. Chill until set, about 2 hours, and serve with or without whipped cream.

How to add roasted blueberries: Preheat the oven to 350°F. Line a baking sheet with aluminum foil and lightly coat with nonstick spray. Spread 1 cup of blueberries (fresh or frozen) and roast for 15 minutes. You're watching for the blueberries to swell—and for some to burst (that's okay). Remove from oven and divide among the 4 serving containers. Ideally, if you'd like roasted blueberries with your custard, start with this step, divide the blueberries among the containers, and then pour in the warm custard. Serve warm, as is, or chill and serve cold. Both versions are absolutely delicious—may you eat with joy!

The Village Blend's Corn Muffins with Caramelized Bacon

The day Matt surprised Clare by opening the shop for her—and letting her enjoy a rare few hours of extra sleep—he brought her this muffin for breakfast. The shop routinely sells out of these by midmorning, and it's no wonder. They make a fast, tasty breakfast for workers on the go. They're great with coffee, and the muffin batter can be stirred together quickly in one bowl. The only issue you may have is whether or not to include sugar.

In the not-too-distant past, throngs of New York office workers ordered corn muffins for breakfast at corner delis. The muffins were split, buttered, and lightly toasted on a short-order grill. As a morning pastry, enjoyed with a fresh cup of coffee, they were baked on the sweet side. On the other hand, you may prefer your corn muffins with little or no sugar. If so, simply reduce or omit the sugar in this recipe. Either way, these muffins are a wicked good breakfast treat.

Makes 12 muffins

For the Caramelized Bacon

6 slices maple or smoked bacon
(if using thick sliced bacon, reduce to 4 slices)
6 teaspoons light brown sugar

For the Corn Muffins

2 large eggs
¾ cup milk (whole, or 2%)
½ cup sour cream (regular, not low fat)
½ to ¾ cup white granulated sugar (or to your taste)
1 teaspoon kosher salt (or ½ teaspoon table salt)

5 tablespoons vegetable or canola oil (see my note below)*
2 teaspoons baking powder
½ teaspoon baking soda
1½ cups all-purpose flour
¾ cup yellow cornmeal
** If you like, use bacon grease in place of all or some of the oil*

Step 1—Make the caramelized bacon bits. First preheat the oven to 350°F. Using kitchen shears, cut 6 slices of bacon into small pieces. Sauté until half-cooked—still soft and flexible with the fat just beginning to change color. Drain the fat. Add the light brown sugar (1 teaspoon for each slice of bacon). Continue stirring and cooking until the bacon bits are cooked through. Transfer to a flat surface to cool and break up any clumps into a single layer.

Step 2—Mix the batter using the one-bowl method. In a mixing bowl, whisk together the egg, milk, sour cream, sugar, salt, and oil. Next whisk in the baking soda and baking powder. Now measure in the flour and cornmeal. Switching to a spoon or spatula, stir well to create a lumpy batter. All visible flour should be incorporated, but do not overmix or you will develop the gluten in the flour and your muffins may bake up tough instead of tender. Finally, fold in the caramelized bacon bits you made in Step 1.

Step 3—Bake. Coat muffin cups with nonstick spray or insert paper liners and spray the papers. Divide the batter among the muffin cups. Bake in the preheated oven for about 18 to 25 minutes. When a toothpick inserted in the center comes out clean, remove from the oven. (Tip: When baked muffins remain in their hot pans, the bottoms may become tough so be sure to remove the muffins from their pans fairly quickly.)

New York "Hot Dog" Onions à la the Papaya King

On the night of the Central Park Festival, Clare and Mike enjoyed a late-night bite at a humble hot dog stand, and Clare expressed her love of New York Onions, a sweet-and-savory relish that's delicious on hot dogs and hamburgers.

For decades, these onions have been part of the city's hot dog–eating tradition. At one time, almost every vendor had his own recipe. This is the one Clare makes at home, and it's very close to what you once found at New York's hot dog carts and stands, including the still-standing Papaya King's hot dog "palace" on Manhattan's Upper East Side.

Alas, the quality of this condiment now varies widely in the city from good to . . . not so great. Likewise, the jarred version of these onions (that you may see on store shelves) is nowhere near the delicious quality of a freshly made sauce, so buyer beware—and consider making your own!

Makes about 2½ cups

2 teaspoons olive oil
5 large red onions, sliced thin and chopped fine
1 (11-ounce) can vegetable juice (V8)
½ cup water
1 teaspoon ketchup
2 teaspoons sweet paprika
½ teaspoon white granulated sugar
½ teaspoon cornstarch
½ teaspoon salt
½ teaspoon red pepper flakes
3 tablespoons apple cider vinegar

Step 1—Sauté the onions. In a medium-sized pot, heat the olive oil over medium heat. When the oil is hot, add the chopped onions. Cook uncovered for 10 minutes, stirring frequently. Reduce the heat to low and let the onions sauté slowly for 20 to 25 minutes, or until the onions are translucent.

Step 2—Start the simmer. Add the vegetable juice, water, ketchup, spices, and vinegar and cook the mixture over low heat for 1½ hours, stirring often and making sure nothing sticks to the side of the pot.

Step 3—Serve. The perfect sweet-spicy garnish for hot dogs, hamburgers, sandwiches, or crackers. New York onions are traditionally served hot, but they are just delicious at room temperature.

"Fryer" Tuck's Ale-Battered Onion Rings

Ale-battered onion rings were one of the rare "vegetable entrées" served at the Meat-dieval Tournament and Feast, former Giant Dwayne Galloway's super-sized action-packed dinner theater. While you may have heard of "beer-battered" onion rings, Dwayne's Meat-dieval kitchen makes them with ale, a darker beer brewed from malted barley and brewer's yeast. The yeast quickly ferments and gives the beer a sweet, fruity taste. Most ales also contain hops, which impart an herbal, earthier flavor that balances the malty, yeasty sweetness. Those aggressive tastes are what dominate these different yet delicious battered and fried onions.

Serves 4

2 large sweet (Vidalia) onions, cut into rings
*¾ cup + 2 tablespoons cake flour**
¼ cup cornstarch
½ teaspoon baking powder
½ teaspoon finely ground sea salt
6 to 8 ounces cold ale (a British or American dark brown is best)

***A note on cake flour:** Because cake flour has a low gluten content, when you combine it with the cornstarch, it will give you a crispier onion ring than all-purpose flour.

Step 1—Heat the oil and cut the onions. Heat the oil to 350°F. Cut the onions into rings of about ¼-inch thick. Toss the rings in the 2 tablespoons cake flour and set aside.

Step 2—Make the batter. When the oil is hot and ready for frying, add enough *cold* ale to the ¾ cup cake flour and the rest of the dry ingredients to make a loose batter. (*Note:* The coldness of the ale helps increase the viscosity of the batter, and the thicker the batter, the better it will stick to the onion rings!) For best results, do not make the batter in advance. Mix it up *just before* frying.

Step 3—Batter and fry the onions. Coat your onion rings with batter and cook at once. Fry until golden brown, about 3 to 4 minutes. Serve piping hot!

Bosnian "Frisbee" Burgers (Pljeskavica)

In the Balkan countries of Southeastern Europe, they like their burgers big, and they don't get much bigger than pljeskavica *(roughly pronounced pee-es´-ka-veet-sa). Clare shared this juicy grilled delight with Eldar, a Bosnian livery driver familiar (perhaps too familiar?) with the two female crime victims.*

This Frisbee-sized mixed-meat patty can be made with ground beef, lamb, pork, and veal, but beef and lamb are traditional. The addition of egg white keeps the patty firm and together—an important point when you're flipping a burger built for two!

While pljeskavica *will fit on a split round of grilled pita bread very nicely, it's traditionally served on a Bosnian bread called* lepinja, *along with a layer of* ajvar, *a spicy pepper and eggplant spread (see the recipe below), and chopped raw onions. A heady cheese-butter called* kajmak *is another traditional condiment. There's really nothing like* kajmak, *but for a close substitute, try a dollop of the Italian soft cheese mascarpone.*

Makes 6 Frisbee-sized patties

2 pounds lean ground beef
1 pound ground lamb (or veal or pork)
2 egg whites
1 tablespoon extra-virgin olive oil
6 cloves garlic, chopped fine
1 tablespoon paprika, sweet or smoked
1 tablespoon sea salt
1 teaspoon black pepper

Step 1—Blend the ingredients. In a large bowl, mix all the ingredients, making sure to thoroughly incorporate the egg white. Seal in an airtight container or bowl covered with plastic wrap and refrigerate at least 8 hours or overnight. The longer the meat rests, the more the flavors blend and the mixture firms.

Step 2—Form the patties. Using slightly damp hands, form the meat into six 9-inch patties about ½-inch thick (the size of a small Frisbee). If you have trouble forming patties, sandwich the meat between two sheets of waxed paper and roll it out, or place it between to sturdy dishes and press hard.

Step 3—Grill or fry. Grill, broil, or fry about 3 to 5 minutes per side, flipping only once (the large size makes this step tricky, but the egg will firm the patty enough to keep it together).

Step 4—Serve hot. *Pljeskavica* is traditionally served on a Bosnia *lepinja* bread, but you can substitute a split pita-bread round that's been warmed or grilled. Traditional sides include chopped raw onions; *kajmak*, a rich, creamy cheese-butter (for a close substitute, use a dollop of the Italian soft cheese mascarpone); and a red pepper and eggplant spread called *ajvar* (see the recipe following this one).

Queen Catherine's Ajvar (Pepper-Eggplant Spread)

The Queen Catherine Café is named in honor of Blessed Catherine, the celebrated Last Queen of Bosnia. Clare visited the Queen Catherine in search of a Bosnian livery driver, and ended up rediscovering this wonderful Eastern European variation on Russia's Poor Man's Caviar. Ajvar *(roughly pronounced eye-var) is a roasted red pepper and eggplant dish that can be served as a relish, a vegetable, or a spread on sandwiches. Smoking eggplant and sweet peppers is an autumn tradition in much of Eastern Europe, and you'll find the smoky, earthy flavor of* ajvar *is a great complement to grilled or roasted meats, and it's especially savory with lamb.*

Serves 6

1 eggplant, 1 to 2 pounds
3 pounds sweet red peppers
½ teaspoon sea salt
½ teaspoon black pepper
2 cloves garlic, finely chopped
½ cup extra-virgin olive oil (plus more for coating the eggplant)
1 teaspoon lemon juice or red wine vinegar

Nontraditional additions and variations include chopped hot red chili peppers and onion.

Step 1—Roast the peppers. Preheat the oven to 425°F. Cut the sweet red peppers in half, and discard the seeds. Coat with olive oil and place on a foiled cookie sheet, skin side up. Roast on the middle rack for 20 to 30 minutes or until the skin blisters and blackens. Let the peppers sit for 20 minutes or until they are cool enough to handle. When cool, peel the blackened skins off the peppers using a paring knife.

Step 2—Roast the eggplant. Half the eggplant lengthwise, remove the seed core, and score with a knife. Coat with 1 tablespoon of olive oil and a pinch of salt. Place the halves on the baking sheet skin side up. Bake for 25 to 35 minutes, until the skins turn black. Remove the eggplant pulp with a knife or spoon and discard the skins. Coarse-chop the eggplant.

Step 3—Blend. Place the eggplant, peeled peppers, salt, pepper, chopped garlic, and olive oil in a food processor. Pulse the mixture until you get the smoothness you want. Traditionally *ajvar* should be a bit lumpy.

Step 4—Simmer and serve. Dump the mixture into a pot. Over medium heat, simmer for 30–35 minutes. Let the mixture cool, then stir in the lemon juice or red wine vinegar. Serve hot or cold, with toasted bread, as a spread on sandwiches, a relish with roasted meat, or a tasty side dish.

Spicy, Creamy Buffalo Chicken Salad with Gorgonzola Dressing

Clare discovered this deliciously spicy, creamy salad at a pretty spicy location—an exclusive underground speakeasy nicknamed the Prince Charming Club. While she didn't sneak into the club for a free meal, the elaborate buffet table was pretty hard to resist.

This is a wonderfully light and healthy way to enjoy the classic taste of Buffalo chicken. The boneless breasts are skinless and the marinade imparts wonderful flavor. Quick tip: Don't cut short the suggested time on the marinade. The lengthy bath in spices is what makes the chicken delicious, not just on the surface but all the way through. You'll find the traditional flavor of celery in the mixed green salad and the classic "blue cheese dip" is reflected in the creamy Gorgonzola dressing. May you eat with joy—Clare certainly did!

Serves 6

3 to 4 pounds skinless boneless chicken breasts
2 cups Louisiana hot sauce (divided)
1 tablespoon scallions, chopped fine
1 clove garlic, chopped fine
1 tablespoon extra-virgin olive oil
1 teaspoon fresh lemon juice
¼ teaspoon white pepper
¼ teaspoon sea salt
¼ teaspoon cayenne pepper (optional)
4 tablespoons butter
a crisp salad of mixed greens (your choice)
celery and carrot (peeled into thin strips)
black olives
Gorgonzola dressing (see the recipe following this one)

Step 1—Prep the chicken. Cut the breasts into long strips, about 1-inch thick. You will get 5 or 6 strips per breast. Set aside.

Step 2—Marinate. In a covered container large enough to hold all the chicken, combine 1 cup Louisiana hot sauce, scallions, garlic, olive oil, lemon juice, white pepper, sea salt, and cayenne pepper (if using). Blend well, add the chicken strips, and cover. Marinate in the refrigerator for at least 8 hours or overnight.

Step 3—Cook the chicken. Preheat oven to 350°F. Remove the chicken from the marinade and discard the liquid. Place the chicken in a baking pan lined with foil and coated with nonstick spray. Bake for 1 hour or until the internal temperature reaches 165°F. Remove from the oven and let cool. At this point, you can continue with the recipe or store the chicken strips in a clean, sealed plastic container in the refrigerator for up to 24 hours.

Step 4—Make the salad. Make a salad of your favorite mixed greens. Shred a celery stalk and carrot into thin strips using a good-quality peeler. Garnish with olives.

Step 5—Finish the chicken. Melt the butter in a skillet and add the remaining 1 cup of Louisiana hot sauce. When the mixture simmers, roll cooked chicken strips in the pan, coating evenly with sauce. Continue cooking until the chicken is warmed through. Serve hot over salad with Gorgonzola dressing (see the following recipe).

Clare's Creamy Gorgonzola Dressing

Gorgonzola is a lovely Italian blue cheese. This is a smooth and creamy dressing that's easy to whip up. The scallions provide freshness, and the lemon juice gives the zip that usually comes with the addition of vinegar. It's versatile, as well. You can make it pourable for a salad dressing, or make it on the thicker side as a veggie, chip, or chicken wing dip. Enjoy!

Makes 1½ cups

4 ounces Gorgonzola cheese, crumbled
1 tablespoon scallions, chopped fine
6 to 8 tablespoons mayonnaise

1 tablespoon extra-virgin olive oil
1 to 2 tablespoons sour cream
1 teaspoon fresh lemon juice
¼ teaspoon white pepper
¼ teaspoon sea salt
1 anchovy, mashed (optional)

In a large bowl, mix all the ingredients and blend until smooth and creamy. To thin the dressing out, add milk, 1 tablespoon at a time, and whisk with a fork until you are happy with the consistency. You can also serve the dressing as a tangy dipping sauce for buffalo chicken wings or raw vegetables.

Babka's Shrimp Kiev

The legendary Babka's eatery became famous for its gourmet comfort foods. Some of its menu items are also twists on old-fashioned New York favorites, as well as the owner's versions of recipes from famous restaurants that came before hers. This Shrimp Kiev is a good example. The dish was invented at the legendary Four Seasons restaurant. Jumbo shrimps are stuffed with herb butter in the manner of a classic Chicken Kiev. Babka's recipe boosts the flavor of the original dish with the addition of tarragon. Like her underground restaurant, the recipe is far from kosher, but it is delicious.

Serves 4

4 ounces (1 stick) unsalted butter, room temperature
1 clove garlic, minced
1 scallion, minced
½ teaspoon fresh parsley, chopped
½ teaspoon fresh lemon juice

½ teaspoon sea salt
¼ teaspoon dry tarragon (or Old Bay Seasoning, but not both)
¼ teaspoon white pepper
24 jumbo shrimps
1 cup all-purpose flour
4–5 large eggs, beaten
4 cups plain bread crumbs
vegetable oil for frying

Step 1—Create the herb butter. Place the butter in a mixing bowl with the garlic, scallion, parsley, lemon juice, sea salt, tarragon (or Old Bay Seasoning), and white pepper. Using a fork or an electric mixer, cream the butter and herbs. Cover the bowl with plastic wrap and cool the butter in a freezer while you prepare the shrimp.

Step 2—Prep the shrimp. Shell and devein the shrimp and remove the tails. Split the shrimp on the vein line, taking care not to cut all the way through the meat. Gently butterfly the shrimp by using your hand to press and flatten each one on a plate, taking care not to tear the delicate meat (or you can place shrimp between two sheets of waxed paper and gently roll them flat). To see step-by-step photos of this process, see the Italian Fried Shrimp recipe at coffeehousemystery.com.

Step 3—Stuff and bread the shrimp. Dip each flattened shrimp in flour, lightly coating both sides. When all the shrimp are floured, place a chilled butter mound between two flattened shrimps (about a half-teaspoon), making sure the butter is completely enveloped by the meat. Using both hands, hold the shrimp sandwich halves together as you flour again, dip in egg, and finally the breading. Place the finished shrimp on a waxed paper–covered plate and freeze for 1 to 2 hours. This freezing will help keep the stuffed shrimp together while cooking. (If storing longer, place shrimp inside a freezer-safe plastic bag.)

Step 4—Sauté and serve. Pour about 1½ to 2 inches of oil into a deep skillet. Heat to about 370°F and quickly deep-fry the frozen shrimp sandwiches for about 3 minutes, until golden brown. Do not crowd the pan or the oil will drop in temperature and your shrimp will be greasy instead of crispy. Drain lightly on paper towels and serve piping hot.

Clare Cosi's Dr. Pepper Glazed Chicken

Swapnil Padmanabhan of Columbia University's Sleep Studies Lab, aka Dr. Pepper, helped Clare to unlock the mystery of Matt's "magic" coffee, along with the secret behind her bizarre and frightening visions. That—and the doctor's special "KISS"—proved to be lifesavers. After the crime was solved, Clare discovered the good doctor's nickname was more than a soft drink mnemonic. His favorite cold drink was a bubbly glass of Dr Pepper soda over crushed ice. Since he also enjoyed American barbeque, Clare decided to thank him by creating a BBQ chicken dish in his honor. This Dr Pepper Glazed Chicken is so sweet and savory that Clare's real Dr. Pepper proclaimed the dish "wonderfully good."

Makes 4 to 6 servings

3–5 pounds chicken parts, skin on
2–4 tablespoons olive or vegetable oil
1 (12-ounce) can Dr Pepper soda (regular, not diet)
¾ cup dark brown sugar
2 tablespoons honey (use a local raw honey)
1 tablespoon ground cumin
1 tablespoon ground chili powder
3 scallions, chopped
1 tablespoon Dijon mustard
½ cup Heinz Natural Ketchup
1 tablespoon cornstarch

Step 1—Mix and heat. In a large saucepan over medium heat, mix the Dr Pepper, brown sugar, honey, cumin, chili powder, chopped scallions, Dijon mustard, and ketchup and bring mixture to a boil.

Step 2—Reduce and simmer. Reduce the heat and simmer, stirring often, for three to five minutes. Now add the cornstarch a little at a time while continuing to simmer until the mixture thickens enough to coat the back of a spoon. Remove from heat and set aside.

Step 3—Prepare the chicken. Preheat oven to 350° F. In a large skillet, heat the oil over medium heat and brown the chicken for 8 to 10 minutes, turning often. Place the browned chicken parts in a foil lined 13 × 9 baking pan, and pour the sauce over the chicken, coating each piece. Bake for 60–70 minutes, until the chicken has reached an internal temperature of 165° F. Serve immediately.

Clare Cosi's Poor Man's Caviar
(Baklazhannaia Ikra)

Poor Man's Caviar is a traditional Russian dish that contains no caviar or fish. So why is it called Poor Man's Caviar? According to legend, the fishermen who harvested caviar sturgeon in Georgia, the Ukraine, and Russia were too poor to eat their catch, so they peddled the fish and concocted a savory topping for their bread using the ingredients at hand.

When Clare and Eldar dined together at the humble yet cozy Queen Catherine Café, Clare remarked how ajvar *(a condiment served on her Bosnian burger) was similar to this traditional Russian delicacy. In the end, Clare suggested that Mike's luxury-loving ex-wife give this recipe a try—for reasons more philosophical than culinary.*

Makes about 4 cups

2–3 large eggplants (about 3 pounds)
1 cup olive oil (divided)
1 large onion, chopped fine
1 green or red pepper, chopped fine
3 cloves garlic, chopped fine
6 ounces tomato paste
½ teaspoon sugar
2 teaspoons coarse sea salt (or 2 ½ teaspoons Kosher salt)
½ teaspoon freshly ground black pepper
½ teaspoon lemon juice

Step 1—Prepare the eggplants. Preheat oven to 350°F. Prick the eggplants all over with a fork, then coat them with olive oil. Place whole eggplants on a foil-lined baking sheet and roast in the center of the oven until soft, about 1 hour. Place the eggplant in a colander so the juices will drain. When cool enough to work with, press the excess liquid out of the eggplants to reduce bitterness. Cut the eggplants in half and scoop out the flesh. Discard the skin and any large seeds. Chop the flesh finely, but do not puree. (You want the dish to have texture and not be the consistency of baby food.) Set aside.

Step 2—Sauté the veggies. In a large skillet over low heat, add ½ cup olive oil. When the oil is hot, add the chopped onions, green or red pepper, and garlic. Stirring occasionally, cook until the onions are translucent and the peppers soft, about 20 minutes. Finally add the eggplant to the onions-pepper-garlic mix, along with the tomato paste, sugar, salt, and black pepper.

Step 3—Finish the dish. Reduce the heat to low and cook, stirring frequently, for 15 minutes. If necessary, add more olive oil to prevent sticking. When finished cooking, transfer the mixture to a heat-proof bowl and let cool. At room temperature, stir in the lemon juice. Cover and store in the refrigerator. *Baklazhannaia Ikra* stays fresh for up to 5 days.

Clare Cosi's Iced Gingerbread Cookie Sticks (Edible Coffee Stirrers)

This was the very recipe Clare used to create "beanstalk" cookie sticks for the Fairy Tale Festival. Little did she know it would be Matt's "magic beans" that would bring her Giant trouble. These cookies, on the other hand, were designed to bring joy.

At the Village Blend, Gingerbread Cookie Sticks dipped in vanilla glaze or melted chocolate make a fantastic winter treat for Clare's customers. During holiday parties, she dresses them up by rolling the newly glazed (or chocolate-dipped) cookie sticks in a variety of garnishes, including crushed candy canes, marshmallow bits, cinnamon candy hearts, colored sprinkles, coarse finishing sugar, or even a bit of crystallized ginger.

See photos of this recipe at coffeehousemystery.com.

Makes about 48 cookie sticks

2¼ cups all-purpose flour
¼ teaspoon table salt
½ teaspoon baking soda
2 teaspoons ground ginger
1 teaspoon cinnamon
¼ teaspoon ground allspice (or ⅛ teaspoon ground cloves)
10 tablespoons (1¼ sticks) unsalted butter, softened to room temperature
⅔ cup dark brown sugar, firmly packed
¼ cup molasses (unsulphured, not blackstrap)
⅓ cup whole milk (or brewed coffee)
glaze and garnishes (optional)

Step 1—Assemble the dry ingredients. In a mixing bowl, whisk together the flour, salt, baking soda, ginger, cinnamon, and allspice (or cloves). Set aside.

Step 2—Make the dough. Using an electric mixer, cream the softened butter and dark brown sugar; add the molasses and coffee and blend again. While continuing to beat at a low speed, slowly add in your dry ingredients, blending just enough to make a smooth dough. Do not overbeat.

Step 3—Wrap and chill. The dough will be very sticky. If it seems too wet, blend in a bit more flour. Form into 2 balls and flatten into disks. Wrap the two disks in plastic and refrigerate for at least 1 hour; overnight is fine, too. (Or make the dough 1 or 2 days in advance and store in the refrigerator.)

Step 4—Roll the dough. First, preheat the oven to 350°F. Remove the chilled dough disks from the fridge and allow to warm long enough to become pliable. Place the dough between two sheets of lightly flour-dusted parchment paper. (This is a great method for rolling cookies because you will only need the lightest dusting of flour, which will keep the cookies from toughening up.)

Thickness: Roll your dough between ⅛ inch and ¼ inch. The thinner version will create crispier cookie sticks; the thicker version will make softer sticks. Experiment with what appeals to you.

Troubleshooting: The biggest issue you'll have in rolling this dough will be the dough's stickiness. When finished rolling, do not remove parchment paper. Slip the flat sheet onto a pan and place the pan in the fridge or freezer for 10 minutes. Once the rolled-out dough is chilled, it will firm up and easily separate from the paper.

Step 5—Cut the cookies. Remove the top layer of parchment paper. Use a pizza cutter to clean up the edges of your rectangle and slice into sticks. Do not move the sticks off the bottom parchment layer or their straight shapes will bend. Simply slip the entire sheet of parchment onto a cookie sheet.

Step 6—Bake. Bake for 8 to 10 minutes. When the cookies are finished baking, you will need to recut them while still warm. Simply slide the entire sheet of parchment paper onto a cutting board and use your original slicing lines as a guide. (The pizza cutter will make quick work of it.) Allow the cookie sticks to cool before handling or they may break.

Step 7—Glaze or dip and garnish. Once cool, you can serve as is, dust with powdered sugar, or dip the top half of the sticks in Clare's Vanilla Glaze (see the recipe below) or try melted chocolate (white, milk, or dark). To make the cookie sticks even more festive, roll dipped cookies in fun finishers such as crushed candy canes, marshmallow bits, pearl sugar, coarse finishing sugar, chopped nuts, crystallized ginger, colored sprinkles, or cinnamon hearts. Use an empty mug or glass to stand the sticks upright while the glaze or chocolate dries.

Clare's Vanilla Glaze

2 tablespoons butter
1 tablespoon milk (more or less)
1 cup powdered sugar, sifted
½ teaspoon vanilla extract (for a whiter glaze, use clear vanilla)

In a small saucepan, over medium-low heat, melt the butter into the milk. Add the sifted powdered sugar, a little at a time, and fork-whisk until smooth. When all the sugar is melted, remove the pan from the heat and stir in the vanilla. If the glaze seems too thick, whisk in a bit more milk. Once the cookie stick ends are dipped, stand the sticks upright in a mug or glass to dry. If you prefer, use a fork to drizzle the glaze over the sticks as they lie on a flat surface. Allow the glaze to cool and harden before handling. For garnishing ideas, see the last step of the Gingerbread Cookie Sticks recipe (preceding this one) and eat with fairy-tale joy!

Don't Miss the Next Coffeehouse Mystery by Cleo Coyle

Join Clare Cosi for a double shot of danger in the next Coffeehouse Mystery!